HOLLOW

Books by Lynette Eason

WOMEN OF JUSTICE

Too Close to Home
Don't Look Back
A Killer Among Us

DEADLY REUNIONS

When the Smoke Clears
When a Heart Stops
When a Secret Kills

HIDDEN IDENTITY

No One to Trust
Nowhere to Turn
Nothing to Lose

ELITE GUARDIANS

Always Watching
Without Warning
Moving Target
Chasing Secrets

BLUE JUSTICE

Oath of Honor
Called to Protect
Code of Valor
Vow of Justice

Protecting Tanner Hollow

PROTECTING TANNER HOLLOW

FOUR ROMANTIC SUSPENSE NOVELLAS

LETHAL HOMECOMING
LETHAL CONSPIRACY
LETHAL SECRETS
LETHAL AGENDA

LYNETTE EASON

Revell

a division of Baker Publishing Group
Grand Rapids, Michigan

Published by Revell
a division of Baker Publishing Group
PO Box 6287, Grand Rapids, MI 49516-6287
www.revellbooks.com

Printed in the United States of America

Library of Congress Cataloging-in-Publication Data
Names: Eason, Lynette, author.
Title: Protecting Tanner Hollow : four romantic suspense novellas / Lynette Eason.
Description: Grand Rapids, MI : Revell, a division of Baker Publishing Group,
    [2019]
Identifiers: LCCN 2018057257 | ISBN 9780800736460 (paper)
Subjects: LCSH: Murder—Fiction. | Love—Fiction.
Classification: LCC PS3605.A79 A6 2019 | DDC 813/.6—dc23
LC record available at https://lccn.loc.gov/2018057257

ISBN 978-0-8007-3716-0 (casebound)

19   20   21   22   23   24   25   7   6   5   4   3   2   1

To my family,
who believes in me 100 percent.
I love you.

To Jesus.
I love you more today.

CONTENTS

LETHAL
HOMECOMING

ONE

Bad things happened in the dark.

At least that's what Kallie Ainsworth had learned. She'd always hated the dark and that childish fear had followed her into adulthood.

Which was why she'd planned to be home in Tanner Hollow, North Carolina, before the sun fell. Unfortunately, the flat tire had delayed her, and now she was on a back-mountain road that led to a place where she was unsure of her welcome. Since she'd been gone for six years, she couldn't hush the uncertainty that simmered just beneath the surface.

Christmas music flowed from her radio and the words reminded her why she was making the trip back to the place from which she'd run. The place she'd vowed never to return to until it was safe.

And now it was.

A lifetime ago her stepfather's abusive actions had sent her running, but now he was dead and had no more ability to instill fear in her.

Anticipation hovered.

She'd dreamed of this moment. Not necessarily Rick's death, but of coming home and being reunited with her family. It had been bad enough that Rick had moved in on her mother and she'd married him, but he'd also insinuated himself into her father's law firm. She still wasn't sure how that had happened. It didn't matter now. He was gone. Forever.

Mature pines to her left led to her family's backyard, and a sheer drop-off to her right made her nervous in spite of the guardrail. She pressed the gas a little harder, focusing on the road in front of her and not the darkness surrounding her.

A sudden impact from behind threw her forward. Kallie screamed as the car swerved and she jerked the wheel to keep the tires on the road. Heart pounding, she managed to right the vehicle only to feel a second slam, this time to her left rear.

The edge of the road. Again. If she went over, she was dead. Kallie didn't have to see the drop-off to her right to know it. Fighting the force of the hit, she pulled on the wheel and stood on the brake. Squealing tires finally gripped the asphalt. The vehicle shuddered to a stop and shut off.

Her attacker shot past her and Kallie saw his brake lights come on. Wait—he was coming back?

Tremors shook her. She twisted the key and the engine ground but didn't catch. She tried again. And again. The car in front of her had turned around and was heading back toward her.

"No," she whispered. She scrambled out of the passenger door. The cold hit hard, stopping Kallie for a split second. Her heavy winter coat rested on the back seat. She looked back at the car that had hit her, now idling in the middle of the road. The driver's door opened, but the interior light didn't come on.

The attacker planned to continue the chase.

Kallie ran to the back of her car and crouched behind it. Darkness covered her, and she hoped he couldn't see her. At the trunk, she paused, her pulse thundering in her ears. *Think, think.*

Footsteps.

He was coming for her.

Terror spiking, she looked at the drop-off. It wasn't as sheer here as it was in some areas, but one misstep could send her to the bottom. There were some trees not too far down. Could she find a hiding place behind one of them?

Her mistake was clear. She should have rounded the back of the car and beelined across the street for the wooded area that led to her backyard.

Now she was a sitting duck.

Footsteps crunched closer.

"I know you're there," a voice whispered.

Kallie's breath caught in her throat. She whispered a prayer for protection. The figure moved along the edge of the street. Kallie could see him looking over the edge. If he looked to his right, he would see her.

Could she move without attracting his attention?

A shudder ripped through her and she tried to think.

She couldn't stay here. She had to try.

Keeping her eyes on the figure at the front of the car, she took a step back, then another. His focus stayed on the drop-off.

Once on the other side of the vehicle, she paused and looked at the open space between her and the cover of the trees. It was only about ten yards, but it might as well have been ten miles. With one more glance over her shoulder to confirm he wasn't looking her way, she darted for the trees.

"Hey!"

His shout spurred her on, his running footsteps sending another splash of terror shooting through her. Kallie's only goal was to escape him and make it to the back door of her childhood home.

She knew this area. She'd played in these woods since the day her mother had finally decided she could explore on her own—within shouting distance.

Now all she had to do was find the path before he found her.

Detective Nolan Tanner stood in the living area of the Goodlette home and scanned the solemn faces before him. Kallie Ainsworth's family.

Sharon Goodlette, Kallie's mother, was still beautiful in her early fifties. If he remembered correctly, her youngest daughter, Megan, was twenty-three and the exact opposite of Kallie in physical appearance. While Kallie had straight blonde hair and blue eyes, Megan had dark curls that reached to her mid back. Her eyes shone like black onyx and her full lips showed a permanent pout.

And then there were the stepchildren. Rick's two grown sons and one daughter—James, Richard, and Shelley.

Right now they all stared at him like he'd grown an extra head.

Rick Goodlette, Kallie's stepfather, had been dead for three days, and his funeral was the day after tomorrow. The reading of the will would take place immediately afterward, and the family had swooped in like the vultures he'd heard them to be.

"I hate to deliver this news at this point, but it might mean you have to delay the funeral."

"What?"

"No!"

"Are you crazy?"

The chorus of objections met his announcement as he'd predicted. He sighed. "Look, I'm sorry, but the evidence says that Rick's death was not an accident."

"But it was a car wreck." Sharon stood and paced to the mantel. She turned. "A car wreck. On a curving mountain road."

"There was a bullet hole in the windshield."

Her jaw dropped and several gasps echoed around the room. "What?"

Sharon Goodlette was either an Academy Award–winning actress or she truly had no idea her husband's death could have been anything but an accident. She stumbled back to her seat and slumped into the wingback chair. "But . . . no. What?"

"Someone reported hearing a gunshot about the time of the wreck. I didn't connect the two until just this morning and, on a hunch, had the vehicle examined a little closer. Initially, the broken and cracked windshield looked like the result of the wreck, but when we went looking for it, the bullet hole was there."

"I can't believe this." She raked a hand through her hair.

"I know this is hard," he said, "and I promise to do my best to wrap this up as quickly as I can."

"Kallie will be here soon."

Nolan's heart thudded. "Kallie?"

"Yes, why?" Megan asked. She sidled up next to him.

A hint of spicy perfume reached him, and he thought it was the same scent she'd worn in high school. He hadn't been fond of it then and found his opinion hadn't changed.

He stepped back. "Ah, I just suppose that surprises me. I didn't think they were that close."

"They weren't."

But she was still coming home for her stepfather's funeral? Probably to be support for her mother. Rumors of Rick and Kallie's arguments rolled around in his head. And the fact that she'd just up and left one morning with no word to anyone, not even him.

He'd missed Kallie. They'd been friends since high school. Friends, then more. But she'd left and taken his heart with her. He gave his head a slight shake. He couldn't think about that right now. "Do you know when she'll be here?"

Sharon looked at the clock on the mantel. "She should have been here about an hour ago but texted and said she would be delayed because of a flat tire."

Nolan frowned. "Is she all right?"

"Yes. At least she didn't say she wasn't." She pulled her phone from the front pocket of her black slacks. "I'll try calling her again." She dialed the number and listened. Then shook her head and hung up. "Nothing."

Megan walked over to stand in front of him. She looked up at him with big dark eyes. "You don't think anything happened to her, do you?"

"No, of course not."

She turned to her mother. "Maybe we should go look for her."

Her mother sighed. "Let's give her a few more minutes. Maybe she just doesn't want to answer the phone while she's driving."

Megan frowned and nodded. "All right, but if she's not here soon, I'm going looking."

Nolan thought of the girl he'd once loved and said a quick prayer for her safety. But a small part of him couldn't help wondering if Kallie had thought of him while she'd been gone. He gave a mental sigh. It didn't matter if she had or if she hadn't. She'd left him after he'd asked her to marry him.

She was only nineteen years old. Too young to know what she wanted. But she sure knew what she hadn't wanted.

Him.

And that still hurt.

TWO

Kallie didn't stop at the tree line. She worked her way through the undergrowth, listening intently, yet focused on getting to the other side of the woods. She had to find the path to the house.

Footsteps pounded behind her and adrenaline sent her pulse skyrocketing.

If he caught her before she could reach—

No. Being caught wasn't an option. She dared a glance over her shoulder and couldn't see anything but shadows.

But he was there.

Why? What had she done to merit someone trying so hard to hurt her? Or even *kill* her?

A branch caught her in the face. Pain sliced through her cheek and warm blood trickled down to drip from her chin. She winced but ignored it.

Kallie reached a large tree with a wide trunk. She slipped behind it to catch her breath. Her regular runs and workouts at her company's gym meant she was in great shape, but there she didn't have terror making her weak. The cold sent shivers through her, but the running kept her from feeling too chilled.

Her lungs grasped for air even as her ears listened for the sound of footsteps.

Nothing.

Not even the crunch of the underbrush to indicate he followed her.

She dragged in another breath and started to move. Then stopped. What if he was listening for her? Indecision held her still. Fear wanted to simply freeze her. The longer she stood there, the colder she got.

How she wished she had her cell phone, but there'd been no time to grab it from the passenger seat.

What should she do? Move or stay still?

The flicker of a light caught her attention. It moved from side to side, advancing slowly.

Then she heard the soft crunch as his footsteps brought him closer. Her heart thundered in her ears. She watched him and realized he was searching every tree close to the path.

She'd have to chance it. She stepped back onto the path and moved as quickly as she could, making as little noise as possible.

But he still heard her.

The footsteps picked up speed.

Kallie doubled her efforts. Just a little farther. And then she was there. She broke through the tree line and released a gasping sob of relief as she stumbled into her childhood backyard.

A hand fell on her shoulder. She screamed and spun, lashing out with the palm of her hand. She connected with supple flesh covering hard bone and her attacker grunted and cursed. His fingers tightened around her upper arm and another scream ripped from her.

His other hand went around her throat.

Tight.

Choking.

She brought a knee up hard and caught him in his upper thigh. He stepped back, but his grip never lessened. Kallie's nails dug into the hand squeezing the life from her. He flinched and his fingers flexed, giving her a precious gulp of air for one brief moment.

The back floodlight flipped on, blinding her for a moment.

"Is someone out here?"

18

"Help me!" Kallie forced the words from her tight throat, grateful they came out louder than a whisper.

"Hey! What's going on?"

She lashed out one more time and caught his shin with the toe of her boot. He cursed and stumbled back. The vise grips on her arm and throat released. She fell to the ground and her attacker bolted.

"Police! Who's there?"

She recognized the voice now. Nolan? Nolan Tanner? Kallie rolled to her feet, swallowing hard. "It's me. Kallie." Her voice came out hoarse, rough, but loud enough. "He's getting away!"

Nolan rushed down the steps toward her. "Kallie? Who's getting away?"

"The guy who tried to kill me." She took off after him.

"Kallie, wait!"

He fell into step behind her as she figured he would. Nolan hadn't been able to see what had happened on the fringes of the spotlight, but now that he was behind her—and armed—she felt a bit braver.

Kallie darted back into the trees and stopped. She had no light, no way to see in the inky blackness. He could be hiding anywhere. Behind any tree.

She stood still, listening, but only heard Nolan's running steps that led him to her. "What's going on? Who tried to kill you? And why?"

"I don't know," she whispered. "Did you see him?"

"I saw something."

"His car is parked just through the woods. He hit my bumper, tried to run me off the road, but I got out and ran."

Nolan pulled his phone from a clip on his belt to call for backup, and she scanned the woods, trying not to miss any sign of light or movement that would indicate her attacker was still nearby.

When Nolan hung up, he activated the light on his phone. "Help is on the way, but show me what you're talking about."

"This way." She stepped ahead of him onto the path and retraced her steps, reaching the road more quickly than she'd expected. She supposed the terror made the run seem like it lasted forever. Seconds before she stepped out of the woods and onto the asphalt, she heard an engine crank and a car pull away. "That's him. He's leaving."

"Maybe," Nolan said.

Her car still sat there, but the one her attacker had driven was gone. They'd missed him by seconds.

A tremor shook her and she shivered. Kallie wrapped her arms to hug herself against the chill.

He rested a hand on her shoulder. "Where's your coat?"

"In the back of my car. I didn't have time to grab it. Or my cell phone."

"Let's get it. You're freezing." He jogged over to the open back door of her car and pulled out her coat. When he returned, he wrapped it around her. Shaking, she slid her arms into the sleeves and let the warmth envelop her. She pulled the gloves out of her pockets and slid them onto her hands.

"What now?" she asked.

"You said the guy bumped you?"

"Slammed me is more like it. Twice. In the back."

He walked to the rear of her car and used the light on his phone to inspect the damage. "Got you pretty good, didn't he?"

"Unfortunately." The shaking began to ease. The fact that she was safe allowed her adrenaline surge to slow.

And gave her a chance to notice the man who'd come to her rescue. Nolan Tanner. "What were you doing at my mother's house?"

He straightened. "It's a long story. Let me call this in, then we'll get you back to the house and I'll explain everything."

He dialed another number and gave her pitiful description of the car that had tried to run her off the road to the person on the other end of the line. "Keep an eye out. Stop the driver and question him. See if there's any collision evidence on the front of his vehicle. If so, take him in and I'll be there to question him." He hung up and nodded to Kallie. "All right, do you think you can drive back to the house, or do you want me to?"

"I don't think it'll start."

"Give it a try."

Kallie climbed in her car and cranked it. Nothing. She sighed. "The battery's dead, I guess." Which was why she hadn't been able to get away earlier.

Once again he pulled his phone from the clip on his belt and she heard him ask someone about a tow truck and meeting him at the garage tomorrow morning.

He hung up. "Do you want me to call someone to come get us and take us back to the house? There's no need to call anyone to come to the scene as I can take the accident report. But if you don't feel like walking, I can get us a ride."

"No, I can walk." She hoped her legs were steady enough. "I'll need my suitcase, purse, and cell phone, though."

He pulled the suitcase from the trunk and set it on the ground while she snagged the phone and purse from the passenger floorboard. She supposed they'd fallen there when her attacker had hit her.

"You're not planning to stay very long if that's all you brought," Nolan said.

"I'm a light traveler. And I pack well. There's enough in there for five or six days and then I can always wash it."

"Impressive."

His matter-of-factness added balm to her frazzled nerves. As a recently graduated lawyer, she was used to working under stressful conditions. She could keep her cool in most situations—including all the mock trials she'd participated in. But this . . . this was different. Someone had targeted her and it scared her. A little shakiness could be understood, right?

And Nolan Tanner.

She'd figured if she ever saw him again, he'd hate her. The fact that he'd acted cordial, concerned, even friendly, allowed a piece of her heart to heal.

He took a long look at her. Long enough to make her uncomfortable and wonder if she'd made a snap judgment about what he thought of her. She shifted, her mind grasping for something to say to break the silence. But then he turned without a word and started off for the path through the woods. She fell in behind him.

Kallie wanted to say something. Anything. But what did a girl say to the only man she'd ever loved—and left?

THREE

Once they reached the house, Nolan led her up the back porch steps to the sliding glass doors. When they stepped inside, Kallie paused just to take everything in. Memories flowed. Good memories—and bad.

"I don't care," her mother was saying, "It's her—"

Nolan cleared his throat.

Kallie's mother spun to simply stare at the two of them.

"Kallie," she breathed. "Oh, my dear girl." Then she was across the room with Kallie in her arms.

Kallie clutched her mother's shoulders and buried her face against the woman's neck. Her heart constricted as she breathed in the familiar smell. Sobs clawed at her throat, but she refused to release them. If she started crying, she might not stop.

After a minute, her mother stepped back to cup her cheeks and simply stare at her. "You're here. I can touch you."

Kallie nodded and swiped a few tears that escaped despite her determination. "I know. FaceTime just isn't the same, is it?"

"No."

Kallie glanced over at the young woman behind her mother. Her sister. "Megan."

She'd changed, matured. The last time Kallie had seen her in person, she'd been just seventeen. Watching her accounts on social media and the occasional FaceTime conversation hadn't adequately prepared her for the difference.

23

"Hi, Sis. Welcome home." Megan crossed the room and embraced her.

Then her mother turned to Nolan. "What happened outside? You said for us to stay here." Her gaze slid to Kallie. "Was that you screaming?"

Kallie ran a shaking hand through her hair. "Yes. Someone attacked me." She shuddered and felt her neck, wondering if she'd have bruises in the morning.

"What?" Her mother reached out and touched her face. "You're hurt."

Kallie frowned, then registered the pain in her cheek. "A branch got me while I was running."

"Let's get that taken care of. It's a small cut, but still bleeding a bit." She looked at Nolan. "Do we need to call the police or will you take care of this?"

"I'll take care of it. I've already called for someone to be on the lookout for the vehicle that rammed her car. Hopefully, we'll hear something soon."

Kallie's heart thumped in her chest while her mother slipped into the kitchen and returned with a small first aid kit. Her overloaded senses almost couldn't take in the events of the night and being reunited with her family. She drew in a deep breath.

Her stepfather was gone. No, not just gone. Dead. He was no longer a threat. She and her mother and sister could now get on with their lives and be a family once more.

Once her mother finished with Kallie's wound, Nolan cleared his throat. "Where did the others go?"

"What others?" Kallie asked.

"Rick's children."

Kallie gaped. "His kids are here?" They'd never shown any interest in their father, as far as she'd known. Her mother had tried to reach out to them, but they'd rebuffed her every overture, angry that he'd divorced their mother and married again.

Of course they'd show up for the reading of his will. For the first time since she heard of his death, she wondered about the money. The money that was her mother and father's to begin with. Not Rick's.

Rick had nothing before he married her mother—except a law degree and a drinking habit. Surely he didn't have control over any portion of her mother's money to give to his children, did he? What had her mother chosen—or been pressured to do—in the last six years?

Megan snorted. "They went to their rooms when Nolan ran out the door."

Nolan blinked. "Seriously?"

Her mother shook her head, lips pursed, eyes narrowed. "They said it was probably just a stray cat."

"I wasn't finished talking to them," Nolan said, "but I suppose the rest of it can wait until tomorrow."

"There's more?" Megan asked.

"More what?" Kallie asked. "What's going on?" She let her eyes swing between her mother and Nolan.

"We're not sure your stepfather's accident was really an accident," Nolan said.

"Not an acci—what? If not, then what?"

"Murder," her mother whispered.

Kallie's lungs closed in and her knees went weak. She sank onto the nearest recliner. "Murder?"

Nolan stepped up and rested a hand on her shoulder. His familiar touch sent warmth shooting through her chilled body. "We just got the report back on the car. The brake line was cut."

"But . . . why would you even check for something like that?"

Nolan sighed, looked at her mother, then back to her. "Your stepfather had an argument with his business partner, Clyde Durham, two days prior to his accident. His secretary overheard the man say something to the effect that he wouldn't live to regret his decision. She called the sheriff, and the sheriff asked me to look into it."

Kallie stared at him, then moved her gaze to her mother, who'd lowered herself onto the love seat opposite the recliner.

"Clyde would never do anything to hurt anyone," her mother said. "I've known him as long as I've known Rick. We all graduated high school together. Clyde and Blake played golf every chance they got. They were big buddies. When Blake died and Rick stepped in to help with the company, Clyde said he didn't know what he would have done without the help." A frown creased her brow. "Rick didn't say anything about an argument. He was moody and cranky the day before the wreck, but I just—" She shook her head. "I didn't really pay that much attention, I suppose. When he got like that, he liked to be alone, so I left him to himself." She covered her mouth with her fingers. "I don't believe this."

"We're still investigating, Mrs. Goodlette. I'll keep you updated."

"What about the funeral? It's the day after tomorrow."

"Keep your plans for now. I'll let the sheriff know what's happened here tonight with Kallie and get his feedback on where he wants to go from here."

Kallie's mother nodded. "All right. Thank you."

The doorbell rang and Megan started. "That's probably Brian. We're going out for a late snack and I'm not even dressed yet."

She left and returned with a young man in tow. He was only slightly taller than Megan, with dark hair and eyes and a lanky build. "This is Brian," she told Kallie, "a good friend and co-worker." Brian smiled down at Megan, and the look in his eyes said he wanted very much to be more than just a coworker.

Megan was employed at their father's law office—and had been since she'd turned sixteen. Even after their father's death a year later, she'd continued to work there part-time while working on her accounting degree.

Kallie and Brian shook hands.

Brian shoved his hands into his coat pockets. "What's going on around here?"

Nolan cleared his throat. "I'll let them explain, but I need to get going so you all can . . . uh, enjoy your reunion. I'll need to talk to everyone again tomorrow, if that's all right."

"Of course," her mother said. "Why don't you come by for breakfast and I'll make enough for us all?"

Nolan locked eyes with Kallie. "Thank you, I appreciate that." Then he headed for the door.

Kallie swallowed, remembering the times he'd come over for breakfast on Saturday mornings. But only when her father was alive. Rick had ruined Saturday mornings when he'd married her mother. "I think I'm going to put my stuff in my room—or maybe in the guest—" She looked at her mother. "Mom, where am I staying?"

"In your old room, of course."

Kallie nearly wilted. She still had a room here. Her bruised throat grew tight, and once more, she refused to give in to the tears.

She grabbed her suitcase, hugged her mother and sister once more, and walked down the hall off the den. A right turn took her past the media room where she'd watched Disney movies with her friends. She kept going all the way to the back of the house and into her childhood bedroom.

She dropped her suitcase to the floor, sank onto the taupe-and-white comforter, and finally released the tears.

FOUR

Nolan tapped the steering wheel and sat outside his home. He'd stopped by the station to finish the paperwork on Kallie's attack and the hit-and-run. He'd also called Clyde Durham and gotten the man's voice mail.

And now he was running the details over and over in his mind.

Something just didn't feel right to him.

He sighed. Nothing had felt right for the past six years since Kallie had taken off and left him with a broken heart. Not that he stopped living. He'd just had to learn to live without her.

Only now she was back, stirring up all those old feelings and emotions.

And someone had tried to kill her. The car bumping her once *could* have been an accident, but twice? No way. And the bruises on her neck were just added confirmation.

So who could want her dead?

A rap on his window spiked his adrenaline even as it jerked him from his thoughts. He looked up to see his brother Jason staring at him with a frown. Nolan lowered the window.

"You okay?"

"You scared the fire outta me."

"Sorry. I called your name, but you didn't answer."

"Didn't hear you."

"Hence the knock on the window."

Nolan rolled his eyes.

"What's got you so preoccupied?" his brother asked.

"Kallie's back."

Jason blinked. "Kallie? As in . . . *Kallie* Kallie? That Kallie?"

"That's the one."

"Whoa." Jason shivered. "Can we go inside? I'm freezing."

Jason worked with the Hope County Fire Department. He'd been on for the past thirty-six hours and was probably ready to crash.

"Someone tried to kill her tonight," Nolan said.

"What? Kill who?"

"Kallie. Her birthday is two weeks away. Did you know that?"

"No. What's that got to do with anything?" He slapped the door of the car. "Dude, get out of your truck and come inside. You're not making any sense."

"Yeah." Nolan opened the door, grabbed his stuff, and followed Jason into the house. Roommates, brothers, and best friends, Jason knew the history with Kallie. It had been Jason who'd helped him work through his grief and anger at losing her.

Once inside, Jason went to the hall closet to drop his gear and Nolan headed for the kitchen. "I asked Kallie to marry me on her nineteenth birthday, did you know that?"

"Ah. Now I understand. Yeah, you told me. I'm sorry, man."

"Forget it. It's not important. What have we got to eat in here?"

"Why are you asking me? I'm the one who's been working," Jason called from the closet. Nolan hoped he was arranging the gear so it wouldn't fall on his head the next time he opened the door.

"Ha. Right. You're the one that gets to sleep on the job, you mean."

It was a familiar argument. A comfortable one.

Jason appeared in the doorway. "So what happened with Kallie? I didn't even know she was back."

"She just got home today. Came home for her stepfather's funeral." He pulled out a tin-foil-covered casserole dish and sent up thanks for some of the older ladies in the church who'd adopted him and Jason.

"Huh. So, are you going to pick up where you left off?"

Nolan shot him a frown. "No. We left off with her leaving, remember?"

"You know what I mean."

"Yeah." He shut the refrigerator door. "I don't like it."

Jason dipped a hearty spoonful of the chicken casserole onto his plate. "Don't like what?" He set the timer on the microwave and turned.

Nolan shook his head. "Everything that happened tonight. Something feels off."

"So what do you want to do?"

Nolan sighed. "Eat. For now. And plan."

Kallie tried to sleep, but the terror of the evening wouldn't let her keep her eyes shut for long. She kept envisioning the man chasing her, feeling his hand around her throat. If it hadn't been for Nolan—

She shuddered and rolled out of bed to cross the room and push aside the curtains that had hung at the window since she was a small child. The moon cast some light onto the backyard, but not much. French doors opened onto the back deck that led to the pool. As a child, she'd loved this room even though her father—her *real* father, not her stepfather—had installed safety locks on the doors so she couldn't get out that way. Still, she'd enjoyed looking out and simply seeing the pool and imagining the fun times to come.

As a teenager, she'd taken many a late-night swim with her friends. Now she wished she was on a second floor. Or simply somewhere else.

Was he out there? Was he watching? Or had the whole thing just been something out of a nightmare? Had she just been in the wrong place at the wrong time? Had she simply been an easy target for someone waiting on the little-traveled back road?

Maybe.

Kallie slipped into her robe and slippers and stepped out of the bedroom. She figured Rick's children were in the other wing on the opposite side of the house where the guest quarters were, so she wasn't worried about waking them with her nocturnal activities. The house might be only one level, but it was quite large. A sprawling structure that she used to pretend was her castle. Once Rick had moved in, it had become her prison.

Shoving the memories aside, she made her way into the kitchen and turned on the Keurig. She wasn't interested in coffee, but tea sounded good and the machine made hot water fast. She rummaged through the drawer and found several bags.

While she waited for the "ready" signal, she crossed her arms and leaned against the wall. Her gaze landed on the water just beyond the backyard. The lake, the dock, the boathouse—all of it—held some wonderful memories. Her father had loved the water and had instilled that same love in his two girls. Kallie especially.

Being on the water meant spending time with the father she adored. And then he'd died and Rick had moved in and stolen whatever peace she'd been able to find in the sanctuary she called home.

Had someone really killed Rick by cutting the brake line on his car? Who had he made mad enough to do that? It could probably be anyone.

"Honey?"

Her mother's voice warmed her. "Hi."

"Can't sleep?"

"No."

"Mind if I join you?"

"Of course not." Kallie realized the water was ready, filled the mugs, then dropped tea bags into the steaming liquid. She set one of the cups in front of her mother before taking the seat opposite her and bouncing the tea bag in the water. "You can't sleep either?"

"I have a lot on my mind."

"Anything you want to share?"

Her mother ripped a napkin into shreds before looking up. "I've done things I'm not proud of, Kallie."

Kallie stilled. Then nodded. "Okay. You want to tell me about them?"

A laugh escaped her. A low sound with no humor. "Not really, but I'm thinking that some of those things are coming full circle to let me know that my sins aren't forgiven after all."

"That doesn't sound like you," Kallie said. "You know God doesn't hold grudges." She frowned. For as long as she could remember, her mother had always been self-assured and confident. The uncertainty in her voice shook Kallie.

"I know." She offered Kallie a weak smile. "Never mind. The past few days have been horrendous and I'm not thinking clearly. We'll talk more after Rick's funeral."

"Mom?"

"Yes?"

"What's in the will? Why would Rick's children show up at this point other than to attend the funeral?"

"He left them some money."

"I see."

Her mother studied her, then tilted her head thoughtfully. "But it wasn't his money to leave. Is that what you're thinking?"

"Something like that. Unless it *is* his money." Kallie sighed. "I'm not worried about myself, Mom. I've done well. I don't need your money anymore. I told you that three years ago." And yet,

LYNETTE EASON

her mother continued to have money deposited into her account each month like clockwork.

"I know. But sending you that money was a way of feeling like I was taking care of you, I suppose." Then realization flickered across her features. "You're worried about me, aren't you?"

"Yes."

Tears sprang to her mother's eyes and Kallie blinked at the flash of emotion behind them.

"Mom?"

She sniffed. "I'm sorry. It's just that it's been a while since . . ." She waved a hand. "Never mind."

"What? No. Tell me."

"I'm just not used to people worrying about me, I guess."

"What about Megan?"

Lips twisting, her mother shook her head. "I wonder about that girl sometimes. She's so intense and focused on climbing the corporate ladder that she doesn't have time to worry about other people."

"She's an accountant for the law firm. What corporate ladder?"

"Head accountant for the law firm—and a large pay raise."

"I see. Doesn't she have enough money off the allowance she gets?" After her father had died, he'd left Megan and Kallie both a nice trust fund that they received on their twenty-first birthday. Nothing extravagant, but enough to ensure they would be able to pay off any school loans they might incur. Kallie had paid her loans off the day after her twenty-first birthday.

"You would think so. She also mentioned doing some other work on the side. I don't know. She's never satisfied and always looking for the next best thing." She paused and sighed. "As for Rick . . . I know what he did to you and that was horrible. He was a monster, Kallie. He had me fooled for a long time—up until a few weeks after we were married—but once I figured him out . . ." She sniffed and ran a hand down her face. "He didn't like that. For

33

some reason he felt threatened by it. Then when I started believing you over him—and calling him out on his lies—he finally just took off the mask completely."

"Which is about the time he hit me and the reason you sent me away."

She hesitated. "Yes, partly." She offered a sad smile to Kallie. "But I learned from you. It didn't take me long to figure out his children are no better. They're greedy and will do whatever it takes to get their hands on whatever money is available."

"All three of them are like that? There's not a good one in the bunch?"

"Shelley is the least offensive of the three. Just watch your back, honey." She stood.

Kallie shuddered at the ominous words, and she didn't like the look in her mother's eyes. "Don't be mysterious. I've already had one person try to kill me tonight. Please, explain yourself."

"I wish I could. That's the problem. I don't know how to. Or even what to tell you other than they never once spoke to Rick over the last six years, but they called me on a regular basis."

"Asking for money."

"Yes."

"Did you give it to them?"

"Sometimes. Just don't trust them. Okay?"

She wouldn't have, even without her mother's warning, but now she'd be doubly guarded. Kallie gave a slow nod. "Okay."

"Now I'm going to bed. I'll see you in the morning."

She left and Kallie bit her lip. What was that all about? Her mother was worried about Rick's children doing her harm, but all three had been inside at the time of the attack.

So, while Rick's offspring might not want her here, someone else didn't either.

And was willing to kill her to prove it.

Kallie made her way back to her bedroom and sank onto the bed. Exhaustion swept over her. She needed to sleep. And think.

And not think.

About Nolan Tanner.

But not thinking about *him* left her thinking about the man who attacked her.

She stood and paced the floor.

Until she heard the creak of the floorboard outside her room.

FIVE

Nolan sat in his truck outside the Goodlette home and tapped the steering wheel. What was he doing? He should be home and in bed. Only he couldn't stop thinking about Kallie.

So he'd sat up doing some research and found quite a bit of interesting information on Rick Goodlette and his children. Information that made him nervous for Kallie, her sister, and their mother. Rick Goodlette had not been a nice guy. Before he'd married Kallie's mother six years ago, his ex-wife had filed charges for domestic abuse before dropping them and leaving him. He'd also been skirting along the bankruptcy border. It looked like he'd done some fancy financial shuffling to stay afloat long enough to land a rich widow.

Kallie's mother.

In his conversation with her, he'd learned that Rick's children were just as bad. Except maybe the daughter. On the surface, it appeared she just went with the flow. But all three of them were having financial issues. And this was the first time they'd come to visit their father since he'd married Kallie's mother.

To attend his funeral and the reading of his will. Interesting. Telling. Bloodthirsty vultures.

"Here."

He took the thermos cup of coffee from Jason and sipped the hot brew. "You didn't have to come with me. I know you're wiped out."

"Yes, I am." He leaned his head back against the seat. "That's why I'm going to take a little nap while you realize your poor, bleeding heart is making you act like a lovesick teenager."

"I've always loved her," he said. And seeing her again had brought all the old feelings to the surface.

"I know. Even when you were dating her sister, you couldn't take your eyes off Kallie."

He grimaced. "Which is why I had to break up with Megan."

Jason chuckled. "Yeah. Your personalities never had a chance of meshing. She was way too controlling and high-maintenance for you."

"Shut up and go to sleep. I'll wake you if I need you."

Kallie opened the door for the third time since she'd heard the floorboard creak and still saw nothing in the hall. With a sigh, she shut it again and locked it. It must have been Megan coming in from her late-night date with Brian.

Tired, throat hurting, and still shaking from nearly dying, she crawled back under the covers and let herself drift.

The creak outside her door woke her. She glanced at the clock out of habit and saw she'd been asleep for close to three hours.

The wood floor gave another soft groan, and Kallie swung her legs over the side of the bed and sat up. Heart thudding, she crossed the room to her carry-on and grabbed a pair of sweatpants. She threw a sweatshirt over the T-shirt she'd fallen asleep in and crept back to the door. Hearing nothing more, she unlocked it and cracked it open.

She peered out into the hall and saw nothing but thought she heard noises coming from the kitchen. Which was weird. Someone would have to be talking really loud for her to hear them. Megan's room was next to Kallie's. Maybe she'd caused the floor to creak on her way to get a snack? Megan had always been a night owl, preferring to sleep in whenever she could.

On bare feet, doing her best to be as quiet as possible, Kallie slipped down the hall toward the kitchen.

As she got closer, she could hear voices. Loud voices.

Arguing?

Kallie crept closer. ". . . don't deserve to be here. You need to leave and go home."

Megan?

"We have every right to be here," Shelley said. "He's our father, remember?"

"Oh please. You're just after the money and we all know it. Well, it doesn't belong to him. It belongs to my mother and your simpering isn't going to get you one red cent."

Kallie flinched at the venom in her sister's voice.

"You know"—a male voice carried an intimidating tone—"someone tried to kill Kallie tonight. You might want to be careful he doesn't turn his attention to you."

Megan gasped. "Are you threatening me?"

"Of course he's not threatening you," Shelley said. "I think he's just saying things are tense around here and we're all on edge. If someone would attack Kallie, who else might he come after?"

A hand dropped on Kallie's shoulder and she gasped, then spun to come face-to-face with her mother. "You scared me to death."

"I'm sorry. I couldn't sleep. I was walking around and heard voices."

"Join the club," Kallie muttered.

"Who's there?" Megan asked.

Her mother stepped forward. "It's just us." Kallie followed her into the kitchen, weariness dogging her footsteps. She wasn't up to a confrontation with her stepsiblings.

Apparently, they felt the same as they filed past, one by one, to return to their rooms.

Megan crossed her arms and glared at her and their mother. "Why did you allow them to stay here?"

Kallie's mother swept a hand through her disheveled hair. "I don't really know, Megan. I suppose I thought I should in honor of their father's memory."

"Well, see, that's what I don't get. There was nothing honorable about him. He was a bully and a jerk and those are the nicer things I can say about him. There's no need to honor his memory by letting his brats stay in this house."

Kallie blinked at her sister's venom. "Wow."

Megan turned her glare to her. "And you. You leave and we hardly ever hear from you, but as soon as the money is up for grabs, you're all about coming back."

Kallie's jaw tightened. "I left because I was told to leave and I came back because I was asked to."

"And you just naturally follow orders," she snapped.

"Of course not—"

"Girls, stop."

Kallie snapped her lips shut and flinched when her mother turned weary eyes on her. "You did the right thing, Kallie. I promise."

Megan actually stomped a foot. "How can you—"

"Megan, shut up!"

Her sister's mouth formed a perfect *O* at their mother's sharp reprimand. Without another word, she turned on her heel and stormed back toward her bedroom.

Kallie's mother sighed. "I'm sorry. She's angry."

Kallie thought about the argument she'd overheard. "Well, I suppose she has a right to be."

"Yes. Yes, she does."

"I thought Rick liked Megan. Why would she describe him like that? I never remember him being ugly to her."

"He wasn't at first. He treated her well. Doted on her, as a matter of fact."

"What changed?"

"Megan did. At seventeen, when he first moved in, she was fine. They got along great. Then she started questioning his authority and bucking his heavy-handed parenting."

"Sounds like normal teenage angst to me."

Her mother shrugged. "I don't know. There seemed to be more to it than that, but neither one of them said so. In the last year or so, Megan stayed away most of the time. Working, college, or hanging out with friends, so things were less tense between them when she was around." She sighed and kissed Kallie's cheek. "It's complicated, I guess. And I'm too weary to think about it anymore. I'm going to go back to bed and try to sleep. You should too."

"I will in a few minutes."

Kallie waited until her mother disappeared down the hall, then walked to the refrigerator and removed a packet of ham, some cheese, mayo, and a bottle of orange juice. Carrying her loot to the counter, she started throwing together a sandwich.

Just like she used to do before being forced out of her own home by the man who'd so quickly become her stepfather. Her father hadn't been buried three months before her mother married Rick. The memories were still raw even after all this time. At first, she'd simply been in shock at the hasty marriage. Then angry. She'd lashed out at Rick one too many times and he knocked her into a wall.

That was it for her mother. "Go," she said. "I've made a huge mistake, honey. Done things I'm not proud of, and now I'm paying for them. But you don't deserve this." She'd handed Kallie ten thousand dollars in cash and Kallie had driven away from the only home she'd ever known.

And away from the only man she'd ever loved.

Nolan had called and texted, but she hadn't been able to explain why she'd left, to voice her shame that her stepfather hated her while he doted on her sister. That her own mother had had to send her away in order to keep peace in the house. Or the yearlong relationship that had ended because he'd become verbally abusive and Kallie had to walk away with more dreams, hopes, and self-worth dashed into a million little pieces.

Kallie bit into the sandwich, leaning over the napkin to catch anything that might drip out.

The window behind her shattered and a bullet planted itself in the cabinet above her head.

SIX

Nolan nearly dropped his thermos at the loud crack. "What was that?" He screwed the top back on the bottle and set it on the floorboard.

Jason had bolted upright out of his nap. "Was that a gunshot?"

Nolan reached for the door handle. "Yeah. It came from the back."

He quickly put in a call for backup and they both bolted from the vehicle. Nolan followed Jason, who headed toward the rear of the house. "Jason, you stay back."

"No way."

"You don't have a weapon. Stay back!"

Nolan rounded the side of the house to see a figure flee into the woods.

"I got him," Jason said. "You see if anyone is hurt."

"Ja—"

But his brother was already pounding toward the woods. Talk about a role reversal. Nolan growled and vowed to have a word with Jason as soon as possible.

The only thing that brought him comfort was the fact that Jason was a seventh-degree black belt and had graduated from the police academy before deciding to be a firefighter. He could take care of himself in a fistfight, but a bullet would end things fast. And not in his favor.

Sending up a silent prayer, Nolan climbed the deck steps for the second time that night and knocked on the door. Kallie's blonde head appeared from around the back of the recliner where she crouched. When her eyes locked on his, she gave a small cry and raced toward him.

She threw open the door, grabbed his wrist, and yanked him into the den. He shut the door behind him. Her scared, pale face wrenched something in the vicinity of his heart.

"Are you okay?"

Tears stood in her eyes. "Barely. Someone shot at me, Nolan."

"Where are the others?"

"I don't think anyone else heard it. I ducked behind the recliner and called 911."

"Okay, stay here. Backup is on the way."

"Wait! Where are you going?"

"After the guy that did this. He ran into the woods and Jason went after him."

She gasped. "Jason? Your brother?"

"Yes."

"But he's not a cop."

"No kidding. Stay put. Tell the cops what happened when they get here. I'll be back."

He slipped out the door before racing down the deck steps, across the yard, and into the very woods Kallie had come from only hours earlier. Someone had just tried to kill Kallie—again.

He dialed his brother's number while he searched the area, aided by the dim light of the moon. Jason's phone rang and he finally picked up. "Hey."

"You find him?"

"No. He slipped away from me. I'm sorry."

"It's okay." Relief and disappointment warred within him. Relief that there wasn't a showdown between the man with the gun and an unarmed Jason—and disappointment that the shooter had gotten away. "I'll meet you back at the house."

43

"Heading that way now."

Something slammed against the side of Nolan's head and he cried out as he went to his knees. His phone fell from his fingers. Running footsteps reached his ringing ears, along with the sound of sirens. His head spun and he struggled to his feet.

"Nolan!"

Jason's voice was squawking at him from the phone he'd dropped. He snagged it from the ground. "Yeah?"

"You okay?"

"He doubled back or something. Knocked me in the head. I'm seeing stars that aren't in the sky right this minute."

"Can you make it back to the house?"

"I can make it."

He retraced his steps, tension in every muscle, pulse pounding in his head. He half expected the guy to try to hit him again and breathed a relieved sigh when he made it back to the house without another incident.

Before knocking on the door, he called in an update to the officers now arriving on the scene. He'd have to give a report, but for now, he wanted someone combing the woods behind the house.

Kallie opened the door to him and he stepped inside. She gasped when she caught sight of him. "Your head!"

"It's okay."

"No, it's not."

Megan entered the room, pulling her fleecy pink robe around her. "What's going on?"

"Someone shot at me while I was in the kitchen," Kallie said.

"What!" Megan's eyes widened and her face paled. "Who would do such a thing?"

"If I knew that, he'd be in jail," Kallie said and ran a hand over her eyes.

Jason stepped into the den long enough to meet Nolan's gaze.

He gave a slight shake of his head to indicate he still hadn't been able to catch up to the suspect—even having his new location.

"And Nolan, you're hurt!" Megan rushed over to him and took his hand. "Come into the kitchen and let me get that cleaned up for you."

"I'm fine."

"You're not fine. You're bleeding. Now come here."

"The kitchen is a crime scene, Megan. We need to stay out of there."

"Then I'll get the kit out of my bathroom. It'll be like old times when I used to patch you up after one of your boxing matches."

She left and Nolan went to open the front door for the officers while the rest of the family filed into the den, questions pinging from them. He heard Kallie explaining the incident. Her mother cried out, and he turned to see her stumble.

—

The officers stepped inside the house just as Kallie caught her mother before she sank to the floor. She guided her to the brown leather love seat and helped her sit. Her mother leaned back and closed her eyes. "Shot at you? Someone shot at you?" she whispered.

"Yes. But he missed. By a lot." Well, not really, but right now she'd say just about anything to see some color come back into her mother's face.

"Obviously you need to upgrade the security around here," Richard said. As Kallie remembered from the wedding, he had helped install security systems for a while. No surprise his mind would jump to that.

She rolled her eyes. "Mom, just breathe. It's going to be okay."

Her mother opened her eyes. "That's twice someone has tried to hurt you tonight. Someone is after you. Who? Why?"

Megan had returned with the first aid kit and was pestering

Nolan about letting her help clean his wound. So far he'd put her off and she had that half scowl, half pout on her face that boded trouble for someone if she didn't get her way soon. Nolan must have recognized the look, because he finally relented. He didn't resist the ibuprofen she handed him either.

Rick's children must have lost interest in the chaos, because as soon as they gave the officers their "I didn't hear or see anything" statements, they disappeared back to their rooms, and the officers left with promises to keep in touch with anything they found.

Nolan pinched the bridge of his nose. "I'm going to grab some coffee. Anyone else want any?"

"Maybe in a minute," Kallie said.

Nolan nodded and headed for the kitchen.

Kallie rubbed her tired eyes for the hundredth time that night and sat on the couch beside her mother. "Coming home might have been a bad idea."

"No." Her mother shook her head. "It was time."

"But look what I've brought with me."

She clasped Kallie's hand and turned to look her in the eye. "Did you bring it with you or was it already here?"

Kallie frowned. "What do you mean?"

Her mother stood. "This conversation will have to wait. Let's get this taken care of, then we'll have a talk."

"Fine," Kallie said. But her mind spun. What could her mother possibly have to talk about?

After the crime scene unit left, Kallie joined Nolan in the kitchen. "What time is it?"

He nodded toward the window. "Time for the sun to come up."

Megan swept into the kitchen, fully dressed and made up. "Brian's picking me up." She smiled at Nolan. "He's taking me to the little café down near Red's. Remember that place?"

His cheeks flushed and he cleared his throat. "I remember it."

Kallie raised a brow at the interaction.

"Anyway, I don't know when I'll be back." Megan winked at Nolan. "I'm sure I'll be reveling in all the good memories. We had some good ones, didn't we?"

"We did."

She sighed. "I don't know who wants to shoot Kallie, but I sure hope you find him fast."

"I plan to."

"Last night was horrid." She shuddered.

Kallie stood and hugged her sister. "I'm sorry to have brought this home with me."

"Just be careful and watch your back."

"I will." She studied Megan. "Are you and Brian serious?"

"Serious? Nope. Not at all. He's just someone to have fun with right now."

A knock on the kitchen door pulled them apart.

Brian stepped into the room and nodded. "Morning."

"Good morning," Kallie murmured.

He turned his gaze to Megan. "You ready?"

She swept past Kallie and Nolan. "See you later. Stay safe."

And then she was gone, leaving Kallie alone with Nolan. Her heart thumped a bit harder as she took her seat. "How's your head?"

"Pounding. But I can ignore it for the most part. How's your throat?"

"Sore." She smiled. "But I can ignore it for the most part." She glanced at the door one more time. "How serious was it between you and Megan?"

"Not as serious as she just made it sound."

"Are you sure you're remembering that correctly?"

He snorted. "I have a perfectly fine memory of the times I spent with Megan. We had fun, but that was it."

"I think she wanted more. The way she was flirting with you just now says she still might."

"I don't know. It doesn't matter. Not in that way anyway." He paused and swallowed, then met her gaze. "Why'd you leave, Kallie?"

She didn't have to ask what he meant. Her mind tumbled back to that awful year her father had died and her mother had married Rick. "I had to. Rick was very abusive toward me. Verbally and physically." There, she'd said the words aloud for the first time.

He fell silent, then cleared his throat. "Why didn't you tell me?"

She shrugged. "I was . . . embarrassed."

"What? Why?"

"I just was."

"But that wasn't your fault. What about Megan?"

"He didn't touch her," she whispered, "just me." She lifted her gaze to meet his before looking away. What was it about her that was so unlovable? What was it about her that caused men to want to abuse her? The relationship she'd broken off a year ago had been emotionally devastating. She'd done a lot of healing in the time since, but that question lingered in the back of her mind.

Nolan grasped her fingers and she jumped. "Sorry, I got lost for a few seconds."

"I've never stopped loving you, Kallie."

She blinked. "Oh."

"I just thought you should know that."

Tears gathered. She forced them away, unable to deal with the raw emotions sitting on the surface of her nerves. "How did you get here so fast?"

"What do you mean?"

"I mean the person shot at me, and seconds later, you were at my door. And Jason too."

"We were watching the house."

"Oh. Really?"

"Yeah. The events of last night just didn't sit well with me. I decided to come stake out your house, and Jason insisted on coming along."

A tear spilled over. "Thanks."

Footsteps echoed on the hardwoods, and she swiped away the tears as her mother entered the kitchen. "May I come in?"

"Of course," Kallie said, even as her mind still reeled at Nolan's words. He'd never stopped loving her? But . . . she was unlovable, right?

Her mother fixed herself a cup of coffee and joined them at the table. She sat silent as Kallie exchanged a look with Nolan. He raised a brow and she shrugged.

"What is it, Mom?"

With a heavy sigh, her mother lifted the coffee cup and took a sip. "I have a secret and I think it's time to tell it."

"A secret?" Nolan asked.

She nodded. "I've racked my brain to try to figure out how someone would know it and why it would be something someone would want to kill Kallie over, but I just can't think of a reason."

Kallie swallowed hard. "Okay. So . . ."

"So, I think I need to tell you my story and see if you can figure it out. I'm afraid if I wait too long, someone will hurt you, but at least if I tell you the truth, you may have a fighting chance."

A fighting chance?

SEVEN

"Go on, then," Kallie said.

Her mother twisted her fingers, then ran a hand through her hair before she cleared her throat. "Um . . . okay, this is hard."

"Just tell us, Mom."

"Right. Twenty-four years ago, I went to my high school reunion. Blake was out of town. Again. Kallie was just barely a year old, and I was tired of being a single parent. I asked your grandmother to stay with you and looked forward to the night out. I never planned to—" She looked away.

"Planned to what, Mom?" Kallie glanced at Nolan. The intensity on his face sent shivers down her spine.

Her mother rubbed her forehead as though to massage away a headache—or her memories. She sighed. "I never planned to meet up with Rick—and have a one-night stand."

Kallie gasped. Then gaped. "What?"

Tears leaked down her mother's cheeks. She raised a shaky hand to dash them away. "It sounds horrible, doesn't it?" She laughed. A humorless sound that caught in her throat. "What am I saying? It *was* horrible."

Kallie swallowed, her throat tight. "Go on."

"I don't know, maybe I did plan to meet him. We'd dated in high school, you know. We'd been *the* couple on campus. Everyone looked up to us, envied us, wanted to *be* us." She shrugged. "I had seen Rick often over the years. It's hard to avoid anyone in Tanner Hollow when you go into town to do grocery shopping or attend church."

"But?"

"But that night was different. We started chatting, standing in the gym of the high school where we'd spent a lot of time together, talking about old times, reliving old memories"—she gave a small shrug—"and old feelings resurfaced."

"That's understandable, I suppose," Kallie said slowly, "but you don't act on them when you're married to someone else."

"I know. And I . . ." She frowned. "I didn't mean to. But I just . . . I don't really remember a whole lot about the night after a certain point. I guess I drank too much, although I only remember having two cups of the punch they were serving, but the next morning, I woke up and Rick was there beside me. In the bed."

Kallie flinched but didn't think her mother noticed. She had a faraway look in her eyes, as though seeing the events play out in her mind. "My clothes were on the floor." Tears spilled over her lower lashes, yet she continued her story, her voice thin but steady. "When I realized what I'd done, I was mortified. I had betrayed my husband, my vows, my child. Everything I believed in. I ran out of there, got in my car, and drove home. My mother was furious with me. She'd been calling all my friends. She really let me have it once she realized I wasn't lying dead in a ditch somewhere."

Kallie could see that happening. Her grandmother could be a formidable woman. "Did you ever tell Dad? About that night?"

"No." Pain flashed. "I couldn't. I was just so ashamed. And then . . ." She drew in a deep breath.

"Then what, Mom?"

"Then I found out I was pregnant."

"With Megan."

"Yes."

Kallie almost couldn't think, couldn't breathe. "Is she Rick's daughter?"

Her mother hesitated, then sighed. "Yes. Without a doubt she is Rick's."

Pain crashed through Kallie. She simply stared at the woman she thought she knew.

"Don't look at me like that. I don't even remember . . ." She shook her head.

"It sounds to me like you were drugged." Nolan spoke for the first time since her mother had started talking.

"What?" Her mother looked up at him, blinking away her tears. "What do you mean?"

Nolan leaned forward and clasped his hands in front of him. Kallie studied him. He'd grown from the boy she'd loved into a very capable man . . . who said he'd never stopped loving her. She focused on his words.

"You said you were drinking, but not a lot, and that you don't remember anything until you woke up. Is it possible he put something in your drink?"

Her mother rubbed her head. "Anything is possible. Yes, of course he *could* have."

"It sounds to me like he did."

"But why?"

"I don't know. Could he have been targeting you for a reason?"

"What reason? I was nobody." She grabbed a napkin off the table and swiped her nose. "I'm still nobody."

"That's not true. You were married to a rich older man and were the sole heir to his fortune."

Kallie gaped at Nolan, her jaw dangling. She snapped it shut. "Of course. You're right. I've seen it frequently in some of the cases I researched for the lawyers while getting my degree. Girls at parties or bars wake up to find they've been raped and robbed. Men and women meet a friendly person on the beach who offers to buy them a couple of drinks and the next thing they know, they wake up and are victims of a crime—if they wake up at all."

Her mother covered her mouth and sat in silence while she digested this. She moved her hand to her eyes and pressed. Finally, she looked up. "I don't know. Why would Rick do that? I mean other than the obvious. Why do that, then wake up and tell me he loved me and that he'd never forgotten me? That he had hoped and prayed that he'd run into me at the reunion, and when I walked in, it was as if we'd never been apart. Just . . . why?"

"You had an affair with him, didn't you?"

"Yes." Her mother wouldn't meet her eyes. "Every time your father was out of town, we found a way to meet. At first I said no, but . . . well, there's no excuse. I eventually did and this is where we are."

"No wonder Dad was barely in the grave when you married Rick."

Her mother flinched. "Yes. I know. But Rick convinced me there wasn't any need to wait." She rubbed her hands together. "I was engulfed in guilt. Hated what I'd done to your father. I suppose I thought by marrying Rick so quickly, I could pretend like I hadn't been unfaithful, that I could deny my sin." Her voice dropped and Kallie had to lean in to hear her. "He'd tried for years to get me to leave Blake, but I wouldn't."

"Why not?" Nolan asked.

"I don't really know. I suppose most people would think it was because of his money. Rick believed that, even though I tried to explain it wasn't. At least not completely." She sighed. "As crazy as Blake made me and as much as I hated myself for what I was doing to him, I just didn't want to leave him. It was bad enough I was cheating on him, that I'd had another man's child and let him believe she was his, but if I left him . . ." She shook her head. "I simply couldn't do it—and I couldn't do that to you. You adored your father."

Yes, she had. And if her mother had left him for another man, Kallie wasn't sure what she would have done. "Did Dad suspect?"

"I don't know. He never said a word. Never treated me any differently, but sometimes there was this look in his eyes."

"What kind of look?" Kallie asked. Her emotions were all over the place, and she just wanted to walk from the kitchen and bury herself in her bed. Instead, she straightened and forced herself not to fidget.

Her mother looked down, and Kallie caught the sheen of tears before her lids hid all expression. "I would catch him looking at me. Sometimes it was just a quick meeting of our eyes, and for just a moment, there would be a look of sadness and pity that he couldn't quite hide before he'd look away—or force a smile." She laughed a short huff that held no humor. "I thought he knew. I was almost sure he did, but I was never brave enough to say anything. I used to wish he would just confront me, but he never did."

"So when he died, you married Rick."

"Yes. To my everlasting regret."

"What happened, Mom? What's the story behind that? You've never told it."

She flinched before shaking her head. "In the beginning Rick was great." She lifted her hands. "He was wonderful. Attentive and acted like he was crazy about me. He made me laugh and told me I deserved the moon and he wanted to give it to me. He swept me off my feet, I'm ashamed to admit." She sighed. "At least I thought he did. Why would he drug me when he didn't have to?"

"Maybe he didn't realize he didn't have to," Nolan said. "And it could be that he had the drug with him and was prepared to use it on the first person he had access to. But I don't think so. My gut is screaming that he had this planned from the get-go. He knew you had money, the two of you had a history, and he knew just how to play you."

"But it wasn't even *my* money."

"But it would be if your husband was out of the picture."

Kallie went still, one part of her brain shouting at her, another part trying to push away the horrible thought. But she couldn't ignore it. "What if Dad's heart attack wasn't a heart attack?" she whispered.

"What?" Her mother blinked at her. "Of course it was. He'd had heart issues since his early twenties when he was diagnosed with cardiac syncope."

"What's that?" Nolan asked.

"It's when the heart doesn't pump the right amount of oxygen to the brain and you can pass out. He got a pacemaker and seemed to be doing fine. Then the heart attack hit and—he was just gone."

Kallie stood to pace. "I don't like this. I don't like any of it. Something's not right." She turned back to her mother. "Go back to when Rick changed. What triggered that?"

"Shortly after we were married—just a few weeks—he got a call and I heard him cursing a blue streak. When I asked him what was wrong, he told me to mind my own business and hit me."

"Mom!"

"I know. I was stunned. I didn't know what to think."

Kallie blinked. "What was the call about?"

"I don't know, he wouldn't tell me and I was too afraid to ask, but the mask was off. He was so awful." She reached out and grasped Kallie's fingers. "Awful to me and to you." Tears slipped down her pale cheeks. "I'm so sorry."

Nolan cleared his throat. "I'll look into Rick's background again as well as his offspring's. Why are they here again?"

Her mother sighed. "Rick requested it. He and his lawyer were pretty tight, so the lawyer called them. In a moment of weakness, I said they could stay here." Her eyes narrowed. "I knew they were bad news, but I didn't realize to what extent, until after they were already here. They wouldn't have anything to do with him while he was alive, but they'll show up when they think they're going to get their hands on my money because their father was married to me."

"And will they?" Nolan asked.

"I truly don't know what is in Rick's will. I know how much money I have and I know how much he had. I suppose they'll get that. But we signed a prenup, so there's nothing of Blake's or Kallie's and Megan's that they can get their hands on."

"A prenup?" Kallie asked.

"It was Rick's idea. I told him that even without a prenup, he wouldn't have access to certain funds because they were set aside for the girls. He said it didn't matter, he wanted to sign one anyway. At first I thought it was because he was trying to reassure me he wasn't after my money, but later I figured out it was because he was afraid of what other people would say since we were marrying so quickly after Blake's death. So I agreed." She shrugged. "He was right too. I had people comment that if they hadn't known he signed a prenup, they would have just thought he married me for the money." Her lip curled. "People are so self-righteous."

"And Rick cared that much about what other people thought?" Nolan asked.

"Very much so. He was always so conscientious about it. In public, he was the doting, loving husband and father. In private . . ." She shuddered.

"I see," Nolan said. "So, with the prenup in place, why do his children think they're going to get anything?"

"I don't know—because their father married a rich widow, I suppose."

"He must have led them to believe they would get something in the event of his death."

She gave a slow nod. "Yes, he must have. How odd."

"Anything else?"

"Not really. Once I saw his true character and his spendthrift habits, I started holding back. Of course that made him angry." She rubbed her eyes, then looked at Kallie. "That was the time he hit you and pushed you into the wall. I refused to give him money."

"And then you sent me away."

"Yes. He told me every time I refused him what he wanted, he'd take it out on you."

Kallie gasped. "I didn't know."

"I couldn't tell you. I couldn't admit that I'd allowed this to happen, that I'd brought that monster into the family."

Kallie held on to her anger. Her mother was to blame. Sort of. Yes, the affair was wrong and she'd paid dearly for her actions, but Rick had been clever. A manipulator.

"And," her mother continued, "what his children don't know—and what Rick didn't know before he married me—is that Blake arranged for you and Megan to be taken care of no matter what."

Kallie frowned. "What do you mean by that?"

"That you and Megan don't have to worry about Blake's money going to Rick's kids."

"Okay," Kallie said slowly. "Because of the prenup, I get that. That's good, but that doesn't explain why someone is trying to kill me."

"What if one of Rick's children knows about the will and thinks that by getting Kallie out of the picture, he—or she—would have easier access to the money?" Nolan asked.

"I don't really see how they could know anything about our finances unless Rick told them." She shrugged. "And I don't see that happening. He never talked to them about finances, other than to assure them they were in his will. At least not that I knew of."

But he could have without her knowing about it. That was the thought that made Kallie uneasy.

"Who gets Kallie's share of the inheritance if she's gone?" Nolan asked.

"I do. And if something happened to Megan, I'd get hers too. But I'm not trying to kill Kallie." She paused. "And no one's tried to hurt Megan."

"So, it's just me. Like it's always been just me."

EIGHT

Nolan could almost see Kallie's brain spinning. Hurt rolled off her in waves. She'd been the one Rick had abused, she'd been the one who'd had to leave her mother and the only home she'd ever known. And now she was the only one who was a target of a killer.

Jason stepped into the room and Nolan realized how long he'd kept his brother waiting outside. Time to wrap up. Besides, his head was killing him. "I've got enough for now. I'll get this in to my supervisor and take it from there. I'll also see if we can get someone to watch the house 24/7 until this is resolved."

"I think that's a good idea," Kallie said.

Nolan and Jason finally made it to the car once they'd ensured sufficient safety measures were in place. Jason paused as he opened the door. "You've still got it bad for her, don't you?"

"What?"

"Kallie? You're still in love with her."

Nolan sighed. "Yeah."

His brother blinked. "Wow. Didn't think you'd actually admit it."

"Why bother denying it? It's true."

"So what are you going to do about it?"

"Nothing. Right now. Except keep her safe."

"So what now?"

Nolan pulled his phone from the clip on his belt and checked for missed calls. "I still haven't heard from Clyde Durham."

"The partner?"

"Yeah, the one the secretary overheard arguing with Rick two days before he died."

"Where does he live? We could run by there and see if he's home."

Nolan sat for a moment, then nodded. "I've been trying to get ahold of the secretary again and she hasn't returned my calls. I think paying a visit to Clyde is a good idea. Let's do it."

Within seconds, Nolan had the guy's home address from the police software. He took the next right, and ten minutes later they were parked on the curb of the lawyer's large home.

Jason let out a low whistle. "Nice."

"Very."

"These guys don't just practice here in Tanner Hollow, do they?"

Nolan laughed. "No, they just live out here where there's lots of elbow room."

"And it's pretty private. Might make it a little harder to track them down if someone wanted to find them."

"True."

They stepped out of the car and Nolan led the way up the brick front steps to the large oak door. He pressed the bell and waited.

Nothing.

"Guess he's not here," Jason said.

"Guess not."

"Who else lives here? Anyone?"

"Not that I was able to find out. I know Mr. Durham's divorced. He and his ex-wife have three children. They're grown and gone, and his wife moved back to San Diego shortly after the divorce was final." He grasped the knob and gave it a twist. Locked. "Garage door is shut."

"Yeah, all three of them."

"Let's check the back."

Together, they walked around the side of the house. The sun-porch sprawled along the back. Nolan approached the door, then stopped. "Uh-oh."

"What?"

"Look."

Jason peered around him and flinched. "Ugh."

"Yeah."

"Is that him?"

Nolan pulled out his phone. "Guess we're going to have to find out." While he placed the call to dispatch, requesting help, he couldn't help but wonder who had put a bullet in the forehead of the dead man in the sunroom.

———

The day of the funeral arrived swiftly. Nolan stood at the back of the church next to the front door, watching each person who came through it.

Rick's casket sat on display in the front of the church. The man's death had been officially ruled a murder, due to the over-whelming evidence. Clyde Durham, the dead man in the sunroom, had also been been murdered and positively identified by his son. Nolan had heard this morning that a fingerprint had been pulled from the bullet, but no match had come up when they'd run it through AFIS.

Worried about the secretary, Lisa Cleveland, he'd had an officer go by her house, but she hadn't been there. And she wasn't answering her phone. He had a bad feeling about that and had requested everything be done to track her down. So far, no word yet.

Nolan's mind spun through the other information he knew. The argument had occurred, Rick had left the office and gone home. He'd died two days later because someone had cut his brakes. Durham could have cut the brake line that night, but witnesses put him at the hospital with his sister all night. She'd had chest pains and he'd gone to her house and picked her up. The sister's neighbor confirmed this, as did the sister.

Nolan knew alibis could be fabricated, but now that Durham was dead, this case had just taken a turn for the confusing. Of course Durham could have hired someone to do his dirty work, but did it matter now? Yes. It did. He wanted to know who'd killed both men. Had the same person committed both murders? And he wanted to know where Lisa Cleveland was. Nolan sighed and rubbed a hand over his weary eyes.

As soon as the funeral was over, they'd head back to the house for the reading of the will. The lawyer had offered to wait, but everyone clearly wanted it all over and done with.

"We have jobs to get back to," Richard had stated. "Putting it off isn't going to help anyone. Least of all those of us who need to travel."

So Kallie's mother had agreed.

Priorities. Nolan gave a mental roll of his eyes and shook his head. Whatever. He'd be there and he'd have other officers stationed around the house and grounds to make sure no more attempts were made on Kallie or her family.

And that the contents of the will didn't incite a riot. If it did, he'd be there for damage control.

Rick's children all sat at the front of the church behind Kallie, her mother, Megan, and Brian. Rick had specified no graveside attendance, just the church service. Nolan had to wonder why, then figured it was none of his business.

He stood at the back of the sanctuary and watched the service, his eyes scanning for anything out of the ordinary. His gaze landed for a moment on the other officers but couldn't keep from sliding back to Kallie. She had her blonde hair plaited in a French braid down her back. Wispy tendrils escaped, softening the look. There'd been no more attempts on her life, but Nolan wasn't fooled into thinking the would-be murderer had simply dropped out of sight.

No. He was here. Somewhere.

The music played softly, people got up to speak, painting Rick as a stand-up guy, a charitable man who was always doing good things for others.

Kallie dropped her head, then rose and walked toward the exit.

———

She was going to be sick. She couldn't sit there another minute and listen to people praise the man who'd stolen her family—and her self-esteem.

With all eyes on her, she slipped out the back of the church and gulped in the cold air while bracing herself against another wave of nausea.

"Kallie?"

She sucked in another breath and turned at Nolan's voice. "I know. I was horribly rude to get up and walk out, but I couldn't listen to another glowing word."

"No. It's okay."

She tried to find some guilt about the fact and, much to her surprise, found none. "Yes, you're right. It is okay. Do you know Mom told me that Rick had planned his funeral several years ago? That he handpicked each person to speak, the music, everything. I see why now. He was afraid if Mom did it, there wouldn't be much of one."

"He was really terrible to you, wasn't he?"

"Yes, he really was. He basically shattered my self-worth."

Nolan flinched. "But you don't believe anything negative he ever said about you now, right?"

"Not when I'm consciously thinking about it. I wasn't around him long, but it was enough to do damage and sometimes his words still haunt me. I second-guess myself even when I know the right decision to make. Sometimes I feel like I'm not good enough for much of anything, then I realize where that's coming from and I pray against it. Every day."

He wrapped his arms around her and she stiffened. But she decided not to fight it. She burrowed into his embrace and relished the feel of it. Of him. She drew in a breath and his familiar scent washed over her. How she'd missed him!

And then people were filing out of the church. She wondered if God felt like he needed the place cleaned now. "How can people actually get up and lie like that? I mean stand in a church pulpit and *lie*?"

"Maybe they knew a different man than you did."

That was true. Of course, Rick would have only shown his "good" side to those in the church. "They saw what he wanted them to see. He was very good at deception."

"He obviously had your mother fooled."

"Yes, he did. In the beginning anyway."

Nolan took her hand. "Come on, let's get back to the house."

"I don't even want to be there," she said. "But I'll go for my mother and Megan. And if those vultures try one thing, you cannot hold me responsible for what I'll do."

"I think you're going to have to be the cool-headed one in this situation, Kallie."

She sighed. "Probably."

He lifted her chin. "I'll be there for you, I promise."

Tears wanted to flow at his gentleness. He would be beside her, lending his strength to get her and her family through it. Tomorrow it would all be over.

At least this part.

Then she wanted to know if someone had murdered her biological father. And she wouldn't rest until she found out.

NINE

Back at the house, Nolan ushered everyone in. He noted the security, glad his boss was willing to grant the manpower for this. He had a feeling they were going to need it. One by one people filed into the living area. Don Grayson, the lawyer hired by Rick, stepped quickly to the small table near the fireplace and set his briefcase on it. Richard and Shelley, Megan, Kallie, and finally their mother took seats facing the lawyer.

Richard sat on the edge of one of the wingback chairs and rubbed his palms on his thighs. Shelley lounged in hers. James chose to stand next to the mantel, hands shoved in the front pockets of his black slacks.

"This is so stupid," the man muttered under his breath.

Nolan raised a brow at him.

He shrugged. "Well, it is. It's like some scene from one of those old eighties movies or something. The family gathers in the den for the reading of the will." He snorted. "Ridiculous."

"Rick requested this," Sharon said. "I'm simply honoring that request."

"Why? He wouldn't have done it for you."

Kallie's mother flinched. "Be that as it may, I'm doing it. Now be quiet or leave."

James snapped his mouth shut and turned his glare to the lawyer.

Sharon nodded to Grayson and he pulled a manila folder from his leather briefcase. "Well, this shouldn't take long." He cleared his throat. "As you know, Rick signed a prenup before he and Sharon married—"

"What?" Richard jumped to his feet. "I didn't know that." He turned to his siblings. "Did you two know that?"

Shelley frowned and straightened, her faux nonchalant pose gone. "No. I didn't."

"Me either," James said. "So what does that mean?"

"It means you don't get a dime." Megan laughed.

Richard lunged at her and Nolan stepped between them. He placed a hand on the agitated man's chest and gave him a light shove. "Don't do it."

Richard gave a low growl but backed off. Nolan turned in time to see Sharon place a hand on Megan's arm and shoot her a frown. Megan rolled her eyes and settled back against the couch. Kallie simply waited.

Mr. Grayson cleared his throat again. "Shall I continue?"

"Of course," Kallie said.

"So the prenup excludes any of Mrs. Goodlette's money that is in her accounts. The only money Rick had access to was what was in the accounts in his name. And now, he left explicit instructions for me to read this as is, so I will . . . apologize . . . in advance. I asked him not to do this, but he insisted."

Nolan's pulse hummed. This wasn't going to be good.

"To each of my brats—"

Shelley gasped. "How rude."

"—I leave the sum of one thousand dollars each—"

"What!"

"Are you kidding me?"

"—to be paid over a one-year period in equal monthly installments."

Richard and James spoke over one another. Shelley simply rose and smiled. "Well, I guess that teaches us." She walked out of the room without a backward glance.

The brothers fell silent and stared at one another, matching expressions of fury on their faces.

"Please continue, Don," Kallie's mother said, her eyes hard, voice flat.

━━━━━

Kallie nearly fell out of her chair. She looked at her mother. "Did you know he was going to do that?"

"No."

"To Megan, I leave the rest of my assets. Megan, you might be a brat at times, but at least I kind of liked you. I can't stand the other three. Use the safe-deposit key and that will give you access to everything. Sharon's name is on the box. She can access it and give you the contents."

Richard bolted to his feet and James took a step forward. Once again, they raised their voices at the lawyer.

"Hold it down!" Nolan stepped in between the men and the lawyer, once again facing the siblings. "Shut up or I'll throw you out!"

The brothers gaped, then stepped back. Richard took his seat once more and James crossed his arms, still muttering, his face pale. Richard looked the most outraged. Fury glittered in his brown eyes.

James shook his head, his anger dissipating as quickly as it had erupted. "I'm leaving. I'll be gone within the hour." He looked at Kallie's mother. "I . . . thank you for your hospitality. Thank you for all you've done for me over the past several years. I wish . . ." He sighed and shook his head. "I appreciate it."

"Of course, James." Surprise coated her words. "You're very welcome."

He nodded, then without another word or a backward glance, he walked down the hall toward his room.

"He knew," Kallie whispered. Her gaze snagged her mother's frantic one. "He knew." Her mother shook her head, eyes pleading.

Megan raised a brow at her mother. "Knew what?"

"Nothing." She waved a hand. "Keep going."

Mr. Grayson shrugged. "There's nothing else. That's it."

"That's it?" Megan said. "What do you mean that's it? What about Kallie? Why would he leave everything to me and nothing to Kallie? I'm not even his child."

Kallie pressed her fingers to her lips to keep from blurting out the truth. Her stepfather had known Megan was his. But Megan didn't know who her biological father was, and Kallie wouldn't spill her mother's secret.

Mr. Grayson held up a hand. "Could you debate the whys of that later? I'd like to finish this up."

"Yes, please," Kallie said. Had her mother not filled her in on the events that took place the night Megan was conceived, Kallie might wonder the same thing. But Rick knew Megan was his—and had chosen her over his older children. How had he known?

The lawyer finished up, gathered his briefcase, and shook her mother's hand. "Let me know if you need anything else."

"Yes. Thank you."

"I'm going to pack." Richard stormed out of the room.

Kallie sat back on the couch and lifted her eyes to the ceiling as though she'd find answers written there. "So, Megan gets everything and someone is trying to kill *me*."

Truly she didn't care about the money. Her mother had made sure she had more than enough to be comfortable while she got her law degree. And, of course, she wouldn't wish this on Megan. It was just—why?

Because, obviously, it wasn't about money.

At least not anymore. She'd wondered if one of Rick's children thought they would get more if she were out of the picture, but she'd dismissed that idea almost as soon as it popped into her head. After all, she'd had absolutely zero contact with the three of them. In fact, the only time she'd met them had been at the wedding six years ago. Why would one of them want to kill her? The idea was ridiculous. Wasn't it?

Nevertheless, someone wanted her dead.

And she had no idea who it might be.

Once again Nolan found himself sitting in his car outside the Goodlette house, sipping hot coffee from a thermos. Jason was working tonight, so Nolan was flying solo.

But Nolan had been busy after the reading of the will. While there was excellent protection for the family and no real chance of someone getting inside the house, he'd taken it upon himself to do a little research. He was glad for the little bit of information he discovered but was still frustrated and felt like he was missing something. Something in the story Kallie's mother had told them.

Rick had drugged Sharon Goodlette and then raped her. She thought she'd had too much to drink and the next morning remembered nothing of what had happened. Rick had been aware of Sharon's dissatisfaction with her husband, because Clyde Durham and Blake had been good friends. It was possible Blake had confided his marriage troubles to Clyde, and Clyde had passed that on to Rick, his high school best friend. Then Rick could have started planning how to break them up so he could move in. The more Nolan thought about it, the more convinced he became that this was how it all started.

Then came the argument between Clyde and Rick.

Clyde had an airtight alibi for the night Rick had the wreck. But that didn't mean he couldn't have hired someone. And then that someone decided to get rid of the one person who knew what he'd done? It was far-fetched, but not impossible. But still . . . Why?

He thought about Kallie's whisper. "He knew," she'd said. Rick knew Megan was his. And truthfully, if Rick and Megan were in the same room, one would notice the resemblance. She didn't look a bit like Blake Ainsworth, the man who'd been a father to her until his death.

Lisa Cleveland was Rick and Clyde's secretary. He'd left her numerous messages and she had yet to call him back. After their initial conversation when she'd disclosed the argument, she'd all but disappeared. He'd had several officers drive past her house over the course of the last two days, and they hadn't reported seeing her come home or leave. And now darkness had fallen. It was getting close to midnight. Would she be home?

Nolan nodded to the officers on duty and decided Kallie and her family would be safe for the short while he'd be gone. He cranked his car and drove to the address he'd visited the day after Rick's death. When he pulled in front of the house, all the lights were off. The open carport stood empty and the place looked deserted. Nolan debated his next move as he climbed out of his vehicle, praying he wouldn't find another dead body.

A hand clapped over her mouth and Kallie woke with a gasp. "Shh," the voice whispered in her ear. "If you wake anyone, they'll have to die. Understand?"

Sleep fled. Terror quickly took root. Kallie lay still, feeling something against the base of her neck. A gun. Her heart thudded and a fear-generated weakness flooded her. Who—?

"Get up," the person behind her said, "and move slow."

Kallie did as ordered, her mind racing. How had someone gotten inside with all of the security?

As fast as the question blipped through her mind, the answer came. No one had *gotten* in. Whoever was behind her was *already* inside.

One of Rick's children?

But which one?

"Move," the voice hissed. "Out the French doors."

"The alarm will sound."

"No, it won't."

So, the person knew the code. She was sure her mother had given the code to her stepsiblings, but Richard had taken the first flight out to return home, after his disgust with the reading of the will. And James—true to his word—had left the home within minutes.

That left Shelley.

"Why?" she whispered. "What did I do to you?"

"You exist. Now move." Shelley—if it was her—pressed the weapon harder against her neck.

Kallie flinched and thought fast. As soon as she walked out those doors, she was dead. "I need shoes and a coat. Please. If you want me to walk, I have to protect my feet."

Kallie had fallen asleep in sweatpants and a short-sleeved T-shirt. With the outside temperatures in the low thirties, she'd freeze without covering. She spoke in a whisper, heart thudding in her ears, while her frantic brain tried to figure out what to do. All she knew was that if she got a chance to run, she'd definitely have a better chance of escaping with shoes on her feet.

A sigh reached her ears. "Get them and let's get going."

"Where are we going?"

"Away from here."

Kallie dressed quickly, ever aware of the gun aimed in her direction. She thought she saw a silencer on the end and wondered why the person hadn't just shot her in her sleep.

Then she realized that would spark an intense investigation of everyone under the roof.

What would happen if she put up a fight?

"If you don't hurry it up, we're going to walk down the hall and I'll put a bullet in your mother, then we'll visit each and every room until they're all dead. You understand?" The husky whisper didn't sound much like Shelley, but if not her, then who?

"I understand." Her only hope was to attract the attention of one of the officers watching the house.

The gun pressing against the back of her head directed her to the door. She unlocked the deadbolt and twisted the knob. Cold air rushed in, sucking the breath from her. *Oh, God, please protect me.*

"Why are you doing this?"

"Because I hate you." The whispered hiss ricocheted through her mind.

TEN

When he reached the back door into the kitchen, Nolan found the handle broken, the latch knocked off. Instincts screaming, he opened it slowly, not wanting to catch a bullet, should the secretary have a weapon on her. "Lisa? It's Detective Nolan Tanner. We spoke the other day about Rick Goodlette. Are you home?"

Silence echoed. He flipped the light switch and bathed the room in a soft glow. Stepping inside, he let his gaze run over the countertops. Clean except for a mug and saucer. He examined the contents of the mug and saw that it was half full. And the porcelain was still warm.

"Lisa?"

If he hadn't felt the warm mug, he wouldn't think she was there, but his gut instinct told him she was.

With careful steps and a listening ear, he pulled out his maglite and continued to search the house. It wasn't a large space, but Lisa had a keen eye for what went together and she was neat. No clutter—everything had a place. Which probably meant she'd heard him drive up and had darted somewhere to hide. At least she was alive.

"Lisa, please. I'm not here to hurt you. I just want to talk." He cleared the first two bedrooms, then slipped into the master bedroom at the end of the hall.

A rustle from the open closet caught his attention. "I'm Detective Nolan Tanner," he said again, just in case she hadn't heard

72

him when he'd entered the house. "I'm sorry to enter your house like this, but I need to know you're all right."

Stillness. Then more noise as she stepped out of the closet. He turned the light on and she shielded her eyes. "What do you want?"

"To talk. That's it. Could we sit in your den?"

Lisa hesitated and lowered her hand to meet his gaze. She looked worn out, like she hadn't slept in days. And terrified. "What do you want to talk about?"

"I think you know."

Her face crumpled and tears leaked down her cheeks. "They're dead, both of them."

"Clyde and Rick?"

"Yes." She swiped a hand across her face, then grabbed the tissue box from the nightstand. "Come on."

With quick steps, she left the room and headed down the hall. Nolan hurried after her. Once in the den, she perched on the end of the love seat and motioned for him to take the chair next to the fireplace.

"Why were you hiding in your closet?" he asked.

"Someone tried to break into my house yesterday. When I heard you come in, I was afraid that person had returned. Even when you called out, I wasn't sure it was really you and not someone trying to lure me out of hiding."

"You're scared whoever killed Clyde and Rick is coming after you."

She nodded. "I just put it together. It's because Kallie is turning twenty-five and will inherit the law firm—or at least a large portion of it."

Nolan blinked. "What?"

"Last week, I found Megan going through her father's files, one by one. At first, I thought she was just looking for money or something, so I didn't say anything, but then I caught her in his private file folder. No one had touched his office except for Clyde, who'd removed all of the clients' information and passed it on to others to handle. But even his wife, Sharon, hadn't come to clear out Blake's personal effects. I mean, it's been six years and his office is like a shrine to him." She shrugged. "I mentioned to Megan one day about a month ago that Sharon probably needed to clean it out. She agreed. The next thing I know, Megan's in there going through his stuff." She flushed.

"What?"

"I . . . uh . . . well, she left one of the files open and rushed out of the building. I could tell she was upset, so I went in the office and read the file. It was Blake's will."

"I see. What's this about Kallie turning twenty-five?"

She pressed her fingers against her eyes. "She gets the whole thing, partner rights, everything. Megan gets nothing."

"And Megan knew this?"

"Yes. She figured it out when she was going through his stuff."

"And Sharon knew this?"

"Well, of course. I mean, I would think so. Blake didn't have a public reading of his will like I heard Rick did, but Sharon would know about it."

But it had never occurred to her that someone would be after Kallie for her share of the company. They'd been so focused on Rick and his death that they hadn't seen what was right in front of their faces. Well, Sharon hadn't anyway.

"Rick and Clyde were arguing two days before Rick died. Are you sure you didn't notice anything else?"

"No, but Clyde recorded every meeting he had. If you can find his cell phone, it'll be on there."

"Why didn't you tell us this earlier?"

"I didn't think of it the day you interviewed me. I was just in shock, I suppose. I thought about the recording yesterday and was going to find a way to tell you about it, but I've been afraid to leave my home. I think the police are watching because they scared off an intruder last night. I feel safe here because the cops are outside. But if I leave, I'm afraid of what might happen."

"Did you get a look at the intruder?"

"A glimpse when he was looking in my window and then again when he ran across the yard to get away from the cops."

"Could the person have been a female?"

She paused. "Yes, I suppose. The person was thin and not too tall."

It *could* be Megan.

He couldn't take a chance. He dialed Kallie's number and it went straight to voice mail. Then he called her mother. Also voice mail. Of course, they would be sleeping. He hoped.

Kallie shivered as she walked the path directed by her assailant. When they'd stepped out of the French doors and onto the deck, there'd been no sign of any security. They were probably huddled down in their cars, but more than likely, Shelley had timed their perimeter checks and had found a hole to slip through.

The wind whipped her hair around her face and she burrowed deeper into her coat. Her eyes scanned the area, seeking escape any way she could get it. "How can you do this, Shelley? What did I do to make you hate me?"

"You think I'm Shelley?" Her captor spoke in a normal voice for the first time since entering her bedroom.

She frowned. She didn't recognize that voice. Wait. Yes, she did. "Brian?"

"You thought I was your stepsister?"

"Yes, why?"

"That's funny."

She wasn't sure why he thought that was so amusing but didn't bother asking him to clarify. "How'd you get in the house? There's no way you got in with all the cops that are watching it."

"True. I have a key and I know the passcode to the alarm system."

75

I simply left the funeral early, telling Megan I had business out of town and would see her later. I let myself in, reset the alarm, and found a hiding place. It wasn't hard to find one in that mansion."

Giving him the perfect alibi if someone questioned her sister.

"Why are you doing this?"

"Because Megan has worked her whole life for that firm and all you have to do is have a birthday to get it."

"What are you talking about?"

He laughed and jabbed her forward once more with the weapon. "You don't even know, do you?"

"Apparently not."

The lake loomed closer.

"Megan found your father's will. Blake's, not Rick's."

"I'm well aware of who my father is, thanks." Never once had she considered Rick as a father.

"She was devastated that you would receive the firm."

Kallie and her father had discussed working together. The topic had been frequent in their conversations while fishing, boating, just hanging out together. He had been so excited when she'd taken the first steps and started on her pre-law track at school.

"So she killed him?"

"Of course not. She just found out about the will a week ago."

Kallie arrived at the edge of the dock. "Then who killed him?"

"I don't think anyone did. I think he simply had a heart attack."

So . . . it hadn't been murder. That comforted her somewhat.

"But you have to die so Megan can get the firm."

Comfort fled.

Rick's death had definitely been murder. "What about Rick? Did you have some reason to cut his brake line?"

"Yes."

"Why?"

As long as he was talking, he wasn't pushing her toward the dock. What did he have in mind? Drowning? She shuddered.

"Because he knew."

"Knew what?"

"Go." He gave her another shove and she stepped onto the dock. "And Clyde?"

"He wanted to call the cops."

She was going to punch him. He was talking in circles.

She drew in a deep breath, trying to calm her racing heart and shaking knees. "Call the cops about what?"

"Keep walking. I'm done talking."

"Call the cops about what? Why not just tell me?"

She was almost afraid to push him, but what did she have to lose at this point? She took three more steps and that seemed to pacify him.

"About the embezzling. Clyde discovered that Megan was stealing from the firm, and he was going to the cops."

"Megan? Stealing from the firm? I don't believe it."

"Of course Megan wouldn't do something like that." He shook his head. "Rick said there was no way she would do that and he'd handle it."

"So it wasn't Megan who was stealing, it was you?"

"Bingo."

"That's what they were arguing about two days before Rick died?"

"You're clever, I'll give you that. Now we're finished talking. Get the keys."

Three machines were anchored to the dock, their keys locked in a small box with a code she just had to punch in. A speedboat, the pontoon, and a Jet Ski. All of which would take her away from her family. Away from safety. Away from Nolan.

"Which one?"

"The fast one! Quit stalling."

Kallie's fingers trembled as she tapped in the code that would release the keys.

Once he had them in hand, he shoved her toward the speedboat.

The one she and her father used to take out on the lake to fish or ski. Kallie's heart pounded. If she got in the boat, she was as good as dead.

He gave her another hard push and she tripped over the coil of extra rope. She landed hard onto the nearest seat and lost her breath for a moment. He was busy untying the boat. Kallie scrambled to her knees and lunged for the ignition with the spare key she'd palmed from the box.

———

Nolan pounded on the door and rang the bell to the Goodlette home. He'd already alerted the officers on duty that they needed to keep their eyes open. Although he could wait until morning to come by the house, he just couldn't get the thought out of his head that Megan had something to do with the attempts on Kallie's life.

And if that was the case, he didn't want her under the same roof with the woman. Two officers stood at the base of the porch.

The light came on and the door opened.

He thought he heard a motor start and motioned to the nearest officer. "Check the back of the house, will you?"

Sharon Goodlette, wrapped in a robe about two sizes too big, stared at him like he'd grown another head. "What's going on?"

"I need to know that everyone's all right in here."

"Of course. Why?"

"Just check Kallie's and Megan's beds."

"Police! Freeze!"

"Help me!"

The shouts came from the officer who rounded the house—and Kallie? Sharon gasped and spun to dart back into the house. She slapped the wall beside her and floodlights blazed, bathing the exterior of the home in light, including the area around the dock. Nolan bolted in the direction of the yell and turned the corner to see Kallie in the motorboat with a man holding a gun on her.

The shout from the officer had come just after she'd cranked the engine. Brian looked up, swore, and dove into the boat, never losing his grip on his weapon. "Drive!" He turned and aimed the weapon at the officers at the edge of the lake and fired.

Kallie flinched and jerked the wheel. Brian stumbled and cursed her. "Drive in a straight line!" He caught his balance and fired again. It gave her an idea.

Kallie looked back over her shoulder while the wind cut through her jacket. Brian stood, weapon aimed. He was leaning forward, and with another jerk of the wheel, she cut the speedboat into a sharp left. Brian cried out and went over. She spun the wheel once more and headed toward the dock, her heart pounding over the sound of the motor.

Rapid gunshots pelted the side of the boat.

The motor sputtered, then quit. "I'm going to kill you!" His manic scream sent fear shuddering through her.

He continued to fire at the engine, and with growing terror, she realized he was trying to hit something to blow up the boat. And if that didn't work, he was going to hit her.

Without another thought, she dove over the side.

The water closed over her head and cold hit her like a hammer to the chest.

So cold.

Swim.

Safety lay just ahead if she could make it.

She shrugged out of her heavy coat and started stroking, aiming for the dock. Surprisingly, her dash in the speedboat hadn't taken them too far from the shore. Mainly because she'd driven in circles in spite of Brian's order to drive straight out of the cove.

A hand clamped on the back of her neck and shoved her under.

Kallie stifled the scream that wanted to escape. If she opened her mouth, she'd drown. She spun under the water and wiggled to get away from Brian. A muffled sound reached her ears. A motor?

She fought her way to the surface and Brian lunged for her once again.

Kallie kicked away from him, terror making her strokes weak. Panting, she pulled hard, her only thought to make it to the dock. A hard hand on her head sent her under.

With his fingers wrapped in her hair, she couldn't pull away. Her lungs screamed for air. She kicked again and again. Dark dots danced before her eyes and she knew she was seconds away from passing out.

And then she was free.

She reached the surface and pulled in a gasping breath. The dots faded. Kallie spun at a harsh shout. Seated on the Jet Ski, Nolan had Brian trapped in a headlock. The smaller man fought him, but Nolan held tight, having the advantage of a firm anchor. Brian thrashed, his cries of fury sending shudders through her.

"Kallie!"

"I'm okay," she sputtered. "I'm okay." But tremors shook her and her clothes weighted her down.

Kallie gathered strength from somewhere and dragged her weary, half-frozen body over to the Jet Ski. She grasped the footrest and held on. With Nolan's grip cutting off his air, Brian's struggles weakened until he finally went limp. "Hold on, Kallie."

"I'm holding." Barely. Freezing, she shook so hard, she almost lost her grip on the Jet Ski.

The pontoon pulled up beside them and Nolan passed his prisoner to the two officers leaning over the side. They hauled him up onto the end of the boat.

Then Nolan turned to her and pulled her up behind him. "It's over. Let's get you home."

ELEVEN

Six hours later, after a hospital visit that confirmed Kallie's assertion that she was fine, just cold, Kallie sat in front of the fire and sipped hot coffee.

Nolan tried to get the story straight. He looked at Megan. Still pale and shaky, she, too, gripped a coffee mug in both hands. Other officers stood, taking notes. Brian had been hauled off to jail where he'd get a lawyer, but Nolan didn't think he'd be free anytime soon, since he'd spilled the whole sordid story on the ride to the jail. His backseat confession would go a long way toward a guilty verdict. "So, you found your father's will."

"Yes." She shrugged. "I was being partly nosy and partly helpful. I thought if I cleaned out some of Dad's things from his office, Mom wouldn't have to. I knew she'd been putting it off, not wanting to face it. I figured six years was long enough. In the process, I came across it."

Kallie's mother rubbed her eyes before looking at Megan, then Kallie. "It never occurred to me that this was about the firm or preventing Kallie from reaching her twenty-fifth birthday. Not once did that cross my mind."

She was beating herself up for not thinking of it too, Nolan thought.

Sharon looked at her youngest daughter. "I didn't want you to know, Megan. Not yet. Blake didn't want either of you to know about the things you'd be inheriting until your twenty-fifth birthday. I was trying to figure out how to explain what Kallie would get on her birthday without telling you about your part, but I couldn't figure it out. I'd done so many things wrong, was a horrible wife in so many ways—" She broke off and shook her head. "Suffice it to say, I wanted to honor Blake's wishes." She pushed a strand of hair behind her ear. "And almost got Kallie killed because I kept my mouth shut." She sighed.

"Wait a minute," Megan said. "What are you talking about? Tell me about what part?"

"Blake did the same for you. When you turn twenty-five, you will also get a partnership and shares in the company."

"What?" She sat up straight. "I didn't see that. Just the part for Kallie."

Sharon frowned, then her eyes widened. "He amended the will shortly before he died. You must have found an old copy."

Megan sat back with a slump. "Oh."

"You were so young, but when you started working there and he saw how much you loved it, he added that to the will to give you the same thing as Kallie, should you want it."

Nolan figured she wasn't going to tell her she wasn't Blake's child. And really, at this point, why should she? It wouldn't serve any purpose other than to hurt her. "When you turn twenty-five," Sharon said, "you won't ever have to work again if you don't want to. Blake didn't want you to know this because he was afraid you'd waste your lives in the meantime, just waiting for the day the money landed in your lap." She drew in a breath. "Blake was very adamant that you girls work, that you learn the value of having a job and being responsible. He figured by the age of twenty-five, you would have that. Had he lived, it wouldn't have been an issue. He would have just brought Kallie in as a partner with the firm, and then, when Megan turned twenty-five, the same thing, and that would have been it. However, he made

82

the provision that should Megan die before Kallie's twenty-fifth birthday, well, she would get everything. If Kallie had died before her twenty-fifth birthday, Megan would have inherited Kallie's part in the firm."

"But I didn't know that part. And when I vented to Brian about the fact that Kallie was going to get everything when I'd worked so hard, he . . ."

"Took action," Nolan said. "He was so in love with you that he would have done anything for you."

"Including kill," Sharon murmured. "He didn't know Megan would get her share when she turned twenty-five. He just thought she was being shafted. He killed Rick and Clyde because they knew about the embezzling. When he found out about Kallie, what was one more death? Especially when it was for Megan."

Megan flinched and Nolan wished she hadn't worded it quite like that.

"Yes," he said. "Clyde found the discrepancy in the numbers and thought Megan was responsible for it since it was done on her computer. Rick said he'd take care of it. Clyde was going to the cops."

"Wait a minute," Kallie said. "How did Brian even find out that they knew what was going on? That they suspected someone was embezzling?"

"That was probably me again," Megan said softly.

"How's that?" her mother asked.

"Rick came to me and told me what Clyde had told him—that someone was embezzling and he thought it was me because it came from my computer." She shook her head. "I knew it wasn't me, but never suspected . . ."

"You told Brian?" Nolan asked.

"Yes." She sighed and closed her eyes. "I was upset that Clyde would suspect I'd do something like that. I mean, we butted heads constantly about stuff, but I thought we were closer than that. He was like another father, and for him to suspect that I would steal from the firm . . . yeah. That hurt."

"And Brian was a sympathetic ear."

"Yes."

Sharon shook her head. "I still can't wrap my mind around it."

Nolan was glad Rick wasn't there to terrorize his family anymore, but he wouldn't have wished death on the man. On Clyde either. He was just glad the truth was out and Kallie was no longer in any danger.

"Brian was the one embezzling from the company," Megan said. "How did I not know? Why didn't I have some kind of sense that he was so devious? So evil?"

"People like that are good at hiding their true selves," Nolan said. "You can't blame yourself. Those who do wrong, those who do evil are the ones responsible for the wrong and the evil. You're a victim. There's no blame to be placed on you." He looked at Kallie. "On any of you."

Kallie swallowed hard. She got what Nolan was saying. None of what she'd gone through was her fault. She wasn't unlovable, she was just a victim of another person's choices. Well, she might be a victim, but she didn't have to live like one.

She lifted her chin. She'd been running far too long and it was time to change the way she viewed herself. Rick's partiality to Megan and her mother sending Kallie away had influenced the way she not only viewed herself but others too—and clouded the way she thought they viewed *her*. Especially Nolan, who'd never stopped loving her. At least that's what he'd said. And if the look in his eye was any indication, he meant it.

Kallie pulled the blanket from the back of the couch and wrapped it around her shoulders for a double layer. "Excuse me."

She stepped out onto the porch and walked over to the hammock.

It hit the back of her legs and she lowered herself into it. She used to spend hours in this very spot, overlooking the lake and simply staring at the stars. Her father sometimes joined her, and they would plan the future of the firm.

The door opened and shut. "Are you all right?"

Nolan.

"I'm fine. Or no, that's not quite true. But I will be. It's going to take some time."

"Is there enough room in there for me?"

"Of course." She scooted over and he slipped in beside her. Kallie spread the blanket over both of them and he lay on his back with his hands behind his head.

"It's peaceful out here when no one's trying to kill you."

She choked on a surprised laugh. "That's one way to look at it, I suppose." She sighed. "I love it out here. I think it feels a little bit like Christmas now. Maybe this one will turn out to be a good one after all."

"None of what happened was your fault. You know that, right?"

"So you said."

He turned on his side and braced his head on his right hand. "I mean it. It wasn't your fault when your mother sent you away either. You're not unlovable." He leaned over and kissed her.

Surprised, she simply stayed still. Then warmth infused her and she scooted closer to cup his chin and return his kiss. "I never stopped loving you either," she said when he pulled back. "But I'm not the same person I was when I left here."

"Neither am I, but I think we have a good place to start, don't you?"

She cut her eyes toward him. "Start what?"

A slow smile tilted the corners of his lips. "You know what. Start over. Start getting to know one another again. That is, if you want to."

"I want to."

He nodded. "Now that I'm not working on any kind of investigation into your family and friends, will you go out with me, pick up where we left off? Left off, as in the fun, good stuff. Not as in the whole you-leaving thing."

"I'd love to go out with you." She frowned. "I hope Megan's okay with that. She's always had a slight crush on you, you know."

"I know, but Megan's like a cat. She'll land on her feet. And she will find someone to love. In her time."

"And God's."

"Yes, and his." He paused. "So . . ."

"Yes?"

"Are you moving home?"

She laughed. "Yes, I am. Just as soon as I can get everything taken care of back in Tennessee."

He wrapped his arms around her and pulled her close once more for a tight hug. "I'm so glad."

"Me too."

"Welcome home, Kallie."

Yes. Welcome home. *Finally.*

LETHAL
CONSPIRACY

ONE

Firefighter Jason Tanner held the hose on the flames that threat-ened to consume the two-story Victorian home. Normally, he worked in Tanner Hollow, North Carolina, but his station had been called to Elk's Corner, forty-five minutes away, to help with this blaze.

The garage door caved in and fell away with a crash and a shower of sparks. He turned the hose on it. Only to notice something shin-ing through the smoke and dark. "Hey, Mike!"

Mike Justus shifted the hose and turned. "Yeah?"

"Are those lights?"

Squinting, Mike moved two steps closer. "They're headlights!"

Jason motioned to his captain, who jogged over. "Hold this, Cap. I think someone's in there!"

"Be careful. Cookie, go with Jace!"

Cookie hurried over and Jason donned his mask. Together they strode toward the garage while water rained down on them along with ash and other debris. The flames had burned the wooden garage door, but not the interior. Yet.

Jason placed a gloved hand on the hood of the vehicle and looked at Cookie. "It's running!"

Smoke obscured his vision and he couldn't tell if there was anyone in the car. But why would it be running with no one inside?

Hefting the ax in his left hand, Jason stepped toward the

passenger door while Cookie worked his way around to the driver's. Jason leaned in and spotted someone stretched across the front seats. Her dark hair fanned around her. The driver's and passenger's windows were cracked—not enough to reach in and unlock the door, but enough to let the fumes leak slowly into the vehicle. "There's someone in there," Jason said. "We've got to get her out!"

Jason tried the passenger door. Locked. He lifted the ax and smashed the window, then reached around and unlocked the doors. The woman didn't move.

Cookie opened the driver's door. The big man leaned in and hefted her slight form from the seat, then headed out of the garage with her cradled in his arms. Jason hurried after him. Once away from the danger of the flames and smoke, Cookie laid her on the ground and bent over her. His eyes caught Jason's. "She's got a pulse, but she's not breathing. Do your thing while I get the rest of the equipment."

They were all trained as EMTs or paramedics, but Jason had more medical experience than most of them. He ripped off his mask and laid it aside.

Jason settled one hand at the base of her head and tilted her chin upward. He opened her mouth and placed the CPR Resuscitator mask over her nose and lips. As he blew life back into her, her chest rose and fell. He continued to breathe and check her. "Come on, sweetheart, *breathe*," he begged between puffs. Jason worked for the next few seconds, his heart thumping as he realized she might not make it. He might be too late.

And then she gasped.

She choked and gagged, and he quickly rolled her on her side as her body reacted to the carbon monoxide she'd inhaled.

When the spasms stopped, he took the wet cloth Cookie handed him and cleaned her face. She blinked, her eyes foggy and unfocused.

But at least they were open and she was breathing.

Paramedics arrived and Cookie waved them over. Within seconds they had her strapped on the gurney with the oxygen flowing. How long had she gone without breathing? Would she have brain damage?

"What's your name?"

She didn't respond.

Jason watched her, drawn to her fragile beauty, but also something more than that. She looked so helpless and he wanted to help her. Protect her.

He shook his head. What was wrong with him? He'd thought he'd seen everything when it came to fires and people in trouble. This victim shouldn't be having such an effect on him.

But she was.

Her eyes flickered and she gave a low groan.

Jason reached around the nearest paramedic and grasped her hand. "It's going to be okay. They're going to take you to the hospital."

Their eyes met. The desperation there latched on to his heart and he found himself unwilling to let go of her fingers.

"Jason. Jason!" Cookie pulled him from her and gave him a slight shake. "What's wrong with you, man?"

Jason cleared his throat. "I have no idea."

He raced over to grab another hose and turned it back on to the fire. His heart thundered at the strange encounter, but he had to ignore his odd reaction and help put out the flames still licking away at the home.

And he needed to put away the image of the beautiful dark-haired woman on the gurney who had somehow managed to worm her way into his heart.

Lilly struggled up from the darkness. Fear clamored inside of her, but she wasn't sure why, she just knew she had to get away.

But from what?

Him. He wanted to hurt her. But why?

Why were her thoughts so jumbled? Why couldn't she think?

Was he there?

It would help if she could open her eyes. His blurry features swam in her mind. She wanted to see him. Not the scary guy, but the nice one. The one whose face she'd seen for a few moments before the ride in the ambulance.

She kept seeing his face, dreaming he was there, taking care of her.

But that was impossible. Wasn't it? She didn't even know who he was.

Where was she? Why couldn't she wake up?

Why had she been in an ambulance?

A hand gripped hers and she floated closer to the edge of consciousness.

Lilly lifted a hand to her face and felt the rubber tubing running out of her nose. She became aware of the air forced into her nose, the bandage around her forearm.

She blinked and her surroundings slowly came into focus. A hospital room. With effort, she turned her head to look at the person holding her hand.

And gasped.

The man from her dreams. His blond hair lay in disarray, like he'd run his fingers through it numerous times. Long, dark lashes lay against his cheeks and his chest rose and fell with easy breaths.

But who was he?

And why did his presence ease the fear beating through her?

Lilly closed her eyes, weakness assaulting her. What had happened? She'd been hurt, obviously. But how?

Images flashed at her.

The man who'd broken down her door.

The gun.

The terror.

He'd shot her.

She flinched and opened her eyes.

The man sitting next to her squeezed her fingers as he straightened and rubbed his face with his free hand. "You're awake," he said softly.

"Who are you?"

He smiled. A beautiful upturn of his lips that revealed a deep dimple in each cheek. "I'm Jason. What's your name?"

"Lilly . . . Peterson."

"Good."

She squinted at him. "But you knew that."

"Your purse was in the back seat of your car. I retrieved it and found your driver's license."

"So why did you ask?"

"You were exposed to quite a bit of carbon monoxide."

The memories swept over her in full force. "He . . . shot me." Her hands came up and explored her body over the gown, but she felt no bandages.

Her words brought a frown to Jason's face. "What? Who?"

"I don't know."

"What do you mean, he shot you?"

"He came to the door, I opened it, and he had a gun. He shot me." This time, she pushed the gown off her left shoulder. "There."

He looked. "It's red. Looks like a mosquito bite or something, but it's not a gunshot wound." Jason met her gaze. "Did you try to kill yourself, Lilly?"

The raw compassion in the question prompted tears. And a raging anger. "No," she whispered. "Never."

"It sure looks like it."

"Because that's what it was supposed to look like. Just like Jenny's death."

"Who's Jenny?"

Lilly pressed her fingers to her eyes, trying to hold back the tears. "My best friend . . . who got into her car last week, turned it on, and died of carbon monoxide poisoning."

"Just like you."

"I didn't believe she would do such a thing. I couldn't believe it. And now I know exactly what happened to her. She was murdered— and I was supposed to die just like she did."

Jason frowned at her. "That's a pretty incredible story."

A harsh laugh escaped Lilly and she grimaced. "I know. It's okay if you don't believe me. I'm not sure I would believe it either if I hadn't lived it."

"They think you were trying to kill yourself."

"Who? The doctors?"

"Yeah."

"I'm sure they do. That's what they're supposed to believe." She blinked and bit her lip, trying to organize her scattered thoughts.

"They want to keep you for an evaluation, make sure you're not a danger to yourself."

She stilled. "They want to lock me up?"

"Just long enough to do the evaluation."

Sheer terror froze her. She swallowed and glanced at the door.

"There's a guard on your door," Jason said. "Just in case."

"In case I try to hurt myself?"

"In case you try to leave without getting help."

Oh boy. The more they talked, the more her mind started work- ing again. She studied the handsome man at her side. "Why are you here?"

His gaze locked on hers. "I don't really know. I just knew I couldn't leave you alone."

Her heart thudded at the look in his eyes. Part confusion, part sorrow. "You pity me."

"Maybe that's part of it. At least when you were unconscious and almost dead. But then when you were loaded into the ambulance . . ."

She remembered the look. The connection that had passed between them. "I remember," she whispered.

"Really?"

"Yes." For a moment, neither spoke. He cleared his throat. "Your house is gone. The fire pretty much destroyed it."

"It wasn't my house."

"Which explains why your address on your driver's license didn't match the home address."

"No."

"In fact, the address on your license is a piece of undeveloped land not too far from here."

She glanced away then back. And sighed. "I know."

He looked surprised that she didn't deny it. But why bother? They'd found her now—and she was going to have to run if she wanted to live another day.

TWO

Jason scratched his chin as he studied this intriguing woman. "Okay . . . So are you in the witness protection program or what?"

She pursed her lips and shook her head. "Not exactly."

"Are you going to tell me?"

Fear flashed across her features. "I want to," she said softly.

"But you don't trust me."

"It's not that, it's just . . . well, yes, I guess it is partly that. I'm sorry." Tears gathered in her eyes and Jason frowned.

He sat in silence for a moment, then said, "You don't know who to trust, is that it?"

Her gaze snagged his and with a slow nod, confirmed his suspicions.

"Who are you running from?" he asked.

Lilly blinked, then flushed even as the fear in her eyes doubled. She gripped the sheet covering her legs and twisted it, then smoothed it back out. She ran a hand through her dark hair and shook her head. "Whoever has finally caught up with me."

A knock on the door sounded and she flinched as the doctor walked in. He appeared to be in his midfifties with salt-and-pepper hair and a trim build. Light blue eyes noted Jason's presence and then turned on Lilly. "Glad to see those eyes open."

"Thanks."

He pulled a penlight from his pocket. "I'm Dr. Fields. You mind if I take a look?"

"That's fine."

As he examined her, he asked several questions. Jason took note of the answers.

The man finally stood back. "You must not have been in the vehicle very long. Just long enough to pass out. I don't think you'll have any permanent effects from the carbon monoxide. You're very fortunate."

"Yes, I am. Thanks."

The doctor blinked as though her answer confused him. "I'm going to notify the on-call psychiatrist," he said. "With any attempted suicide, we have to order an evaluation. You understand that, right?"

"I didn't try to kill myself."

Dr. Fields raised a brow at Jason, who shrugged and frowned. "I don't think this is a suicide attempt, Doc."

"No? If not, then what is it?"

Jason said nothing and the doctor drew in a breath as he looked back at Lilly.

"An accident?"

Lilly shook her head.

"Because if that wasn't a suicide attempt or an accident, then" —he paused—"are you saying someone tried to kill you?"

She met his gaze. "Yes. That's exactly what I'm saying."

"I . . . uh . . . I see. Well, from what the police say, it's a suicide attempt, so we'll still need that evaluation. Someone will be here soon to transport you to the floor where they do those."

Lilly paled but gave a slow nod. "All right."

The fact that she didn't protest surprised Jason. The doctor left and she looked at him. "I didn't try to kill myself."

The quiet intensity of her words slammed him. And he realized something. He believed her. Fully and completely. And he was going to help her. "Hold on a sec." He bolted for the door.

When he opened it, the guard was at the nurse's station talking to the pretty blonde. Just past him, the doctor was going over a chart with two others dressed in white coats. "Dr. Fields?"

The man turned. "Yes."

"Lilly doesn't need an evaluation. I'm going to be taking care of her."

Lilly blinked at Jason's sudden departure, but took advantage of the moment to throw back the covers and swing her legs over the side of the bed. Dizziness hit her and she closed her eyes, holding on to the rail until the room stopped spinning.

On shaky legs, she crossed the floor and opened the closet door. Her clothes were there. They smelled of smoke, but they would do for now.

Quickly, she changed into them, stopping every few seconds to cough and gather her strength. Her arm throbbed, but she was able to ignore it. Once she had her clothes on, she set her tennis shoes on the bed and sank into the chair next to it.

Spent, Lilly closed her eyes and leaned her head back to rest a moment. But tension hummed through her. She had to get out before anyone came back.

But what about the guard? How would she get past him?

She'd have to fake a faint or something.

Now that she had a plan, she just had to implement it. Only she didn't have the strength to move.

But she had to. The events of the night were foggy and trying to remember exactly what had happened caused her head to pound. She just knew she was in danger and had to get away.

The door opened and she gave a mental groan. Too late. She'd waited too long. She opened her eyes and focused on the man in the white coat. "I'm not going to a psych ward."

He stepped closer and Lilly's internal alarm clanged. She stood and he struck. Quick as a snake, he grabbed her by the forearms and tossed her on the bed. She didn't even have time to scream before he pressed the pillow over her face.

Once Jason realized he couldn't change the doctor's mind, he stopped trying and walked back to Lilly's room. He frowned at the absence of the guard and determined to speak to someone about that. Jason knocked and pushed open the door.

Only to see someone hovering over Lilly on the bed.

No, not hovering.

Smothering.

Jason raced to the man, grabbed him by the upper arm, and pulled him off Lilly. A swift punch sailed toward his head and Jason ducked, stepped back, spun, and kicked out. His right foot connected with the attacker's left cheekbone and the man went down. His head cracked against the tile floor, and Lilly sat up gasping.

Jason checked to make sure the would-be killer wasn't going to cause any more problems and found him unconscious but breathing.

He looked at Lilly. "Are you okay?"

She gave a short nod, her face as pale as the pillow that had almost ended her life.

Jason pulled his phone from his pocket and dialed his brother's number. Nolan answered on the second ring. "What's up?"

"I just stopped a murder."

A pause. "What?"

"I'm at the hospital, room 4 in the Emergency Department. The guy's on the floor, unconscious right now, but I really need you to come get him."

"Call hospital security. I'm on my way."

Jason hung up and found Lilly on her feet. "The cops are on the way," he told her.

"Good. Now I have to leave. Can you help me get out of here

before they come to take me to the psych ward? Once I'm locked up with no escape, I'm dead."

The door opened and two officers entered, hands on their weapons. The man on the floor stirred, and Jason glanced at the first officer. He looked familiar. "Robby?" He'd met the officer a few months ago at the annual softball game the police department put on to raise money for the local children's hospital.

"Jason?"

"Yeah. How'd you guys get here so fast?"

"We were already in the hospital on another matter when the call came over the radio. What's going on?" he asked, his gaze landing on the body sprawled at Jason's feet. The officer with him knelt next to the man and checked his pulse. "He's still alive," Jason told him. "I came back into the room after talking to the doc and this guy had a pillow over Lilly's face trying to smother her."

Robby lifted a brow at Lilly and she shuddered. "He's been stalking me for weeks," she said.

"A stalker, huh?"

Lilly nodded. "I can't get away from him. Everywhere I go, he shows up."

"And this time he must have decided to end it for her," Jason muttered. "There was supposed to be a guard on her door, but he was too busy flirting with the nurses down the hall."

The man shifted with a groan and lifted a hand to his head.

"I didn't check to see if he had any weapons," Jason said.

The officer quickly patted the man down and paused at his right hip. He pulled out a gun and passed it over to Robby, who handed his partner his cuffs.

With the man's hands secured behind his back, Jason felt slightly better. Lilly's attacker opened his eyes and blinked a few times before he focused on the people in the room. Then his gaze went dark and he tried to lunge at Jason. The two officers restrained him.

"Calm down!" Robby gave him a hard shove, knocking him back to the floor. His partner yanked the attacker to his feet and shoved him into the chair next to the bathroom. Robby held him there with brute force.

Jason simply stared at the man. "You need to leave Lilly alone."

Dark eyes glittered at Jason. "You have no idea what you've just landed in the middle of."

"That's true. But it doesn't change the fact that you tried to kill her. And failed. She's safe now and you're off to prison. Hope your sick obsession was worth it."

Lilly's sharply indrawn breath caught Jason's attention, and he glanced at her. She shook her head and frowned. She clearly didn't want him to antagonize the man.

"It's no obsession," he said. "She's just a job."

THREE

Once the officers removed the man who'd tried to kill her, Lilly looked at Jason. "Do you believe me now? That I didn't try to kill myself? That I was set up?"

"I believe you. I believed you before the attack. And I think the doctor will too."

She glanced at the door where her attacker had been escorted out. "But they're getting desperate. They don't care if it looks like suicide or an accident anymore. They just want me dead."

"They? I thought it was just a stalker."

She raked a hand through her hair. What was she going to do now? Where would she go? Where *could* she go? "No, I just said that for now. And I don't have time to talk to the cops or jump through the hoops they're going to want me to jump through. I have to leave."

"And go where?"

"I have no idea." She gave a half laugh that held no humor. "But the good thing about that is, if I don't know, neither do they."

"I know."

"Know what?"

"I know where you can go."

"Where?"

"With me. Come on."

His phone buzzed and he took a second to glance at the screen. "Nolan's on his way. Maybe we should wait for him."

"Nolan?"

"My brother. He's a cop."

She shifted uneasily, glanced at the window, then the door. "No, I can't wait. I can't stay here."

"Fine. We'll let him know where we are once we get there." He grabbed her purse from the nightstand and handed it to her. She slipped it over her shoulder, letting him take her hand before he pulled her out of the room.

The officer who had been assigned to her room was there, just outside the door, sitting in the chair and reading a magazine.

"Hey, where are you going?" the man asked. He stood and rested a hand on his weapon.

"I'm leaving. I've been discharged." The lie came easily to her tongue. The pang of guilt that stabbed her heart wasn't quite as easy to deal with. She hated lying, and circumstances had forced her to become a liar.

The officer frowned. "No one said anything to me."

Jason sighed. "You want to check with the nurse?"

"Yeah. Hold on a second."

He started down the hall, then paused and turned back. "Why don't you come with me?"

"Fine." Lilly gripped Jason's hand and fought the desire to bolt toward the exit.

Which was exactly the direction he was leading her. She followed him, and as soon as the officer had his back turned once again, Jason opened the door and motioned for her to slip inside. She did and the door shut with a light click. "Go up," he said.

Lilly didn't hesitate. She ran up the stairs to the next floor and heard the door open below them.

Jason pulled her to a stop and held a finger to his lips.

"Hey! Hey, police! Stop!" The officer's footsteps descended and

Lilly breathed a sigh of relief. She and Jason stepped out onto the new floor. At the end of the hall, they found another stairwell.

This time they went down. It led them straight to an exit that took them outside onto the hospital sidewalk. "Where's your car?" she asked.

"On the other side of the hospital. You want to wait here? Hide in the bathroom?"

"No. I'll go with you. They'll probably sound some kind of security alert and start searching for me."

"Right."

Together, they walked half the perimeter of the hospital with Lilly glancing over her shoulder every few seconds, certain she would be caught and stopped.

"Who's after you?" Jason asked as he led the way into the parking lot near the emergency room. He lifted the key fob and clicked it. His Jeep Wrangler chirped and she darted for the passenger seat.

"A really desperate person." She clicked her seat belt and looked over her shoulder while Jason climbed behind the wheel. Hospital security drove past in the little car with the flashing yellow light on top. The driver paused when he saw them and lifted his radio to his lips. "He's calling us in," she said.

Jason started the Jeep and backed out of the parking lot. "No doubt he was looking for my car. Make sure your phone's GPS is shut off, then power the whole thing down."

She did as he said while he left the parking lot and merged into the traffic passing the hospital.

"How would he know what to look for?" she asked.

"Easy. He simply called it in and got my name from the officers who took the report on your attack. A quick search and they have my vehicle make, model, and license plate."

"Great." She sighed. "I'm so sorry I got you into this."

"You didn't get me into it. I volunteered. Now sit tight and let me get us out of here."

Sit tight. Yes, she might just have to do that. She drew in a breath and coughed. Her lungs still ached, as well as her head, her arm, and just about every joint in her body. It would take a while for the carbon monoxide to leave, and she'd just have to deal with the effects. Nausea rose. She swallowed and leaned her head against the window, not sure whether to be grateful for Jason's timely intervention—or scared to death he would be the next one to die.

Jason glanced at his silent passenger and figured she'd fallen asleep. That very fact gave testament to her complete exhaustion, and he wondered how long she'd been running before the person who'd tried to kill her had finally caught up with her.

The purple shadows under her dark lashes were still there and he vowed to find a way to help her get rid of them. Make her feel safe. Questions haunted him. Who was she running from? And why? He didn't think she was a criminal, but the thought pressed in on him. He dialed Nolan's number and his brother answered on the first ring.

"Where are you?"

"You haven't tracked my phone yet?" He kept his voice low so he didn't disturb Lilly. She didn't move when he started talking.

"That's next on the list."

"I'm on the road. I need you to run a background check on Lilly Peterson."

"The woman from the hospital?"

"Yeah."

"The one that's suicidal and you helped break out of the hospital?"

"That's the one."

Nolan's big sigh filtered through the line. "Jace—"

"Don't start, Nolan. She didn't try to commit suicide. Someone tried to kill her, and she needs help. There's something going on here that's bigger and deeper than it looks. I'm going to find out what that is."

His brother's hesitation came through loud and clear. "Are you sure?" he finally asked.

"I'm not sure about anything right this second except the fact that I'm supposed to help her."

"Then that's what we need to do."

"We?"

"I have a feeling you're going to need some law enforcement on your side."

"Probably."

"Okay, where are you going to hole up for the night?"

"I think you can figure that one out."

A pause. "You don't want to say?"

"No. And I'm going to turn off my phone's GPS until I get a chance to get more of her story. But it's obvious someone wants her dead. The guy in the hospital room laughed when he was accused of being a stalker. He described her as 'a job.'"

"A professional?" Nolan's quiet question held a world of concern.

"Yes, that was my impression. And now they know she's with me, so they'll try to track her through me."

"Okay. Stay safe, and I'll start running her information." Nolan blew out a breath of frustration that came through the line.

"How's Kallie?" Jason asked.

"Ready to give birth any day now."

Terror and excitement mingled in his brother's voice and a twinge of envy ran through Jason. He pushed it aside. Right now, the sleeping woman in the seat beside him needed his help. He'd have to worry about his love life later.

"I'll use the pay phone to keep in touch. Talk to you later."

"Right. The pay phone. Use the code if you need to."

The code to signal he needed help and couldn't say so.

106

"I will."

Jason hung up and pulled over, leaving the engine running. He turned off the GPS on his phone, then shut the device off completely. He then pulled back into the lane, drove two miles, and got off the highway, crossing the bridge before turning left to get back on the interstate going in the opposite direction.

Now, he could focus on getting Lilly to a safe place while Nolan worked on things from his end.

FOUR

Lilly woke when the car rolled to a stop. She blinked several times and was horrified to realize how deeply she'd slept.

"We're here."

Her heart thudded at his words. "I'm sorry I conked out on you."

"You needed it."

"Yes, but I shouldn't have taken it. I should have been watching to make sure we weren't followed."

"We weren't."

She eyed him, comforted by his calm assurance, but not quite sure she believed him. "How do you know?"

"I did a stint in Iraq before coming home to fight fires. Trust me, we weren't followed."

Lilly raised a brow, then nodded. "All right. Then where are we?"

"At a little cabin in the woods." He smiled. "It's my family's place. We use it year-round, but mostly in the summer. We get everyone together and spend a few weeks playing."

"Playing?"

"You know, boating, skiing, swimming." He shrugged. "Since it's only a couple hours away from Tanner Hollow, everyone comes and goes as they can—or want. I think my aunt and uncle were just here last week."

"Nice."

They climbed out of the vehicle and he grabbed several fast-food bags. "I swung through the drive-thru and grabbed some burgers and fries. I also got a couple of salads because I wasn't sure what you would eat."

"Anything is fine, thanks." She was hungry, but frowned. "Please tell me you used cash."

"I did."

He led the way to the front door. "There are some things in here that we keep for guests, like a toothbrush and soap, but we'll have to figure out what to do about clothes for you."

She really wanted to change, but wasn't interested in trying to find an open store. All she wanted was a bed and some more sleep. If it would come. And food. Yes, food would be good.

They stepped inside the cabin and instant coziness surrounded her. "Oh, wow, it's lovely."

"It's not much, but it serves the purpose."

"Not much? Looks wonderful to me." The walls were made from smooth wood, probably maple. Reds, greens, and golds blended to form a soothing and relaxing atmosphere. The large living area held a full-sized sofa and matching love seat artfully arranged in front of the television mounted over the fireplace. To her right, the living area flowed into the kitchen. Bar stools surrounded the large island, and all of the appliances looked brand new.

"My mom and aunts and uncles got together last year and up-graded everything," Jason said, "so it feels kind of weird to walk in here and see it like this. It's nicer than it used to be, that's for sure." He laughed. "Anyway, it's got three bedrooms down here and two bathrooms. Upstairs there's a kind of loft that has another sleeping area and a bathroom. You can have your pick of rooms. Sherry and Gail, my cousins, usually sleep in the room at the end of the hall because it has a queen bed and a set of bunk beds in there. There might be some clothes in the closet that could work for you if you want to check."

She dropped her purse on the leather sofa and turned to meet his gaze. "Thank you."

"No problem."

"Yes, actually, it is a problem. I'm a problem." She sighed. "And I'm afraid you've just inherited my problems."

"Will you tell me what happened to bring you to this point?"

Should she? Her best friend had been killed because of what Lilly had seen, and she sure didn't want to drag another innocent person into the danger that stalked her at every turn.

And yet, if she didn't tell him, she might be endangering him even more. Warning him was probably the best thing she could do for him.

"Sure. Let me get a quick shower and find something to wear and we'll have a little talk while we eat." The nap in the car had helped. The shower would revive her for a while longer.

"Fine. I'll see if there's anything in the refrigerator. We have some food to last us a couple of meals, but after that, we'll have to figure something out."

With one last pause and a search of his guileless green eyes, Lilly headed for the bedroom at the end of the hall.

Jason stepped into the kitchen, placed his hands on the granite countertop, and pulled in a deep, steadying breath. What was he doing getting mixed up in her problems? The question almost made him smile. Almost.

He couldn't help it. If he came across a woman in distress, he had to help. It was one of his downfalls. And it usually came back to bite him in the end, but all the same, he couldn't *not* help.

His brother Nolan seemed to have the same complex. Only he'd married the last woman he'd rescued. Jason gave a light snort. He wasn't in the market for marriage.

Shaking off the thought, he walked over to the refrigerator. A quick perusal didn't bring good news. But it wasn't awful. He had condiments and some milk that had expired a week ago. He smelled it. "Ugh. Nasty." He dumped it down the sink and went back to rummaging. Peanut butter, grape jelly, butter, mayo, mustard, and ketchup. There wasn't a whole lot he could do with that without some bread. He finally shut the door with a sigh. The freezer revealed a bag of chicken, some frozen veggies, and half a gallon of mint chocolate chip ice cream.

They could get a couple of meals out of that, but if they planned to stay more than a day or so, he'd have to run into town—which he'd have to do anyway if he wanted to check in with Nolan. And he did.

He returned to the counter and placed some of the fast food on a couple of plates, filled two glasses with water, and set everything on the table.

The bedroom door opened just as he finished getting the silverware out of the drawer.

Lilly walked into the kitchen, freshly showered and dressed in a pair of sweatpants, a long-sleeved Michigan State T-shirt, and socks. She'd not bothered with her tennis shoes. "There were quite a few things to choose from in the closet. Thanks."

"Of course. Ready to eat?"

"More than." She slid into the chair and placed her napkin in her lap. "I could have helped you with the food."

"It wasn't any trouble. You want to talk while we eat?"

She drew in a deep breath and nodded. "Fine. You deserve to know the whole story, but just understand that the people I'm running from are dangerous and well connected."

"Connected to what?"

"People. Like assassins."

He blinked. "Okay. Like the guy who came after you in the hospital."

"Yes. He might be in custody, but there will be others."

"Why?"

"Because I saw a murder and I saw who did it."

Jason paused. "Whoa. Okay, then. Why don't you start from the beginning?"

FIVE

Lilly ate three bites and chased them with water before she spoke again. "I work for my father, Congressman Tyler Maloney."

Jason jerked and sat up straight. "Congressman Mal—I've heard of him."

"Most people have. He's big on making sure he stays in the limelight since he's running for a seat in the Senate."

"Why do you sound like that's a bad thing?"

She shrugged. "My father and I have our issues. He can be very demanding and domineering, but as soon as the camera is on him, he's all charm and polish."

"I see. But you work for him."

A sigh escaped her. "It's just my father and me, you see. My mother was killed in a car accident when I was four."

"I'm so sorry," he murmured.

"Thanks. I was in the car, too, but was thrown clear. I had a broken collarbone, but that was it. Anyway, my father is a good man deep down, I just don't get to see it very often. He's simply so busy he doesn't have time for anything—or anyone—else."

"Like you?"

"Yes." She shot him a sad smile. "I know he loves me, but he was so shattered by my mother's death that he's never been able to recover. I feel guilty when I wish he was more like his brother, my uncle Reggie, but the fact is, I do."

"What's Reggie like?"

"Kind, gentle, attentive, creative. He never makes you feel like you're in the way or that he'd rather be someplace else." She shook her head. "All that aside, while my father and I have our differences, one thing we agree on is his work, his goals, and the people he helps—the people *we* help. I love the work we do together and being a part of the greater good." She cleared her throat. "I'm in charge of directing his charities."

"Sounds important."

She laughed without humor. "I like to think the work being done, the children we're helping, and the people whose lives are improved due to the foundation's gifts are important, yes. Anyway, Tuesday night, six days ago, I left his office after picking up some signed documents for a family who had just received word that their terminally ill child was to receive his dream ski trip to Vail, Colorado."

"Impressive."

She gave him a wan smile. "The family sure thought so."

"Wait a minute. Where did all this take place?"

"In Washington, DC, at my father's campaign offices. I don't work out of that building—I have an office not too far from there. But I needed his signature on those papers, and I needed it immediately or the processing would be held up, so I took them over to him. My friend Jenny, who was an attorney and worked nearby, was going to dinner with me that night. I called to say I'd be late and would just meet her at the restaurant. She said no, she'd meet me in the parking garage and pick me up instead."

"Okay, go on."

"It was late. Almost everyone had gone for the day, but there's security in the garage. Cameras, a guard at the gate." She shrugged. "I don't mind coming and going after dark."

"But something happened."

Though her appetite was fading with the telling of her story, she took another bite as the memories washed over her. "Yes, something definitely happened. Jenny texted and said she was parked near the elevator on the third floor. I told her I'd left my purse in my car and needed to get it, but to just wait, I'd be there in a second since I was parked on the same floor."

"So, you'd grab your purse and get in her car."

"Right. We weren't going far, so it wasn't an inconvenience for her to drive us and then bring me back. It's much easier to find one parking spot in downtown DC than two."

"I can see that."

"I got the papers from my father and headed to the parking garage. There was some construction, or renovation or something, going on in that part of the garage and Jenny said she didn't want to drive around it to park because it made it a longer route to get out of the garage. I told her to just sit by the elevator." She swallowed and looked away.

"What?"

"I stepped off the elevator and ran to get my purse, then headed back to her car. I was halfway there when I heard a loud noise. Like a pop or a crack."

"A gunshot," he said.

She nodded. "I thought maybe someone had set off a firecracker and didn't think much about it. Then someone screamed. I ran toward the sound and a woman was standing there. Kind of weaving, holding a hand to her side." Lilly remembered the blood on the woman's fingers. "She went to her knees. And the sound came again."

"He shot her again?"

Tears gathered in her eyes. "I moved to see who it was, and he was just standing there holding the gun over her, aiming it at her." Her voice dropped, almost to a whisper. "And then he pulled the trigger a third time, but there was no need. She was already dead. Inside, my brain was screaming at me to run, to get out of there, but I couldn't move, I was just . . . frozen."

He reached over and gripped her fingers. "I don't think that's very unusual."

She appreciated his offer of comfort even while her mind played out the events of that evening. "I must have made some kind of noise. He looked up, locked his eyes on mine, and we simply stared at each other for a good three seconds. Then he lifted the gun and aimed it at me."

He tensed.

"Time seemed to start back up again at that point, and I ran," she said. "The bullet missed me by a fraction of an inch. I threw myself into Jenny's car and yelled at her to go. She knew something was terribly wrong and didn't hesitate. We made it out of the garage and drove around for several minutes before I was able to think coherently. I told her to go to the police station, that he'd seen me."

"And you saw him," he murmured.

"Yes."

"Did you call 911?"

"I tried. I actually had the phone out, but Jenny made a quick turn and hit a curb. My phone flew out of my hand and hit the floor, then slid under the seat. I was searching for it when she pulled into the parking lot of the police station. The parking garage was just a few blocks away, and at that time of the evening, there wasn't a lot of traffic."

"So you went inside."

She nodded. "I was a little hysterical, and I'm not sure I made much sense at first. It took me a little bit to get the story out."

"Understandable."

"So the police raced over there to the scene and—"

She remembered walking up to the place where she'd seen him shoot the woman. Remembered staring down in stunned shock at what she saw. Or didn't see.

He squeezed her fingers. "And?"

"Nothing . . ."

"What do you mean, *nothing*?"

"It looked like nothing had happened. There was no body, no blood . . . nothing." She met his gaze. "It was like it never happened."

"But you know it did."

"Yes, of course, but . . ." Lilly shook her head. "I don't understand how he could have cleaned everything up so quickly. I mean, there were other people in the building, people who would come down and get in their cars. How could no one have seen anything?"

"Where was the security guard?"

"He said he never heard anything."

"But he was in his little booth on the bottom floor. You were on the third." Jason shrugged. "It's possible he didn't hear anything. If he had the doors and windows closed on the booth."

"And he probably would, since it's so cold outside."

"What about cameras? Security footage?"

"They looked. And it showed nothing. By the time it was all over, the police thought I was in need of psychiatric help—or had a grudge against my father and was trying to damage his campaign."

"What did your father say?"

"He said he knew I'd never do anything to damage his campaign, that I was as passionate about the work we did as he was. And while he didn't understand what was going on, he'd look into it. He also told me that I should keep quiet about the whole thing until someone found evidence of what I'd seen." She rubbed her eyes and realized tears had leaked down her cheeks. "But the police aren't *looking* for any evidence. That's the problem."

"And your father hasn't been able to find anything out?"

"No. And I'm not sure how hard he's trying, to be honest."

"Why?"

"My father doesn't like conflict. I think while he believes that I saw something, he also just wants it to go away."

Jason frowned. "But he handles conflict all the time."

"Yes. Political conflict. And he takes that head on. But personal conflict is another story."

"I see. What about the woman who was killed? Surely she had to be missed by someone. Any missing persons report?"

"I didn't know her, so I don't have a name. If she's been reported missing, I haven't seen a news report on her."

"Would you recognize her if you saw a picture of her?"

She shuddered. "Yes. I'll never forget her face."

"Lilly, who was the shooter?"

She hesitated.

"You knew him, didn't you?" he pressed.

"Yes."

"Who was he?"

"Franklin Rutherford, my father's campaign manager."

―――――

Jason sat back with a hard thud. "Wow."

"I know." She sniffed and grabbed a napkin to blow her nose. "I can't believe it either. And while my father's initial reaction was disbelief, he agrees that I wouldn't react that way without provocation. But what can he do? There's no proof."

"So, we have to find it."

She blinked. "What? How?"

"The woman. We track the victim down."

"Again, how? I don't know her name or anything."

"I'd be interested in seeing that security footage. If she was in the parking garage, she could have been in the building at some point."

"Maybe. Jenny wasn't. She was just there to meet me."

"Good point." He went back to eating while he thought. After several minutes of silence he looked up to see her plate was empty except for a few crumbs. "How big is the building?"

"Twelve floors with offices on each floor. There's a cafeteria and a small convenience store on the bottom floor. My father's campaign offices take up the entire fifth floor."

"I want to call Nolan and fill him in on all this." He paused. "What's your real name?"

"Lillian Maloney, but just call me Lilly. I'm kind of getting used to it."

"All right, Lilly, would you be all right with him coming up here and hearing your story?"

"I guess."

"In order to call him, I have to head into the town. There's a small mom-and-pop store with a pay phone. I don't want to use our cell phones unless it's an emergency."

"Mine is a burner phone, but it's possible they could have somehow gotten the number and that's how they found me."

"Where did you get all this stuff? Fake ID, a burner phone?"

She bit her lip. "A friend," she said softly. "Six days ago, I witnessed the murder. The next day, Jenny was dead. As soon as I learned of her supposed suicide, I realized I was going to be next. My only option was to run before they killed me. I went to my friend who works with rehabilitating convicts. Her name is Alicia Day. She got a name and address for me from one of the men she works with, and I went to see him. For a price, he's willing to make you into whoever you want to be."

He nodded. "Would he also be willing to sell that information to whoever came asking?"

Eyes widening, she gave a slow nod. "Probably, but how would anyone know I went to him?"

"I don't know. If these people are as determined to kill you as it appears they are, then they'll have their resources. They'll be talking to any and all of your friends. Is it well known that you're friends with Alicia?"

"Yes," she whispered. "She and Jenny and I were very close."

He nodded. "Then they'll talk to her. Probably already have." He rose and went to one of the drawers in the kitchen and returned with a pad of paper and a pen. "Give me Alicia's address as well as the name and address of this guy who made the ID for you."

She did and he wrote it down.

"You sound—and act—like a cop," she said, "not a firefighter."

He laughed. "It comes from living with two of them. And . . . I graduated from the academy myself. But my father was a cop before he died, and then there's my detective brother, Nolan. We were roommates until he got married, and he often bounces his cases off me."

"Makes sense."

"So, will you be all right if I go into town to make that call?"

She blinked. "Now?"

With a raised brow, he leaned forward. "Someone's trying to kill you. It's not like we have a lot of time to waste."

She sat back and drew in a breath. "Of course. You're right."

"There's not an alarm system, but there's a bell that'll tell you if anyone drives up."

"A bell?"

"Yeah. Mom wanted it installed. She hates being surprised by a sudden knock on the door. She always needs a couple of minutes to prepare for whoever is coming."

"Makes sense."

He scanned her face, the tense set of her shoulders, and the way she pushed the crumbs around her plate.

"Lilly? What is it?"

"What if they don't drive up the driveway?"

"Then . . . yeah." There would be no warning.

Looking up, she sighed. "I want to go with you."

"I'm not sure that's a good idea. Someone might recognize you."

"But what do I do if someone shows up here? Where do I run?

You'll have the only vehicle. I don't know this area, and I have no way to defend myself."

While he saw her point, he really didn't think anyone had followed them. Then again, he couldn't say he was a hundred percent certain of that fact. He gave a slow nod. "All right. You can come with me." Not that she needed his permission. "I'll buy us pay-by-the-minute phones while I'm there. I think Henry carries some in his store."

"Does he have the smartphone kind? And prepaid credit cards?"

"Yes, I'm sure he does. Why?"

"I like the features available on the smartphone. I have some cash."

"When do you want to leave?"

She carried her plate to the sink. "I'm ready when you are."

"Are you going to put shoes on?"

She looked down at her socked feet. "Yes. And see if I can find my brain while I'm at it."

SIX

She was so tired. Physically, emotionally, mentally. At some point, she was going to break. But it couldn't be now. When she finished brushing her hair and putting her shoes on, she walked into the den to find Jason.

But he was nowhere to be seen. Panic hit her. He hadn't left without her, had he? She raced to the window and shoved aside the curtain, then dropped onto the couch.

His truck was still there. Her heart finally slowed, and she laid her head on the back of the couch to catch her breath.

The stairs creaked and she looked up to see him coming down from the loft area. He'd cleaned up a little, and his handsome features hit her. He really was a good-looking man. But he didn't come across arrogant or cocky. He was just confident in who he was. She liked that.

He smiled when he saw her and heat crept into her cheeks. Turning to hide the blush, she ordered herself to get it together. She was on the run from a killer. Being attracted to the guy who'd saved her life—twice—was probably completely normal and would pass once the danger was over. Assuming she lived through it.

"Ready?" Jason asked.

"I'm ready."

They headed to his truck, climbed in, and pulled away from the cabin. She fell silent on the ride, but Jason apparently felt the need to talk. "So," he said, "we need to know the identity of the lady who was shot. We need to know what Franklin Rutherford was up to shortly before and after the incident."

"The murder," she said quietly. "It was more than an incident."

"Yes, sorry. The murder. And we need the security footage. I'll ask Nolan if he can get a copy from the garage. What else?" Before she could answer, he said, "We need to ask Nolan if there's a way for you to view recently reported missing persons."

"We can try that, but I doubt she's listed as missing. I've been diligent about watching the news, and there have only been two women reported missing since that day. Neither one of them matches the description of the woman I saw."

"Okay, we'll keep that in mind, but I still think we should check."

"Sure. It can't hurt."

"We also want to know who the guy in the hospital was working for."

"I can tell you who he was working for—Franklin Rutherford."

"Then we need to connect them somehow."

"Oh." She glanced at him from under her lashes. "Are you sure you're not a cop at heart?"

He shot her a grin. "Maybe. It was a toss-up for me between the police force or firefighting."

"And you chose firefighting?"

He shrugged. "It's hard to explain. I just felt like my talents would be better used in that area. I was fascinated with fires when I was a kid. Not starting them, but how they worked."

"How they worked? Don't they just burn?"

With a laugh, he shook his head. "No. Sometimes it seems as if they have a mind of their own. Even as a cop, I was studying them all the time, following arson cases and volunteering at the fire station. It finally occurred to me that firefighting was really where I wanted to be. I just need to take the captain's exam and I can move up."

"Wow. Good for you."

"Thanks." He cleared his throat.

"But why go to the police academy at all then?"

He shrugged. "Because I thought that was what I was supposed to do. When you come from a family of cops, sometimes it's hard to believe you can actually do something else."

"Well, I for one, am grateful you chose firefighting." He smiled and she found she had to look away from his captivating eyes. "So . . . what else do I need to tell Nolan? I should have written all of this down at the cabin."

"I think that probably covers it for now."

"Good, because we're here."

━━━━━

"Stay here, okay?" Once she gave him a nod, Jason grabbed some change from the cup holder, climbed from his Jeep, and shut the door. The pay phone was off to the side near the entrance to the store. After lifting the receiver, he dropped quarters into the slot. He dialed Nolan's number and was gratified when his brother picked up before the first ring stopped.

"Are you okay?" Nolan asked.

"For now, but you've got to get up here and hear her story. Something crazy is going on, and if we don't help her, she's going to wind up dead like one of her friends. And I need you to bring a way for her to view photos of recent missing persons."

"I could bring my laptop and she could do that on there, but Jason, I . . . uh—"

"And we need security footage from a particular parking garage." He gave Nolan the address, date, and approximate time. "And—"

"Jace!"

"What?"

"I don't want to leave Kallie, man."

"Oh. She's not due for another week."

"I know, but she's been having contractions off and on for the past two days."

Jason raked a hand through his hair. "Fine. I understand. Is there someone else you can send?"

"Hold on a second." Jason heard voices in the background, then Nolan came back on the line. "Never mind. Kallie told me to get myself together and help you. I'm leaving in ten."

"Great. Tell Kallie thanks."

"Yeah, yeah." Nolan fell silent.

Jason rubbed his eyes, then filled Nolan in on everything Lilly had told him. When he finished, Nolan gave a low whistle. "Wow."

"I know, right? So, the guy in the hospital said Lilly was a job. Someone hired him. Most likely Rutherford if Lilly is to be believed. And I think she is. These people aren't playing around, Nolan, and they know I'm with her."

"Then they're going to be looking for you too."

"Exactly. And they'll find me eventually, but hopefully we have enough time to come up with a plan that will allow us to find them first."

Nolan sighed. "All right. I get what you're saying. Have an escape plan and stay safe until I get there."

"Will do. Oh, and Nolan?"

"Yeah?"

"Bring me a gun."

Silence echoed back at him. Then he heard his brother take a deep breath. "All right. Is your permit up-to-date?"

"Yes, you know it is."

"See you soon."

Jason hung up and walked back to the truck. "I'm going inside the store to grab a few things, all right?"

"Hold on, I have some cash."

"So do I. Hang on to yours for now. You may need it worse than I do."

She bit her lip and nodded.

It didn't take Jason long to do his shopping. At the register, he nabbed two of the pay-as-you-go smartphones and set them on the counter.

He didn't recognize the cashier. "Where's Henry?"

"He has the night off. I'm CJ." He flashed a bright smile. "Henry hired me about six weeks ago. You have a place up here?"

"My family does. I'm just here for the night."

"Cool." The young man placed the items in the bag and took the cash Jason handed him. "Have a good night."

"Thanks."

Back at the vehicle, Jason climbed in. Lilly glanced at him. "Well?"

"Nolan's going to meet us there."

During the drive back to the cabin, she was quiet, yet definitely not relaxed. Her eyes moved from mirror to mirror.

"I'm going to make sure you're safe," he said softly.

She sighed. "Safe is good. But the only way that's going to happen is by putting Franklin Rutherford behind bars."

"Then that's what we're going to do." When he pulled into the drive, he didn't turn the engine off. "Go inside and pack a bag. Whatever clothes you can find that you think you can use for a couple of days on the run."

"What are you thinking, Jason?"

"I'm thinking I want to keep you safe, and to do that we have to be smart. Smarter than the people who are after you."

She huffed a sigh. "All right."

"I'm going to park outside your window. Throw your bag out and I'll put it in the Jeep, then I'll get myself a little bag too."

"You think they can find us here?"

"I'm going to assume they can."

126

"Good, I'm glad to hear that, because that's my assumption too."

She climbed out and shut the Jeep's door. He watched her dash into the cabin and sent up a silent prayer that God would protect them.

Because he had a feeling things were about to get ugly.

SEVEN

Lilly hurried to pack a small bag she found in the closet. She tossed in two changes of clothes, some undergarments, and the small bottles of shampoo and conditioner someone had collected and stashed under the sink.

She stepped back into the bedroom and strode to the window. With a quick flip of the latch, she unlocked it and opened it. She tossed the bag out. Jason caught it and put it on the front floorboard of the passenger seat.

"I'm going to owe one of your cousins some clothes," she said.

"Don't worry about it. I doubt either one would miss them." He left the doors open and disappeared around the side of the house. Lilly heard him come in the front door and lock it.

She met him in the den and he handed her a phone. "Let's get these set up and each other's numbers programmed in. I'll give you Nolan's number too."

For the next few minutes, they worked with the phones. When they were finished, she leaned back and closed her eyes.

"You okay?"

"Yes, just really tired."

"You're probably still suffering some of the side effects of the carbon monoxide. Tell you what. I'm going to clean up any evidence that we were here. I'm going to wash the dishes and burn the trash. If they get here after we're gone, I don't want it to look like we were ever here."

"I'll help."

"Nope. I'm going to take care of it. It won't take me but maybe ten minutes. Why don't you go lie down and I'll come get you when Nolan gets here? He's going to be another hour at least."

She nodded. "Okay, if you're sure."

"I'm sure."

"All right. I think I will, then. Thanks." Dropping the phone in the front pocket of her sweatpants, Lilly walked down the hall to the bedroom. The window was now shut and locked tight, but it didn't give her much comfort. Glass was easily broken. By a fist or a bullet. Either one would achieve the end result. She pulled the blinds and lay down on the bed.

Sinking into the softness, she closed her eyes. Only to have them pop right back open. How could she possibly sleep? And yet fatigue pulled at her. With a concentrated effort, she closed her eyes once more and sent up a prayer of gratitude for Jason Tanner.

She must have fallen asleep, because when a hand fell on her shoulder, she sat up with a start.

"It's just me, Lilly," Jason said.

Heart thundering, she settled back and let her pulse begin to slow. "Sorry, I guess I'm a little jumpy."

"With reason."

"Is your brother here?"

"Yes. We've been talking and letting you rest. No sign of company yet."

She swung her legs over the side of the bed and slipped her feet into her shoes. "Let me freshen up a little and I'll join you."

He left and she scrubbed a hand down her face. Thankfully, her chest felt less tight and most of the dizziness had passed. The sleep had helped.

When she entered the living area, she found the two men sitting on the leather sofa, talking and sipping from cans of soda. An open laptop rested on the coffee table in front of them. "Hi," she said.

Nolan stood and offered his hand. "Nolan Tanner."

"Lillian Maloney. But just call me Lilly." She shook his hand.

"Sorry about all the trouble you're having."

"Thanks." She seated herself on the love seat opposite the sofa.

"So, Jason's been telling me more about your adventures. I've been doing a little research myself."

"Have you found anything interesting?"

"A few things, but first, why don't you take a look at this list of nationwide missing persons. I've narrowed it down by age and gender. There aren't many—which is a good thing."

Lilly pulled the laptop over and scanned through the photos. There were twenty-three of them. Not many, but twenty-three too many. Some had disappeared before the date in question. She scanned them, but focused more on the most recent disappearances. And stopped at one. "Wait a minute."

Jason leaned forward. "You recognize one?"

"Yes. She hasn't been on the news, though. At least not in the last two days or so. It says here that her name is Melissa Miller."

Nolan looked at the one she indicated. "Who is she?"

"Franklin's new secretary. I heard her name mentioned in passing, but I've never met her."

"Your father's campaign manager has a secretary?"

"Maybe assistant is a better description. But that's who she is. When was she reported missing?"

"Yesterday morning."

"It's been a week since he killed her and they're just now reporting her missing?"

Nolan pulled the laptop closer and clicked a link to access the details of the report. After scanning the file, he glanced back at Lilly. "Seems like her family thought she was on vacation to the Caribbean with a new boyfriend. She was supposed to arrive home day before yesterday. When she didn't check in, they got concerned. They called the local police and a couple of officers checked out her apartment. It was obvious she hadn't gone anywhere. The open suitcase on the bed was their first clue."

"Where's her family from?"

"Um . . ." Nolan scanned the report again, paused, and pushed the laptop aside. "Los Angeles. From what I gather, Melissa has always been involved in politics and wanted to move to Washington to work with the big players."

"Wait a minute. Even though he lives in DC, Franklin flies out to LA quite often. He has a second home there. You think it's possible the two of them met there and he brought her here for closer access?"

"That's certainly a possibility. Says here she was hired four weeks ago, moved out here, got an apartment, and started working for Rutherford."

"And went on vacation three weeks after being hired?" Jason asked.

Nolan clicked his tongue. "They say it's who you know."

"I guess so," Jason said.

"And he shot her," Lilly said softly. "Three times. How did he leave no trace that anything happened?"

"I have a friend with the police department in Asheville. His name is Greg Masters. There's nothing he can't do with a computer, and he does all of their forensics stuff. I called and asked for the security footage, and since nothing had come of it originally, and it's not involved in any ongoing investigation, they were willing to share it with me. Greg is going to see what he can come up with."

"You think it was tampered with?" Jason asked.

"It occurred to me."

Lilly nodded. "But it still doesn't explain the lack of evidence at the garage. I mean, I was with the officers and"—she spread her hands—"even I can't explain it."

"There's an explanation," Nolan said. "We'll figure it out. For now, you two lay low and get some rest. I'm going to keep working. I think now that we know who the victim is, that's going to change the course of this."

"What about Rutherford?" Jason asked.

"I did a little digging into him as well while I was waiting on your call. He's squeaky clean on the surface."

"And underneath?" Lilly asked.

"Seems like his wife filed for divorce a couple of years ago. Infidelity."

Lilly flinched. "He had an affair?"

"That was her grounds for the divorce."

"But she didn't go through with it. They're still married."

"True. I'm not sure what happened with that. I'd need more time to get the details."

"He smooth-talked her into staying with him," Lilly said. "He's like my father. Big on appearances."

"In the short time I had, I couldn't find anything about a mistress, and unless I can get access to his financial records, I won't know if there have been any exchanges of funds. And I'd need a warrant for that."

"And you don't have enough evidence to get one of those," Lilly murmured.

"No, sorry."

"Then we'll just have to get the evidence," Jason said.

"But how?"

He scratched his chin. "I'm thinking."

A bell chimed and both Nolan and Jason tensed, then stood. "Someone's coming," Jason said.

EIGHT

Nolan already had his phone out and was punching in numbers. "I'm calling for backup, you two get out of here."

Jason frowned. "What about you?"

"They're not after me."

"But they're after us, and if we disappear together, they may think they can use you to *get* to us."

"Just go. Local cops will be here any minute. I have your numbers memorized." He glanced out the window. "They just cut the headlights and it looks like they're pulling off the drive into the wooded area. And now I can't see a thing. They're definitely not friendly." He turned. "Go on, get out of here. I'm going to be right behind you."

Jason grabbed Lilly's hand and pulled her toward the back door. Glancing out, he didn't see any movement, but that didn't mean someone wasn't out there.

"The window?" she asked.

"Yeah," Jason said.

"My truck is just outside the door," Nolan said. "I'm going to go out and get in it. Real casual, like I don't have a care in the world. Maybe by keeping their attention on me, it will take it off of you."

"Keep your truck between them and you."

Nolan turned the porch light on, and Jason knew it was so whoever was watching would have a clear sight of Nolan exiting the house. He grabbed his laptop. "Get going and call me when you get settled." He slipped out the front door.

Jason guided her toward the back of the house, making a bee-line for the window in her bedroom.

"You knew this would happen," she said.

"It pays to be prepared." The fear behind her words made him glad he'd listened to his gut. He opened the window, climbed out, and turned back to help her through it. "Quick. Into the Jeep."

Jason slid over to the driver's seat. Lilly didn't waste any time, but quickly followed and shut the door.

The first bullet pinged off the passenger side mirror and Lilly jerked. Jason reached out and shoved her down so her head rested against his thigh. "Stay down."

The engine roared and they shot backward. Jason heard another shot and felt the bullet slam into the back of the Jeep. He continued in reverse and saw Nolan with his weapon raised and aimed at the man now chasing them on foot.

The intruder had pulled his SUV off the drive and into the woods, so Jason's path was clear. Another shot, then another.

At the end of the long drive, just as the back tires hit the road, Jason spun the wheel to the right and came ninety degrees to the drive. Then he shifted into drive and hit the gas once more.

No more bullets came their way, but they met sirens and flashing blue lights as they raced away from the cabin—with someone behind them. Lilly sat up and he glanced at her. "Call Nolan. Make sure he's okay. There were two of them."

She dug the phone out while he continued to drive and watch the rearview mirror.

"Nolan? Are you okay?"

"I'm all right. I got the one shooting at you, but the other was sitting in the car and is coming after you. I called it in and you should have the cops on your tail as well. I've got to stay here and clear this up. Let me know where you land."

"We will," she said. "Thank you." She hung up. "He's okay, but he shot one of them."

"I kind of figured that when the bullets stopped coming our way."

"Where are we going?"

After another glance in the rearview mirror, he sighed. "I'm not sure, but it doesn't matter until we get rid of our shadow."

For the next several minutes, she fell silent as he drove. Finally, he made a sharp left turn and the SUV behind them shot past. She saw the brake lights go on just before they disappeared. Jason made another left and another. Then pulled into the driveway of a home, circled to the back, and shut off the lights.

"What if someone from the house sees us?" she asked, her words hushed as though the occupants of the home might hear her.

"I'll just explain we're running from a killer."

"Hmm. I'm sure that will go over well." Her adrenaline continued to pump through her body.

"I'm thinking we need to take a road trip," he said.

"To where?"

"Washington, DC."

Lilly raised a brow and he shrugged in response.

"That's where all this started, right?"

"Well, yes."

"Then I think that's where we're going to find our answers."

Once he was sure they'd lost whoever had been on their tail—including the police—he'd let Lilly take the wheel, and the seven-hour trip had passed without incident. Jason was exhausted and knew his limits. It was either let her drive or find a place to crash for a while. But since both of them wanted to get as far away as possible, Lilly had insisted she was fine to drive and he was able to grab a few hours of sleep.

He woke slowly and rubbed his eyes. "How far out are we?"

"About two hours."

"Oh man, I'm sorry. I must have been more tired than I thought."

"It's fine. I wasn't sleepy."

"What about now?"

She shook her head. "The closer we get, the more my adrenaline rushes."

"Yeah."

"I want to go to my place," she said. "Do you think it's safe?"

He thought about it for a moment. "I would think that would be the last place they'd look for you."

"Unless Rutherford has someone watching just in case I return." She bit her lip and fell silent. "But even if he does, I can probably get in without anyone knowing."

"How?"

"I'm in a condo building on the top floor."

He raised a brow. "No way. I wouldn't have pictured you as a condo girl."

She laughed. "I actually love it. The building has a ton of amenities." She sobered. "As well as several exits and entrances. We simply go in one of the doors to the side, maybe?"

"It's possible."

"I can call Uncle Reggie and see if he can scope the place out for us first."

"Tell me a little more about your uncle Reggie."

"He's fabulous. He's the man who taught me what a real father is like. While my father was working, Reggie took me on trips to the zoo, zip-lining in the park, and ice-skating in Central Park."

"Central Park? That's not in Washington."

"I know. It was a weekend trip." She laughed. "He even took me to France for my sixteenth birthday."

"What does he do?"

"Washington high-priced real estate. He owns the building where I live."

"Nice."

She smiled. "Yes. His condo is next door to mine."

"Is that weird?"

"Not really. We're both so busy, it's rare that we see each other unless we make the effort. And for the cut in rent, I'm willing to overlook the fact that he probably did that so he could keep an eye on me." She frowned. "And yet, look what happened. I'm sure he's frantic. I called him once to reassure him that I was all right and I think that's how they found me in North Carolina."

Jason frowned. "They tapped his phone."

"Yes. It's the only logical explanation for how they were able to track me down. And once they had that number, they could just follow the trail."

He fell silent for a moment, then said, "So, if you call Reggie now, they'll know."

Her shoulders slumped. "Right. Even though I have a new number now, they'll probably try to trace it because it'll be one they're not familiar with. And then they'll know I'm in Washington." She sighed. "So, it's best not to call him. At least not from my phone."

"No, not your phone, a pay phone."

"Two pay phones in one day. I didn't think those even existed anymore."

"A few. We'll see if we can find one." He paused. "What do you think about calling the press and giving them an exclusive?"

"What do you mean?"

"I mean, if this is all out in the open—you tell your side and what you saw—then I would think Rutherford and his hired goons would have to back off, wouldn't you?"

She blew out a slow breath. "Maybe, but it would also be the end of my father's campaign. He'd be ruined. And furious. He'd never speak to me again."

"Hmm. Sounds like he has his priorities messed up."

"Well, I can't argue with that, but I think calling the press is out, regardless. I have absolutely no proof to back up the story."

"Which brings us full circle. We have to get the proof." He pursed his lips. "I have an idea. It's kind of a crazy one, and I probably should have thought of it earlier."

"What?"

"Nolan has friends in high places in law enforcement. What if we get our own crime scene tech out to the scene and let that person go over it like it's never been looked at?"

She blinked. "That would be great, but does he know anyone out here who could do that?"

"If not, we could fly someone in. We took the long way. It's only an hour or so flight from Asheville."

"I don't know . . ."

"I'll help pay for it. I know it would be expensive."

"That's not why I was hesitating. I'm not worried about the cost."

Not worried about the cost? Interesting. "What is it, then?"

"I'm just worried about bringing someone else in on this. I'm scared that if I do, that person will be a target."

He sighed. "Yeah, I get that, but I think we need to do it."

She nodded. "All right. Make your calls. We'll be there in about an hour and a half."

NINE

Lilly had turned into the underground garage and pulled out her key card to swipe it when Jason grabbed her hand. "Wait."

"What?"

"That might not be a good idea."

She blinked. "Why?"

"Because if these people are as good as you say they are, they're going to know when you swipe that card."

Her heart sank, but he was right. "All right. So, how do we get in?"

"Let's find a place to hide the car relatively well and think for a while. I messed up. We shouldn't have come here in this vehicle." He swiped a hand over his face. "But hopefully they're not looking for it here in Washington."

"Okay." She pulled away from the parking garage and drove to the intersection, making a right, then another right into a gas station parking lot. She'd come here often, but since she wouldn't be going inside, she didn't think anyone would recognize her. Instead of stopping in the front, she drove around to the back and parked in the employee lot so the vehicle wouldn't be visible from the street.

"I need to start thinking like a cop," Jason said. "More than I have been." He leaned his head back and closed his eyes. "All right. Question. How did they find us at the cabin?"

"Either they searched property records and traced the cabin to your family or they traced the call from the store somehow," she said.

"If it was traced from the store, they'd have to have Nolan's phone bugged somehow. A property records search would probably take too much time for them to act this quickly. So, once they got my information from my vehicle tag at the hospital, they simply put together who my relatives were and the most likely one I'd contact was Nolan."

"And they managed to trace his phone."

"It's the only thing I can think of."

She groaned. "So, no more communication with him for now."

"Right."

"Which means we have another problem," she said.

"What's that?"

"The key card not only gets me in the parking garage, but it's the only way to get in the building."

He winced. "All right. We may have to get creative."

"Reggie has a key," she said. "To the building and to my apartment. But, like we said earlier, it might be a risk to even call him."

Jason thought for a moment. "Okay, it's not like they're going to know every number he calls or receives calls from. He's a realtor, he'd get calls from all over. Including from different parts of the country from people looking to move, right?"

"Sure."

"However, a local call might still be the better idea."

"Probably." She let out a slow breath. "Okay, I think we have to chance it. It's the least risky option."

"I don't see a pay phone, so I'll just go inside and buy another pay-as-you-go phone. One with a local area code. Hang tight."

And then he was out of the car before she could comment or protest.

He returned about five minutes later with a phone and a pocket knife. Once he had the package opened and the phone set up, he handed it to her. "It's got some battery life. Go ahead and see if you can get Reggie."

She dialed the number and it went to voice mail. Lilly hung up.

"Try again."

She did.

"Reggie Maloney."

"Uncle Reggie?"

"Lillian! Oh thank goodness! Where are you? Are you okay? I've been worried sick. Your father is beside himself and said if we hadn't heard from you by the end of today, we were filing a missing persons report. He was worried you might be depressed or having some kind of psychotic break. Especially after Jenny . . ."

Her father was worried about her to the point that he was ready to file a missing persons report? A lump rose to her throat and she cleared it away. "I'm okay." For now. "Did he tell you what happened? What I saw?"

"What you saw? No. I hadn't heard from you or seen you in a couple of days, so I went to your father. He just said that you needed some time away but would be back soon. Although he thought it would be a lot sooner than this."

Lilly frowned. Reggie had been the first one she'd wanted to call after the murder, but her father had convinced her to keep it quiet. He hadn't thought Jenny's death had been an accident either. "I don't know what's going on, Lillian," he'd said. "But let's keep our heads down until we can figure it out. If they're willing to kill Jenny, as you think, then the more people you talk to, the more people you put in danger." So she hadn't told Reggie anything.

She cleared her throat. "There's a little more to it than that. I need your help getting into my condo."

"Are you locked out?"

She gave a low, humorless laugh. "Something like that."

"Where are you?"

"Across the street."

"I'll let you in."

"Thanks." She started to hang up, then stopped. "Oh, and Reggie?"

"Yeah?"

"Meet us at the back entrance, where—"

Jason placed a hand on her arm and shook his head. "We're going in the front."

She blinked. "What?"

"Just tell him. Trust me. And tell him not to speak to you when we enter, and to wait about three minutes before coming up on the elevator."

"Um. Sure. Did you get that, Uncle Reggie?"

"Yes, the front, don't speak, wait, then come up. What is this all about? Who's with you?"

"I'll explain everything when I see you. Just do as he asked, okay?"

"Lillian—" He gave a sigh. "All right. See you in a minute."

She hung up and nodded to Jason. "He's going to do it."

He slipped a credit card into her hand. "Pretend to use that just before Reggie opens the door."

"To make it look like I used my key to anyone who might be watching?"

"Yeah."

They climbed out of the car and he draped an arm over her shoulder. His nearness was like a balm to her ragged nerves. He might just be trying to make anyone watching think they were a couple, but Lilly had to admit, she liked it. She liked him. Was it because he'd saved her life a few times? That probably had something to do with it.

Snugged up under his arm, they hurried back to the front of the store and across the street. As they headed toward the front door, he leaned his head over hers. "Laugh like I'm saying something funny. And then I'm going to kiss you, okay?"

"Uh, what? Why?"

"Just do it, okay?"

She forced the giggle and he kissed her temple, then her lips. Dazed, she froze, then forced herself to relax. If it hadn't been for the fact that she might have killers watching her, she would have gotten swept away in the moment. Instead, she palmed the credit card and held it, ready to pretend to use it when she saw Reggie through the glass door.

And there he was, striding across the lobby floor and reaching for the door. Jason lifted his head and stared at her for a moment before clearing his throat and nodding. She held the credit card to the device that would unlock, should she be using her key, just as Reggie pressed the button from his side of the glass.

The lock clicked and Jason pushed it open. Without looking directly at Reggie, she said, "Go get a cup of coffee at the bar, then come upstairs to my door."

She and Jason walked past him and to the elevator.

Lilly remained silent and tense. And she hadn't made any effort to move away from his one-armed embrace.

The elevator stopped and the doors slid open.

Her shoulders rose and fell as they stepped off together. Then again and once more. "Breathe, Lilly."

"I'm breathing."

"No, you're getting ready to hyperventilate. In through your nose, out through your lips."

She followed his instructions and drew in one final breath, letting it out slowly. She cleared her throat. "I'm okay. I'll be okay."

Another chime sounded the arrival of the next elevator. Jason tensed and stepped in front of her. Then relaxed slightly when Lilly said, "Uncle Reggie." She went to her uncle and wrapped her arms around him. "I'm so glad to see you."

"You too, girlie."

"Jason, meet Reggie Maloney. Uncle Reggie, meet Jason Tanner, the man who saved my life. A few times now."

"Saved your life?" The two men shook hands, then Reggie narrowed his eyes. "Let's get inside. I want to hear what's going on."

Reggie opened her door and waited for Lilly to step around him and enter first. Before she could do so, Jason snagged her arm and pulled her back. "Let me just check the place, okay?" He pulled his gun from his waistband.

Reggie's eyes went wide.

Lilly shook her head. "We'll check it together."

She followed him and Reggie pulled up the rear.

Her gaze swept the large living area. Her condo was a mirror image of Reggie's. Off to their right was her large kitchen with dining area, while the hall ahead of them led to the four bedrooms and four bathrooms.

"Stay here, please?"

"You're not a cop, Jason."

"I know, but I know how to clear a house as well as Nolan. You learn to do it the right way in Iraq."

While she and Reggie waited just inside the front door, Jason quickly cleared her home. He came back into the living room, tucking his weapon back into his belt.

Lilly walked into her den and straightened the cushions on her couch. Adjusted a painting on the wall. Moved her television remotes back to the coffee table. Suddenly she stopped. "Someone's been in here."

"What?" Jason asked.

Reggie gave a slow nod. "Lilly always leaves her home immaculate."

"Things are different. Moved." She looked around. "It's subtle, but it's there."

Reggie turned to her. "Why would they search your apartment? And how would they get in?"

"I don't know," she whispered.

Jason rubbed his chin. "They were probably looking for evidence of where you would run."

"Oh no." Adrenaline spiked the hair on the back of her neck. She bolted to the kitchen and found the pad where she'd written the name of the man who'd sold her the ID. The top page was missing. She groaned, hoping the guy was okay.

Jason's phone rang. "I don't recognize the number. That's got to be Nolan." He lifted the device to his ear and walked into the den.

Once Jason was out of earshot, Reggie placed his hands on her shoulders and turned her to face him. "I've tried to be patient, Lillian. But talk to me."

She swallowed and nodded. While Jason continued his conversation with his brother, she brought Reggie up to speed on everything. The more she talked, the more color he lost in his cheeks. He staggered to one of the chairs at her kitchen table and sank into it. "I don't believe this. Jenny was murdered?"

"Yes."

His gaze met hers. "Alicia came to me a few days ago and asked if I'd heard from you."

"What else did she tell you?"

"Nothing much. She was extremely evasive." He blew out a low breath. "At least now I know why."

"I'm sorry I didn't come to you. You were out of town when everything happened, and once I realized someone had killed Jenny, I was too afraid to put you in danger by asking for your help. Dad was insistent that you not be involved. He didn't want to put you at risk." She bit her lip.

He rubbed his eyes. "Your father?"

"I think he wants to believe me. But he's denying the whole thing happened. It's going to take some evidence to the contrary to pull him fully over to my side." She shrugged, weariness dragging at her. "And so far, there's nothing."

Jason turned to face her from his spot in the den. "Do you have a laptop?" he called.

"Yes, why?"

"Nolan just texted. Greg sent him the security footage from the parking garage and said for us to take a look at it."

Lilly swung her gaze to her desk in the far corner of the den. "Uh, no. I guess I don't have a laptop after all. It's missing." A sense of fury welled. "I need to report this."

"Not yet," Jason said. "You need to just let it go for now. Whoever broke in was looking for where you would go. But we don't want to draw attention to your condo at this point." He went back to his conversation.

Reggie's jaw looked tight enough to shatter. "I have one. I'll go get it."

"Thanks," she said softly.

Reggie left to get the computer and returned the same time Jason hung up with his brother. "Nolan sent the video to a new email account he created under a fake name," Jason said. "He gave me the username and password. He also said a friend of his will be landing at the airport in a little over three hours. Claire Montgomery. She's with the forensics department in Asheville and said she'd be willing to see what she could find in the parking garage. Said if there was a murder committed there, she'd find the evidence."

"But it's contaminated now," Lilly said. "People have been all over that place since that night. And the construction is probably finished."

"I know. And Claire knows that. We'll just have to hope for the best. We're going to video everything she does so that on the off chance she finds something, we'll be able to share that information with officers. Or in court."

Lilly bit her lip and nodded. Reggie just shook his head. He set the laptop on the kitchen table and quickly typed in the password, then stepped back and motioned for Jason to sit down. "Have at it."

Jason pulled up the email and clicked on it. "And, here we go," he said. The video began to play, and Lilly saw the parking garage come up. The place where she'd seen a woman shot and killed. And then disappear.

"Greg said to watch it carefully."

The construction items were clearly there, like she'd said. There were the orange cones blocking entry into the work area. Just beyond the cones were the buckets for mixing concrete, a ladder chained to the pillar, and a plastic tarp laid out to cover the area that had already been poured.

The video played to the end and she blinked. "Nothing." Her hands fisted. "But I know what I saw. He was on the other side of the orange cones and so was she. She was on the concrete flo—Wait a minute."

"You saw it?" Jason asked.

"She would have been on the tarp." She pointed. "Rutherford was standing here." She pointed to the area on the screen. "And she was right below him because he shot her, and when she fell"—her eyes widened and she looked at Jason—"she would have fallen right on the tarp."

He nodded. "That's what Greg came up with." As he eyed her, she thought she saw something like admiration in his gaze.

"That would have made for some fast and easy cleanup," Reggie said.

"Yes. Yes it would," Lilly said. "I didn't even notice that at the time."

"Greg said they messed with the footage." Jason dragged the cursor back across the bar at the bottom of the screen. "Let's go back to the beginning and play it again. See if we can see what he saw."

Once again, the footage started rolling. All the way to the end. "Let's try slow motion." He played it again, slowing it down.

"There," she said. "Did you see that?"

"I did. It blipped, didn't it?"

Rewind. Play. Blip.

"The tarp is in a different place," Reggie said slowly. "It's close, but you can see the edge of it there, overlapping the first two orange cones."

Jason moved the cursor back and paused it. "And in this section, it's not touching them."

Lilly rubbed her arms, chilled at the knowledge that not only had Rutherford gone to great lengths to cover up this woman's murder, but that he had help. A lot of help. There's no way he could have done all this by himself. But who?

Jason shut the laptop. "I say we get some sleep and, as soon as Claire arrives, head up to the parking garage."

"During the night," Lilly said. "In the dark."

"It's when the garage is empty—or at least has very little traffic."

"Right."

"I'm going with you," Reggie said.

"What? No." Lilly shook her head. "You don't have to do that. We'll keep you updated."

His eyes locked on hers. "I'm going."

She lifted a brow. "Fine."

Reggie nodded. "And then I'm going to find Franklin Rutherford and make him eat his teeth."

TEN

Three hours later, under full cover of darkness and only a quarter moon in the night sky, they picked Claire up at the airport. Jason was impressed with her no-nonsense, professional attitude. Her blue eyes could have resembled a warm summer sky, but instead, Jason figured they would freeze over a small pond with one look. Not that she was rude, or even cold. She was simply on a mission and no one was going to derail her from completing it.

"Thank you for coming," Lilly said.

"I couldn't resist. Nolan knew this would pique my interest, and since there's no open case, there's nothing that says I can't nose around a bit. I just have to fly back out by noon today. Unless I cancel my meeting. Which I can do if absolutely necessary."

"Perfect," Jason said. "Let's get this done."

They'd left Jason's car parked behind the gas station, so Reggie drove. Claire rode in front with Reggie, while Jason shared the back seat with Lilly. He reached over and took her hand. "We're making progress."

"Yes." She squeezed his fingers and shot him a tight smile.

Reggie drove the rest of the way in silence until Lilly sucked in a deep breath. "How are we going to get in the garage? If I use my key, they may know it."

"I have one," Reggie said.

"What? How?"

149

"The woman I've been dating works in this building."

She blinked, then raised a brow. "You've been dating someone?"

"Yes." He laughed. "Come on, I'm only fifty-two years old. I don't plan to spend the rest of my life alone."

Lilly shrugged. "I'm just surprised. You've never seemed interested in anyone before."

"I've just been waiting for the right one to come along." Jason thought the man sounded pensive and a bit sad. "And Beth is a wonderful lady. She's a realtor—albeit for an opposing team—but we get along really well, and I'm looking forward to seeing where it goes."

"Then I'm happy for you."

"Thanks."

Before long they turned into the parking garage. Reggie swiped the key and continued under the electric arm. "Go to the third floor," she said.

"I know," Reggie said.

"I know you know. I'm just . . ."

"It's okay," Jason said. "Hang in there."

———

Around and up they went until Reggie stopped in front of the elevator. Precisely where Jenny had parked to wait for her. He inched forward, and Lily saw the construction equipment was gone, along with the orange cones and plastic tarp.

At least Franklin Rutherford's car wasn't parked in his coveted spot right across from the elevator. She swallowed, the memories rushing over her.

Claire got out and removed her large bag from the trunk. "It's awfully light in here," Jason said.

"Will we need to figure out a way to cut the lights?"

"Maybe." She set the bag on the floor. "I've got some BLUESTAR with me. Its luminescence is brighter and lasts longer. You can even

150

see it when it's not completely dark." She glanced around again. "But this might be too bright. BLUESTAR is good stuff, but let's play it safe and cut the lights when I have it mixed and ready to go."

Claire turned her attention back to her bag. She pulled out a tripod and a video camera. Within just a few minutes, she had it set up and recording.

"You know," Claire said, "any evidence I find may not be admissible in court."

"What do you mean?" Jason asked. "That's why we're doing this the correct way."

"Yeah, but a really good attorney will do his best to get it thrown out."

Lilly sighed. "We'll cross that bridge when we come to it. For now, let's just see if there's anything here. No one else is looking, so what does it really matter?"

Claire shrugged. "Works for me." To Lilly, she said, "All right, show me where you saw her."

As Claire had noted, the parking garage was well lit, and Lilly had no trouble picking out the exact spot where she'd seen the woman lying—and dying. She walked over to it. "Right here."

Claire nodded. "Let me see the security footage Nolan sent you."

"One second." Jason tapped his screen, then passed her his phone. She watched it, her eyes darting from the phone to the scene. Finally, she turned to Reggie. "All right, do you mind participating in a little role playing?"

"Not at all."

"Lilly, show your uncle where to stand."

Lilly placed him where she'd seen Rutherford standing over the body of the poor woman he'd shot. Then paused. Should she lie down? Pretend to be the dead woman? She shuddered.

Hands settled on her shoulders and she jumped. "I'll do it," Jason said. He gently moved her aside and stood in front of Reggie. "Okay, tell me how she was positioned when you saw her."

Lilly shot him a look of pure gratitude. "At first, she was still standing, holding her side. Blood was pouring over her hand. Her left one." Jason placed his left hand on his hip.

"Higher," she said.

He moved it to his rib cage.

"She went down to her knees. Then he shot her again and she fell," Lilly said. "Onto her back." Jason sat and then reclined on his back. Lilly's mind blipped, re-creating the scene in spite of her desire to block it from her memory. "He stood there in his overcoat and hat, arm stretched out, holding the weapon."

"Like this?" Reggie asked. He pointed his finger at Jason.

"Yes," Lilly whispered. "Just like that." She frowned. Something was off. "Wait a minute." She knelt next to Jason and grasped his warm right hand. "Melissa had her hand flung wide." She placed it as she remembered it. "Her arm made a ninety-degree angle to her body. And her palm was up." She blinked. "Why do I remember that?"

Claire actually offered a small smile. "The mind is an amazing thing. Being in these surroundings where the event happened is triggering memories."

"And I remember the plastic now. When he stepped toward her for the final shot, it . . . crinkled . . . or something."

"And she fell near this post?" Claire gestured toward the concrete pillar.

"Yes."

The woman tilted her head and narrowed her eyes as she looked back to Jason. "And that's how she lay? You're sure?"

"Positive."

"Okay, then I would say that he shot her as she walked from the elevator, catching her by surprise."

"The first shot."

Claire nodded. "See how her feet are directly facing that pillar? You said she was standing when you saw her. So she didn't just fall

152

to the ground immediately. She grabbed the nearest thing to keep from falling—the pillar—then stepped back and was ready to run."

"Yes. I remember that now," Lilly said. "She reached out with her hand—the one that had blood on it—and sort of pushed off the post but was still facing him. Like she was refusing to fall. Which was why he had to shoot her again. The shot came *before* she went down to her knees."

Claire nodded. "And that second shot knocked her down and onto her back."

"And the third one was for insurance," Jason said. He sat up, then hopped to his feet.

"Now to prove it," Claire said.

Jason could see the toll this whole role-playing ordeal was taking on Lilly, but he could also see she was determined to be strong and do what she came here to do. He glanced at his watch. "Sun's going to be coming up in about thirty minutes."

Claire nodded. "We need to get moving. We'll do this area first, then move on. How tall would you say the woman was?"

"About my height," Lilly said. "Maybe five feet six or seven."

Claire looked at Jason. "I don't want to take any chances with this. We're going to do this right the first time and put this guy away. How do we get this area dark?"

"You have a flashlight?"

"Of course."

"Get it. When the power goes off, start working. You'll have five to six minutes."

"That should be enough time."

Jason held his hand out to Reggie. "May I borrow your car?"

"Of course." He dug in his pocket and pulled out the keys, which he dropped into Jason's hand. Jason climbed into the car and took off.

ELEVEN

Claire pulled two flashlights from her box and handed one to Reggie and one to Lilly. Next she grabbed a spray bottle and other ingredients. With quick, efficient movements, she mixed the solution. "All right. That's done. I guess now we wait."

"I guess," Lilly said. She turned the flashlight on and Reggie did the same. How would Jason get the lights turned off?

No sooner had she thought the question than the place went dark.

Reggie's beam cut through the sudden darkness. Claire moved quickly, giving instructions on where to shine the light.

She started with the pillar, spraying it from where the top of Melissa's head would have been and all the way to the bottom. She used easy, even strokes to cover the area. Once she had the area sprayed, she lifted another camera from her bag and turned. "The old luminol only worked for about thirty seconds, but this stuff lasts a bit longer. If something shows up, we'll get it on here. Okay, turn the flashlights off."

Lilly clicked hers off and Reggie did the same.

Seconds passed. "And there it is," Claire said.

Blue marks appeared on the concrete column, one in the shape of a partial handprint. Claire snapped pictures until the blue began to fade. "Lights on, please."

Reggie's beam appeared, then Lilly turned hers on. She wasn't sure when Claire had grabbed the Q-tips, but she was busy taking swabs of the concrete column and placing them in small containers.

Another few seconds passed and the lights came back on.

Lilly blinked against the brightness. Claire had started packing up her equipment when Lilly said, "He shot at me."

The woman paused and Reggie paled. "What?" Claire asked.

"He shot at me, but he missed. The bullet should be around here somewhere."

"Show me," Claire said.

"What's going on up here? Are you folks all right?"

The question came from the entrance to the stairs behind Reggie. Lilly forced a smile. "Hi, George."

The sixtysomething man paused, hand on his weapon. "Lillian? That you?"

"It's me."

His hand fell away from the gun and he strode toward her. Six foot three inches tall with a steel-gray buzz for a haircut, George was a former Marine and pure muscle. Sharp blue eyes took in the scene before him and he crossed his arms. "Like I said, what's going on?"

Lilly decided to go with honesty. "We're looking into a murder."

Those blue eyes narrowed. "The murder that didn't happen?"

"Oh, it happened all right," she said.

"Lillian, come on, I've known you forever and your father for longer. The cops didn't find anything the first time you cried wolf, they're not going to find anything now."

Claire stepped forward. "Now wait a minute—"

Lilly placed a hand on her arm as Jason pulled Reggie's car back around. "It's okay, Claire." She turned back to George. "Do you mind if we take a look at one more thing?"

He frowned. "What?"

"The man shot at me that night. The bullet's got to be here somewhere, right?"

"If someone shot at you, yeah, it would be here. Or it could have gone out of the garage. *If* someone shot at you."

Jason came over to her and slipped his arm around her shoulder. "Someone shot at her."

"Who are you?"

"A friend."

"He saved my life, George. A couple of times. And if the bullet exited the garage, wouldn't someone have said something about it?"

"Maybe." He shrugged. "Depends on what it hit. A window? Yes, I would have heard about it. The side of the building? Probably not. But it doesn't matter. No one shot at anyone."

"And if it had hit a car here in the garage, you would have heard about the complaint."

"Absolutely."

Claire was eyeing George. "How tall was the shooter, Lilly?"

"About an inch shorter than George."

Claire nodded and walked over to the man. "Do you mind?"

"What?"

"Role playing."

For a moment, Lilly thought he'd refuse, then he shrugged. "Oh, why not? I got nothing better to do."

Claire smiled. "Thanks. Now"—she took his arm and led him to stand where Reggie, who was only about five feet ten, had stood earlier—"stand here. Lilly, take your spot."

With a deep breath, she did so.

"Now shoot her."

George blinked. "What?"

"With your hand. You know. Lift your arm like you have a gun and aim at her."

"Oh, oh, yeah. Okay." He did.

"Now, Lilly, run the way you did that night, and George, you follow her with your arm like you're aiming to shoot her."

Lilly dashed toward the elevators, because that was where Jenny had been parked.

"Okay, you can stop," Claire called.

Her heart pounding, Lilly stopped. She stood still for a moment while the memory of that night slashed through her. The crack of the gun echoed in her mind and she whimpered.

Then warm arms slid around her and pulled her close. She shuddered.

"You're safe, Lilly," Jason murmured against her ear.

The fear faded, but she couldn't suppress another shudder. "I know. Thanks." She pulled away from him and instantly missed the secure feeling he gave her.

She turned to see Claire running her fingers over the wall, walking down it slowly. Until she stopped. "Here. Found it."

Jason blinked. She'd actually done it. Jason took Claire's kit to her and set it on the floor. While she worked on extracting the bullet, Jason walked over to join Lilly, Reggie, and George.

Lilly looked at him. "Now what?"

"The sun is getting ready to come up. I say we let Claire get back to her lab and do her thing while we hide out and get some sleep."

"Hide out?" George asked.

"The man who killed Melissa is now coming after me," Lilly told him. She'd keep his name to herself at this point. "I'm only barely managing to stay one step ahead of him and his hired killers."

George sighed. "But they never found any evidence."

"He cleaned it up."

"But the security footage—"

"Was tampered with," Lilly said.

"Then you need to go back to the cops," George said.

"I will. When I can prove it." She glanced at Claire. "And I'm getting closer by the minute."

He scowled. "Did you have something to do with the power going out?"

"No. Not me. Exactly."

"I did," Jason said. "I'm a fireman. I know how to cut the power when I have to. Claire needed darkness for about five minutes, so I gave it to her. I simply found the power box and shut it down."

"Could have asked for help. Someone could have gotten stuck on the elevator."

"Sorry about that." He knew he didn't sound too sorry. He'd thought about the elevators but knew it would be only a short time they'd be out of commission. If someone had been on one, the only thing they'd be in danger of was a panic attack. "Look, we're done here. Can you just keep this under your hat for the time being?"

The man didn't answer.

Lilly stepped forward and placed a hand on his forearm. "Please, George? For me?"

"Ah, Lillian." George huffed a sigh. "I guess. For you. Will you promise to be careful?"

"Of course."

"Fine." He shot a hard look at Jason. "But no more tampering with the power."

Jason raised his hand as though taking a solemn oath. "No more tampering. I promise."

"Go on, get out of here." He chucked Lilly on the chin. "Be careful, kid, you hear?"

"I hear. Thanks, George."

"Right." The man went to the exit stairs and disappeared through the door.

Lilly let out a slow breath and Jason cupped her elbow. "Let's go. We've got to get Claire back to the airport."

"Actually, before I go, I need to get a DNA sample from the dead woman. Gotta have something to compare with the blood samples, you know?"

Jason blinked. "How do you plan to get that?"

"I don't know. I was hoping you might have some ideas."

TWELVE

Reggie drove from the parking garage back to the building he and Lilly shared. Claire rode with them, the evidence tucked into her bag.

"You said we needed DNA evidence to prove it was actually Melissa in the garage," Jason said.

"Yes."

He nodded. "What time do you have to be back today?"

"I have a meeting at four this afternoon. Why?"

"What about her apartment?" Lilly said. "We could go there and get the evidence."

"How would we get in?" Jason asked. "It's probably a building like yours. You either have to know someone or live there to get in."

"True." Lilly bit her lip. "All right. What if I got the DNA for you? Could you take it back and see if it matches the blood?"

"Of course. But, again, how?"

"Well, she was just reported missing yesterday. I imagine her desk at the office hasn't been touched yet."

"What are you thinking?" Jason asked.

"What if I go to see my father and simply check her desk? We're women. We always have a drawer for personal things. A toothbrush, hairbrush, fingernail clippers, nail file. Doesn't take much, right?"

"Right," Claire said.

"Can you stay until I can get the DNA?" She looked out the window. "The sun's coming up. I can go at lunchtime. The building will be open, and my father and Franklin will be gone."

Jason shook his head. "I don't know about this."

"I do. I'm doing it."

"Then you're going to need backup."

"No," Claire said, "I'll have to get the sample. To collect it correctly."

Lilly nodded. "Then we'll have to figure out how to arrange that."

Reggie pulled into the parking garage of their building and swiped his card. With a glance at her, he simply shook his head. She supposed everything that had happened in the last few hours was a bit much for the man to take in.

But for now, they'd sleep.

Once she, Claire, and Jason were tucked away in her condo, Reggie slipped down the hall with the promise to pick them up in four hours.

Lilly made sure each of her guests had what they needed for showers and sleep, then walked into her kitchen to check her refrigerator. Everything she'd left when she'd fled a week ago went into the trash except for the condiments. The freezer didn't offer much. That left her with crackers, cheese, and dry cereal. And some peanuts.

With a grimace, she shut the door and decided a drive-thru might be their best option.

"Don't worry about feeding us." Jason's quiet voice behind her brought her head around. "We'll get something on the way back into the city," he said. "For now, you need to rest."

"I guess that's going to have to be the plan for now."

"Exactly." He took her hands and gazed down at her, his eyes dark with some emotion she couldn't name—and wasn't sure she wanted to at the moment. "Lilly, I—"

He hesitated. She squeezed his hands. "I know, Jason," she said softly. "I know."

He leaned over to kiss her. Gently, sweetly—and a bit desperately. His arms slid around her and pulled her closer. Lilly's heart pounded even while her head swirled. She kissed him back, needing the comfort that he so willingly offered. When he lifted his head, his eyes stayed locked on hers. "I know we haven't known each other long, but I really do care about you."

"I feel the same way," she whispered, then cleared her throat. "But let's make sure if we start something, we can finish it without people trying to kill me—or us."

His lips curved. "That sounds like an excellent idea to me."

She nodded, then leaned her forehead against his chest. "Thank you, Jason."

Strong arms held her tighter and she reveled in the feeling. Then he sighed, kissed the top of her head, and gave her a gentle shove toward the hall. "Go. Sleep while you can. Right now, since no one has tried to kill us, I'm hoping they don't realize yet where we are."

"But that could quickly change."

"It could."

"All right. You promise to rest too?"

"Sure. When I get sleepy."

Lilly nodded and headed down the hall to her room, knowing Jason wouldn't be sleeping. He'd had a nice nap in the car and his adrenaline was probably firing nonstop. He'd keep watch and would wake her and Claire should trouble strike. Until then, Lilly would do her best to sleep. Without changing clothes, she lay across her king-size bed and pulled up the fuzzy blanket from the foot of it. She closed her eyes and sent up a prayer that she would get the evidence they needed to put a killer behind bars.

And that no one would have to die to do it.

Jason stood in the doorway of Lilly's room and watched her sleep. She looked so peaceful, he hated to wake her, but it was pushing eleven o'clock and he wanted to get there early. Reggie had come over twenty minutes ago, dropped a bag of fresh fruit, chicken salad, and crackers on the table, and was now pacing a groove in the den hardwoods.

Jason had eaten his fill and fixed plates for the ladies. He could hear the water running and figured it was Claire. Jason stepped inside Lilly's sanctuary and couldn't help taking in her décor. She liked bold colors with milk chocolate walls, white trim, and red curtains. He would never have chosen the colors, but they worked for her. Just another interesting side to her personality. The room was large, with the king bed looking almost small in the space. She had a sitting area off to the left in a small alcove with a television, a recliner, and a sofa.

Feeling a bit like an intruder for lingering and studying such a private area of her life, he moved on silent feet to the bed and touched her shoulder.

With a gasp, she bolted upright, eyes wide and frightened. He immediately sat beside her. "It's okay, Lilly, it's me."

She pressed a hand to her chest and closed her eyes. "You scared me again."

"I kind of figured that out. I'm sorry, I didn't think. I should have called out to you from the door."

"No." She ran a shaking hand through her hair. "It's okay."

"Can you be ready to leave in about thirty minutes?"

"Of course."

He nodded and stood. "Reggie's already here and keeping watch. He brought food so we don't have to stop on the way. I'm going to use the shower you so graciously offered, and I'll be ready."

"Okay. Good. I'm hungry." He helped her to her feet and she shot him a shaky smile. "We can do this, can't we?"

"Yes. We really can."

She hesitated, then shook her head. "Okay. At least I'll be inconspicuous. The people in the building are used to seeing me there. And while I haven't put in an appearance for over a week, that's not unusual. I can easily get Claire into the office as long as it's empty."

"You know, the police may have already been through it."

"I thought about that, but even if they did search it, they were looking for information on where she might disappear to, not something that held her DNA."

"True. Okay. I'm going to get out of here and let you get ready."

Jason left, shutting the door behind him, and walked back into the den to find Reggie at the window, holding a pair of binoculars to his eyes.

"See anything?" he asked.

"No. Nothing that worries me anyway."

"Good. I'm going to jump in the shower, and then we'll head out."

Lilly's uncle nodded. "Go on, I'll stay alert."

Jason studied the man who Lilly trusted without question. While Reggie had given him no cause to suspect he wasn't exactly as he appeared to be—a man worried about his niece—Jason still couldn't help being slightly suspicious. Nothing else had happened since they'd brought Reggie in on everything.

And it made him wonder. He turned the shower on, but couldn't turn his thoughts off. He couldn't figure out what reason Reggie would have to turn on his niece. What was his relationship with Franklin Rutherford besides a mutual love for Lilly? Anything?

He wanted to text Nolan to ask him to look into it. But communicating with his brother was taboo at this point. He'd just have to keep a close eye on Lilly and Reggie both.

THIRTEEN

Lilly stared at the building she was getting ready to enter. The chicken salad and crackers she'd wolfed down sat in her stomach like lead. She smoothed a hand down the silk jacket she'd donned. The matching pants made her feel comfortable, like she was born to wear them. Her flawless makeup and hair simply added to the well-put-together outward package. Jason's jaw-dropping reaction to her appearance when she walked into the den gave her some confidence she desperately needed. Her fingers curled around the new cell phone she'd insisted they stop and purchase. She planned to leave it in her father's office with a request to call her. Maybe if she could tell her father everything they'd found, he'd believe her.

"Okay," Jason said, "in and out. Don't stop to talk to people unless you can't avoid it." He nodded to the parking spot across from the elevator. "Rutherford's car is gone."

"Yeah, he should be at lunch," Lilly said. "He goes every day like clockwork at 11:55. My father often goes with him."

"Where does he park?"

"On the first floor. His car wasn't there either." Her pulse slowed a little. No one would be expecting her to walk through those doors. As far as the people in this building knew, she'd simply been busy, either traveling or attending charity events.

She climbed out of the vehicle. Jason and Claire followed.

Reggie would wait in the car. Once they had the evidence, collected by Claire, she would slip back downstairs to the parking garage and Reggie would take her to the airport.

Lilly led the way. In the elevator, she pressed the button for the fifth floor. "Everyone ready to play their parts?" she asked.

"Ready."

Claire nodded and handed Lilly the bouquet of flowers they'd picked up one street over. "This is the most fun I've had in a while," Claire said. She tilted her head and looked at Lilly. "Minus the part where there's a killer after you."

"Thanks." Lilly liked Claire and hoped to get to know her better. Assuming she lived to see Rutherford behind bars and this whole terrifying ordeal come to an end.

When the elevator opened, she, Claire, and Jason stepped off onto the floor and turned right. In the car, Lilly had gone over the location of Melissa's desk and the quickest route to find it.

Lilly would provide a distraction—as would Jason, should he be needed. Franklin's office was two offices in one. Franklin occupied the larger one, of course, which housed a mammoth-sized desk and leather chair. He had a sofa and two wingback chairs in the sitting area opposite the desk. His secretary worked in the area outside Franklin's office. Her door usually stood open. However, it could be closed off for privacy when Franklin deemed it necessary. For now, as long as he was out of his office, Claire shouldn't have any trouble slipping inside and searching Melissa's desk.

Lilly would keep anyone who came near the office busy. Somehow.

"Lillian?"

She turned. "Hi, Miranda."

"Oh, Lillian, have you heard about Melissa?"

Lilly frowned and nodded at the dark-haired woman. "I have. Has anyone heard anything at all from anyone?"

"No, the police are looking into it. In the meantime, the show must go on. What are you doing here?"

"We're here to deliver flowers to Franklin and I need to get something out of my father's office."

Her father's office and Franklin's were right next to one another.

Miranda's gaze flitted from Jason to Claire. Lilly pasted on a smile. "Miranda, forgive my manners. Meet Jason Tanner and Claire Montgomery. They're getting to know the work we do and the charities developed by my father. I'm just giving them the full tour."

"Welcome," Miranda said. Her smile blossomed, and she let her gaze linger on Jason's face. Lilly wanted to tell her to back off.

Instead, she cleared her throat. "I'm assuming my father's at lunch since I didn't see his car in the garage."

"Of course. A creature of habit."

"Of course." Lilly gestured toward the nearest door. "This is Franklin Rutherford's office. He's my father's campaign manager."

Jason nodded. "Your father's going for the Senate, I hear."

"Indeed."

"Well, I'll just let you three get back to it," Miranda said. "Very nice to meet you all."

As soon as her back was turned, Claire slipped into the office. Lilly placed the flowers on the table just inside the door and stood there while the woman hurried over to the desk.

From the corner of her eye, Lilly saw Miranda heading back toward her. She turned to Jason. "Ah, Mr. Tanner, if you'll just wait here a moment, I'll be right back. Once Ms. Montgomery is finished in the restroom, we'll continue."

Jason clued right in. "Of course." He took her spot in the doorway, leaned against the doorjamb, and pulled his phone from his pocket.

Miranda kept walking even though she allowed her eyes to linger on Jason.

Lilly gave a light snort and headed for her father's office. Once inside, she stopped and looked around. It was familiar and comfortable even though the man who occupied the space often felt distant and foreign to her. She sighed. Losing her mother had changed him into a workaholic, she supposed. Reggie said it was because he loved her so much and her death nearly killed him. Working had been his way to survive—and then it had just become habit.

A pang shot through her. She'd always been driven to gain his approval, and when she finally took her present position, she thought she'd achieved that goal. Maybe. The fact that she wasn't sure bothered her.

She walked around to stand behind his desk. Taking a pen from the holder, she pulled a pad of sticky notes in front of her and wrote down the new cell number with the words "Call me, please" under it. She placed the cell phone next to the note and drew in a breath. She wasn't sure if Franklin had managed to bug her father's phone, but she wouldn't put it past him.

Hearing voices in the hall, she quickly stepped to the door and slipped out of the office.

Claire and Jason faced her, talking to a man who had his back to her. But Lilly had no trouble recognizing him.

Franklin Rutherford.

Jason saw Lilly's terrified expression, then her face hardened and her shoulders straightened. "Hello, Franklin."

The man went rigid and all color drained from his face. Then his features smoothed out and he dipped his head as he turned to face Lilly. "Lilly, how dare you show your face here after what you've put your father and me through?"

She swallowed, but lifted her chin and narrowed her eyes. "What I've put you through? You're going to deny that you killed Melissa? That you had my best friend, Jenny, murdered, and that you almost succeeded in killing me?"

A gasp pulled Jason's attention from the seething campaign

manager. When he turned, Miranda and four coworkers stood there gaping. Miranda turned her gaze to the man. "Franklin?"

"It's lies," he snapped. "All lies."

"No, it's not," Lilly said, "and I'm going to prove it."

Rutherford pulled at the sleeves on his coat. He finally sighed. "Lilly, I don't know what's happened to bring you to this state of madness. I just pray that someone can get you the help you need before further damage is done."

"I don't need help. But you're going to."

Rutherford's eyes snapped to someone in Miranda's little group. "Who do you think you're calling?"

The man with the phone pressed to his ear chuckled. "My boss. I'm a reporter for the *State*. This one is too good to pass up, sorry. Tell Maloney good luck getting that Senate seat now." He shook his phone. "Got the whole thing on video." He smirked at Lilly. "Thanks!" Then he turned on his heel and strode off.

"Oh no," Lilly whispered. "What have I done?"

Jason stepped around Rutherford and grasped Lilly's arm. "I think our work here is done." To Rutherford, Jason said, "That didn't go exactly as planned, but if Lilly dies now, guess who'll be the first suspect?"

The man looked like he might have a coronary. Claire joined them, and without another word to the glaring man, Jason escorted the two women down the hall toward the exit.

Rutherford didn't say anything else, but his expression said this wasn't over. Not by a long shot.

Once in the car, Lilly put her head in her hands and was silent. "Oh boy. I messed up."

Jason rubbed her back. Reggie's fingers tapped the wheel. He obviously wanted to know what had happened.

"No, you didn't," Jason said. "But things might get interesting."

"What was he doing there?" she said. "This is a disaster. The press is going to have a field day with this."

"The press?" Reggie asked.

Jason told him what happened. Reggie blanched. "Whoa. Tyler is going to have a fit."

"Or a coronary," Lilly said. "And he'll probably disown me. Claim I'm not his and that I was switched at birth or something because no offspring of his would ever behave so."

Reggie looked in the rearview mirror and Jason caught the odd expression in his eyes.

Lilly gasped and leaned forward from the back seat. "Claire, I've been so focused on my mess-up . . . Did you find anything?"

Claire turned with a smug smile. "Indeed I did. I even videoed the collection of it—all proper and done right."

"What did you find?"

"A hairbrush that had her name on the handle. No way to argue that it's not hers. Once I get home, I can process this right away."

Lilly sat back and closed her eyes. Jason curled his fingers around hers. "I can't believe it," she said. "We actually did it."

"Yeah," Jason said. He lifted her hand to kiss her knuckles. "We make a great team."

FOURTEEN

Back in her home, Lilly couldn't sit still. Reggie had left to take Claire back to the airport, and Jason had taken an incoming call into the bedroom with orders for her to keep the blinds shut and her distance from the windows. She figured it was Nolan calling him. Jason must have told him it didn't matter now because Franklin knew they were here in the city. He was probably planning her demise even as she paced her den, trying to figure out what to do next. She glanced at her phone and was actually surprised it hadn't rung yet. She kept expecting her father to call, if only to rake her over the coals for her stupidity. The fact that he hadn't concerned her.

So she forced thoughts of her father from her head and allowed the events of the afternoon to move in. What had Rutherford been doing there? And where had her father been, if not eating lunch with his campaign manager?

The television played in the background. The video of her yelling at Franklin in her father's offices played nonstop. News anchors speculated—and made things up. She shook her head. Even with the video, they had to put their own spin on everything.

Her phone buzzed and she froze. Only four people had that number. Reggie, Jason, Nolan, and now her father. She glanced at the screen and recognized the number belonging to the new phone she'd left on his desk. She took a deep breath and prepared herself for the coming tirade. Then tapped the screen and answered. "Hey, Dad."

"Hello, Lillian."

She frowned. "Franklin? How did you get this number?"

"From your father's desk."

Her stomach clenched. She looked at the screen again and tapped once more. She lifted the phone back to her ear. "And where's my father?"

"Safe. For now."

"What does that mean?" A chill swept through her. She knew what it meant.

"I assume you've seen the news."

"Of course. And for whatever it's worth, I never meant for that to happen. I was doing everything I could to keep it away from the media. I had no idea that reporter was there."

"Well, you messed up. So there's only one thing to do."

"What?"

"You have to fix it."

"Fix it? How? There's no way to fix it."

"You will or your father is a dead man."

Her phone buzzed again, and she lowered the device to look at the picture. Her father was in his office bent over his desk working on some papers.

"I can get to him any time," Franklin said. "You know he trusts me with his life. In spite of your silly story about me killing some-one."

Lifting the phone back to her ear, she said, "You won't get away with this."

Silence echoed back at her. Then Franklin said, "Recant what you said earlier."

"What?"

"Recant it or he dies. It's really that simple."

"But—"

"Hold a news conference and admit that you lied, that you were holding a grudge against me because you wanted this position as campaign manager and your father gave it to me. Admit that you thought by smearing my name, you'd simply take over. Apologize and do some groveling and I might let your father live."

Lilly swallowed. "And if I don't? You'll kill him? You think you can get away with that?"

"I've already gotten away with one murder, what's going to stop me from getting away with it again?"

The silky confidence in his voice sent shudders racing through her. "But my father will just turn you in once I tell him about this conversation." The whole thing was just preposterous.

"Lillian, Lillian. What does your father care for most in this world?"

"His career," she whispered.

"And how much does he want that Senate seat?"

Lilly closed her eyes and dropped her chin to her chest. "With everything in him." Her father loved her, but not more than his career. If this could save it, he'd follow Franklin's lead.

"So, now you know your role. You're the poor daughter who has developed a terrible mental illness. You've been off your medications and you've slandered a good man with your lies."

"And my father is the compassionate, loving man who is determined to make sure his poor daughter is taken care of," she whispered. His plan wasn't so hard to figure out.

"You always were smart. So, do we understand one another?"

"We do."

"And if you tell anyone about this, your father will die."

"But if you kill him, where does that leave your career?"

He actually laughed. "You don't know who you're dealing with, little girl. We've already gotten forged hospital records with evidence of your mental instability, a lifetime of medication, and a history of delusions. Once we release that to the press, I become a victim of your lies. And your poor, heartbroken father will commit suicide. Just like your best friend."

Panic welled inside her. He had this all planned out, and she couldn't see a way around it. She had no doubt he had the records. If she didn't do as he asked, not only would her father die, she would, too. Eventually.

"And," he said, "with all the publicity that is going on right now due to your little outburst being splashed across national television, once you retract your words and admit to your lies, I'll have the sympathy of everyone and be able to write my own ticket."

"What's to keep you from arranging my death once I do this?"

He snorted. "Nothing, I suppose. You'll just have to take that chance if you want to save your father."

Lilly's hands were tied. "Where do I go for this press conference?"

He gave a low grunt of satisfaction. "I thought you might see it my way. Be in front of campaign headquarters in thirty minutes. And if I see anyone with you, your father is done."

"I don't have a car," she said.

"There's one waiting just outside your building. Go get into it. Now. And don't hang up until you start talking to the reporters."

Quickly, she grabbed a pen and a sticky note.

"Come on, Lillian. I don't hear you moving."

"I'm thinking."

"Don't bother, it's only going to get your father killed."

Lilly paused only a brief second before dashing off a seven-word note to Jason. *At the office, stay hidden. He's watching.*

With an agonized glance toward the bedroom where Jason was still talking, she grabbed her purse and slipped out the door.

———

Jason stepped into the living area and found it empty. "Lilly?" Maybe she was in her room. He went to knock on the door and found it standing open.

The room was empty.

Bathroom?

He checked. Also empty.

His pulse picked up speed and he walked back into the den, his eyes going to the coffee table where Lilly had dropped her purse upon arriving home.

It was gone.

She'd left.

He pulled out his phone, grabbed his car keys, and dialed Reggie's number. Just as he went to open the door, he skidded to a stop. A sticky note was pasted at eye level. He read it and his blood ran cold.

Somehow, Rutherford had contacted Lilly and she was going to meet him.

And it was up to Jason to figure out how to save her.

─────

The black SUV pulled to a stop at the curb and Lilly climbed out, phone still in hand. "I'm here." And so was the media. In full force. She shuddered and searched for the courage to do as instructed. The reminder that her father was counting on her gave her the strength to straighten her shoulders and lift her chin. She had a plan. It was risky, but it was the only option she had on the table. She hung up on Franklin and opened an app on her phone. It took her only a few seconds to find what she was looking for.

With another deep breath, she stepped up to the microphone. Reporters shouted questions at her and she simply stayed silent until they stilled.

Lilly cleared her throat and leaned in. "Thank you for coming." Franklin appeared to her left, and she shot him a glare for a full ten seconds. He was the first to look away, and she took another moment to enjoy the fact that it was caught on camera.

Her father soon joined him, and Lilly once again had a moment of self-doubt. No. She had to do this. It was the only way to save her father from a madman. She took a deep breath, then leaned once more into the microphone.

"As you know, I made some comments this morning that were recorded without my knowledge. As a result, an unauthorized video has been released. News outlets across the country have picked it up and are playing it nonstop. I have no excuse for what I said so publicly. If I had accusations to make, I should have done so behind closed doors. Unfortunately, it's too late now. The damage is done, and it's up to me to undo it."

Franklin made a small motion with his hand as though to encourage her to hurry it up.

She looked back at the eager faces before her. All of them hungry for a good story or blood. Or both. "So, I'm here to say that every word I said to Franklin Rutherford was true and I will not recant it."

The crowd roared. Franklin's eyes flared and he laid a hand on her father's shoulder. "In fact, I think you should hear for yourself exactly why I said what I said." She hit play on the app that recorded phone conversations and held the device next to the microphone.

"And if I don't?" Lilly's voice filled the air. "You'll kill him? You think you can get away with that?"

"I've already gotten away with one murder," Franklin said in that smooth, arrogant tone. "What's going to stop me from doing it a second time?"

The reporters roared. Franklin ran. Jason shot out from the crowd and tackled him. He held him there until the police, who'd shown up for security reasons, could reach him and cuff him.

Lilly turned back to the reporters. "The rest of the recording will be available at a later time."

Her eyes collided with her father's. He stared at her, his expression unreadable. Then he turned on his heel and pushed his way through the teeming chaos to disappear back into the building.

Lilly's heart pounded with the pain of his reaction, but she loved him. And she'd done the right thing for him. Maybe one day he'd come to understand that.

And if he didn't, at least he was alive.

FIFTEEN

Jason sat next to Lilly in the café where they'd managed to snag a seat in a secluded corner. It had been two weeks since the dramatic arrest of Franklin Rutherford, and Jason had just returned that morning from Tanner Hollow.

"How are Kallie and the baby?" she asked.

Jason grinned. "Doing great. Nolan Jr." He shook his head. "He's got some big shoes to fill."

"Nolan will be a wonderful dad. He'll teach him all he needs to know."

"Exactly." He took a sip of his coffee and watched her expressive eyes. "What is it?"

She shrugged. "Nothing really."

"Something really."

Lilly chuckled. "I'd like that one day."

"What?"

"A husband, a baby or two. A family." A sigh slipped from her. "I've been so focused on work, work, work that I've neglected the part of me that wants more than that."

Jason took her hand. "I think you're on the right path."

She smiled. "You think?"

"Yeah."

"Yeah." She peered up at him, her smile lingering. Then she frowned. "I almost didn't live to tell you that. I can't thank you enough for everything."

He squeezed her fingers. "You don't have to keep thanking me." He shrugged. "And it must be we're meant to be together. If that electrical box at your rental hadn't shorted out and caught fire at the exact time it did, we wouldn't be sitting here having this conversation."

"It wasn't my time yet."

"Exactly. And I, for one, am very grateful." He cleared his throat. "So, I don't mean to spoil the mood, but I have something I probably need to share with you."

"What's that?"

"Nolan got an update on the case. They found Melissa."

Lilly drew in a swift breath. "Where?" They'd searched Franklin's property and turned up nothing.

"She'd been dumped in a lake about four miles from Rutherford's house. He'd wrapped her in the plastic from the parking garage and tossed her in his trunk. Then he drove straight home, took weights from his home gym, and tied them to her, using the rope from the tire swing in his backyard. The rope came loose from the tarp and she floated to the surface. A fisherman reeled her in yesterday afternoon."

Lilly closed her eyes and swallowed hard. "Her poor family. But at least now they know for sure."

"And the evidence Claire collected is probably going to be admissible. Add that to your testimony and the recording you had the genius to make, Rutherford's going away for a long time."

"What about the guy who attacked me in the hospital?"

"Also going to be behind bars for years. They're rounding up evidence on other murders he'd committed as well. Apparently he's the politicians' hit man."

She grimaced. "That's awful."

"I know." He gripped her fingers. "I'm sorry."

"I am too."

"Did you ever figure out why Rutherford was at the office when he was supposed to be at lunch the day you confronted him?"

"He'd been expecting a document that he needed my father's okay on. Miranda had called and told him it came in, so he came back to get it."

"Wow. Bad timing."

"I don't know. It all worked out. In an unexpected, crazy way, but it worked out nonetheless."

He smiled. "True enough. So, have you convinced your father to come out to eat with us tonight?"

Lilly shook her head. "No. He says thanks, but no thanks. He's grieving the loss of his campaign manager, even though he says the man is where he deserves to be."

"Try one more time."

"What?"

"Let's go to his office and try one more time. I plan on being in your life a very long time and I want to know him."

"Jason, it might be an impossible—"

He gave her his best puppy-dog look. "Please?"

She groaned, then laughed. "Fine. Let's go talk to him, then."

Lilly held Jason's hand as they walked the short distance to the building she still saw in her nightmares. Once on the elevator, she rubbed sweaty palms on her slacks and decided she would do as Jason wanted—try once more to convince her father that he needed to spend time with the man she had come to care about very deeply in a short time. Jason and Reggie had hit it right off, and she desperately wanted that for her father and Jason. But the truth was, she wasn't going to hold out hope for it. Or let it ruin the joy she found in being with Jason.

They stepped off the elevator and made their way down the hall to her father's office. The door stood open, but he wasn't inside. "I guess he stepped out for a few minutes. We can wait inside."

Jason followed her in and took a seat in the nearest wingback chair. Lilly went to her father's desk and picked up her favorite picture. One of her mother. It was the only picture he had on his desk. She'd been hurt by that once upon a time, but had come to accept it as just part of who he was.

"I used to come here as a kid and sit in his chair. I'd feel so important."

"You're important to me no matter what chair you sit in."

She laughed. "Thanks." Lilly took a seat in the large leather chair. The shredder was in the way, so she moved it back to its spot on the end of the credenza before pushing off with her feet to spin the chair in circles. "I used to do this as a kid too."

Jason's laughter echoed hers.

And then her eyes fell on the credenza behind her father's desk. A yellow sticky note. The one that was missing from the stack near her phone. Puzzled, she picked it up. And found another piece of paper below it with Jenny's home address on it.

Dread curling in her belly, she looked at the next piece. The address where she'd been staying when the man had drugged her and tried to kill her. It had been a cash-only rental in a rather skanky part of town, but it had suited her purposes.

"Lilly?"

Jason's voice dragged her gaze away from the evidence she wanted to deny.

Her father stood in the doorway, his face pale, features tight.

"You were in on it," she said.

He stepped inside and shut the door. "Franklin came to me the night he killed Melissa." Her father ran a shaky hand over his face. "I couldn't believe he'd do such a stupid thing, but he was in love and she'd tossed him over for a younger man. Said she was quitting the job and would clean her desk out when she got back from vacation with the new man. He lost it and shot her. We had to act fast to clean up that mess."

"She wasn't a mess, she was a person," Jason said.

"And the security footage?" Lilly said.

"Easy enough to bribe someone to fix that."

"Who? Not George?"

He shrugged. "No. Paul. It happened on his watch."

Lilly stood. "And me? I was a part of that *mess* too. You just gave him the green light to kill Jenny and me?"

"No, of course not. But Franklin was adamant that if this got out, our careers would be ruined."

"So, in order to keep your precious career, you were willing to let him hire someone to kill your own daughter? How dare you! How could you?" She flew at him, unsure what she planned to do when she got her hands on him, but Jason stepped in and caught her before she could find out. She struggled for only a moment before she collapsed against him. "I hate you! You're a monster! I'm your daughter!"

"No you're not!" Red flushed in his cheeks while his eyes narrowed and his nostrils flared.

Lilly froze. Blinked. Gaped.

Her father did, too.

"What did you just say?" She finally managed to get the words past her lips.

He sank onto the sofa. "Why couldn't you just mind your own business?"

"I was minding my own business when I saw a murder, remember?"

When he didn't answer, Jason looked ready to pounce on the man.

She shook her head even as pain raged through her. "All my life I've tried to please you, but it was never enough. I convinced myself that you loved me even though you loved your work more. I finally came to be able to accept that as an adult. I thought if I worked with you, was as passionate about your charities and politics as you were, that I'd finally receive your stamp of approval." She choked out a humorless laugh. "But I guess not. I'll never receive that love or approval because I'm not your child." She swallowed and gathered her strength, her emotions. "So, whose child am I?"

"Mine."

Lilly turned at the new voice and tears welled. "Uncle Reggie?"

He'd opened the door and no one had noticed. Now, he stepped into the office and shut the door behind him. "I've wanted to tell you forever, but I promised your mother I wouldn't."

"But why?"

He smiled. "Because she loved you more than life itself and knew your father would make you pay if she said anything. She didn't want his wrath coming down on you."

Lilly swung her gaze back to her father. "And you agreed?"

"Of course he agreed," Reggie answered for him. "Can you imagine what it would have done for his image if word of his wife's infidelity with his own brother had gotten out?"

Her father lunged at Reggie and swung. Reggie spun and the punch went wide. Jason caught her father around the middle and yanked him back. He landed on the sofa.

Reggie shoved his hands in his pockets and shook his head as he studied his brother. "You're a fool."

"Get out of my sight."

"She loved you, you know," Reggie said. "Olivia had eyes for no one but you. Until you grossly neglected her."

"And you were right there to pick up the slack, weren't you?"

Reggie shrugged. "It wasn't an intentional thing. It was more an accident than anything. But after the first time, she realized I loved her more than you ever would."

"But she stayed with me," her father snarled.

"Because she knew she was sick and probably wouldn't live long after Lillian was born. And then she was granted four years with her daughter and she never took a moment of that time for granted."

"What?" Lilly gasped. "But my mother died in a car accident."

"One in which you were supposed to die too," her father said. Rage burned in his eyes. He looked manic. Or mad. Lilly couldn't decide whether to cry or run.

"You killed her," Reggie stated quietly, his expression deadly. "I always wondered but could never prove it."

"She kept throwing you in my face. 'Why can't you be more like Reggie?'" he mocked. "'Reggie would never talk to me that way.' I finally couldn't stand it another minute. I cut the brake line and sent her on an errand."

"I'll kill you myself," Reggie ground out.

"No, you won't," Jason said. "Lilly needs you."

Reggie flicked him a brief glance before turning his gaze back on his brother. "And you wanted Lillian dead too? What kind of monster are you?"

Her father's nostrils flared. "A very powerful one. One who knows how to turn any situation to his advantage. After the wreck, everyone was so sympathetic. The poor widower-slash-single-father thing worked well. My popularity grew by leaps and bounds. So I put up with having a brat on my heels and nannies in the house."

"And if I hadn't been useful?" she whispered. "You would have gotten rid of me, wouldn't you?"

His jaw worked and he looked away.

"The police are on the way," Reggie said.

Her father didn't move.

"I can't believe this," she said. "And yet I can. I think I'm actually surprised it wasn't your idea all along."

His eyes rose to meet hers and instantly she knew.

"You lied. Franklin didn't put the hits out on me, did he? You didn't just *go along* with him. It was you the whole time."

Pounding on the door jerked her attention to it. "Police! Is everything all right in there?"

Her father leapt off the couch and darted for his desk. Faster than she thought possible, he was behind it. "No! Dad!"

He lifted his hand, pointing a gun at the three of them. Jason, who had raced to stop him, pulled back, hands up. He deliberately stepped in front of her. "Put it down, sir," he said. "It's over."

More pounding. "Police! Open up!"

"What are you going to do, Ty?" Reggie asked. "Shoot us all?"

Her father's hand trembled, his desperation clear. "No. I just need enough time to get out of here."

"He's got a gun!" Reggie cried.

The door flew inward. Officers swarmed the office and zeroed in on the gun in her father's hand.

"Put it down! Drop it!"

Their voices crashed around them.

"Dad, please," Lilly cried. "Please."

His eyes lifted to meet hers. "I can't go to prison."

"No," she whispered.

But she knew what he was going to do. He turned the weapon on the officers and Jason yanked her to the floor as the shots rang out.

"Don't look," he whispered. "Don't look."

EPILOGUE

Six months later

Lilly lifted her face to the sun and smiled. Today was her wedding day. It had been a tough six months, but Jason and the man she now called Dad had gotten her through them.

Claire had reported back that the DNA had been a match to Melissa Miller, but with Franklin in prison on a full confession and Tyler Maloney dead, there'd been no more need for the evidence.

Kallie stepped into the church parlor with Nolan Jr. on her hip. The baby clapped his hands and held his arms out to Lilly. She took him, unconcerned that he might disturb the pearls on the front of her dress. "He gains a pound every time I hold him."

"I know." Kallie grinned. "You look amazing."

"Thanks."

"I'm so glad you chose to get married here in Tanner Hollow instead of in Washington."

"Me too." Soon, she'd walk down that aisle, then she and Jason would be off for a cruise to Alaska. Just the two of them. For two weeks.

She handed the baby back to her soon-to-be sister-in-law. "All right, my friend, let's get this show on the road."

"After you."

Lilly stepped out of the parlor and walked down the hall to the door that led into the sanctuary. It was a small wedding, attended by a few people she loved—like Reggie and his fiancée, a woman who would soon be her stepmother. Lilly had loved Beth from the moment she'd met her. It was like Reggie had finally decided he could put Lilly's mother to rest and move on with his life.

Miranda and several others from the office had flown in, and they'd had a grand time the night before.

But now it was time. She was going to marry Jason and live in Tanner Hollow. For as long as life kept them there. She'd already started three charities in the time she'd been there and was currently raising money to build a teen center for students who had nowhere to go after school. It was going to be a good life.

The music started and she took a deep breath. Reggie, the man who'd been a father to her all her life even though they'd never lived in the same house, stepped up next to her. "You ready for this?"

"Beyond ready."

"You look beautiful."

"Thanks, Dad."

His throat worked. "Every time you call me that, I feel blessed."

She kissed his cheek, and the doors opened.

At the end of the aisle, Jason stood confident and handsome in his black tux. She wanted to run the length of the church and throw herself into his arms. Instead, she grinned. He grinned back, but she thought tears might have been in his eyes. "Come on, Dad, let's go. Walk fast. None of that wimpy, slow stuff."

He laughed. Together, they walked the aisle in record time and totally out of sync with the rhythm of the music.

She didn't care a bit.

Jason took her hand and her dad stepped back. "You're gorgeous."

"So are you."

Nolan stood beside him. "Glad you could make it."

She laughed and looked into Jason's eyes. "There's nowhere else on earth I'd rather be than right here at this moment."

"Ditto," he whispered.

The pastor cleared his throat and they turned to face him as he began his message. Jason leaned over and kissed her temple. "I love you."

She grinned up at him. "And I love you."

He kissed her.

The pastor stopped talking. "Uh . . . we're not to that part yet."

Jason lifted his head. "Then let's get there."

Lilly laughed from the sheer joy racing through her. And sent up a silent prayer of thanks for God's protection and provision, and for bringing her to this moment.

She took a deep breath and said the vows that would take her into the future. A future that would include the man at her side—and more love than her heart could possibly hold.

LETHAL
SECRETS

ONE

Honor McBride tightened her grip on the steering wheel. A glance in the rearview mirror confirmed she wasn't being followed. Right now. Unfortunately, she wasn't sure how good of a job she'd done when it came to covering her tracks. Looking over her shoulder was going to be a minute-by-minute activity.

"Are we almost there?" said a tiny voice.

"I'm hungry."

"I'm tired."

"How much longer?" Christopher was the last to voice a complaint. Almost thirteen, the blond slumped against the passenger door and groaned.

"I told you, we should be there in about ten minutes," Honor said.

"That's what you said thirty minutes ago," Gus piped up. "I may just be seven, but I can tell time, you know."

"I know, Gus." She tried to sound soothing, but her ability to speak without gritting her teeth had ended about six hundred miles ago. "The GPS took me the wrong way. The lady at the gas station said to go this way." She waved the paper at the rearview mirror.

"I'm famished," Beth Ann said, her lisp making it come out *famithed*. This from her five-year-old with a dictionary obsession. Beth Ann had started reading at the age of two and a half.

Three years later, she'd acquired a vocabulary worthy of an English professor.

"We're all hungry. Surely we'll be there in time to make a run to the grocery store before it closes." She glanced at the dashboard clock of her 1980s station wagon. Almost thirty-five years old, the Mercury Colony Park was the only thing on the lot she could afford with her limited cash reserves. She took it because it was big enough for her crew and their meager belongings.

Honor took another quick look in the rearview mirror at the three in the back. Carbon copies of each other, every one of her children sported white-blond hair and blue eyes like their mother. Not much of Lorenzo to be seen in them. Honor knew that had been a topic of conversation for some people. Not that she cared anymore. She knew the truth, and that was all that mattered. And besides, they didn't get her pale, sun-sensitive skin. They all tanned a beautiful brown in the summer. Compliments of their father.

She refocused her gaze on the road before her, pushing aside memories of a dead husband and desperate times—and the fact that she and her children were in danger. That was the most worrisome part.

"Hey! Stop it! Mom, Samuel hit me," ten-year-old Harry whined.

"Did not," Samuel, Gus's seven-year-old twin, protested. "It was just a light shove because you're hogging the seat again. Move over. Please."

Tears crowded behind her eyeballs, pushing to be released. Having learned the hard way that crying helped nothing, she refused to let them fall. But for the millionth time since they'd started this journey eight days ago, she wondered if she'd made a huge mistake in running.

No, she'd had no choice. Not after the latest incident—someone trying to run her off the road—and the implied threat against her children.

He'd come to her house that sunny Sunday afternoon.

"Lorenzo owed me," he said. "You're his wife. Now you owe me."

"I don't have that kind of money."

"Then you better find it. You have five days to get the money together, then I'll be back to collect it. Sell one of those brats—they're worth a lot on the black market. And keep this to yourself, understand? If you bring cops into the picture, your kids'll pay." He stepped close, crowding her against the wall in the kitchen and raising a hand to trail a finger down her cheek. "Or maybe I'll just take you. You're probably worth the fifty grand." She shoved him away and he let go, but those hard eyes remained locked on hers. "Five days."

Terrified, she'd immediately packed a few necessary items—including the legal papers that could mean the difference between life and death—grabbed her kids, and hit the road.

She was the only parent they had left and she was determined to live to watch them grow up. Another glance in the mirror assured her yet again that she wasn't being followed. At least there was no one she could see.

"Y'all be quiet," Christopher demanded of his siblings. "Mom's tired."

"We're all tired," Harry said, his tone sullen.

"And starving!" Beth Ann added.

"Hey, little people, look!" Relief poured through Honor's wilting veins. "There's the sign."

Beth Ann read, "Welcome to Tanner Hollow."

"What a crummy name for a crummy town," Harry said.

The corner of Honor's mouth crooked up for the first time in a very long time. "You gotta work on all that optimism, Harry."

She turned left, then made another right, following the signs into downtown Tanner Hollow. At four thirty in the afternoon, the sun had started its downward descent. It would be chilly when darkness finally fell, but thank goodness, November in the south would be as warm as it was in the panhandle of Texas. The kids pressed their noses to the windows. Pleasant surprise curled through her at the quaint stores lining the streets. Some were already decorated for Christmas, and it wasn't even Thanksgiving yet. Several people walked the sidewalks, others sat on benches in front of the stores, dressed in warm coats, gloves, and knit hats.

"It's pretty," Christopher finally said.

"Look at that toy store!" Beth Ann said. "It has a plethora of lights. I wonder how many. Can I count them?"

Hope had started to spread in her chest when the loud pop made Honor jerk. The station wagon lurched, then listed to the right. She screamed and the kids echoed her. Honor slammed on the brakes.

Despair clawing at her, she threw the car in park and opened her door, terror chasing the breath from her lungs. He'd found her. He'd shot at her. She needed to hide, protect her children, but how? Her forward momentum carried her around the front of her vehicle to discover a flat tire.

Not just a low-on-air flat tire.

But a flat-as-a-pancake, not-going-anywhere, you-ran-over-something-sharp flat tire.

Or a bullet went through it.

But how would he know? How could he have beat her here, managed to find a hiding place, and then shot out her tire?

She pressed a hand against her beating heart and took three deep breaths.

No one had shot at her.

It was just a flat tire. The tires had needed to be replaced when she'd purchased the car. It had just been a matter of time.

They were still safe.

Sobs choked her. But she couldn't let them out. Not yet.

"Um, ma'am?"

Honor whirled. And looked up. And up some more. With wide

shoulders and a head full of red hair, a decidedly handsome man stared down at her with emerald-green eyes and worry creasing his forehead.

Oh my.

Honor suddenly realized she was ogling the good-looking giant in front of her—and he was staring back. She sucked in an embarrassed breath and smoothed her cherry-red long-sleeved top over the waistband of her jeans. "Yes?"

He shifted, then waved toward her traitorous vehicle. "You seem to be having a problem here. Can I help you?"

She cleared her throat and surveyed the tire. Everything in her wanted to tell him she could handle it. Instead, she swallowed her pride. "I would be most grateful." She started to turn back to the car when she caught movement from the corner of her eye.

Tilting her head, she looked around the man who hadn't budged and saw she'd attracted the attention of quite a few townspeople. A sign above their heads said Dot's Delicious Diner.

Keeping her groan of embarrassment locked inside, she gave everyone a weak smile. "Sorry about creating a ruckus out here. This nice man has just agreed to change my tire, and then we'll be on our way."

"Where you heading?" her would-be rescuer rumbled.

Christopher spoke up from behind her. "Not heading nowhere. We're here, thank goodness."

The man rocked back on his heels. "Here? In Tanner Hollow?" The puzzlement in his bright green eyes didn't appear to faze Christopher.

"Yes sir, we're moving in today," Christopher said.

"And I'm still hungry, Mama." Beth Ann poked her head around her older brother to peer up at this stranger while directing her words to her mother.

"Me too," Gus declared.

"Me three," Samuel added.

"Food's probably as crummy as the name of this crummy town." Harry crossed his arms and poked out his bottom lip.

Honor sighed against the sheer exhaustion and constant fear that threatened to turn her into a blubbering mass of insanity.

"Hey, Dot!"

Honor's adrenaline spiked at the man's sudden bellow.

"Yeah, Eli?" A large woman straight from one of Beth Ann's storybooks stepped from the crowd of onlookers. She had a mess of gray hair that didn't look like it had seen a comb since early that morning, rosy cheeks, and sparkling blue eyes. Immediately Honor thought of Mrs. Claus. However, the apron around her middle proclaimed "I'm Dot."

"Why don't you feed these kids while I change their mama's tire?"

"Why sure thing, darlin'." She turned to the kids. "Y'all hungry?"

A chorus of yeses immediately filled the air. Without another glance at their mother, they turned to follow Dot into the restaurant.

Honor shook herself from her weary state and realized the last of her money was walking away from her. "Wait a minute! We . . . no . . . I mean . . . they can't . . . I can't . . . ."

What could she say that wouldn't sound like she was denying her children food?

The desperation flashing in the woman's pretty, yet fatigued, eyes tugged on heartstrings he'd thought long gone. Eli Marshall ignored the strange thing his heart was doing and focused on the worry and indecision playing across her features.

"Make it the two-dollar specials, Dot, okay? They look mighty hungry."

"You got it, Eli." Understanding flickered as she met his gaze, then Dot ushered the last child into the restaurant. Eli turned back to catch the relief spilling over the woman's face. He'd guessed right when he figured she was wondering how she was going to pay for her five kids to eat dinner at the diner.

He held out a hand as he assessed the newcomer. "I'm Eli Marshall."

She blinked and gazed up at him. "I'm Honor McBride."

"Have you come a long way?"

"From Texas. Amarillo."

A whistle escaped his lips. "That's a doozy of a trip."

Wryness chased the weariness away for a brief moment. "Try making it with five kids."

He winced. "You deserve a medal."

She shrugged a thin shoulder. "Aw, they're great kids. Couldn't ask for better. I'm just tired and grumpy and so are they."

He grinned. "Happens to the best of us, ma'am." He glanced at her car. "Now, let's get that tire changed." He turned back to the onlookers. "Y'all go on and finish your supper, I've got this taken care of."

Diner patrons shuffled back inside, and the moment fizzled. Eli grinned at her. "We haven't had this much excitement since the Carson brothers dressed up Old Man Heriot's prize bull in a pink tutu and turned him loose on Main Street."

A sound bubbled from her throat that he thought might be a giggle, but she turned away too fast for him to be sure.

"Where's your spare?" he asked.

"Probably buried under all this junk back here." She opened the hatch of the station wagon and proceeded to pull out suitcases and boxes and set them on the ground beside her.

Eli noticed her graceful movements and the fact that in spite of having five kids, she was as slender as a reed—and pretty. Definitely pretty. He didn't have any business noticing that about her. She had five kids. Which meant she probably had a husband around somewhere. But she wasn't wearing a ring. Which could mean absolutely nothing.

He moved to give her a hand at the same time she turned to say something to him. Her nose smacked the fourth button of his red plaid flannel shirt.

"Oh!"

His hands came to rest on her upper arms.

Stepping back, she raised a hand to rub her cute, if slightly pointed, nose and flushed a deep shade of red. His hands dropped to his sides. He wanted to laugh, but the look in her eye said he might not live to regret it if he did. He cleared his throat. "Sorry about that. I was just trying to help."

Her red cheeks glistened. "I know, and it's all right. If you'll just back up a minute, I can get this stuff out of the way." Her eyes darted to the road behind her, then traveled in a full circle before landing back on the vehicle.

"I'm sure you can, but there's no reason for you to have to if I can do it for you. Let me take care of it, all right?"

Not giving her much choice, he elbowed his way into the back of the station wagon to finish unloading the stuff. Then he pulled the carpet up to find the spare.

Busying himself with changing the tire, he couldn't help but be aware of her watching. Not just him, but everything. Everyone. The tension running through her had to be as exhausting as driving thirteen hundred miles with five kids.

Several times, she walked to the door of the diner to peek in—to check on her kids, no doubt—then returned to her post to watch him.

He looked at her and caught her eye. "I promise I know what I'm doing."

She froze, then rubbed a hand down her cheek. "I'm sorry. I don't mean to be rude," she said. "It's been a really long, long day, and I very much appreciate your help."

"Nothing to it."

Finally, he got the last lug nut on tight and everything packed back inside the car. Eli motioned to the damaged tire. "I'll take that over to Billy Joe's, and he can probably patch it for you. Keep you from having to buy a new spare." He scrutinized the rest of the tires mounted on her vehicle. "You might want to consider getting all new tires, they're looking pretty worn. That could be dangerous, especially in rainy weather."

She shot him another embarrassed look and bit her lip. "I'll keep that in mind. I'm really grateful for your help. Do I . . . um . . . need to pay you anything?"

TWO

"You're welcome. And you don't owe me anything. It's the neigh-borly thing to do." He cleaned his hands on the baby wipes she offered him.

Even though she no longer had a child in diapers, she still car-ried the handy wipes.

When he finished, he dropped them in the trash can next to the diner. "Now, where are you spending the night?"

She blew out a sigh. "My great-aunt, Wilma Estes, willed me her house. We're here to move in this afternoon." Thank good-ness, the attorney had gone ahead and mailed her the key. Since the house was paid off, there'd been no mortgage transfer to hold things up. She glanced at the sky, then back at him. "Only now, it's probably going to be tonight."

Shock darkened his features. "You're going to move into the Estes place? Are you serious?"

"Yes." She frowned. "Why?"

"It's been empty since she died. There's no telling what you'll find out there."

"I think it'll be all right." But she couldn't help the little niggling of worry. Frustrated with herself for what she felt was weakness, she placed her hands on her hips. "I called three days ago and had the water, power, and phone turned on. We'll be fine. Once again, thank you. But now, I need to get my children, get to a grocery store, and head to the house."

"You better make sure you've got power before you go to the grocery store."

Honor pulled up short and forced a smile. "Like I said, I appreciate your help, but I think I can take care of things from here."

Eli held up a hand in surrender. "Why don't you follow me out to the Estes place? I live nearby, so it's not any trouble to lead you."

Honor shifted. Did she want to accept any more help from this man? A man whose green eyes awakened an attraction like she hadn't felt in years? Maybe ever? The instant connection she'd felt scared her almost as much as the fact that she had someone on her tail who wouldn't think twice about killing her. However, it would be nice not to have to worry about getting lost. "How far away is it?"

"Just off Main Street here. About a mile."

"Oh, wonderful." She nodded. "I could probably find it, but if it's not any trouble, I'll take you up on your offer."

That little dimple in his right cheek peeked out at her. "No trouble at all."

"Hi, Mama, we had apple pie and 'nilla *ithe* cream!"

Honor looked down at Beth Ann and cringed at the sight of her sticky face. She grabbed Beth Ann's hand and hurried inside the restaurant to see the rest of her children wolfing down huge slices of the dessert. "What? I thought you were just eating dinner."

"We did, then we got pie. It's yummy," Samuel said.

Visions of her meager stash of cash rapidly dwindling to nothing made her cringe. She gave a smile that she hoped was stronger than it felt. "Sweetie, I didn't say you could have dessert, just the two-dollar plate."

"Oh, it's all right, ma'am," Dot said from behind the counter. "I heard you talking to Eli about moving to town. All visitors get their first meal on the house." She winked. "It keeps 'em coming back for more." She pulled a bag off the counter and handed it to Honor. "And here are some goodies to keep you going until you get to the store."

Honor gave the woman a smile of gratitude as she grabbed a napkin from the nearest table, dipped it in Harry's water glass, and mopped up her daughter's face. When she finished, she turned to Dot. "I truly don't know how to thank you," she whispered.

"You can thank me by bringing those kids back so I can feed 'em again." She pressed a napkin-wrapped item into Honor's hand. "It's a ham biscuit. I'm assuming you're hungry too."

"Yes. Thank you. How much—"

"On me. But come back to eat soon, okay?"

"Okay, then. We'll be sure to do that." And she would. After she found a job. Or something.

The children voiced their approval of the idea.

Honor nodded at them. "Of course." Tossing a relieved smile back to Dot, she said, "Thank you. Again." She turned to the five pairs of blue eyes watching her. "Come on, you guys, we need to get going."

No one argued. They were full and tired and as ready to be done with the travel as she was. But she still shot each one a look that said they'd better mind their manners.

One by one, her children turned an angelic face toward the kind woman who'd just filled their bellies and offered her a whole-hearted "thank you."

Beth Ann darted forward to wrap her arms around the woman's ample waist. "Thank you so much. You're a very accomplithed cook."

Dot's jaw dropped, then she laughed and hugged the child. "Oh my goodness, aren't y'all just the sweetest things?"

"Not always," Beth Ann said. "Thometimes we're downright ornery."

Honor shook her head and, with one last smile, herded her brood outside the restaurant and back into the station wagon. Eli waited in his truck, the engine idling.

Okay, they'd all go see the house, then come back into town and do a little grocery shopping. Exhaustion didn't begin to describe the fatigue seeping through her bones. At least a mile wasn't that far.

Once everyone was loaded up, she followed her rescuer down the remaining block of Main Street. At the corner of Hawthorne and Main, he took a left onto a side road that led to the edge of town.

Less than a minute later, she turned down a dirt road that she realized was her driveway. A barbed-wire fence lined the road, and land stretched to blend into the trees beyond the property line.

But it was the house that caught her attention.

She slammed on the brakes and, ignoring the indignant protests of her children, stared at the sight before her.

Full-blown depression hit.

For the first time since her husband's funeral, she gave serious thought to praying.

"We're living here?" Christopher climbed from the vehicle, his eyes taking in every detail.

Forcing cheer into her voice, she said, "Yep, we sure are. It looks like we have some work ahead of us, but it's nothing we can't handle."

Glad she'd decided to forgo the groceries—something she'd never admit to the man who was parked next to them—she shoved aside a sinking feeling, inhaled a fortifying breath, and took the plunge.

Pulling the key from her purse, she approached the front door.

"Uh . . ." Eli's voice drifted up to her and she paused to look back at the man who stood by his truck, one hand on his hip, the other scratching his head. "You want me to check it out before you go in there?"

The dubious look on his face shot determination through her. She didn't need his help or advice. Well, she might, but she had to learn to do things on her own, because she wasn't going to have someone offering to help her each time she found herself faced with a problem. She forced another smile. "I can handle it, but thanks."

"That porch doesn't look very safe." He strode toward her, hand outstretched.

"I said I've got it!" The sharp crack of her voice snapped him to a halt.

Slapping his extended hand to his jean-clad thigh, he shook his head. "Right."

She clapped a hand to her mouth, then lowered it. "I'm so sorry, I didn't mean to snap. I really didn't." Tears clogged her throat and the feeling once again surprised her. She wasn't a crier, but lately, it's all she'd wanted to do. "It's just been a very long day. I think the porch is fine, all right?"

He frowned, but then shrugged. "Sure."

Wooden steps sagged beneath her weight, and she stepped carefully onto the porch. When she didn't plunge through to the ground below, she reached for the screen door.

A gentle tug brought it crashing down beside her. Beth Ann squealed, and Honor turned to see her latched on to Eli's leg. Suppressing another urge to scream, Honor inserted the key into the lock.

She breathed a sigh of relief when the key worked. The door swung inward and—miraculously—stayed on the hinges.

The kids crowded near the bottom porch step, anxious to get a look at their new home. "Stay there," she said. "Understand?"

They nodded. She looked past them and didn't see Eli. Had he left? His truck was still parked in front. She shrugged and stepped inside, stifling her groan as she took in the den area. Dead bugs and the smell of rotting trash greeted her. It was all Honor could do not to voice her own disgust at the sight. But she held it in.

"Can we come in now?" Samuel asked.

She turned to see her brood standing in the open doorway. "Thought I told y'all to stay put."

"We got scared," Beth Ann said. "Eli thaid he'd be right back, but he's not."

A glance to her right revealed an open-concept kitchen with a back door that had seen better days.

A creak from upstairs froze her. "Hello? Is someone here?"

No answer, but a scraping noise sent her adrenaline pumping. She stepped farther inside. Could be a rodent. A big one.

"Mama?"

"Stay back, Christopher. I think someone's upstairs."

"Then get out of the house, Mom!"

"It could just be a rodent."

"I'm getting Mr. Eli," Samuel said.

"No, Samuel—"

But he was already gone.

Honor grasped the iron poker from the fireplace set and crossed the wood floor to start up the stairs. A figure appeared at the top. Dark eyes stared down at her.

Christopher gasped. "Mom . . ."

Honor swallowed her scream. "Hi," she croaked.

The man bolted toward her and Honor stepped back just in time to avoid being mowed down. He raced out the kitchen door and Honor drew in a deep breath while Christopher steadied her.

She coughed. Dust and stale body odor assaulted her.

"Honor? You okay?"

She turned and blinked when she saw Eli standing in her doorway. "Oh, I thought you'd left," she said. Relief worked its way up her spine. She had to admit she was glad he was still there.

"No, ma'am, I was just checking the perimeter of the house when I heard the back door shut."

"A man was here. A-an older man. Dark eyes, scraggly beard. Smelled like he'd been swimming in a sewer."

"Ah, that sounds like Zeb Young."

"Who's that?"

"One of our homeless fellows. I haven't seen him in a while. Guess we know why now."

"There are homeleth people in Tanner Hollow?" Beth Ann asked. "We need to find him. He can stay here with us."

"No, honey. We can't just take in a homeless person."

"Why not?" Innocence shone in her blue eyes.

"Because—"

"Because he would probably kill us in our sleep," Harry grumbled.

Beth Ann gasped. "Kill us? Like, dead?"

Harry rolled his eyes. "That's usually the way it works."

Honor sucked in a deep breath. "No one's killing us," she said. At least not a homeless person. "Harry, stop talking like that. We probably scared him as much as he scared us. Right now, we need to make sure there are no more squatters in here, figure out what we're going to do, and how long this will take us to clean up."

A chorus of groans greeted her announcement.

Examining their tired faces, she sighed and looked at Eli, defeat poking its head around her defenses. "I guess you were right. I suppose I should have planned to stay somewhere else until I was able to see what we were getting."

"There's a nice little hotel right back up the road—" He stopped at the negative shake of her head.

"No, that's just not an option right now. On the way out here, I had to replace the brakes on the car, pay for extra hotel rooms . . ." She trailed off with a little shrug. "Nope, we don't have a choice. We'll just have to be fine right here." Darkness was falling, and they were going to need light to clean by. She reached over and flipped the light switch.

Nothing.

Okay, maybe *fine* was stretching it a bit.

THREE

Uncertainty held Eli frozen in the doorway. He wrinkled his nose against the odor, then took a shallow breath to do some silent observations of the McBrides' new home.

What he saw worried him. *Okay, Lord, you dropped this family right in my path, not to mention my neighborhood. What do you have in mind?*

"Wanna help me find my room?"

Eli looked down to find the pint-sized Beth Ann had crossed the room and was staring up at him with trusting blue eyes. She really was a cute thing. Probably would grow on him if he let her. Which he didn't plan to do.

He squatted down to her level. "I think your mom will help you with that."

"But I want you to help me." She leaned against his leg and tilted her blonde head. A crack formed in the ice around his heart.

Gus stepped forward. "Leave him alone, Beth Ann."

Harry grunted. "What a crummy house. This place is a dump."

A light flashed toward him. Since they had no power, Honor had used her phone's flashlight feature to work her way through the house. He had his on too. In her left hand, she carried candles. "All right, guys," Honor said from the bottom of the stairs, "from what I can see, it's actually worse down here than it is upstairs. There are four bedrooms and three bathrooms. The mattresses and all the furniture even had plastic over them, so we don't have to worry about bugs in the beds."

"Bugs?" Beth Ann's eyes went wide.

"Right. There aren't any, okay?"

"Okay, Mama."

"The steps are sturdy enough. It's only 7:00. If we get busy, we can have this place cleaned up in no time. We'll set these candles around so we'll have some light to work by." Groans greeted her, and Eli waited, wanting to jump in, but bit his tongue. Wasn't his place. She stared at her children and waited for the rumbling to cease, then said softly, "Come on, guys, I'm tired too, but let's do what we can do, all right? We're a team, remember?"

"Mom's right," Christopher said. "We have to stick together. Let's do this, people."

They clumped their way into the kitchen. Rummaging under the sink, Honor found leftover cleaning supplies and even some sponges still in plastic wrap. "Christopher, you get a room to yourself. Harry, you, Gus, and Samuel are in the next room because it has a double bed and two twins. Harry, you get the double. Beth Ann, yours is the last one. I'll be up to help you in a minute, but do the best you can for now, all right, hon?"

Beth Ann nodded. "I can do it. I don't need any help."

Honor passed out the supplies and sent them on their way.

"What about me?" Eli asked.

"You?"

"I'm pretty handy when it comes to cleaning and fixing things."

"Oh, well—"

A knock on the door interrupted her. "Yoo-hoo. Anyone here?"

Honor's startled gaze shot to his. "Who's that?"

"That sounds like Mrs. Styles. Edna Styles was your great-aunt's best friend."

"But how . . . ?"

He smiled at her befuddlement. "It's a small town, Honor."

In the foyer, they found Mrs. Styles standing in the doorway with a horrified look on her face. "Oh my, this place is awful. I didn't realize it had fallen into such disrepair."

Honor cleared her throat. "Yes, ma'am, but we're working on it."

"Well, this just won't do. Won't do at all." She flipped the switch on the wall and got the same results Honor had only moments before.

"And no power?" Edna pressed a hand to her chest.

Beth Ann popped her head in. "Hi."

Mrs. Styles's wrinkles crinkled even more when she spotted the child. "Oh my goodness, aren't you the prettiest little thing ever?"

"Yes, ma'am," Beth Ann said with a firm nod.

Eli choked back a laugh and Honor nudged her daughter. "That's supposed to be 'thank you.'"

"Thank you, ma'am," Beth Ann said dutifully.

Mrs. Styles flipped the switch again as though she might get a different result. She didn't. "No power. Unbelievable. And you with little ones? Well, we'll just see about this. I'm Edna Styles and I'm thrilled to meet you. I have to run; I'll be back for a more proper introduction once I get this taken care of."

She whirled and exited before Honor had a chance to blink. When she turned her gaze back on him, Eli lifted his shoulders in a shrug.

Honor shook her head and went back to the kitchen only to reappear with a broom. He took it from her in spite of her protests.

"Come on," he insisted. "I've got nothing waiting on me except my dog, Lady."

"You're not married?"

"No." He left it at that.

"Oh." He could see her bite her lip against the questions. But she didn't ask.

"What about you?" he asked.

"What about me?"

"You've got five kids, but no ring on your finger. Where's their father?"

"He died five months ago."

Eli winced. "I'm sorry. What happened?"

"A car accident. Maybe."

"I'm so sorry." *Maybe?*

She nodded. "I am too. About a lot of things."

For the next hour, they worked in their separate spaces, with Honor running around clucking over her young ones and praising them for their efforts. He was surprised at how fast the house started to gleam with everyone pitching in. Her kids were busy little bees. The smell of lemon cleaner had overpowered the unpleasant odor, and Eli could see her hopes rising.

"What are you going to do about no power?" he asked.

Blowing out a sigh, she stopped scrubbing the oven and looked at him through a hank of hair that had fallen over her left eye. "We'll survive until morning."

"But—"

"Seriously, we'll be okay."

"It's going to be cold tonight."

She stood up and looked around. "There are blankets in the closet that have been zipped up in plastic bags. We'll use those. Plus, I can start a fire in the fireplace."

Eli stared at her, trying to decide if he'd ever met anyone more stubborn. "Let me get the fire started for you then," he finally said.

"No. I'll do it in a few minutes. Please, you've done enough."

"But I don't—" In the flickering candlelight, her narrowed eyes shut him up. "All right then. I can see you think you have something to prove. I guess I'll just, uh, head home then."

Flushing under his gaze, she mumbled, "It's not that I think I have something to prove, it's just—" She shook her head. "I'm going to check on the kids." She walked to the stairs, then turned back and caught his eye. "Thank you, Eli. I apologize if I've offended. Once I get some sleep, my nerves won't be strung so tight."

He nodded and swallowed. She looked so beautiful with the shadows dancing on her features. Exhausted, true, but still beautiful, and he wanted to help her. To come to her rescue. But she didn't want rescuing—and he wasn't in the rescuing business anymore. "I'll see you tomorrow then?"

"Yes, probably, in this small town. I imagine you see most people on a daily basis?"

He laughed. "If you venture outside."

She ran a hand over her messy ponytail. "We have water, we have firewood, and we have food—thanks to Mrs. Dot. I grew up camping out. Tomorrow will bring new opportunities—and hopefully electricity."

He smiled. "All right then. Holler if you need anything."

"I will."

He walked to the door and grasped the knob, then turned back. "Look, you can come stay at my house. It's small, but it's warm. I have a guesthouse down the hill that's not being used. I can stay there."

Her eyes widened and she looked horrified at the suggestion. "Put you out of your house? I couldn't do that, but thank you for the kind offer."

"Not even for the kids?"

Her lips snapped shut and flattened into a thin line. "The kids will be just fine. Like I said, we have everything we need."

Once again he nodded and decided to give it up. "I'll check on you tomorrow."

"Really, it's not necessary."

He tilted his head, then shook it. "All right, then. Good night, Honor."

"Good night, Eli. And thank you again."

"You're welcome." He shut the door behind him and heard a

loud clunk. He turned to see the doorknob resting on the rickety porch. He rolled his eyes. Stubborn woman.

Interesting woman.

Interesting woman with five children.

That made her off-limits right out of the gate.

He walked down the rickety steps, careful where he placed his feet. The last board snapped, and he nearly fell on his face. He caught himself, muttered under his breath about stubborn women, and pulled his toolbox from the back of his truck. Chilling wind blew across the nape of his neck. An eerie quiet surrounded him. Where were the night sounds? It was only quiet like this when something was around. Or someone. Was Zeb out there watching? Angry that his shelter from the cold had been taken away from him?

Maybe.

Or was it something else? Something to do with the pretty woman and her five children?

He shook his head. He'd fix the doorknob whether she liked it or not, then he'd go home and get some sleep.

And try to ignore the nagging in his gut that danger had just rolled in to Tanner Hollow.

The question was, what kind of danger? Danger to his heart? Definitely. But there was something more. Something that said Honor McBride had so many layers he could spend a lifetime peeling them back and he'd learn something new every day. His phone rang.

"Hello?"

"Hey, it's Billy Joe."

"What're you doing up so late?"

"Couldn't sleep, so I'm down in my garage working. Found something interesting."

"What's that?"

"Can you keep a secret?"

"Of course. What is it?"

"I called Nolan, but he said to call you too."

"Come on, Billy Joe, what is it?"

"That woman's tire you changed?"

"Yeah."

"She didn't run over a nail."

He frowned, biting back his impatience at the man's dragging out of the information. "Okay, what'd she run over?"

"A bullet."

Eli paused for a moment to let that sink in. "You care to elaborate?"

"Someone shot her tire out. I pulled the bullet out just a few minutes ago."

———

Honor watched him go after he'd fixed the doorknob. She wanted to call him back, but he'd worn a frown the entire time he was working, and she wasn't sure why. He'd started to say something three times, then snapped his lips together like it was an effort to keep the words from spilling out. So she'd let him fix the knob, biting back the desire to ask him to stay.

Quite frankly, this independence stuff was exhausting, and she couldn't say she liked it very much. Then again, maybe she just needed to get used to it. One would think that five months of widowhood would be enough time to adjust, but truthfully, she wasn't sure she ever would. And maybe that was the way it worked. Time would tell. More time.

Honor went into the newly cleaned master bathroom just off the bedroom and drew in a calming breath. The scent of lemon still hung in the air. By candlelight and the light of the moon filtering through the now-sparkling window, she brushed her teeth, then stared at herself in the mirror. Her blonde hair hung limp and the dark circles under her eyes betrayed her exhaustion.

No wonder Eli had been reluctant to leave her. She looked like she was about to keel over. Which she was. She glanced at her watch. Midnight. They'd worked on the house for close to five hours, but it had paid off. They had a clean, if not yet warm, home.

Her bed called to her, but there was no way she could sleep with her hair so ratty. She found her shampoo and conditioner in the bottom of her overnight bag and turned the water on in the sink. Leaning over, she scrubbed her hair until she got out every last bug, cobweb, and who knew what else. Then she wrapped her cold, wet hair in a towel.

And realized she was freezing. Shivering, she picked up the candle she'd scrounged from under the kitchen sink and headed downstairs to the fireplace. Though she'd refused to let Eli start the fire, she noticed he'd piled wood and old newspapers into the opening. All she had to do was hold the flame to the paper.

Gratitude at his thoughtfulness made her sigh. Why had she been so insistent on not accepting his help? She was a fool. If he offered to do anything else for her, she wouldn't say no. Maybe. Depending on what it was.

She got the fire going, then went upstairs to check on the kids. All five of them were sleeping deeply, snuggled under the blankets. Their sweet, innocent faces reminded her why she'd run, and her spine stiffened. She could do this. She could. They were the reason she had to stay strong. And stay alive.

The alternative was too awful to consider.

Honor walked back into the master bedroom and crawled into the bed. The sheets could use a spin through the dryer with some fabric softener, but tonight she didn't care. They felt so good after the long drive and the impromptu cleaning spree.

As she lay there, a small flicker of something that might have been pride ignited inside her, and she let her lips curve into a small smile. She'd done it. She'd really done it.

Then the memory of why she'd had to leave returned, and her

smile flipped. She was a good mother. At least most of the time. And in spite of everything, she'd thought she was doing a fairly decent job. Not that Lorenzo had noticed or cared. The only time he'd had kind words for her had been when she'd told him she was pregnant. And he'd never raised a hand to her for the duration of those nine months. When he died, she thought she was finally free.

But with Lorenzo's death, she was trapped in a danger that could kill them all. So she'd run.

Her eyes closed. No one was going to hurt her children. No one. Not as long as she had breath left in her body.

FOUR

Eli tossed aside the covers and padded to the window on bare feet. The hardwoods were cold, but he didn't care. Lady, his golden retriever, lifted her head from her bed on the floor. Her eyes followed him even as she shifted into a more comfortable position. "Sorry, girl, I can't sleep, so I guess that means you don't get to, either."

His sermon notes lay scattered on the small desk, and once again, a pang of guilt hit him. He had no business preaching, but he'd promised his brother he would do so for the next two months while the man tried to put his marriage back together. Just because Eli had been to seminary didn't mean he was supposed to preach—no more than the fact that because Hudson was a preacher meant he was supposed to have a perfect marriage.

Seminary had been the only thing he could think of that was the antithesis of the environment he'd grown up in. And while he'd enjoyed his time there, he'd been drawn back to the bank he'd worked at during high school. Getting his MBA in finance had been an afterthought when he'd decided against full-time ministry. But his desire to help people still drove him. Owning the only bank in town allowed him to give his customers a personal touch. And take a chance when he felt like it was merited.

Which led to him helping his brother. He simply couldn't say no. Not to Hudson. Growing up in their home had been tough, but they'd survived because they'd had each other. Maybe if they'd had a mother like Honor, things would have been different.

Honor. She'd been on his mind since he'd left her house. She intrigued him. And troubled him. Obviously, she was on the run from something. Someone. At least that's what the bullet in the tire seemed to indicate.

Or had some kid been playing with his daddy's rifle and thought it would be cool to shoot someone's tire?

Nolan, Eli's cousin who was the sheriff of Tanner Hollow, was looking into it. He'd told Eli to keep his mouth shut about it until he had some answers. There was no sense in scaring her if it turned out to be an accident.

Eli walked to the window. If he positioned himself just right, he could see the top of her roof through the trees this time of year. In the daylight. All he could see now was a soft glow that probably came from the light on her porch.

He stiffened. That wasn't possible. She didn't have electricity. So, where was the light coming from? And why was it flickering like that?

Fire.

Moving quickly, he grabbed his phone and called 911 even as he shoved his feet into his boots and grabbed his coat, cell phone, and truck keys. He made sure Lady couldn't get out the doggie door to follow him, then climbed into his truck.

The drive to her home took less than thirty seconds. He pulled in front of the house and snatched the fire extinguisher from the back of his truck about the time the first fire truck screamed to a stop in front of Honor's home.

Four firemen spilled from the interior, and Honor's front door flew open with Christopher, Beth Ann in his arms.

"Go through the kitchen!" Eli cried.

Christopher spun away from the flames and disappeared back

into the house. Eli raced around the side to the kitchen door. It flew open and Christopher stumbled outside, clutching his sister.

Eli hurried to the teen. "Where's your mom and the others?"

"Still in there." Christopher shoved Beth Ann at him and started to race back into the house.

Juggling Beth Ann's slight weight with one arm, Eli reached out with the other to grab Christopher's bicep. "You're not going back in there."

The boy jerked against Eli's tight grip. "I have to!" Christopher cried. "She needs help."

"Help is here." He handed a crying Beth Ann back to her brother. "Hold on to her and stay put."

Without waiting for an answer and holding the hem of his shirt over his nose and mouth, Eli darted inside the kitchen.

Honor clutched the twins' hands in her left hand while she pressed the wet towel against her nose with her right. Fear hammered at her as she tried to see through the haze of smoke in the hallway. The moonlight wasn't much, but it was better than nothing. On the next step, she tripped, her ankle turning, fear sputtering.

"Mom?"

"I'm okay, Gus. Keep shining the flashlight in front of us." The towel slipped and smoke hit her full force. "Keep going, hon," she croaked, pulling the towel back in place with one hand. She didn't dare let go of a child to keep the rag over her face.

Putting one foot in front of the other, she shoved down the panic that wanted to explode.

She thought she heard flames crackling, but so far she hadn't seen any fire. About two minutes ago, Beth Ann had jumped into her bed, waking her up, complaining about her room being smoky. When Honor had flipped on her flashlight, the upstairs had looked like a foggy morning in the path of the beam. She'd awakened the boys. "Get wet towels from the bathroom and keep them over your nose and mouth. Then get outside! Go! Hurry!"

Christopher had grabbed Beth Ann and bolted down the steps about five seconds ago. Harry was right behind her with orders not to let go of her sweatpants waistband. Ankle throbbing, she made her way down the steps and found the room even more smoky—and engulfed in flames. *No, oh no.* Tears leaked from her eyes, blurring her vision. She blinked them away, desperate to hold on to her building terror. *Think about the kids. Get the kids out.* Her ankle gave out once more and she landed in a heap at the bottom of the stairs.

"Honor!"

"Eli?"

And there he was, a white knight in the midst of her overwhelming fear. He pulled her to her feet, then hoisted Gus into his arms. "Go through the kitchen!" Blinking, trying to see and breathe, she tightened her grip on Samuel's hand and followed him as he made a slight left into the kitchen. Together, the five of them raced out the door into the night.

Christopher, still holding Beth Ann, let out a glad cry and stumbled toward her. The fear on his young face wrenched her heart.

"We're okay," she called to him. "Get back!"

Harry let go of her and raced over to his brother and sister while Honor ran her hands over Samuel's face. "You're okay?"

"I'm okay, Mom." He coughed and swiped a hand down his sooty cheek.

"Gus?"

"He's fine," Eli said. "But let's get you looked at." He waved two firefighters over and they jogged toward them.

"I'm Jason Tanner, ma'am," the first one said. "Come with me."

Making sure she had her brood within sight, Honor let the man lead her to an ambulance that sat a good forty yards away from the burning home. Beth Ann reached for her and she lifted her daughter's small body to her chest.

"Is my room gone, Mama?"

"I don't know, baby, but that doesn't matter," she said. A paramedic probed her ankle. "All that matters is we're safe. The house can be fixed." She caught sight of Eli standing silently next to one of the paramedics who'd motioned her children into the back of the ambulance.

"I think it's just a slight sprain," the young man said. "I'll wrap it to give it some support. Just be careful not to twist it again."

"Thank you." Once he was finished, she walked over to Eli. "What happened? Why is my porch on fire?"

"They're still looking into it. Fortunately, the trucks got here fast and it looks like they're getting it under control."

"How did they get here so fast?"

"I couldn't sleep. I happened to look out my window and see the flames."

She raised a brow. "You live that close?"

He smiled. "Just over the hill. Our properties are adjoining."

"Oh." She cleared her throat and kissed Beth Ann's head. The little girl had dropped back off to sleep on Honor's shoulder and her arms ached from holding her, but she'd just have to endure. She shifted the child and Beth Ann gave a low protest.

Eli reached for her. "Let me take her."

"Are you sure? She's pretty heavy."

A low rumble escaped him. A laugh? "I think I can handle it," he said.

Her face grew hot. "Of course you can."

With her daughter snuggled against the big mountain man, she looked tiny—and a lot more comfortable. Warmth suffused Honor in spite of the chilly air. What would it be like to have someone who could help shoulder the burdens of life on a daily basis? She'd never known that kind of support, but she believed it existed because she'd seen it. Maybe one day. If she could get past her lousy judgment when it came to men.

"Mom?"

She turned to find Christopher watching her. "Yes?"

"Just before the fire started, I thought I saw someone in the yard."

A shiver chased away the momentary warmth. "What?"

"Something woke me up, and I got up to look out the window. Someone was standing in the yard. Then he turned and left. I think he walked into the woods behind the house."

Honor looked at Eli. "Could it have been Mr. Young?"

"Zeb?" He shook his head. "I doubt it. He would have probably headed for the diner where he can stay warm."

"No, it wasn't him," Christopher said. "This guy was bigger. Taller. And he didn't have a beard. He had a ball cap on, though."

Honor locked eyes with Eli and he frowned. "Let's mention it to the sheriff."

The firefighter Honor had seen earlier walked up. Jason. "I think the fire's out," he said. "We'll stay here the rest of the night to ensure nothing sparks again, but you'll need to find a place to go for the next few weeks."

She closed her eyes and swallowed her pride. "I have no money," she finally said, her voice so low. "I can't afford to go anywhere else. We'll just have to make do."

"She can stay at my place," Eli said. He held up a hand when she started to protest. "You can't stay here. There's no way to know that the electrical hasn't been compromised by the fire and water. I know you won't take my house, but the guesthouse is sitting empty and ready for use. It's got two bedrooms, a great room, and a kitchen. All of you can fit there with some creative arranging. I've got a couple of air mattresses the kids can use. I can't force you to, of course, but I really wish you would. It'll be tight, but at least it's safe and warm."

Beth Ann lifted her head and cupped his face. "Does it have a bed?"

"Yes, ma'am. It has three beds."

"Then we'll stay there. This whole ordeal has been *exhauthting*." She laid her head back on his shoulder and Honor huffed a small laugh.

She looked at Samuel, Gus, Harry, and Christopher. They simply watched her, but she could see they wanted her to agree. Defeated, Honor gave a slow nod. "Okay. Thank you. We'll take you up on your kind offer."

Eli smiled and her kids' shoulders wilted with relief. Honor hated that they had to deal with this, their innocence slowly being destroyed thanks to their father's actions—and the actions of whoever had decided to come after her.

Jason glanced at Honor. "I'll go call Nolan and get him to come out here and talk to your son. Maybe he can figure out who it could have been."

She bit her lip. "Nolan?"

"Oh, sorry," Jason said. "He's the sheriff now. He's been in law enforcement for years, but when our sheriff retired four months ago, Nolan took over. He's a good man. And I'm not saying that just because he's my brother."

"Okay. Thank you."

"It's two in the morning," Eli said. "Tell him to come to the guesthouse. We can get the other kids settled in so Honor can focus on the conversation."

"Got it." Jason pulled a phone from one of his many pockets and dialed a number.

Eli turned to Honor. "I've got whatever you need for tonight. Tomorrow, we can come back out here and see if you can salvage some of your things."

That sounded like an excellent plan to her. All she wanted was to get her kids back in a bed and deal with everything else in the morning. The two hours of sleep she'd managed to snag before Beth Ann woke her had recharged her a bit. She wasn't tired at the moment, but she figured as soon as the adrenaline crashed, she'd be ready to do the same. She shot another glance at her smoldering home. While she was grateful that she and her children were safe, she had no doubt the man who'd threatened them had found them—and was letting her know it.

FIVE

Eli opened the door to the guesthouse, and Honor slipped inside. She shrugged out of the heavy coat he'd loaned her and hung it on the wall rack. The kids' coats were next. They stood quiet, blue eyes wide, mouths tight, lined up against the wall and staring at their new temporary home.

His gut tightened. Kids weren't supposed to have to deal with this kind of stuff. "All right, guys, we'll have you set up with the air mattresses in a moment. Beth Ann, go get in the bed in the big room on that side." He pointed. "You'll share that with your mom, okay?"

Beth Ann shoved her thumb into her mouth, nodded, and walked into the bedroom without a backward glance.

The four boys watched him. He opened the hall closet and pulled out a twin air mattress and a pump. "Okay, guys, you get the second bedroom. There are twin beds in there and the air mattress can fit near the window. Someone can take the couch if that's all right."

"I'll take it," Christopher said.

"Unfortunately, there's only one bathroom between the bedrooms, so you'll have to take turns."

"It's fine," Honor said. "Thank you."

"I'll take the air mattress," Harry said. "Gus and Sam can have the beds. I just want the bathroom first."

Once the boys were tucked in under a mountain of covers, Eli headed for the door.

Then stopped. He looked at Honor. "Do you want to sit out on the sunporch and wait for Nolan? The door closes and we can talk without little ears overhearing."

She hesitated, then gave a small nod. "Sure. Just let me check on Beth Ann."

When she returned, Eli had her coat ready. "It's an enclosed sunporch," he said, "but it can still be a little chilly. I'll turn the space heater on if we need it."

"This is fine," she said. She slipped her arms in the sleeves and buttoned the top button. "Beth Ann wanted to know if she could still go to school tomorrow."

"I think it would be all right if she missed. It's been an adventurous night for sure."

"It would be fine with me, but she was insistent. I told her if she was awake early enough, I'd see if I could get her there. On that note, she fell asleep. Won't be long before the rest of them are too."

Out on the porch they sat in the hanging swing he'd built last summer.

"This is nice," she said. "Feels like you're outside, but not."

"I like it." He paused and wondered if he could ask her what was going on with her and the kids. Would she get mad if he pried? "You don't have to answer this if you don't want, but you've been antsy and on guard from the moment you drove into town," he finally said. "And Christopher thought he saw someone outside before the fire started. What—or who—are you running from, Honor?"

She sighed and looked away, pulling the edges of her coat tighter around her throat.

She looked so small and frightened. He reached out before he realized what he was doing, gripped her fingers, and gave them a gentle squeeze. She jerked, eyes wide and filled with a mixture of surprise and fear. He immediately released her hand. "Whoa. Sorry. I didn't mean anything."

She flushed. "No, I'm sorry. I'm not used to . . . comforting gestures, I suppose."

"Tell me about your husband."

Her blue eyes slid from his to study her hands. A shoulder lifted in a slight shrug. "What can I say? He was not an honorable man. I thought he was when I married him, but I soon learned that he was very good at wearing masks and putting on a façade."

"Ouch."

"Yes. When he died, he apparently owed some unsavory people a lot of money. One of them came to me to collect it. When I told him I didn't have it, he threatened me. And my children." She fell silent.

"I see." A pause. "Why do I have the feeling there's more?" he asked.

A short, humorless laugh escaped her, and she bit her lip. "I overheard my in-laws talking one night a couple of weeks ago. They have decided to fight me for custody."

"Was that a surprise?"

"No, not really. I can't say I didn't expect them to pull something like that. I left before they had a chance to file the paperwork. I was hoping if they filed after I was gone, it would just look like they were being petty about me leaving."

"Why would they do that? You're a great mom. Anyone can see that."

This time it was she who reached over and took his hand to give it a squeeze. "Thank you. But I don't think it had anything to do with my parenting skills."

When he realized he was glad she didn't withdraw her hand and that he noticed how small her fingers were next to his, a dart of fear shot through him. In the few short hours since he'd met her, he was already starting to care about her, and that just wasn't an option. He'd sworn off women with children after Audra had left and taken Jackson with her, crushing his heart and dreams of family.

So, no women with kids. Especially not five kids.

Five cute kids, though.

It didn't matter. While she appeared to be openly sharing everything with him, he still sensed she was keeping something else hidden. "What else?"

Her gaze locked on the area where her home would be. "And then someone tried to run me off the road."

He jerked. "What?"

Before he could ask her for details, Nolan pulled up, parked at the top of the drive, and climbed out of his cruiser.

"That didn't take as long as I thought it would," she said.

"It doesn't take long to get anywhere around here," Eli murmured.

They didn't speak again until Nolan stepped up onto the porch and took the rocker next to the swing. After Eli made the introductions, Nolan nodded to Honor. "You want to tell me what's going on?"

"We've been sitting here talking," Eli said. He caught his cousin up to the point where Honor had said someone tried to run her off the road.

Nolan's eyes narrowed. "Tell me about that."

"I was driving home from the bank last week when a car came out of nowhere and rammed into the back of me. I managed to keep it together long enough to pull over, and the person who hit me took off without looking back."

"Are you sure it was deliberate?"

"I'm sure."

The quiet certainty in her voice speared Eli, and he exchanged a glance with Nolan. "Okay. Is that it?" Nolan asked.

A shudder ripped through her. "Pretty much. Between my in-laws' plans to file for custody and the people who're looking at me to pay Lorenzo's debt, I didn't know what else to do. So I left. Unfortunately, it looks like they may have followed me."

"Why do you say that?"

"I'm not sure the fire was an accident."

Nolan and Eli exchanged a look she couldn't quite decipher. "What is it?"

"We don't think it was an accident, either."

"And why is that?"

"Because your tire had a bullet in it."

She blinked, then drew in a slow breath. "I see."

"You're not surprised," Nolan said.

"I . . ." She shook her head. "No, I guess I'm not. I wondered about it when it happened. It was actually the first thought that went through my head—before I even hit the brakes. And then Eli was there to help, and I . . . I guess I just decided that it was an accident. That I'd managed to pick up something during the drive or I'd rolled over a nail. It was what I wanted to believe, anyway." She looked up. "It was easier to believe that."

"As for the fire," Nolan said, "I'm having someone from Asheville come down to take a look and see how it started."

She nodded.

Eli gave Nolan the description of the man Christopher had seen in the yard prior to the fire starting. "Does that sound like anyone you know?"

"That's a pretty vague description," Nolan said with a shake of his head. "Could be any number of people around here."

"Yeah, that's what I was afraid of."

Nolan looked at Honor. "I think it's best you stay here for the time being. At least you'll have Eli here to keep an eye on things. I'm assuming you have insurance on the house?"

"Yes. The house itself is paid for, and apparently, before she died, Wilma put it in my name. The taxes and insurance are paid through the end of this year." She'd been the one to get the mail the day she had received the notice from her aunt's attorney about the house. "It was like a gift from out of nowhere." At least until Lorenzo had found the letter.

"You're going to sign over the deed, and we're going to sell that place! We need the money," he'd said.

"I won't."

"You will or—"

"Or what, Lorenzo?" She didn't give him a chance to answer. "It's mine. My name, and my name only, is on it. Not yours. And I'm not signing it over to you."

"We'll see about that." His soft words sent fear shooting through her, but she lifted her chin and left the room. He had died in the wreck the next week.

"Honor?"

She blinked the memories away and focused on the men in front of her. Nolan and Eli were both frowning at her. "Are you okay?" Eli asked.

"Yes. Sorry. I got lost in the past a bit."

"You need to get some rest," Eli said. "I think we all do."

"I need to register the kids for school at some point," Honor said. Horrified, she realized something. "Clothes."

"What?"

"My children need clothes for tomorrow." She groaned. "I'm going to have to go back down to the house and get them some. And they'll probably need washing and drying." Fatigue sapped her.

"You're going to make them go to school tomorrow?"

"No, of course not, but they still need clothes to wear. We'll have errands to run, and I won't leave them here alone."

Eli stood. "We'll take care of everything tomorrow. For now, you get some rest. I'll leave Lady here with you. She'll alert you if there's anything to be alarmed about."

"Are you sure?"

"Of course. She's a retired search-and-rescue dog. I adopted her when her hip started giving her trouble and her owner decided he couldn't keep her any longer."

"That was kind of you."

He shrugged. "I live by myself. I was lonely and she's good company."

Nolan stood too. "I'm going to have the night shift swing by here a few times. I've got to get home or Kallie's going to be calling out the search party."

"Kallie?" Honor asked.

"My wife." He said it with such pride and love that Honor was speechless for a moment as a dart of longing pierced her.

She cleared her throat. "Of course. Thank you so much for coming out."

"Don't hesitate to call if you need anything else or have any more trouble, okay?"

"I won't. Thanks."

Nolan left and she turned to Eli. "How come you're not married?"

The shutters came down over his eyes and he shrugged. "Just hasn't worked out for me yet."

"I sure understand that. Being single is far better than being unhappily married." She shook her head and sighed. "Marriage wasn't anything like I'd envisioned."

"You think you'll ever do it again?"

She laughed. "Oh, I don't know. I'm not against the idea. I've seen happily married couples, so I know it can happen." Sadness flickered and she shook her head. "I guess I just don't know if it's supposed to happen for me."

"Yeah. Right there with you."

"What happened with you?"

He sighed. "I was interested in a woman, and she decided she wanted a career more than she wanted me."

"I have a feeling that's the short version."

"Something like that. She came to me for help and I wound up working to get her out of an abusive relationship. Once her boyfriend was arrested, she decided she—and her son—didn't need me anymore and moved on."

"Oh dear. That had to hurt."

"It did." He shrugged. "It was a year ago. I've healed."

"Hmm." She stood. "We're a pair, aren't we?"

"Definitely. I think it's time to turn in." He opened the door and let out a low whistle. "She'll be fine in the little doghouse off to the side."

"Can't she just stay inside with us?"

"Sure. Wasn't sure you'd want her to."

"Of course. We love animals."

He whistled again, and in a few seconds, a beautiful golden retriever bounded toward them.

"She doesn't look like her hip's bothering her," Honor said.

"She had surgery on it about six months ago and she takes medicine for arthritis. It keeps her mostly pain free and happy."

"Good to know. I'll put some water out for her."

After Eli left, Lady followed Honor into the kitchen and waited while she filled a bowl and put it on the floor.

Honor then made the rounds, checking on her sleeping children— her precious, innocent children. Panic hit hard. He'd found her. But how? Was there no place she could go that he wouldn't follow? She gave serious thought to praying, but what could she say? Would God even listen after she'd blamed him for everything that had gone wrong in her life? She sighed and rubbed her eyes. *Oh please, God, tell me what to do.*

Because if she didn't figure something out fast, she was going to be dead, with her children left to the mercy of the man who talked so easily about selling them. They must be kept safe. She drew a deep breath and vowed to find a way.

SIX

Eli slept. A little. He'd gotten up throughout the night to look out the den window at the little guesthouse thirty yards away. Every time he checked, it was quiet. And Lady hadn't notified him that anything was wrong. So, he should have been able to sleep soundly.

Only now it was seven thirty, and the sun was already shining high in the sky. And unfortunately, Honor and her kids weren't the only thing weighing on him. His brother had texted twenty minutes ago and said things weren't exactly going the way he'd expected. His wife of three years had decided she needed a break. From everything. But mostly her husband. Hudson was heartbroken. Eli texted his brother.

> Come home.

Hudson
> No, not yet. Thanks for all your help.

> Of course. Everything's under control here.
> Take care of yourself and let me know what you
> need me to do.

Another reason not to trust fickle females. His gaze went once more to the guesthouse. Fickle or not, Honor was one female he intended to keep safe. Then he'd quietly step out of her and her kids' lives. He could step out now before he got in too deep, but he'd never be able to live with himself if he didn't keep an eye on her and something happened to her.

Absolutely not. Not on his watch.

But it didn't mean his heart had to do that stupid pitter-patter thing it wanted to do every time he was around her. The front door of the guesthouse opened and Lady dashed out, followed by Beth Ann, who stopped and turned back toward the door.

Honor appeared, and sure enough, his heart pounded a little harder. Ridiculous. She said something to Beth Ann and the child nodded vigorously. He opened his back door so he could hear what she was saying, but it looked like they were done with the conversation.

Lady did her business, then bounded back over to the little girl and licked her face. Beth Ann squealed and laughed and hugged the dog's neck before hurrying back into the house. Honor looked around the yard, stared at the trees bordering his property as though searching for someone—or expecting someone to jump out at her. Then she stepped back and shut the door.

Eli rubbed his face and shook his head as he went to get ready for the day. He showered, shaved, and dressed in record time. Then grabbed eggs, bacon, cheese, ham, and orange juice from his refrigerator and tossed the items in a rolling cooler.

Nolan drove up as Eli stepped outside. "You're here early."

Nolan climbed out of his car and grabbed a bag from the back. "Clothes and her purse. Figured she'd want them for today."

"You went down and got them after you left last night?"

"Yeah. And washed and dried them."

"Have you been up all night?"

"Pretty much. But I didn't want her to have to worry about it and I wanted to check out how bad it was. She's fortunate. Upstairs is just water damage. Downstairs, the family room was charred, but not as bad as it looked when the flames were blazing, and thankfully, the kitchen survived. Still, it's going to take a while to get it all fixed."

"She can stay in my guesthouse for as long as she needs it."

Nolan studied him. A little closer than Eli would have liked. "She's made an impression on you," his cousin said.

"I guess she has." No sense in trying to deny it. He set the bag of clothes on the cooler. "I'll just get this on down there to her."

"And I'm going to see if we have any strangers in town staying at the hotel."

"Good idea."

"See you later."

"Later." Eli made his way down the walkway to the guesthouse and knocked.

The door opened and Harry stood there, a frown on his young face.

"Hi," Eli said.

"Hi."

Did the kid ever smile? "Do you cook?" Eli asked.

"No."

"That's 'no, sir,' mister," Honor said from behind Harry. She scowled at him and the boy flushed.

"Sorry," Harry said. "I mean, 'No, sir, I don't cook.'"

Honor patted him on the shoulder. "That was lovely. Thank you, Harry." To Eli, she raised a brow. "Good morning."

"Morning. No sleeping in this morning?"

"Apparently not."

"I brought y'all some clean clothes and food and your purse." He handed her the bag, then gestured toward the cooler. "Thought y'all might be hungry."

"Starved," Christopher said. "We were going to try fishing in that lake I spotted from the kitchen window."

"Come in," Honor said. She took the bag of clothes and hugged it to her chest. "Thank you so much. When did you do this?"

"Nolan did it last night after he left."

"I'll have to figure out a way to thank him." She stepped back, and Eli rolled the cooler into the kitchen. He unloaded it under the watchful eye of the other children, who'd climbed up on the bar stools on the opposite side of the sink island.

Eli grabbed a big bowl and set it in front of Gus. "Can you crack all these eggs, add some milk, and stir?"

"Me?" The boy's eyes went wide.

"You can do it, Gus," Beth Ann said.

The kid looked doubtful but took one of the eggs and knocked it against the bowl. Shell and yolk fell in. He froze and his face paled. "I'm sorry," he whispered.

"Why?" Eli asked, keeping his voice even and face free of the anger he wanted to direct toward the man responsible for the fear on Gus's face.

"I dropped the shell in it."

Eli shrugged and his eye caught Honor's. She stood in the doorway watching, biting her lip.

"It's okay, kid. Happens to the best of us. If you drop some of the shell in, you just get it out."

"How?"

With two fingers, Eli pulled one of the larger pieces out and efficiently scooped up the smaller piece resting on the bottom of the bowl. "Like that."

The little boy stared at him. "Wow."

Eli knew he should not feel like a superhero at the moment. "It's not that big of a deal."

"You didn't get mad," he whispered in awe.

Clearing his throat to rid it of the lump that had suddenly appeared, Eli glanced at Honor again and caught sight of the tears swimming in her eyes before she looked away. "Mad? That's a silly thing to get mad about." He shrugged. "Besides, I don't mind a little crunch in my eggs."

Beth Ann giggled. And even Harry's face softened from his permanent scowl. Not exactly a smile, but better.

"What are you doing, Eli?" Honor asked softly.

He paused. "Cooking breakfast."

He was glad the words came out low and even, like it was the most natural thing in the world for him to do.

"I want to help," Samuel said.

"Great." Eli passed him the package of bacon and a pair of scissors. "Open that and put the pieces on this bacon cooker here." He passed the device to Samuel, who went to work.

Christopher was in charge of popping the biscuit rolls and placing them on the baking stone. Beth Ann busied herself setting the round six-person table near the window. She paused and looked back at Eli. "We need another chair. There are theven of us."

"Not a problem. I'll get one off the porch in just a minute."

"I'll get it," Honor said. She kept her gaze on his and mouthed "thank you" before backing up and out the door.

Out on the sunporch, Honor drew in a calming breath and placed a hand over her pounding heart. Oh goodness. She couldn't get the sight of Eli cooking at the stove out of her mind. Or the fact that he'd been so kind to her hurting children. Children who were starved for the love and acceptance of a man.

She should tell him to leave. Should warn him that he needed to run as far away from her and her kids as he could and not look back. But she couldn't exactly do that. This was his home.

But she needed to find another place to stay before the danger caught up with him. She couldn't bear it if something happened to Eli because of her. *She* was the one who should be running as far and as fast as she could.

But what was she supposed to do? She had no money, no job, nothing. She was at the mercy of strangers and she didn't like it.

At all. But she *was* grateful. Very, very grateful. Maybe God hadn't forsaken her after all.

Maybe. *Are you there, God? I want you to be.*

"Are you okay out there?" Eli called.

"Yes. I'm coming." She grabbed the old ladder-back chair from the end of the porch and carried it to the door. Movement at the edge of the building stilled her for a moment.

Chills swept up her spine and she shivered. Stared through the window a moment longer. Then hurried inside.

Eli took the chair from her. "What's wrong?"

"Nothing."

"Something," he said in a low voice. With a glance at the kids, who weren't paying him a bit of attention, he said, "What is it?"

"I thought I saw something moving just behind the tree line."

"Something? Or someone?"

"I don't know. It was just a shadow."

He frowned and pulled his phone from his back pocket.

"What are you doing?" she asked.

"I'm going to get Nolan to come out and take a look."

"It might be nothing."

"What if it's not?"

She nodded. "Okay." She carried the chair into the kitchen and placed it at the table. "All right, kids, who's hungry?"

"I think it's a given that we all are," Harry said.

"Right." She ruffled his hair and ignored the fact that he pulled away and rolled his eyes.

Honor went to the window and parted the blinds. A quick scan of the tree line didn't reveal anything more to worry her, but she couldn't help the sick feeling that curled through her. Someone had followed her from Texas. And that someone was now watching.

Waiting to strike again.

Eli stepped up behind her, and she tuned in to the chatter in the kitchen. Kids who sounded delighted and happy. Tears flooded her eyes, and she immediately blinked them back and turned. "I'm starved. Let's eat."

While they scarfed down the fabulous food their host had prepared, Honor's mind was sketching a plan. She stole a glance at Eli and her heart melted at the tender expression on his face. He was having a grand time. His gaze met hers, and she smiled, hoping it conveyed her thanks for his thoughtfulness. And she realized something. She didn't want to leave Tanner Hollow. She wanted this to be their forever home. "I need a job," she said.

The kitchen fell quiet. Eli blinked at her. "Okay, what kind of job?"

"I'm not sure. I don't know much about anything except kids."

"I thought you worked as a secretary or something," Christopher said. "You know, before we were born. Isn't that how you met Dad?"

"Well, yes, but that was fourteen years ago, and I was barely out of high school when I took that job." She looked at Eli. "I had some scholarships to go to college, but not enough." She shrugged. "I planned to work and save and then go, but Lorenzo swept me off my feet." She bit her lip, hoping she didn't sound as bitter as she thought she might have. "Things have changed a lot since then. I'm not sure I'm qualified for that kind of work anymore." She took a bite of the eggs and chewed, savoring the taste.

"I don't know that there's a whole lot of job opportunities around here," Eli said. "I can get the paper and you can take a look at the classifieds. More than likely, you're going to have to drive in to Asheville or Hendersonville to find work."

"How far is that?"

"Hendersonville is closer—twenty to thirty minutes, depending on traffic."

She grimaced. "Well, I'll just do what I have to do. I'll take a look at the paper while these guys are napping."

"Napping?" Harry looked horrified at the idea. "I'd rather go to school."

"Me too," Gus said.

"I definitely prefer going to school," Beth Ann said. "Can we go now?"

Honor looked at her brood. "Is that what you all want?"

Christopher shrugged. "Why not? Beats sitting around here all day doing nothing."

She bit her lip. "You can wait until tomorrow. It was a rough night last night." A rough week. "Tomorrow will be better after a good night's sleep. Then you'll be more awake and focused. You'll make some new friends and have a good time. After all, that's why we moved here, remember?"

"We moved because that uncouth oaf said you have to pay him a bunch of money or he was going to hurt us," Beth Ann said.

Honor gaped. "Uncou—what? How do you know that?"

"I heard him."

Well, obviously. "But when?"

"When he came over last week. Don't you remember?"

Honor pressed her thumb and forefinger to her eyes. "Yes, baby, I remember, but . . ." She drew in a breath and caught Eli's concerned gaze. "Never mind. Fine, if you want to go to school, we'll go to school. Leave the dishes and get dressed. I'll clean everything up a little later. Now, scoot." More moaning and groaning trailed behind them as they all left the kitchen. "Take turns in the bathroom. You know the order. Everyone else start laying out your clothes."

"Order?" Eli asked.

"From fastest to slowest."

"Smart."

"I have my moments." Occasionally.

He leaned forward. "Tell me about this guy who threatened you and your kids."

"I don't know much about him. He's just someone my husband owed money to."

"Does he have a name?"

She shrugged. "Carl Sanchez. I'd never seen him before he came to my house and said Lorenzo owed him fifty thousand dollars and I was to pay up."

"Did he have any proof of this?"

"I don't think he thought he needed proof. I got the impression he was the kind of person who simply stated what he wanted and got it."

"Right. And your husband never said anything about him?"

She sighed. "We didn't talk much in the last couple of years of our marriage. In case I wasn't clear, my husband wasn't a good man. He was clever, he was smart—and eventually, he was predictable. But he wasn't good and he often hung out with people I did my best to avoid."

"I see." He paused.

"What is it you want to know?"

He turned to face her. "How can you have five kids with a man like that?"

Honor struggled not to be offended by the question. She could see he was truly baffled how she could keep having children with such a man. She rubbed her hands together and stared at them for a moment, then lifted her gaze to meet his. "Because when I was pregnant, he didn't hit me."

SEVEN

Honor stepped out of the kitchen to go check on her kids' progress in getting ready, and for a moment, Eli couldn't move. He didn't know why he was surprised by her answer. But he was. And he understood so much more about her now. He wished her husband was still alive so he could punch the man in the face.

With a sigh, he stood, and Lady bounded over to the door, wagging her tail and looking at him with much expectation. He laughed. "All right, you can go." He let her out and she raced to the main house.

He turned to find Honor watching him. "She's a beautiful dog," she said.

"Thanks. The kids about ready?"

"Getting there."

"I'll drive you to the school, then you can see what you can find in the job market if that's what you want to do."

"Don't you have to work?"

He shrugged. "I work from home mostly."

"Doing what?"

"I own the only bank in town. I go in two or three times a week to make sure everything is running smoothly and to sign whatever papers need my attention. The rest of the time is mine."

Her jaw dropped. "You don't look like any banker I've ever seen."

He grinned. "What do I look like?"

"A mountain man. Someone who has a grizzly for a pet and hunts his own food."

Eli couldn't help it. Laughter rumbled from him until he was breathless. "Thanks," he said when he caught his breath. "I needed that."

The kids came into the room one by one. Beth Ann looked bright-eyed and ready to go. He couldn't say the same about the four boys, although they'd all agreed that school was better than being bored all day.

"You only have a week and a few days, then you'll be out for Thanksgiving break. Are you absolutely sure about this? Really, you can stay here and rest or watch some television or something."

Beth Ann crossed her arms and poked her bottom lip out.

"I'll stay," Harry said.

"Me too," Samuel said.

Gus shrugged. "I don't care either way."

"We're going," Christopher said. "Like Mom said, it's only a week and a few days."

"Who made you boss?" Harry asked.

"Guys, please," Honor said.

Christopher snapped his lips shut and glared at his younger brother until Harry squirmed and sighed. "Fine."

Honor blew out a sigh and frowned.

"What is it?" Eli asked.

"Their school records. I'm going to need them, and they were in a box in my bedroom back at the house."

"They burned up?" Harry asked hopefully.

Honor shook her head. "Not if they're in my room."

"May have some water damage, though," Harry said. It was clear the prospect thrilled him.

242

"It doesn't matter," Honor said. "I'll just get them and we can be on our way."

"But we'll be late," Beth Ann said with a glance at the clock on the mantel. "Later. We'll be later. I can't be later. Not on the first day!"

"But—"

"They'll let them in today," Eli said. "As long as you promise to stop by after school with the records."

"Really? Their school back home would never do that."

"Things are a lot more laid-back around here than in your big-city schools. We're a small town with a smaller number of students. There probably won't be more than ten or twelve in each class."

"Wow."

"So, no worries. They'll be fine with you bringing the records later when you pick up the kids."

"Done," Honor said. "Is that satisfactory, Bethie?"

"Perfect." She turned adoring eyes on Eli. "You're a very good man."

Eli flushed to the tips of his ears.

Honor bit her lip on a laugh, surprised she could find anything funny these days. "All right, people, let's go. Eli, can you take us to pick up my car?"

"Let's just get these guys to school so Beth Ann's not any later. We'll come back and get your car after that."

To her surprise, Honor heard herself agreeing.

They piled into Eli's truck. With four kids in the back of the King Cab and Beth Ann buckled in between her and Eli, it was a tight fit, but they made it work. Within two minutes they were in the parking lot of the elementary school, where the youngest four would go. Christopher would be across the street at the middle school. She shook her head as she climbed out. Her oldest was a seventh grader. It didn't seem possible. But it was, and she wanted to live to see him—and her other four—through the rest of their school careers.

It didn't take long to get everyone settled in their respective classrooms, and Beth Ann never looked back once she spotted the bookshelf in the kindergarten class. Honor tucked into her purse the piece of paper with information about how to go online and fill out the mountain of educational paperwork she needed for each kid. Then she hurried back to the truck where Eli waited with Christopher. At the middle school, she let out a slow breath as she watched her son enter the building. *Keep it together.* If she cried, Christopher would never forgive her. He reappeared at the entrance, gave her a cheeky wave, then disappeared once more. With a lighter step, Honor returned to the truck.

Once in the passenger seat, she buckled up. "Okay, I guess you can just take me back to get my car and I'll be good from here."

"I'm headed into town anyway to get some dog food from the feed store. You want to ride with me and pick up a paper? Or I can take you back to your car. Whichever you prefer."

"Um . . . sure. I can ride, I guess. I don't want to be any trouble."

Eli shot her a quick smile and turned the truck toward town. "You're no trouble."

"All right then. Thank you for chauffeuring me."

At the store, she got her paper while Eli headed for the dog food section.

"Eli? Is that you?"

Honor turned to see the woman from last night.

"Hello, Mrs. Styles," Eli said.

"I heard about that poor woman's home. Is she all right? The children?"

"They're fine."

"I've already spoken to the church elders and we're going to get right to working on the house. Paulie's donating the lumber supplies. Gretchen's husband, Howard, is going to do electrical and plumbing. Mike Carter's got the paint covered. And Jimmy's donating new appliances. Have I missed anything?"

Honor stepped forward, stunned. "Are you talking about doing all this for my house?"

"Of course, honey. You're one of us now, and we take care of our own."

"But the insurance company will pay for it."

Mrs. Styles dismissed that with a wave of her hand. "They can take forever. You just let us know when the adjuster's come and gone and everyone will get busy."

"And these are all people in the church?"

"Yes, ma'am."

"I . . . I don't know what to say."

"Nothing to say. Welcome to Tanner Hollow."

She bustled out of the store, and Honor turned to Eli. "What in the world?"

He shrugged. "Welcome to Tanner Hollow." He nodded to the paper. "Wanna check the classifieds?"

Mrs. Styles had knocked Honor for a loop, that was for sure. Eli smiled at the stunned expression that hadn't left her face. He sat across from her at the Main Street Café and sipped his second cup of coffee. She was still on her first, as she'd been interrupted by a call from her insurance company. She placed her phone on the table. "The insurance company's decided they need to investigate to determine if it's arson," she said softly.

"That can take a while."

"If it is deemed to be arson, there won't be a payout. At least not without a long, drawn-out, expensive fight that I may or may not win." She swallowed and looked away.

"Then it's a good thing Mrs. Styles has lined everything up for you, isn't it?"

Her frown deepened. "I'll still have to pay them somehow."

"Ah, I think you must have missed that part. They won't require

245

payment. Widows and children are taken care of in this town. If you had a husband, they'd still help out, just maybe not quite as generously."

"But—"

"You've never lived in a small town before, have you?"

"No." She blinked. "This isn't just a small town, it's like something out of the 1800s when they had a barn raising."

He laughed. "That's one way to look at it, I suppose."

"And the principal told me just to bring the kids' records in tomorrow morning since she had to leave to take her son to the doctor. She also said the kids could ride the bus home. I just find this small-town laid-back attitude and hospitality stuff amazing."

"There are good people in this town."

"I'm seeing that." She cleared her throat. "But it looks like I'm going to be pumping gas for a living."

He frowned. "What?"

She pushed the paper across to him. "My choices are working at a gas station or church secretary."

"Just for the record, I don't think anyone pumps gas anymore for a living—at least not here in the South. You'd be on the register and ringing up items inside the store. But what's wrong with church secretary?"

"I'm not too happy with God right now. I'm not sure I want to work for him."

"What are you mad at him for?"

She frowned. "You really have to ask?"

"Well, it seems to me that he's been looking out for you."

"What?" She scoffed. "How do you come to that conclusion? My husband was a louse, he died in debt to people who threaten children with despicable things, my in-laws want custody of my kids and will probably fight dirty to get them, someone—who most likely had bad aim—shot out my tire, someone tried to burn my house down . . ." She paused to take a sip of her coffee. "Shall I go on?"

He studied her for a moment, trying to come up with the words that would reach her. "I agree that's a lot for one person to handle."

She leaned back. "Why do a I hear a 'but' at the end of that statement?"

"But," he held up a finger, "what if you look at it this way? You don't have to spend the rest of your life with a louse. You got your children away from the man who threatened them. Your in-laws don't have custody, and since you overheard their plans, you have time to figure out how you're going to circumvent those plans should they implement them. And someone had bad aim and shot out your tire."

She frowned at the last one, and he covered her hand with his. "He didn't shoot you or any of your children."

"Right." She shuddered. "There is that to be thankful for."

"And, while your house is damaged, someone already has things in motion to repair that house in record time—and it will be in better shape than when it was first built." He sighed. "It's a fallen world, Honor, I'll give you that. Bad things happen. But it seems to me, God has been taking really good care of you up to this point."

Honor swallowed and looked away. Eli could see the sheen of tears. "You sure do have a way of putting a different spin on things. I'm not sure I like being made to think that hard."

Eli chuckled. "Nothing hard about it. It's all about how you choose to look at things."

She bit her lip and looked down at her hands, wrapped around the mug. "Thank you, Eli," she said softly. "I needed to hear that."

"So, you'll apply at the church?"

A laugh escaped. "I didn't say that."

"Well, you could see if they need help here or at Dot's across the street."

"I just need some income for the next few months. Then every-thing will be fine," she murmured absently, her gaze on the win-dow, seeing something only she could see in the depths of her mind.

"What happens in a few months?"

She blinked. "What?"

"You said you'd be fine in a few months."

"Oh. Wilma's estate will be settled and I'll inherit the rest of her . . . um . . . assets, I guess." She finished the last of her coffee and stood. "Would you like to go with me to the gas station and see if they still need a cashier?"

"Sure."

EIGHT

They didn't. "I'm sorry. I hired someone yesterday. Thanks for stopping by and reminding me I need to take the ad out of the paper."

Honor forced a smile. "Sure thing." She turned and made her way out of the store to find Eli waiting for her. "You know, if you had taken me to get my car, you could be about your business."

"You don't want me around?"

"What? That's not what I meant."

He smiled. "I know. So, what do you think about that church secretary job?"

She sighed. "I guess I'll have to consider it. I really don't want to be half an hour away from my kids." Not when she wasn't sure when the next shoe was going to drop, so to speak.

"So you want the job?"

"Maybe. Depends on what it entails."

"Just answering the phone mostly. Typing up the weekly bulletin and prayer list. Stuff like that."

Honor wondered if she'd be bored out of her skull or if she'd find it fulfilling. She honestly had no idea. She'd met Lorenzo three months after graduating from high school and married him six months later on her nineteenth birthday. Ten months after that, Christopher had come along. For the past thirteen years, she'd been a mother and a wife. Lorenzo had discouraged any activities outside of those two roles, so Honor really had no idea whether she'd like the position or not.

"Honor?"

"Sorry, got a little lost in thought there. But, um, sure. I could probably handle the job. Who do I talk to about it?"

"Well, normally, it would be Pastor Hudson Marshall, my brother. But since he's on sabbatical right now, filling the position falls to me."

She gaped. "You?"

"Yep."

"Why you?"

"Because I'm the interim pastor."

Honor planted her hands on her hips. "You know you could have just told me all this."

"Why spoil the fun?" He shrugged. "And besides, if you didn't want the position, I didn't want to force it on you."

Honor groaned. "Fine."

He laughed. "Come on."

The tour of the old church didn't take long, but Honor noted the place needed some serious repairs. "My uncle was the pastor here and decided he would retire early," Eli said. "When he offered my brother the position, he took it, but he didn't realize the extent of the church's needs. We've been trying to raise the money to do a complete renovation, but people around here are simple folks. They give what they can and it's enough to keep us limping along."

"What about a loan?"

"It's being talked about, but so far no one's come forward to offer to put their name on it."

"What about you?"

"I thought about it, but most of my money's tied up in my land. I make a good salary as the bank owner and manager and have offered to match whatever donations come in. The campaign just

LYNETTE EASON

started a few weeks ago, so we'll see what happens." His phone rang. "Hold on a second and let me get this. It's Nolan."

"Of course."

She wandered down the hallway, hearing the old wood flooring creak under her steps. Pictures of past potlucks and church gatherings lined the wall and she studied them, wondering at the sheer fun most of the people exhibited. She had a feeling it wasn't just the church that inspired that but rather the relationship they shared with one another—and the reason they gathered at the church in the first place. To worship. She found she wanted that. The community. The togetherness. The sense of belonging.

"Honor?"

She turned. "Yes?"

"Nolan said he's been out to your property with the arson investigator and so far, they haven't seen any evidence."

"That's good."

"They're still working on it, so that could change, but . . ."

"Right. Thanks."

"He also said he's going to keep a deputy at the guesthouse 24/7 for the next week or so."

Her throat grew tight. "Thank you," she whispered.

"Sure."

Clearing her throat, she turned and gestured to the building. "It's a beautiful piece of this town's history. Would be a shame to see it close down."

"I agree."

Once inside the small church office, Honor paid close attention to everything Eli told her—and came to the conclusion that even Beth Ann could do the job. "I really don't think you have enough work to keep me busy for eight hours a day five days a week."

"Probably not." He rubbed his chin. "Let's start with twenty-five hours and see how that works out."

"What's the hourly rate?"

He told her, and she did the math in her head. "With no real expenses except food and what the kids need—and the small amount of cash I brought with me—I can probably make it on that for a short time. But I'll have to find something to supplement it when I move back into the bigger house. I'm sure the power bill will be at least one week's pay in and of itself. And then there's water and—" She stopped when he held up a hand.

"I'll announce from the pulpit that you're looking for some part-time afternoon work. You might get some offers."

"That would be great. Thank you." He kept his gaze locked on hers for a few moments. Long enough that she felt a flush start to rise from the base of her neck. "What is it?" she asked.

"I gotta admit that I like you, Honor."

"Um, I like you too, Eli, but I'm not looking for anything more than friendship at this point. And if that's too blunt, I'm sorry. I'm out of practice with this kind of stuff."

He smiled. "Don't worry, I'm not looking for anything more than friendship either." He paused. "But if I was, I'd be looking at you."

Eli thought about those words a week later—and Honor's reaction to them.

"Oh." She'd bitten her lip. "I'm not sure what to say to that."

"I'm not either. I think I need some tape for my mouth." He'd glanced at his phone. "I'll drop you at your house so you can get the papers and your car. I've got a meeting at the bank in an hour."

"All right. Thank you."

And that had been that. In his defense, he hadn't realized the words were going to come out of his mouth until they'd hung in the air between them.

Needless to say, things had been slightly awkward on the ride to her home, but the next time he saw her, she acted fine. And they'd made good progress on becoming friends. On a surface level anyway.

Eli had reminded himself that was just fine and all he needed or wanted. Unfortunately for his heart, the more time he spent with Honor and her children, the more time he *wanted* to spend with them and the deeper he wanted their conversations to go. He told himself to forget it. She had a life to get on with and someone out to do her harm. He needed to focus on keeping an eye on her and the kids and keep his mind off romance. That was easier said than done, but at least she was close by and easy to keep watch over.

Since she lived in his guest cottage, it was easy to see the family's daily routine. Wake up, breakfast, drop the kids at school. Then head to the church for her five hours of work. Once finished there, she would either come home and wait for her kids or run errands and pick them up at school.

But it was obvious Honor was on edge, even though no more incidents had occurred since moving to his guesthouse and having a deputy planted there 24/7. And just this morning Nolan had informed him that he could no longer keep tabs on Honor and the children now that the holidays were approaching. Even deputies liked some time off to spend with their families. Eli understood, but he didn't like it and vowed to make sure he kept an even closer watch on them. To him, it looked like the person stalking Honor was just tormenting her by lying low and planning to strike when she least expected it.

Someone was still watching her. Eli knew it and Honor knew it. Just last night, he'd thought he'd seen someone snooping around the cabin and sent Lady outside. She barked, and the intruder took off. But it made him nervous—and even more determined to watch her back.

Now, on the Monday morning of Thanksgiving week, he found himself observing her from his office desk. Her head was bent over the laptop, and he thought it was cute how she bit the tip of her tongue while she concentrated.

He gazed a few seconds more before she looked up and caught him. "Did you need something?"

"No, just thinking."

"About?"

"You. And your kids. And everything that's happened. Did you notice anyone outside the cottage last night?"

She stilled. "No. I heard Lady barking and looked out the window, but I didn't see anything. I figured if it was something to be alarmed about, you would have told me. Why?"

He shook his head. "There've been no strangers other than family members of the locals who've checked into the town's one hotel for Thanksgiving. I spoke with Marge, the gas station owner you asked about working for, and she hasn't noticed anyone hanging around that she doesn't know."

"What about those family members?"

"No. That's the thing about a small town. Even out-of-town family members get to be well known." He shook his head. "So either the person is staying out of sight in a neighboring town or he's camping out in the woods. Or something."

"Or he's just well known enough not to be considered a stranger," she said softly.

"Maybe. But I don't think that's the case. You didn't know a soul here before you came. Look at all the attention you attracted the minute you rolled into town."

"True. But I also had a flat tire." She sighed and rubbed her eyes. "I don't expect the calm to last long," she said. "Every hour that passes twists my nerves tighter."

"Why?"

"I just . . . feel like time is running out. They have to do something soon."

"They? I thought it was just one guy. Who's they?"

She shook her head and sighed. "Never mind. I need to get this bulletin finished, then be ready to meet the kids when they get home from school."

The door opened and Eli stood. "Jimmy, good to see you. What brings you over here?"

"Heard there's a new family in town who's going to need some new appliances."

"Indeed. Jimmy, this is Honor McBride. Honor, Jimmy Donlan."

"Pleasure to meet you, Mrs. McBride."

Honor smiled. "Same here."

"So, do you like stainless steel, white, or black?"

"Oh. Um. Whatever's cheapest, I guess."

"No, ma'am, I need to know your preference."

"Well, stainless then, but really, as long as they work, I'm not picky."

"I've got you covered." He waved to Eli. "See you Sunday."

"You got it."

Jimmy left and Eli walked over to stand in front of her desk. When she looked up, tears swam in her blue eyes. "What aren't you telling me, Honor?" he asked softly. "What secrets are you guarding so fiercely?"

She looked away and swiped the tears with a shaking hand. "I won't deny I have secrets."

"I'm hoping one day you'll be able to share them with me."

"Maybe." She sniffed. "I just can't believe how kind everyone in this town is. Mike Carter stopped me in the grocery store two days ago and told me to come pick out paint colors."

"He and his wife work with the youth at the church. Your kids will love getting to know them."

Her phone rang, and he motioned for her to take it while he wiggled the mouse and pulled up his email.

"Oh, hi, Mr. Jamison."

Jamison? Quinn Jamison? One of Tanner Hollow's two lawyers?

Eli had gone to school with the man and had a lot of respect for him. But why was he calling Honor?

"Yes, I enjoyed meeting with you yesterday as well."

Eli's brows rose. She'd met with a lawyer? Why? How had he missed that? He knew Nolan had upped the deputies' presence in town, especially when Honor was there, so Eli wasn't so concerned about sticking right by her side every single moment, but still . . .

"Sure," she said. "That sounds great. I'll stop by and sign the papers as soon as I leave here."

She hung up and turned back to her computer.

Eli cleared his throat. "Uh, I couldn't help but overhear that. Is everything all right?"

She smiled. "Yes. Just taking care of a few legal details that need to be addressed ASAP."

"I see."

"How do you feel about being a dad?"

"I . . . uh . . . what?" Where had that come from?

"A father. How do you feel about being one?"

"Oh. I'm not sure. Why?"

"Surely you've thought about it."

Where was she going with this? And why did he feel all flustered at the line of questioning? "Well, yeah. But . . ." He shrugged. "Okay. I don't think I'd make a very good one, so I'm not holding my breath."

"What?" She gaped at him.

"You asked."

"I know, but—"

"I didn't have a very good example, and I'm not really sure I should have kids."

"I think you underestimate yourself. You've been wonderful with mine. Better than any male they've had in their lives to this date." She paused. "You took Harry fishing."

"I couldn't tell if he loved it or was bored to death."

"Are you kidding? I asked him how it went and he smiled. An actual, real smile."

Emotion welled in his throat. He cleared it. "We, uh, didn't talk a whole lot, but he's a neat kid. A deep thinker about a variety of topics. At least that's what I got from what I managed to pry out of him."

"Exactly. And you had tea with Beth Ann. She was very impressed you didn't spill a drop."

"It was pretend tea."

"And you drank it all and asked for a refill. She'll love you forever."

His heart squeezed at the thought of the sweet little girl.

"And Christopher has never been so happy to have someone throw a football with him," Honor said. "And Gus and Samuel are so impressed that you can tell them apart. Lorenzo used to get them mixed up and it infuriated them. Just why is it you think you don't know how to be a dad or that you wouldn't be a good one?"

For a moment, he simply stared at his hands linked together on his desk. Then he looked up. "Because someone I loved told me I wouldn't."

She froze for a split second, then met his gaze. "The woman who left you?"

"Yes. You see, she didn't just want her career, she wanted to be free of me. She was finally honest and said she didn't want to live in a small town with a small-town banker. She wanted more out of life than that—and she wanted a better role model for her son."

"I . . . see."

"She said because I didn't have a good example of what a father and husband should be, she doubted I had what it took."

Honor shot to her feet. "What? That's ridiculous! I'd like to have a few words with her and set her straight."

Eli blinked. Her immediate defense of him soothed his pained heart on so many levels. "It's okay, Honor."

She slapped a hand on the desk. "It's obvious she didn't have a clue about you or know you at all."

"Wow. You can be very spunky, can't you?"

She grimaced. "It's a fault that haunts me."

"No, it's great. I mean, I couldn't tell when we first met if you were just at the end of your rope or if you really were that strong. You see, I grew up in an abusive household. My mother didn't have much . . . spunk, we'll say . . . and my father bulldozed right over her. I watched her become a shell of a woman before she died. His abuse killed her spirit, her laughter. But you're not like that. At all. After years of abuse, you still have your spirit. And laughter."

She shook her head. "It wasn't easy. What would have been easy would have been to allow him to take that away from me."

"Why did you stay?" he asked softly.

"Because he threatened to take my children from me if I ever left him."

"And he had the means to do that?"

"He did."

"I see. And your family wouldn't help?"

Her conflicted gaze met his and she sighed. "I'm an only child. My parents are good people, but they live in their own little world with their high-powered jobs in their nonstop big city."

"So, your parents are career people. What do they do?"

"My father is the CEO of a large manufacturing corporation, and my mother is a lawyer for a cutthroat firm. All I ever wanted was to get married and have a family. They had no idea what to do with that. Or me."

"How did you turn out so . . . you? I would have thought you'd have followed in their footsteps."

"I grew up with nannies so . . . their lifestyle and workaholic ways didn't really influence me. Neither did their love of money. They hoard their money like some people hoard food. So, unless I was willing to pay her the big bucks, my mother would have no more interest in helping me leave an abusive husband and fight for my kids than she would in going camping."

"Wait a minute. You said you grew up camping."

"With my third nanny. She was there the longest and came to be my mother figure. Her name is Sherilyn DuPont. After I graduated from high school, she took a job overseas." Honor wore a sad smile. "But we email quite a bit and stay in touch."

"And college? You said you were working, had some scholarships, but not enough. Your parents wouldn't make up the difference?"

"Actually, they did offer. A college education was definitely a must for their only child." She shrugged. "But I said no. I was done with it all by that point and ready to assert my independence. They had no use for me, and I refused to need them." She shook her head. "I'm not proud of that. It just drove us farther apart. To the point that I'm not sure we'll ever reconcile."

"But you want to."

A heavy sigh escaped her. "Yes. I do. But Mother refused to take my call the last three times I tried to connect, so . . . that's where we stand right now."

"Wow. I see." His eyes narrowed. "Any more secrets you want to share?"

"Some secrets aren't meant to be shared."

"Sorry, I didn't mean to pry."

She uncapped the water bottle on the desk and took a sip. "It's okay. If anyone around here has the right to pry, it's you." She rubbed her eyes. "I think I've figured out how they—um . . . he . . . found us."

He rolled with the change of subject. "How?"

"It has to be through the house. It's in my name now. If he looked hard enough, he'd find it pretty quick, I imagine."

"That makes sense."

"Although I'm not sure how he would have even known to look

for real estate in my name, but if he hired a private investigator, I guess he would have been able to figure it out. And since he wouldn't have known which route I'd take when I left Texas—I did mostly back roads—he could have simply gone ahead to wait on us."

"Well, if someone is here, he's staying under the radar."

"I know. And that's what's got me worried. I've warned the school to keep the kids under tight supervision and they're to leave with no one but me, but . . ."

"You still worry about leaving them there."

"I do. But keeping them cooped up in a cottage is no way to live. And I'm not worried about anyone killing them. It's me they want dead."

"You said 'they' again instead of he. Is more than one person after you?"

She swallowed. "Yes. Probably."

"More secrets you don't want to share?"

Her phone rang, relieving her of the need to come up with an answer that wouldn't leave him with more questions. She smiled at him and took the call. "Hello?"

"Honor McBride?"

"Yes."

"This is Mark Hill, the adjuster with your home insurance. Would you be able to meet me at your home in about an hour?"

She glanced at the clock. "Sure, I can do that. But I thought you had to hear from the investigation first."

"We did. It was ruled an accident, and now I need to do a walk-through."

"Oh! Of course. That's great. Thank you. I'll see you there." She hung up.

Eli frowned. "An accident? What caused it then?"

"You heard the conversation. He didn't say, but I'm going to meet him there in an hour. I can ask him."

"I'll come with you."

"You don't have to do that." She nodded at the calendar where she tracked his bank and church responsibilities. "You have that meeting at the bank, remember?"

"I don't want you meeting with that guy alone. I'll get Nolan to send someone out to be with you."

"Who?"

"One of the deputies." He picked up the phone and within two minutes had it all arranged.

NINE

After her stop at the lawyer's office, Honor pulled to the end of the drive of her damaged home and simply sat behind the wheel staring at it. Her mother had been an only child, but Honor's grandmother had had three sisters. Living so far away, her grandmother had come to visit her only a few times in her life. But the last time had been about six months after Beth Ann's birth, and Granny had brought Aunt Wilma. She and Honor and the children had had a blast that week. Lorenzo had been on some business trip, and they'd had the run of the house.

Aunt Wilma had cried buckets when they'd had to leave and promised to be in touch. And she had. Gifts and cards and Face-Time had brightened all their lives. And made living with Lorenzo slightly better than unbearable. Then Granny had died. And now, Aunt Wilma was gone too.

Honor closed her eyes, and with long-practiced skill, forced the tears away. She just had to hang on until Wilma's estate was finally settled and she would be able to provide for her children with no more stress or worry. At least if her plan worked.

Deputy Trent Linder had introduced himself when she'd walked out of the lawyer's office. Then he'd followed her to the house and parked in plain sight.

Honor got out of her car and gathered her coat tighter around her throat with a gloved hand. The low hum of a motor reached her, and a light brown compact pulled up next to the deputy's cruiser. A man in his early forties stepped out of the vehicle. Deputy Linder opened his door and climbed out as well.

"Hi. I'm Trent Linder. You mind showing me some ID?"

"I'm Mark Hill, insurance adjuster. What do you need ID for?"

"Just keeping an eye on Mrs. McBride and the people around her." He held out a hand.

"Uh, sure." The man patted his pockets and shook his head. "Oh, sorry. My wallet's in the glove box. Hold on a second." He went back to the vehicle, opened the passenger door, and leaned in.

Honor's internal radar started blipping. She frowned. The guy didn't look like an insurance adjuster. Then again, what was one supposed to look like?

When Mr. Hill straightened, he took two steps back, turned . . . and fired the gun he held in his right hand.

Honor's scream lodged in her frozen throat when the deputy crumpled to the ground. She took a step forward, only to stumble to a stop when he turned the weapon on her.

Honor spun and darted for the corner of the house, ignoring the fear that wanted to cripple her. The gun cracked a second time and she waited for the burst of pain—even as she kept going. She racked her brain for a plan, but there was no way to get to her car and she couldn't help the deputy. She needed to escape and find help. And pray. She headed for the woods behind the house.

The third bullet planted itself in the ground beside her. Honor put on a burst of speed, her pulse hammering, breaths coming in pants. She hit the tree line just as another bullet slammed into the trunk beside her. Wood chips stung her cheek and she ducked.

With a low whimper, Honor hurled herself onto the narrow path to the side and raced as fast as her feet would take her. She had no doubt that he would follow her. Where did the path go? She'd had no opportunity to explore these woods and no idea where to run. But it had to end somewhere, didn't it? If she ran parallel to the tree line, would she eventually come out at Eli's guesthouse?

"Stop running, Honor, or I'm going to go after those brats of yours."

Honor ducked off the path and behind a large tree trunk, desperately trying to stifle her gasping breaths while she got her bearings.

From the corner of her eye, she could see him moving along the path. "Come on, Honor. This little game of cat and mouse has gone on long enough. Joe and Elise are not bad people. They'll take care of the kids."

Ha. They'd take care of their money.

"One million per kid, Honor. That's a pretty lucrative business there. How'd you manage to work that out?"

She hadn't known about the money until right after Lorenzo's death when she'd found the letter. She couldn't think about that. Not now. She had to fight to stay alive.

Would Eli be home yet? No, he had a meeting at the bank. She'd scheduled it for him. Pressing her fingers against her eyes, she ordered herself to think. Just beyond the tree line, she could still see her home. And Eli's in the distance. Yes, if she could circle around, staying hidden, she could get to Eli's home and find a phone. Or the guesthouse. They both had landlines. And she knew where the key was hidden for both residences. Her attacker drew closer, and she edged away from the trunk, being careful where she stepped. As long as she could see him, she could make sure he didn't see her. She hoped. Now she just had to avoid doing something stupid that would get her caught. *Please, God, don't let me die. My kids need me. And I want to keep getting to know Eli.*

She darted to the next tree, then the next. And still he followed. She couldn't put enough distance between them to run for it without alerting him to her location. Shivering, she pressed her fingers against her lips to keep the sobs from escaping. *Help me, God.*

———

Eli walked out of the bank and turned to find Nolan bolting from the sheriff's office to his cruiser. He held the radio to his mouth and was talking fast.

"Nolan?"

Nolan looked up. "Trent Linder is down at Honor's place. Shot."

And just like that Eli's world crashed around him. "Honor?"

"I don't know."

Eli ran to the passenger side of the cruiser and threw himself into the seat. "Go!" He buckled his seatbelt as Nolan hit the gas.

"Ambulances are on the way, as are the other deputies."

"School's almost out. The kids'll be on the bus."

"Had Janet call the school and tell them to lock it down and keep the kids there."

"Good thinking."

The drive to Honor's place took less than two minutes, but those one hundred twenty seconds felt like an eternity. When they pulled into the long drive, Eli craned his neck to see the house. It finally came into view and the sight of the deputy on the ground next to his car nearly stopped his heart.

"Stay put, Eli. I don't know where the shooter is."

"I do," he said as he opened the door. "He's wherever Honor is."

"Eli—"

"Take care of Trent. Pop the trunk. I'll take care of Honor."

"You can't use an official weapon."

Eli raised a brow. "I'm not. I'm using yours." He knew that Nolan kept his own personal rifle in the trunk for deer season. He grabbed it and looked around. No sign of her, but her car was there, along with a brown compact. He carefully picked his way into the house and let his gaze sweep it. "Honor!"

No answer.

She wasn't in the house.

He backed out and thought he caught sight of movement in the tree line. He took off at a run. "Honor!"

Honor froze at the sound of Eli's shout. Relief and terror crashed through her. She swung to see the man turn and stalk toward the edge of the trees. Eli continued to race in their direction, completely unaware of the man now watching him.

"Honor!"

Sucking in a breath, Honor bolted toward the man with the gun, even as she watched him lift it and take aim at Eli.

"No!"

She took a running leap and slammed into his back, knocking him off balance and sending the gun to the ground. He hollered and rolled, kicking out and catching Honor in the side of the head. Stunned, she lay still, head spinning. She couldn't stay down. If she didn't get away, he'd kill her. With a groan, she scrambled to her knees.

Only to feel something hard jam against the back of her head. "Don't move." His granite voice stilled her.

And then Eli was in front of her, a rifle raised to his shoulder. "Put it down!"

"You put it down or I put a bullet in her pretty head."

"What is it you want? Just tell me and I'll get it for you, but don't hurt her."

Sirens screamed in the distance. The small town's two ambulances, three fire trucks, and on-duty deputies drew closer. "Well, Honor, looks like I'm going to need a hostage, so I guess you get to live a little longer."

"Why are you doing this?" Eli asked, stepping toward them, the rifle held steady.

"Money. Why else? Now, get us to a vehicle and I won't kill her."

Yes, he would. Honor knew if she left with the man, it was all over for her. "You're not the man who threatened me at my house. Are you working with him?"

He laughed. "He was just a decoy. You were supposed to go to the cops and report it so that when you wound up dead, they'd be looking for him. Instead, you ran. And I had to track you down. I don't appreciate that extra work."

"Honor doesn't have any money," Eli said. "I think you've got the wrong person."

He laughed. "You haven't told him?"

Eli stayed rock steady, his eyes communicating his determination to rescue her. And yet she knew what the man behind her was capable of. Then again, Eli looked pretty capable himself. "Told me what?" Eli asked.

"She's coming into a cool million in a couple of months. And then four more over the next few years. It's all in a nice little account in the bank ready to be disbursed to the legal guardian of those five kids." He shoved her forward. "And I'm here to get my share." He kept the gun steady against her head. "Now we're going to get out of here." His gaze slid to Eli. "I guess you're coming too. You know too much."

"Why would I help you when I know you're going to kill us?" Eli asked.

"Because you get to live a little longer. And if you don't do what I say, I'll just go ahead and kill her." He paused. "One hostage might be easier than two anyway." The gun pressed harder and Honor gasped.

"Stop!" Eli said. "Just stop. Fine. I'll do what you want."

"Eli, go! If he kills us both, no one will know. I need you to go!"

Her pleading got her nowhere. Eli wasn't about to leave her to this man's mercy. "There are cops all over this place," he said. "See them?"

In the distance, red lights flashed in front of Honor's home. Her captor must have realized he'd let the standoff go on too long. His hand tightened on the back of her jacket.

"That's why we're not going that way. I've been living in these woods long enough to figure out the best way out is by your place. Then you can drive us out of this little hick town."

"My vehicle is at the bank. I only have one."

"I'll figure that out! Now, let's go before they start searching these woods!"

But he was too late. Honor heard the ambulance scream off, even as four Tanner Hollow deputies headed in her direction. She realized that they could see her and what was going on. Her captor pulled her deeper into the trees.

Eli's slow, measured footsteps followed them. "Let her go, and I'll let you run."

The man didn't answer, and Honor thought he might actually be thinking about it. Until two deputies closed in from the sides, their weapons drawn.

The gunman whirled and pulled her closer. "Stop!" She winced at his harsh yell. "Come any closer and I kill her! I'm not going to jail."

Eli still had his rifle to his shoulder, unwavering.

"Who hired you to do this?" she choked. "Who?"

"Your loving father-in-law," he spat, his breath harsh. "Apparently, they're pretty close to broke. Like father, like son."

She swallowed. "He never did like me."

Eli's hard eyes met hers. "I wish you could have trusted me, Honor."

She gave a low, slightly hysterical, short bark of laughter. "I did. I gave you my kids."

TEN

Eli barely managed to keep the rifle from jerking. "What?"

But the man behind her was getting more and more agitated as he realized his chance of escape was diminishing.

And then Honor tripped, her foot twisting on a root. For a moment, the man's head was completely exposed. Eli's finger tightened around the trigger.

The man grabbed for Honor.

But a red mist exploded from behind him. His gun dropped to the ground. And he followed. Eli looked past them to see Nolan lowering his department-issued rifle, features hard, eyes flat.

Eli raced to grip Honor's biceps and pull her away from the dead man. Tears streaked her cheeks, and she trembled with uncontrollable spasms. He wrapped his arms around her and held her. Tight. Slowly, he walked backward, wanting to put as much distance as possible between her and the man who'd been trying for weeks to kill her.

He held her while she sobbed and glanced at Nolan as he approached.

"She all right?" Nolan asked.

"She will be," Eli said. "Thanks to you."

"And you. You kept him distracted enough to allow me to take the shot when I had the opportunity."

"He was thinking too much. Trying to figure out how he was

going to escape instead of just running." Pausing a moment, Eli ran a hand down Honor's hair and grimaced. He held the hand up to Nolan, who nodded before jogging back to the cruiser. When Nolan returned, he tossed a towel to Eli. "I'm going to clean you up a bit, okay?"

A paramedic from the remaining ambulance walked over. "I can help with that too."

Together the men cleaned the blood and other matter from her hair, face, and clothing as best they could, but Eli knew she'd want a shower as soon as possible. She buried her face back in his chest after he'd wiped it clean. "Thank you," she whispered.

She stayed still, her sobs having slowed to the occasional hiccup.

"Did you hear all that? About her father-in-law?" Eli asked Nolan.

"I heard it. We'll figure out who the dead guy is and check his bank accounts. I'm guessing whoever hired him paid him some up front. If we can trace it back to her father-in-law, we'll have him."

"Stop calling him my father-in-law, please," Honor said, without lifting her face from Eli's chest. "His name is Joe McBride, and I never want to be associated with him again."

"Of course," Nolan said. "I can understand that."

"Thank you."

Nolan listened to the squawking in his radio, then looked up. "The medical examiner is on the way."

Shudders racked her, and Eli figured it was shock settling in. "Come on. I'm taking you back to my place. We're going to get you warm, and then if Nolan needs you to give any kind of statement, he can come get it from you there."

Nolan nodded his agreement. "I'll drop you off and we'll get your truck to you a little later."

"Thanks." Eli started to lead her to the cruiser, but she resisted. "I have to go to the guesthouse. My kids will be home any second."

"They're at the school. Nolan put it on lockdown until all of this was resolved. It'll be a little bit before they get there."

"How did you know to come?"

"The deputy who was shot faked being unconscious. He figured the guy would just finish him off if he knew he was still alive, so he waited and called it in as soon as he could do it without getting caught."

"I'm so glad he wasn't killed."

He kissed the top of her head. "And I'm glad you don't have to be afraid anymore."

"Yes. I'm definitely grateful for that."

"You want to go get cleaned up so your kids aren't scared when they see you?"

"Definitely." The word came out thick with emotion, and he led her to Nolan's cruiser.

Once they were back at the guesthouse, Eli and Nolan waited for her to get cleaned up. Within twenty minutes, she was sitting across from them. Eli looked at his cousin. "You mind giving us a few minutes?"

"Of course not. I'll be in the cruiser writing up my report. Text if you need me. I'll take you to the bank to get your truck whenever you're ready."

"Thanks." Once Nolan was gone, Eli looked at Honor. "Why didn't you tell me what was really going on?"

She looked away from him to stare at her hands clasped in her lap. "I wanted to."

"But?"

"I was afraid to say anything to anyone. I had become so used to doing things by myself that I wasn't even sure how to reach out or ask for help. Thank goodness you didn't wait for me to do so. But you'd already done so much that I didn't want to drag you farther into my mess." He scoffed and she frowned. "And I was a little afraid of what you'd think of me."

"What do you mean?"

"What if you didn't believe me? What if you thought I was just having children so I could get a big payday?" She bit her lip and looked away.

"I wouldn't have believed that."

"But how was I to know that? I didn't want to take the chance it would disgust you and you'd turn away from us. I . . . I was afraid of losing your friendship, your respect."

"Oh, Honor." He sighed.

"I only found out about the money shortly after Lorenzo died. I was going through his things, sorting what was to go to charity and what to give to his parents, when I came across a letter his grandfather had written. It was one of those official things laying out the terms of their agreement. And written before Lorenzo and I were married."

"What kind of agreement?"

"Lorenzo was an only child. If he died, the family name would have died with him. Apparently, Lorenzo had no intention of marrying and made his intentions known to his family. This didn't sit well with his grandfather, so he said for every child Lorenzo fathered—within the bounds of marriage—he'd pay him one million dollars on that child's thirteenth birthday. And that's why my in-laws are so desperate to get their hands on my kids. Whoever is guardian of the children controls the money."

Eli's breath left him in a whoosh. "That's just . . ."

"I know. There are no words for it. But"—she sighed—"it explains why he never laid a hand on me when I was pregnant. He didn't want to risk causing a miscarriage."

"Unbelievable." He paused. "What did you mean you gave me your kids?"

———

"If something were to happen to me, the way my original will read was that my in-laws would get custody."

"Which explains why they were so determined to do you in."

"Yes. So I visited the lawyer, Mr. Jamison, and had him draw up a new will—naming you as their guardian should anything happen to me."

He blinked. "I don't know what to say!"

"Are you mad?"

"I-I'm speechless." He cleared his throat. "And honored beyond words." He paused. "No pun intended."

The breath left her. "Are you sure? I probably should have asked, but I didn't want to take a chance on you saying no."

"So, that's why you asked me all those questions about being a dad?"

"Yes. You didn't seem so sure about the idea, but I knew you were up to the job if it came down to it."

He leaned over and wrapped her in a tight hug. Then kissed her. A gentle, sweet meeting of the lips that conveyed such deep emotion. It had been so long since she'd been kissed that she almost pulled away, but she stopped and allowed herself to just feel. And was thrilled to find that kissing him felt right. Normal. Safe. When he leaned back, he said, "Let's go get our kids."

EPILOGUE

SIX MONTHS LATER

Eli threw the football toward the young man who had hopes of making the high school team after his last year in middle school. The kid had a good arm and was a natural athlete. Hopefully, the fact that he hadn't played on a team before wouldn't be held against him.

Christopher caught the ball and barreled toward him. Eli had a good hundred-plus pounds on the teen but let Christopher knock him out of the way and cross over into the "end zone." Or in this case, race between the two water-filled milk jugs they'd set out on either end of the field.

Christopher did the touchdown dance, only to be taken down at the knees by a pint-sized six-year-old. He landed hard and Eli winced. But Christopher laughed and rolled while Beth Ann scooped up the football and charged in the other direction.

"Hey," Harry called, "he already scored. We need to kick it off again."

"Gotta catch me first!" Beth Ann called over her shoulder, a mischievous gleam in her blue eyes. She took a sharp right and headed for the chicken coop. The little twerp had made a habit of stealing the football and making her brothers chase her to get it back.

"Beth Ann!" Samuel called. "You come back here! Right now!"

Another giggle answered him, and Eli shook his head when Gus shot him a helpless look. "Aw, let her go. I came prepared today. There's another football in the back of my truck."

The boys high-fived and headed for the truck just as Honor stepped out of the house, wiping her hands on a towel. Saturday afternoons had become his favorite time of the week. Honor McBride had become his favorite person on the planet. Her kids ran a close second. He shoved a hand into the pocket of his jeans and curled his finger around the ring he'd bought on his visit to Asheville last week. Nervousness danced along his spine, but he'd rehearsed this over and over last night and refused to let cowardice get the best of him. He headed toward her.

At the sight of Eli heading in her direction, Honor's pulse picked up speed. She could no more control the pounding of her heart than she could the weather.

He came right up to her and kissed her. She leaned into him, relishing the way he made her feel loved and cherished and like she was the most important thing in the world to him. When he lifted his head, his eyes were twinkling more than usual. "What?" she asked.

"You brought hope back into my life."

She smiled. "I could say the same thing about you."

"Have you had enough time to come to trust me? To know that I'd never do anything to hurt you? On purpose anyway."

"Yes." She wasn't surprised the word came out without hesitation. She'd watched him closely over the past six months. They'd been together practically every waking hour between her work at the church and her habit of setting him a place at the table for dinner each night. He was still the interim pastor, since his brother had extended his sabbatical, but it looked like Hudson's persistence in wooing his wife back was paying off, and they were supposed to return to town at the end of the month. "I trust you. I've spent more time with you in these past six months than I did with Lorenzo in thirteen years of marriage." She shook her head. "I was so young and sheltered. I had no idea what I was doing at the age of nineteen. No idea he was just using me to ensure his financial security." She touched his cheek. "I love you, Eli."

"And I love you, Honor. I think I fell for you the moment the screen door came off the hinges and landed at your feet. You wanted to scream at the top of your lungs, didn't you?"

She laughed. "Yes. I sure did."

"But you didn't. I admired your restraint."

"You would have yelled, wouldn't you?"

"Absolutely." He sighed. "I'm not perfect. I have my flaws. I can be hard-nosed and stubborn."

"I know. I've seen you at your worst, remember?"

He flushed. "That game was not going to get the better of me. At least not without a fight."

"And yet . . ."

"Harry won." He hung his head, then looked her in the eye. "But I've been practicing," he whispered.

"What?"

"Shh. Don't tell Harry."

Honor had no idea the video game she'd gotten her son for Christmas would spark such bonding between the two, but it was the best thing she could have done. Harry actually laughed out loud these days, and his eyes had lost that haunted look she thought he'd been born with. "I won't. What's Beth Ann doing in the chicken coop?"

"Hogging the football she stole from her brothers."

Honor peered around him. "But they're still playing."

"Because I brought another one."

She laughed and sighed with a contentment she didn't think she'd ever known before. The people in the church had been so good to her and her family. Two months after the arrest of her in-laws, who hadn't even tried to deny their involvement in the attempts on her life when the detectives had pointed out the transactions paid to a killer had traced right back to them, she and the kids had moved into the rebuilt house. And when she'd received Christopher's money, she'd made a huge donation to the church, which was now undergoing renovations to give it new life. While she wasn't happy with the way the money had come to be in her possession, she was determined to use it to secure her children's future—and to do a lot of good with it.

"Are you happy, Honor?"

"I am. It's a new feeling."

"I'm glad. I hope I have something to do with that happiness."

She kissed him. "You know it."

"Okay, then . . . um . . . will you marry me? The kids already said it was okay for me to ask. And I wanted to do it here—where we've found so much joy together. I already feel like you and the kids are my family, and I want to make it official. That is, if you do."

Tears formed and spilled over. She couldn't help it. She simply nodded. "I'd be honored to be your wife." She laughed and swiped her cheek. "Pun intended."

Eli grinned, then slid the ring he'd been clutching onto her finger. As he leaned down to kiss her, she found herself thanking God for watching over her and her kids—and for bringing this very special man into her life. She thanked him for not giving up on her and for leading her back to him.

Cheers erupted in the background, and she pulled back to see her kids high-fiving and jumping for joy. Keeping one arm around the man she loved, she held out the other.

"Group hug!" Harry yelled, and bolted toward them. The others followed, and soon she was swallowed up in an embrace of love.

Beth Ann squirmed away and launched herself at Eli. He caught her up against his chest and kissed her cheek. She patted his face. "Does this mean I get to call you Daddy?"

The others fell silent. "Only if you want to," he said.

"I want to."

"Me too," Gus said.

The others echoed their agreement, and Honor thought her heart would rupture with happiness. She knew not every day would bring this kind of joy, so she savored it while she could.

"No more secrets, right?" Eli whispered.

She laughed. "No more secrets. Just love."

"Just love." And to the delight of the kids, he kissed her again.

LETHAL
AGENDA

ONE

It had been a long day, and all Claire Montgomery wanted to do was crash on the couch with her microwave dinner and a cold glass of water—and try to forget the evil in the world. Just for a few minutes. Against her will, her to-do list started running like a ticker tape through her mind and she groaned.

Rest would have to take a back seat to packing. Since accepting the promotion to one of the supervisors for the forensics department in Asheville, North Carolina, three months ago, the commute was taking a huge toll on her, and she'd decided to start house hunting. In fact, if she hadn't been able to continue to work from home two days a week, she'd already be living in an apartment somewhere near her office. But she didn't want an apartment. She wanted a house that belonged to her.

Now her schedule was about to change and she really needed to be in the office five—or more—days a week. Moving was her only option if she wanted the opportunity to enjoy the home she planned to purchase.

Claire parked in the drive. She had to admit her little rental house was the first place that had come close to feeling like a real home. She'd miss it—and her landlord. Mr. Abrams was the best.

"But you have things to do before you can even think about the process of buying a home, so quit wishing and get inside where it's warm."

She grabbed her bag with her laptop and other work notes from the passenger seat, climbed out of the Suburban, and slammed the door. Darkness had already fallen, even though it was only a little after six o'clock, but night came early to the small town of Tanner Hollow during the winter months. And November was forecasted to be extra cold this year.

"I think the weatherman got it right this time," she muttered, shivering as a gust of wind found its way beneath the collar of her heavy coat. She really needed to stop talking out loud to herself. Someone was going to get the wrong idea and call the men with the white coats to come get her.

Claire darted up the porch steps, only to jerk to a stop on the second step and hop back to the ground. She'd bypassed a muddy boot print on the first step.

Weird.

No packages indicating the print could belong to a delivery guy. She noticed the second footprint on the next step. Then more right up to her door.

With a gloved hand, Claire twisted the knob and found it locked. Okay, so someone had walked up on her porch and then left.

"Hi, Claire."

She spun to find Levi Harrison, her next-door neighbor, standing next to her car. Levi had autism—and a fascination with crime, which meant he had a fascination with her. In a totally non-creepy way. It was her job that was the draw.

"Hi, Levi. What are you doing out here?"

"Looking for you." He ducked his head. "I have been waiting for you to get home. I was hoping you would tell me some more stories about the bad guys and the good guys. And how the good guys put the bad guys in prison because the bad guys always leave evidence behind. I want you to tell me about your new microscope again and maybe I can look at it?"

His stilted speech always made her smile. Whenever he actually used a contraction, it threw her. "The new microscope is at my office. And I can't tell any stories tonight, but maybe tomorrow?"

"No. Tonight. Please. And the old microscope is fine. The one in your home office. It is cool too." His eyes focused somewhere in the vicinity of her left ear.

"Sorry, Levi." She simply couldn't talk about her job. Not after today. "But what if you come over tomorrow around lunchtime. I'll take a break to tell you one story, let you look at a slide under the microscope, and might even have a dinosaur for you." The twenty-year-old also had a fascination with all things dinosaur.

"Okay. That is exciting. I can do that. Thank you." He turned to go, and her gaze dropped to his feet. Hiking boots. Her pulse slowed. He'd probably climbed her porch steps to look in the window and see if she was home in spite of the fact that her car hadn't been in the drive. Levi could be very persistent. Most of the time, she was okay with that. Tonight, she had no energy for the young man and was grateful that when she said no, he didn't press.

"Levi, you gotta quit leaving the house without telling me." The snapped words drew her gaze to the other man leaning against the wrought-iron fence that separated the two yards, his glare darting between her and Levi.

Bart Wells, Levi's cousin and guardian. She liked Levi, actually enjoyed his company—and the innocence he brought to their conversations delighted and refreshed her. But his cousin creeped her out a bit. He hadn't been inappropriate in any way, so she wasn't sure why he put her off. She waved anyway, and Bart returned the gesture without smiling. "You shouldn't encourage him," Bart said.

Claire raised a brow. "I'm sorry?"

"Telling him stories, making him think he can one day do a job like yours. He's a good construction worker and he'll make a decent living under my supervision." Bart's construction van sat in the driveway, and she knew Levi helped him during the day. "But

if you keep filling his head with things he'll never be able to do—"
He broke off and curled a strong hand into a fist. "Well, just stop.
It's cruel to encourage that, so just leave him alone." He grabbed
Levi's hand and led him into the house while Claire gaped, then
sighed. Was it cruel?

"Absolutely not," she muttered. Levi had a lot of potential and
remembered every single detail she told him. She could only wish
to have a memory like his. "He'll probably surprise us all and be
my boss one day."

Claire pulled the edges of her coat tighter against her throat
and hurried up the front porch steps to unlock the door. When
she stepped inside, warmth washed over her, soothing her ragged
nerves and barely leashed emotions.

Shucking her heavy coat and hanging it on the rack by the door
took the last of her energy. She stumbled to the couch and crashed
facedown, while she tried to re-center herself. But it had been a
tough day. Tougher than most. Blips from the crime scene flashed
in her memory, and no matter how hard she tried to keep them
at bay, they pushed through her well-formed barriers. A child had
been murdered by his father because the system had failed to protect him. Bile rose in the back of her throat, the past rushing back
to her.

A low thump from the back of the house froze her, the memories
scattering for now. She bolted to her feet, energy returning with
the rush of adrenaline.

Claire put a hand on the weapon at her side and took a step
toward the noise. Paused. Snagged her cell phone and dialed 911.
She might wind up looking the fool if it was just a mouse. Or . . .
something.

Floorboards creaked.

Her heart thudded faster.

Okay, that wasn't a mouse.

"911. What's your emergency?"

"Someone's in my house," she said, her voice low as she backed toward the front door. "I'm leaving, I'll be in—"

A figure in a dark hoodie and a black ski mask stepped from her bedroom at the end. He darted toward her. She raised her weapon, fired. Missed.

He tackled her and she hit the floor with breath-stealing impact.

"Derek St. John. As I live and breathe, I can't believe you came to visit," Sheriff Nolan Tanner said from the driver's seat of the squad car.

"Yep. You've got me for two whole weeks." Derek grinned at him and shrugged. "Why not? You invited me and I needed some time away. Hopefully, you won't feel the need to renege on the invite." The grin faded quickly.

"Not a chance. So, who broke it off? All you said was that you and Elaine had decided to go your separate ways."

"It was mutual. I could tell she knew something was wrong, but she didn't want to address it. I finally brought it up in the form of a question."

"What kind of question?"

"I asked her if she was happy. She said no. We talked and decided it was best for both of us if we just made a clean break."

"Sorry, man. That had to sting."

It had. "It's been seven months, so the sting is gone. Now, I just mostly have regrets that we didn't do it sooner." He paused. "She called me last week to tell me she's engaged to her brother's best friend."

Nolan let out a low whistle. "Ouch. Double sting."

"A little. The funny thing is, I'm actually happy for her."

"You're a better man than I."

"I'm not sure that's possible."

Nolan laughed. "How's that crazy family of yours?"

"Still crazy, loud—and wonderful. They've been incredibly supportive, even though I haven't asked for it. The truth is, I don't know what I'd do without them.

"I know what you m—"

The radio cut him off. While Nolan answered the call, Derek shook his head. While he'd been honest about his feelings where Elaine was concerned, he hadn't admitted what really bothered him. The truth was, he felt like the odd man out in his family. Every one of his five siblings had found their soul mate and were starting families.

Over the last few years, he'd watched his siblings fall in love and marry—and knew his relationship with Elaine was just settling. It was comfortable. And while he wanted to marry and have a family too, he wouldn't do it just because he wanted to fill a void. The breakup *had* hurt, but it had also been a relief. He'd meet someone eventually. Until then, he'd spend his days enforcing the law and helping those who couldn't help themselves.

After he spent his two weeks of vacation relaxing in the quiet town of Tanner Hollow, North Carolina.

The squad car lurched forward and Nolan hit the lights.

"What's up, man?" Derek asked, his pulse picking up speed.

"Someone broke into Claire Montgomery's home and is attacking her. Glad you're a cop because you're going on this call with me. You have your piece?"

"Always."

"Consider yourself Tanner Hollow's newest deputy."

TWO

The intruder had a vise grip on her left wrist and Claire wasn't sure how much longer she could hold him off. Panic thrummed through her and she wanted to scream but didn't have the breath to do so.

After she'd hit the floor moments ago, her lungs had frozen, but she'd swung her hand and caught the man in the temple with the corner of her cell phone. He grunted and jerked away, freeing her for a split second.

In that moment, she dragged in a ragged breath and lurched to her feet, stumbling for the front door. She'd just twisted the deadbolt when he caught up with her and yanked her back to the floor. Now, he straddled her hips, right hand wrapped around her wrist, his left forearm jammed against her throat, once again cutting off her air.

"You're dead, Claire," he said, his dark eyes boring holes into hers. "Finally, it's time for you to die."

With her right hand, Claire flailed, looked for anything that might be a weapon. Tears squeezed down her temples. Dark spots danced before her eyes.

Her hand landed on the wood-and-wrought-iron coat rack. With the last of her strength, she jerked it toward them. It swayed like a tree in a fall wind. Knowing she was only seconds from blacking out, she yanked again. It fell, crashing onto the back of the man on top of her.

He yelped, his arm slipping from her throat. Blessed oxygen filled her lungs, even as he shoved the coat rack from them and stumbled to his feet, his hand pressed against his head. And then he was staggering away, muttering curses and heaping threats.

All Claire could do was gasp in air.

A hard pounding against her front door sent hope flaring.

"Police! Open the door! Claire, it's Nolan. Are you all right?" Nolan Tanner.

"Claire! Answer me or I'm going to kick the door in."

Unable to push any words past her aching throat, Claire scrambled to her knees and twisted the knob before falling to her side, every muscle in her body screaming in pain. Darkness threatened once again.

The door swung in and Nolan stepped inside, followed by . . .

Derek St. John? She blinked and gasped again.

"Claire!" Nolan dropped to his knees beside her.

She rolled to her side and pointed to the back of her house. "Get him," she whispered. "Go."

Agony shot through her throat. Nolan bolted to his feet. "Stay with her and call for an ambulance."

"On it," Derek said. With a gentle hand, he swept her hair away from her sweaty face. "Just hang on, Claire, help's on the way."

Tears slicked down and she bit her lip to stifle the sobs. She wouldn't break down. Crying would hurt her throat too much. She was safe. It was okay. He was gone. She was fine. Alive. She kept up the mental litany, not sure where her words left off and Derek's picked up.

". . . okay now." A pause. "Claire?"

"What?" she croaked.

"You're okay now." He helped her sit up and pulled her into a loose embrace so that her head rested against his chest. "That better?"

"Yes."

Footsteps sounded behind her and she jerked her head around as Derek's arms tightened. "It's just Nolan."

She wilted against him once more.

"Sorry, Claire." Nolan's rough voice vibrated with tension. "He got away."

"Can you stand?" Derek asked.

"Yes. I think so." Now that she could breathe, her strength was returning.

Derek helped her to her feet. "Just take it easy for a few minutes."

"I'll go out to the ambulance," she croaked. "My house is now a crime scene."

"Of course."

Derek held her arm, and while Claire usually took pride in her ability to take care of herself, she couldn't bring herself to pull away. In spite of her assurance that she could stand, she wasn't quite so sure she could walk, but with Derek's assistance, she made it to the ambulance.

"Ms. Montgomery?" the young man in the back said. "I'm Dr. Grant Williams. Let me take a look at you."

"Doctor?" Derek asked. "On an ambulance?"

"It's a new program the hospital's implementing. We trade off going on different calls." Claire sat on the gurney and let the doctor examine her throat. "Cut your air off, did he?"

"With his forearm," she rasped.

"Yeah, bet that didn't feel good." She huffed a sound of agreement. He moved on to her eyes. "No sign of subconjunctival hemorrhage." Once he was finished with his in-depth assessment and she'd answered a bazillion questions to his satisfaction, he sighed. "Nothing's crushed or broken, but you're bruised up pretty good. I recommend cold packs and talking as little as possible for the next twenty-four hours or so."

"What about whispering?" she whispered.

"Occasionally. Mostly, you can write notes."

Claire groaned.

"Who was that guy, Claire?" Derek asked. "Did you know him?"

Derek. She'd almost forgotten he was there. She met his gaze and shook her head. "Never seen him before."

"No talking," the doctor said and slipped an oxygen mask over her face. He turned for a moment, and when he faced her once again, he handed her a pad and a pen. "That'll do for now. Until you can get your phone. Don't people text more than talk these days?"

She gave a small laugh behind the mask, then wrote, "I hate texting."

He read it and shook his head. "Of course you do. The one person in the town."

Dr. Williams nodded to Derek, and Claire focused on the ceiling of the ambulance. Reality crashed in with soul-crushing force. Someone had tried to kill her, and if Derek and Nolan hadn't arrived when they had, he would have succeeded. The problem was, she had no idea who had attacked her—or why.

Derek sat next to the hospital bed, his gaze on Claire. He'd been there since last night. The doctor had decided she needed to stay overnight for observation. Claire had protested at first but had finally given in. When Derek had asked whom he could call, she'd shaken her head and written, "No one. I don't have any family."

Those seven words had punched him in the gut with harder impact than any fist had ever done. He dropped his head into his hands and rubbed his eyes. A knock on the door snapped his attention back up.

Claire's eyes fluttered open. Derek squeezed her hand at the momentary confusion there before he rose to open the door. Kallie Tanner stood there, holding a bouquet of flowers. "Hi."

"Hey. Come on in." He hadn't realized Kallie and Claire were friends, but it made sense. Claire no doubt worked closely with Nolan on any crime scenes that might occur in Tanner Hollow. Being friends with Kallie would come with the deal.

"Nolan said she was all alone," Kallie whispered, "that she didn't have any family coming."

"Hey, what's going on?" Claire's hoarse voice pulled him back to her side, with Kallie following. Claire focused on him. "You saved me."

"Yeah, for once, Nolan and I had pretty good timing."

"Thank you." Her gaze slid to Kallie. "Pretty flowers."

Kallie set them on the counter near the sink. "I thought you'd enjoy them. How are you feeling?"

"Silly. Sleepy."

"They gave you something," Derek said. "You've been out for a while."

"Still don't think I needed to stay overnight," she said with a yawn. "When can I leave?"

"When the doctor says you can," Kallie said.

Derek nodded his agreement.

Claire frowned. Her attention focused on him. "What are you doing in Tanner Hollow? The big city of Columbia, South Carolina, get too boring for you?"

He chuckled even as he gave an inward grimace at the reason for his arrival in Tanner Hollow. "I just needed a change of pace."

"Hmm." Her eyes narrowed. "Why do I have a feeling there's more to it than that?"

He cleared his throat. "Your feeling is correct, but that's a story for another time." Could she really read him that well? They'd had one all-night conversation at a local Waffle House a year ago when she'd come to teach a weeklong continuing education conference on preserving crime scenes. He'd asked her a question, and she'd suggested dinner without it being anything more than her wanting food. "I'm starving," she'd said, "and the answer to that question is going to take longer than five minutes."

Derek blinked himself back into the present. Seeing her again brought back memories he'd had to bury. He found he liked resurrecting them now that he was free to do so.

"Where's your family, Claire?" Kallie asked softly. "Nolan said you didn't have one. That's not true, is it?"

Claire's eyes blanked even as all expression left her face. "They're dead. Most of them anyway. The others I don't speak to."

"Oh." Kallie sighed. "I'm sorry. Not the best time for me to bring it up." She paused. "We've known each other for a couple of years. I can't believe I've never asked you that."

"You asked," Claire said, "I just skillfully avoided answering."

"You did?"

Claire's lips twitched, a subtle smile chasing away the awkwardness her answer had brought. "Like I said. Skillfully."

"Well, then, consider yourself adopted," Kallie said. She glanced at her watch. "I've got to run." She gave Claire a gentle hug and headed for the door. "You've got my number and Nolan's. Use them if you need anything."

"Thank you."

Derek thought Claire might be holding back tears. Once Kallie was gone, he turned to Claire. "She and Nolan are the best."

"I know."

He settled back into the chair beside her. "I've never forgotten that night a year ago," he said. All they had done was talked and it had affected him in a way he still wasn't sure he could explain. "Actually, the whole week."

"Are you still with Elaine?" she asked. "I don't see a ring on your finger, but that doesn't mean much."

"We called it off seven months ago."

"So, she's the reason you needed a change of scenery?"

He smiled, then shrugged. "She might be a part of it, but mostly . . ."

"Mostly what?"

"Mostly, I think I just needed to see you again."

THREE

Needed to see her? Claire leaned back and picked imaginary lint from her blanket. "Why?"

He ran a hand over his chin as though considering his words. Finally, he said, "I've never connected with anyone like that before. Not even Elaine—and . . ." He shrugged. "I don't even know if I can verbalize it. I just knew I didn't want to marry her." He gave a small, humorless laugh. "I was in denial, of course. I figured it was just nerves or something. And then I pictured . . . well, let's just say that I battled a lot of guilt for a while."

"I'm sorry," she whispered. She paused. "Wait a minute. So that time we spent together is the reason you broke up with your fiancée?" She squeaked the last word and raised a hand to her throat.

"No, not exactly. Elaine and I had our issues off and on from the time we started dating. But this time . . ." He sighed. "Basically, she and I talked, shed a few tears, and agreed we'd be much better off just being friends."

"I see." Did she dare tell him she'd thought about that night often? That she'd been heartbroken to learn he was committed to another woman? That she'd left the restaurant and gone home and cried? Her response had floored her. And confused her because it was so out of character.

And now he was here saying he'd felt the same?

Unbelievable.

294

She never would have guessed.

Her already high respect for the man just doubled at how well he'd hidden his feelings from her that night.

"*You see?*" he asked. "That's it?"

He'd put himself out there and was now doubting himself. She hurried to reassure him. "I felt the connection too, Derek, but you have to understand . . . I'm . . . I'm not . . . I can't . . ."

"It's okay if you don't feel the same. I can take it, but I have to know."

She locked her gaze on his. "I just said I *did* feel it. It's not . . ." Claire palmed her eyes and gathered her thoughts. She dropped her hands. "So, you came to Tanner Hollow to see me?"

He hesitated. "I didn't consciously decide to do that, but yeah, talking to you was probably one of the major factors in coming." He shot her a tight grin. "Just don't tell Nolan. It would hurt his feelings."

She gave a short laugh, then winced at the pain in her throat. "Don't make me laugh."

His intense gaze never wavered. "Are you sure you felt what I'm describing?"

"I . . . don't know. I mean, yes, I was really disappointed when you said you were engaged to someone else, but I got over it. Sort of." He winced and she bit her lip. "Sorry, that was a bit blunt, wasn't it?"

He smiled. "Well, I asked for it. And you did add 'sort of' at the end."

She knew she was dancing around the subject, but this topic had completely upended her thinking. She sighed. "Granted, I felt the same way. I'll admit it, but we can't make a decision about a relationship based on one night of conversation."

"It was more than just that one night. We spent the week together in that class. We talked and interacted and . . ." He waved a hand. "Of course you're right. And yet . . ." He sighed. "I'm not really asking you to make a decision about a relationship. At least not yet. I just want to know if we can spend time together. Get to know one another and see if that night was a fluke . . . or not."

"Oh."

"So, will you go out with me?" He took her hand. "I mean, after you're recovered and feel like it." A pause. "Should you actually feel like it. Although, I guess you've got the perfect excuse to turn me down gently if you don't, in that you could just say you don't feel like it."

She frowned. "What?"

He laughed and pinched the bridge of his nose as he closed his eyes. "I'm really bad at this, aren't I?"

"No, it's just unexpected."

"And a little weird?"

"No, not weird exactly." She sighed. "Now I'm making a mess of it. It's that whole 'It's not you, it's me' thing."

"What's you, not me?"

"I have so much baggage in my past," she blurted. She picked at the sheet again before clasping her hands together to keep them still.

"Like what?"

She sighed. "Like a lot of stuff, but since you're being so honest, I suppose I should be too."

"Honest about what?"

"The fact that I've never actually had a relationship before."

He stilled. "You mean you've never dated anyone?"

"I've *dated* in the sense that I've been asked out, picked up, and taken to dinner. But I've never been in a super serious relationship." She cleared her throat. "I . . . tend to either scare off the guys who are initially interested simply due to the nature of my job, or . . ."

"Or?"

"Or I avoid the ones that look like they might really stick around." She closed her eyes and prayed he didn't notice the heat she could feel lighting her cheeks on fire. Then again, she was sure he couldn't possibly miss it.

"Why?"

She peeked at him, saw he wasn't judging her, and shrugged. "I'm not exactly sure . . . I have my theories."

"Care to share?"

"Derek—"

The knock on the door saved her from spilling some of her darkest secrets. Secrets that he could find out with a little digging, but she doubted he'd do that.

Dr. Haddad stepped into the room, a smile on her pretty features. "Well, glad to see you're awake and feeling better."

Claire nodded. "My throat's still sore, but I suppose that's to be expected."

"It is. Any trouble breathing?"

"No."

"You're fortunate. That was our main concern and the reason we wanted to keep you overnight."

"I know."

"All right, then, I'll write up your discharge papers." She hesitated at the door, her gaze gentling. "I'm glad this ended well for you. I hope they catch the guy."

"Thanks, me too."

"Oh, you have a couple of visitors outside. Said they worked with you. I'll send them in if that's okay."

"Oh." She blinked. "Sure."

Dr. Haddad left and the door opened once more. The short, dark-haired, perfectly made-up woman who stepped into the room was in her midforties. The only wrinkle on her face was the one between her brows. When she saw Claire was awake, she rushed to her side. Tara Scholtz grabbed her hand, her green eyes sparkling concern. "Are you all right?" She gasped and lightly brushed Claire's bruised throat. "Who would do such a thing?"

Touched at the woman's distress on her behalf, Claire swallowed the sudden surge of emotion. "I don't know, Tara, but thanks for coming."

The sixty-year-old man standing in the doorway waved. "Hi, Claire."

"Franklin? You came too?"

"Of course." He frowned as though hurt she was surprised by the visit. "We're friends, aren't we?"

Were they? Apparently, he thought so. "Well, thank you, I'm touched. It's very sweet of you to stop by."

The tightness around his eyes eased a bit.

"We heard about what happened from James," Tara said. "We've been working your house for the past several hours."

James Fortune, her boss. "Did you find anything?"

"Nothing we can really discuss without first analyzing," Franklin said.

"Of course." Claire made the introductions, and for the next ten minutes, they all made small talk until Claire's throat demanded she be quiet.

Derek looked at her. "Do you mind if I'm your ride home?"

"Mind? I'd be very grateful."

———

Derek followed Claire into her home and shut the door behind him. Evidence of her attack and the crime scene unit's subsequent presence stopped him in his tracks. "Why don't I take you to a friend's house or a hotel or something?"

"No thanks."

"He made this personal, Claire. I was listening while you gave Nolan the statement at the hospital. You said he used your name."

"Yes." She shuddered.

"So, this wasn't some random attack. I don't think you should stay here alone."

"I've been alone all my life. I'll be fine." She dropped her keys onto the small table just inside the door, then removed her heavy coat.

Derek blinked. The statement punched him hard. If he'd been in the boxing ring, the hit would have put him down for the count. What was even more heartbreaking was that she hadn't made the statement in an effort to gain sympathy or attention, it was just fact for her. She had no idea how sad that made him.

"Claire, everyone has someone. Who's your person?"

She let out a low laugh, then coughed and grimaced. "My person?"

"Okay, that's something one of my sisters would say. How about, who's your best friend?"

Claire shrugged. "My job, I guess." She rubbed her eyes. "That's really pathetic, isn't it?"

"Ah . . . no, it's just . . ."

She rolled her eyes. "Pathetic."

"I wouldn't use that word."

"Well, if it fits—"

The knock on the door pulled his attention from her. Reflex drove his hand to his weapon before he realized her attacker wouldn't announce his presence if he'd returned.

Another knock. This one a little more insistent. "Claire? Hi, Claire. I am here. Are you?" More knocking.

"That's Levi," she said. "My next-door neighbor. He's a great kid. And autistic. He knows I'm here, so he probably won't leave until I talk to him." She walked to the desk in the corner of the room and opened the top drawer. When she turned back to him, she held up a plastic toy. "He's crazy about dinosaurs, so I try to keep them around for him."

Curious, he followed her to the door and checked out the side window. "Young guy, late teens, early twenties, shaggy auburn hair?"

"That's Levi."

He opened the door and Levi stared up at him. "Hi."

"Hi."

Levi shifted from foot to foot. "Claire's here. I want to see Claire, please."

"Sure, she's here."

"Hi, Levi," Claire said from behind him. "Còme on in and have a seat."

Levi stepped inside and his gaze went straight to the bruises on her throat. "You were hurt. The man hurt you?"

Derek's senses snapped to attention. "You saw the man who broke into Claire's home?"

"Bad man." Levi frowned. "This is Claire's house. He should not have come in, but he ran away."

Claire took the young man's hand. "Levi, did you see him?"

"Yes. He climbed out of your window and ran to the car."

"What car?" Derek asked.

"PKL2429. A 2014 or 2015 silver Toyota. Right rear light is broken and there is a dent in the right back passenger door. Michelin tires that are dangerous. They are bald. He should know better than to drive with those. He might have a wreck—especially if it rains. And it is supposed to rain tomorrow."

"Good job, Levi," Claire said. "Good job." She pressed the dinosaur toy into his hand and Levi's eyes lit up. He hugged her and Derek winced when Claire grimaced at the embrace. Her body was still healing, and he was sure it hurt. By the time Levi let go and raced out the door, Derek was on the phone with Nolan, giving his friend the information. He hung up and raised a brow at Claire. "I didn't think people with autism were big huggers."

She started to shrug, then stopped. "Each individual is different. Some hug, some don't."

"I guess all of my encounters have been with the non-huggers." He raked a hand over his hair. "Nolan's running the plates and said he'd call back as soon as he knew something." His phone buzzed. "Guess he knows something."

FOUR

Claire popped three ibuprofen while Derek took notes on whatever Nolan was telling him. She had some stronger painkillers, thanks to the hospital pharmacy, but she'd rather not take them. *"You're dead, Claire. Finally, it's time for you to die."*

She fought the sudden surge of nausea at the memory and pressed a hand against her head, as though she could shove the words out of her mind. It didn't work.

"Claire?"

One of Derek's hands came to rest gently on her shoulder and he turned her to face him. He still held the phone to his ear. "Do you know a guy by the name of Brad Stevenson?" he asked.

She ran the name through her brain, searching, trying to find it. "No."

"That's who the car was registered to. Nolan's getting background on him now but wanted to know if you recognized the name." He turned his attention back to the conversation and nodded. "Okay, thanks. I'm going to stay with Claire for now. Call me when you know something." He hung up and didn't move away from her.

She blinked up at him for a moment, then rested her forehead on his chest. "Brad Stevenson," she whispered. "I should know him, right? Because he obviously knows me."

His hand came up to stroke the back of her head and she al-

302

lowed herself the moment of pure comfort. The split second in time where she felt safe. Cared for.

"My dad killed my mom," she whispered. His hand stilled. "That's why I don't do relationships, I think."

He still didn't move, and his complete frozenness scared her. She started to pull away and he stopped her, holding her tighter against him. "Tell me," he said softly against the top of her head.

"I was ten," she said into his chest. "He was abusive for as long as I can remember. My mother finally threatened to leave him. They argued and he called her all kinds of vile names, then started in on me. She and I were in the kitchen fixing dinner and she just seemed to snap. She threw a can of peas at him. It hit him in the head, splitting the skin. I remember seeing the blood drip down, hit his cheek, then run off his chin."

Derek's hold tightened. Not tight enough to hurt, but tight enough to make her feel secure and able to continue.

"He just stood there, staring at her. Then, without a word, he spun on his heel, walked into the bedroom, and got his gun. When he came back out, my mother hadn't moved. I was sitting on the floor crying. And he just lifted the weapon and shot her in the chest."

"Claire," he whispered. "I'm so sorry."

"Everything's kind of a blur after that. He turned the weapon on me and said if I opened my mouth, he'd kill me too. The cops came and Child Protective Services was called and they put me in emergency foster care. They tried to interview me, but I didn't speak. I couldn't. I wanted to tell them what had happened, but I couldn't seem to get the words out. And honestly, I wasn't even that scared at the thought that he'd kill me. I was, but I wasn't. I don't really know how to explain what I was feeling. I was just . . ."

". . . traumatized."

"Yes, I know that now, but . . ." She swiped a stray tear. "He said she attacked him. That my mother came at him and he was only protecting himself and me." Claire cleared her throat. "She had a history of mental illness and his defense used that. He got off." She huffed a disbelieving laugh. "He killed my mother and walked free. And . . ." She blew out a breath.

"And what?"

"And they gave me back to him."

Derek's heart pounded harder against her ear. "I have no words," he said. "I can't say I haven't seen it happen, but I . . . there just aren't words."

"It's okay. My dad was a great actor."

"A psychopath."

"Oh yes. Completely. We bounced from town to town, job to job for a few years, never staying in one place too long because eventually, there was someone who saw through his act." She swallowed. She'd told him this much, she might as well lay it all out there. "One of the reasons I avoid relationships—I think—is because I'm afraid I have it in me to be just like him."

Derek pushed her away from him, and at first, she thought he was repulsed by her confession. She kept her eyes closed, not wanting to see the look of revulsion that had to be on his face. But he didn't let go of her upper arms. "Claire, look at me."

She couldn't.

He gave her a light shake. "Claire, please, look at me."

She opened her eyes. And caught her breath.

Pure compassion stared back at her. Not disgust or horror or anything else that would have sent her hurrying to bury herself under the covers. "It wasn't your fault that he got off," he said, "and I can tell you right now, you're nothing like him."

"You don't even know him. You don't even know me that well."

"I don't have to. I've worked with psychopaths. I've arrested them and—"

This time it was her turn to encourage him to keep going. "And?"

"And I've even killed a few, thanks to my position on the SWAT team."

Somehow Claire knew he could tell her each person's name. Because taking a life—even if it was so someone else could live—wouldn't come easy to him.

"But," he said, "you were a kid. You lived through a terrifying, horrific thing no child—or adult for that matter—should have to go through. You're a survivor, not a psychopath. And I *do* know you," he whispered. "At least my heart does."

Tears she hadn't realized were forming leaked from beneath her lids to slide down her cheeks.

Derek pulled her close once again and simply held her.

It was exactly what she needed.

Until the window near the fireplace exploded.

Derek yanked her to the floor in one swift move even as he rolled, grabbed the grenade, and threw it back out the window. A millisecond later the explosion rocked the house. Derek's body covered Claire, but she wasn't moving. Or screaming. Or anything.

Shock coated her features, her eyes wide and locked on his. Blood oozed from a cut on her cheek.

"Claire? Are you okay?"

She blinked. "Yes. I think."

The back part of her den was gone, smoldering now, but the brick exterior had protected them enough that, while they had a few bumps and bruises, they were still alive.

He helped her to her feet even while he was thinking. *Four seconds. Four seconds. Four seconds.* Four seconds from pulling the pin to explosion.

"That was a grenade," she gasped. "You picked up the grenade and threw it."

"I know. Come on, we've got to get out of here. It's not safe."

"That was—"

"Dumb. I know."

"Incredible. We'd be dead if you hadn't, but please, don't ever do anything like that again."

"Don't worry, I think that was a once-in-a-lifetime thing. And please don't tell my mother about that." *Please.* Four seconds. He was an idiot. They should have just run.

They never would have made it.

Weapon in hand, he made sure she was behind him as he rounded the doorjamb and stepped onto the front porch. "All clear," he said. "Come on. Head to my truck."

Neighbors stood on their porches. Several held cell phones to their ears and others held them at arm's length. Recording, no doubt.

He caught sight of Levi standing at the fence, clutching his dinosaur, just before Derek helped Claire into the passenger seat of his truck. The young man waved. An older man grabbed Levi's arm and propelled him toward the house.

Sirens sounded. Derek pulled away, not wanting to take a chance that whoever was trying to kill Claire might be lurking and take a shot at her in spite of the number of people on the street.

"Where are we going?" she asked.

"Someplace safe." Derek activated his Bluetooth and called Nolan.

The man answered before the end of the first ring. "I heard. Fill me in."

"Someone tossed a grenade through Claire's den window. I threw it back. Fortunately, the den faces the woods and not someone else's house, so I would think the damage to any other property would be minimal."

"Damage would be—" A pause. "You threw it—" Another pause. "Never mind. Was anyone hurt?"

"A few scrapes and bruises, but we're alive. I've got Claire and we're heading to a hotel where we can regroup."

"Which hotel?" Nolan asked.

"One in Asheville. I think we might have a better chance of hiding out in a bigger city while we decide our next move. So far, all we've been able to do is go on the defensive. It's time for that to change."

"I agree," Nolan said. "Let me know where you wind up and I'll do my best to join you so we can map out a strategy. I've also got some news about Brad Stevenson."

"Anything that can't wait on Stevenson?"

"No. And I've got to catch this other call. Hang tight and I'll see you as soon as you let me know where you are."

"Sounds good." Derek hung up and glanced at Claire. "What is it?"

"I've made someone really mad," she said. "Mad enough to kill. When he attacked me, he used my name, so this isn't some random thing. It's personal." She gave her head a light shake. "All I can think of is that it has to have something to do with my job."

"That's what I was thinking as well. Or . . ."

"What?"

"Something to do with your father?"

She frowned. "I wouldn't think so. He was killed just before I graduated from high school." She shot him a wry smile. "He bullied the wrong person at one of the bars he liked to frequent, and this time he's the one who got shot."

"So much violence in your young life."

She shrugged. "I suppose it was just unavoidable with the kind of parents I had and the type of environment I grew up in. As a result, I was a very angry teenager. I made a lot of bad choices, but fortunately I never got caught and was able to turn my life around with the help of a teacher and his wife. They took me under their wing, convinced me to give God a try. I appreciated them, grew to love them, and wanted to please them, so I kept my grades up and got a full ride to college. They showed me what a real marriage looks like. A God-centered one."

He frowned. "I thought you said you didn't have anyone to call when you were in the hospital. What about them?"

She shook her head. "She has a special needs child and they live too far away. It would be a huge inconvenience for her to travel."

Did she ever put herself first? The more she talked, the more insight he gained into her character. And he liked it. "Was your father the reason you chose the profession you did?"

"Of course. He got off because of sloppy forensic work." She shot him a sideways glance. "Trust me, I've seen the files, and you'd be appalled. I don't know what was going on with the crime scene unit who caught my case, but they cut corners and didn't do their jobs—or handle the evidence—properly. I vowed that I would make sure any case I caught—especially one involving a domestic dispute—would be done right. There would be no chance anyone would get away with murder because I didn't do my job. And I wanted to make sure no child went back to a murderer to live in fear every minute of every day."

With his right hand, Derek squeezed her ice-cold fingers. "We're here. Let's check in to our rooms and continue this discussion."

"That's it. Nothing to continue."

"Hmm . . . somehow I doubt that."

Within minutes he had them registered with connecting rooms. He handed her the key to hers. "We can leave the doors open, but at least this way, we'll have some privacy."

She took the key and bit her lip. "You're a good man, Derek St. John."

He gave a low grunt. "I know some people who might disagree with that."

"Yeah, the bad guys you caught and put in prison."

FIVE

Claire checked out the bathroom and noted the robe hanging on the back of the door in addition to all of the necessary toiletries lined up in front of the mirror. When Derek had checked them in, he'd requested toothbrushes and toothpaste, so she'd be fine except for the fact that she needed a change of clothes.

A soft rap on the connecting door drew her into the main room. Derek stood in the opening. "I just got off the phone with Nolan. He's still at your place. The fire's out, and his friends are boarding up the broken windows and the part of the wall that's missing."

"Please tell him thank you. I'll have to do something special for him once this is all over."

"He's glad to do it. He's also bringing us clothes and food."

She blinked. "Are you a mind reader now?"

"Hardly. I just knew what I needed and figured you probably did too."

She nodded and took a seat at the small table in the corner next to the window. Derek sat across from her. "Can you think of any cases where someone might hold a grudge?" he asked.

"A lot. I testify on a regular basis, Derek. I'm young, but I'm considered an expert in my field—and I'm good at convincing a jury that I know what I'm talking about."

"Have you ever been wrong?"

"Not in the sense that I misinterpreted the evidence or anything. My job is to go where the evidence leads and keep my personal feelings out of it. If the evidence takes authorities to an innocent person for some reason, then I just have to hope and pray that new evidence comes to light before the trial." A pause. "Not that I know they're innocent at the time."

He pursed his lips. "And has that ever happened?"

"Twice. One case was a cop who attempted to frame another when money disappeared from a crime scene. The other was a twin who left his DNA at a murder scene but had an air-tight alibi. The innocent twin didn't and was arrested. Later, security footage showed his brother wearing the same clothes he testified in at the mall where the murder took place. One of the officers recognized the shirt and asked for it to be entered into evidence. The shirt had the murder victim's blood on it."

"Interesting."

"Very."

Derek rubbed his chin. "Can we access your cases and go through them one by one?"

"Well, sure, but what would we be looking for?"

"Someone who doesn't have an alibi."

She gaped. "Do you know how long that would take?"

He sighed. "Gotta start somewhere, right?" He pulled his phone from his pocket and tapped the screen. "And I have a plan to speed things along."

"What kind of plan?"

"The kind called teamwork." A voice on the other end of the line reached her and Derek turned his attention to it. "Linc, what are you and Allie doing in the next few days? Uh-huh. Can you figure out a way to get a couple of days off? I've got a friend that needs some help before the killer who's after her succeeds and I wind up collateral damage." A pause. "Yes, I'm serious. Uh, yeah, great. Thanks." He hung up. "They're on the way."

Her jaw dropped. "Wait a minute," she said. "Linc. I remember that name. A brother, right?"

"Yeah. FBI so he's got federal jurisdiction and can assist in this investigation."

"Nice. Who's Allie?"

"His wife and former partner." He paused. "You'll like her. I think you will relate well to her."

"Why's that?"

"It's a long story, but the gist of it is, her family was murdered by her brother and she tracked him down to get justice."

"Oh." The word was little more than a whisper. Her heart ached for the woman and she hadn't even met her yet. "You're right. I can relate. That's awful."

"It was, but she's very open about everything. She does a lot of speaking in high schools and prisons, talking about what happened. She says if, by talking about it, she can help others come to terms with their past, then it's worth reliving the pain of it."

"Wow. And she and Linc just dropped everything to come here?"

He shrugged. "That's what my family does. Even though they think I'm a little off."

"They do? Why?"

"Because I don't talk to them about much." He rubbed his eyes. "I'm a loner by nature. I don't like asking for help."

"But I'm willing to bet that you're the first one to respond when one of them needs you," she said.

"Well . . ."

"Yes, that's what I thought. And yet, you just asked them to come help us."

He clasped his hands and shot her a wry smile. "I'm trying not to be such a loner. So, let's come up with a plan."

More questions tumbled through her mind, but she let him change the subject. "What are you thinking?"

"That the fastest way to get this done is to set up an office at your work."

"At the lab?" She drew in a breath and thought about it. "Okay, we could use the conference room, I guess."

"That'll work. We'll need computers and access to all of your past cases."

She blew out a low breath. "All right. I'll have to call my boss, but I don't think he'll have an issue with giving you access. Most of my cases are public record anyway."

"Great."

The knock on the door made her jump. Derek rose and strode to the side of the door. "Yeah?"

"Room service."

Derek's shoulders unknotted a fraction. "That's Nolan." He opened the door and his friend stepped into the room, bags in hand. Some delicious fragrance wafted from one of the bags.

Nolan handed it to Derek. "Chicken parmesan and salads, compliments of Kallie."

"You realize you married way above your head."

"Ha. You're not the first one to point that out."

"Just making sure you know."

Claire took the bag from Derek. "Thank you, Nolan. Tell Kallie she's a saint."

Nolan took a seat on the bed while Derek and Claire settled themselves at the table and dug in to the feast. "Okay, first things first. Brad Stevenson. He's an ER doc working long hours, sleeping at the hospital and all that. He never even noticed the car was missing."

"So he has a rock-solid alibi," Claire said.

"It appears that way at the moment. We're still digging, but he's on hospital security footage at the time of your attack. He wasn't anywhere near your house."

"All right, then I guess that's that."

"For now. As for the grenade, it exploded just before it would have gone out the window. That's one reason why that wall was so damaged. It took the brunt of the blast."

Claire shuddered and Derek barely managed to suppress his own flare of remembered terror at what could have been. "Better the wall than us," he said.

"Amen to that. The good news is, your neighbor Levi got a good look at the person and is looking at mug shots of recently released local thugs who might have a grudge against Claire." He offered them a tight smile. "Now, I realize this might not have anything to do with any cases you testified at, but it's the most logical lead we've got, so we're running with it."

"Makes sense," Claire said. She took a sip of water and another bite of chicken. "And Levi will be able to communicate well enough if the person he saw matches up to one of your pictures."

"Do you have any court cases coming up?" Derek asked her.

She frowned. "Two within the next month. One is a murder case and the defendant is very vocal about his innocence."

"Is he?" Derek asked.

"Not according to the evidence."

"Give me that information," Nolan said. "We'll start tracking down alibis for anyone connected to these cases."

Once they talked about Derek's plan and Nolan had everything he needed, he stood. "I'll leave you two to get some rest. Try to keep your heads down until we can get everything set up at the lab." He strode to the door. "My brother, Jason, and I came prepared to stay the night."

"To play watchdog?" Derek asked.

"Yep. With three of us taking shifts, we'll all be able to get some rest while Claire is never left unguarded."

"I like that plan," Derek said. "Good idea."

Nolan shot him a tight smile. "I have one every so often." He gripped the doorknob. "Derek, you take first shift, then call me at midnight. Jason and I will cover the rest of the night."

"Got it."

"I'll get a room and we'll all head to your office tomorrow at eight o'clock sharp. Will that work for you, Claire?"

"Yes, thank you."

Once he was gone, Claire rubbed her eyes. "I need to shower and go to bed before I fall over."

"Same here. You go first. I'll wait until Nolan's on duty to do anything other than guard you." She launched herself into his arms and he held her. Gently. Understanding her need for comfort and reassurance without her having to say a word. "We're going to get him, Claire, I promise."

One way or another.

She looked up, tears swimming in her blue eyes. Curls still dusty from the explosion hung over her right temple. He brushed them back and settled his lips over hers. She went still, then returned the kiss, taking it for what he meant it to offer—he hoped. Comfort—and a promise. And a hint of restrained passion that held a wealth of possibilities of things to come. Like the direction he wanted to take the relationship.

When he broke off the kiss, she blinked up at him, longing and uncertainty clashing in her gaze. He smiled and pulled her back against him and she settled her cheek against his chest. "It's going to be okay, Claire."

"I think I almost believe you," she whispered.

"Believe me." He gave her one last gentle squeeze. "Now go and get comfortable, get some sleep. And take some ibuprofen. There should be some in the bag Nolan brought. You'll feel your bumps and bruises more tomorrow."

"You've thought of everything, haven't you?"

"I'm trying." His phone buzzed and he glanced at it. "Linc and

Allie will be here shortly and they're bringing Daria." He raised a brow. "Now that's good thinking."

"Who's Daria?"

"Daria Nevsky. She's living with Linc and Allie. Her father was a criminal they took down almost three years ago with her help. At the time, she was seventeen years old. She's also a technology genius. I'll introduce you to them all in the morning."

"Thank you."

Her soft words squeezed his heart and he cleared his throat. "You're welcome."

She didn't move.

"Claire?"

"I'm scared I'll dream." The words left her in a rush. "I'm scared to be alone." The last word came out on a choked sob.

His grip tightened. "You're not alone. I'll be right here."

She pulled away and swiped her palms across her cheeks. "I'm sorry. I don't mean to be such a wimp and have a breakdown. I'll be fine."

Derek shook his head. "Claire, you're anything but a wimp. After what you've been through, I'd say you're entitled to a breakdown." He paused. "But if that's a breakdown for you, then . . . well . . . that wasn't a breakdown."

She huffed a short laugh. "How do you do that?"

"What?"

"Make me laugh when I least expect it."

"It's a gift." He traced a finger down her cheek. "Seriously, if you find you can't sleep or the dreams come, I'll hold your hand while you sleep. Who knows? It might help keep my dreams at bay."

"You dream?"

"Almost every night."

"What about?"

"Faces mostly. Of the people I've killed while doing my job for

SWAT. Or the faces of those I've failed because the team didn't get there in time. I dream about being undercover and getting caught. Being tortured." He shuddered. "Nothing I really like to talk about, but I will if it'll help you."

She drew in a deep breath and nodded. "Okay, you can go now." He raised a brow and she shrugged. "I don't know why, but that helps. You don't have to talk about it or give me details. I'm sorry you dream too—I wouldn't wish that on anyone, but it helps that you understand."

"I really do." He paused. "I've even gone to counseling about it." He paused. "I've never told anyone that before. Not even my family."

"Thank you, Derek." She hugged him and he inhaled her scent. There was still a hint of vanilla beneath all the grime and dust. "I think I'll be okay now," she said.

He waited until she was locked in the bathroom before slipping back to his room and pulling the adjoining door almost shut. The small crack would allow him to be on her side within seconds if she needed him for any reason. Even if it was to hold her hand so she could sleep.

Or so he could.

SIX

She hadn't thought it possible, but she'd slept. Hard. When she'd awakened, he was asleep in the chair beside her, hand clasped around hers.

When she pulled free, he awakened and rose. "Thanks," he said.

"For?"

"For letting me hold your hand. It helped." Then he'd slipped into his room to get ready.

Now, she walked between Nolan and Derek while Linc, his wife, Allie, and Daria brought up the rear.

"It's going to be okay," he'd said last night.

She wanted to believe him. More than anything, she wanted to believe everything would be okay. But that's what the social worker had promised her before the trial, and it had definitely not been okay.

Nolan held the door for her, and she stepped into the building that had been her home for the past five years. She was sad to realize work felt more like home than the small house that had just gotten blown up, but . . . it was true. This was where she'd thrived.

Being promoted had been an honor and a bit of a surprise, as she'd figured Franklin Greene, a longtime employee, would have been first choice. But she'd been the recipient of the offer and she'd taken it without hesitation.

Only now she wondered.

What if Franklin wasn't as okay with her getting the promotion as he'd appeared to be? Claire led the way to her office and stopped. Derek nearly ran into her. "What is it?" he asked, placing his hands on her shoulders.

"Nothing, just a thought."

"About?"

"Claire!" Tara raced over to hug her.

Claire froze, then raised her arms to gently pat the woman on the back. "Hi."

"It's so good to see you back this fast. I can't believe everything that's happened." She stepped back. "Are they any closer to finding out what happened or who did it?"

"That's what we're getting ready to start working on. Is Brandon around?"

Tara's dark head nodded to the break room. "He just went to grab some coffee."

"Thanks." Claire introduced Tara to Linc, Allie, and Daria. "Tara's got a keen eye for ballistics." They all shook hands, then followed Claire to the break room while Tara rushed off with a wave. Claire pushed the door in and found Brandon Jennings leaning against the counter, watching the coffeepot fill up.

He turned. "Claire, glad you felt well enough to make it." She made more introductions and Brandon gestured to the door. "I got your text and think we've managed to get everything set up in the conference room. We'll do whatever it takes to get this guy."

Brandon had been a good boss before she'd been promoted. Once she moved up, he made no secret he was interested in her.

And she made no secret that she didn't return the feelings.

It hadn't seemed to faze him or cause any awkwardness between them, but now she couldn't help looking at him in a different light. Was there a hidden resentment that would push him to do such a thing?

Claire walked into the conference room and closed her eyes.

She needed to get a grip. She had to quit looking at everyone with suspicion. Then again, someone *had* tried to kill her.

"Claire?"

All eyes were on her and she realized she'd been standing there with her eyes shut. "Sorry, just thinking." The table held four laptops, set up and ready to find the person who had a grudge against her. She rubbed her hands together. "All right, if you guys want to see what you can find, I'm going to check in with my crew and see what I can do to play catch-up on a few things."

Derek frowned. "You're not going to stay here?"

"No, but I'll be close by if you have any questions. And I promise I won't leave the floor without checking in with you."

He relaxed a fraction. "All right, I suppose that's acceptable."

She shot him a small smile. "Thanks."

For the next hour and a half, Claire checked in with those under her supervision, then cleared her neglected email inbox. She sipped on a second cup of coffee, doing her best to ignore her aches and pains.

Her throat was sore, but she was surprised at how much it had improved in such a short time. While her voice still had a rasp, she figured it wouldn't be too much longer until she was back to normal. Whatever normal was.

She leaned back in her chair and stretched.

A loud clatter behind her sent her to her feet and spinning to confront the threat.

"Sorry, sorry, sorry." Gilly, the janitor, held his hands in front of him as though she'd drawn a weapon on him.

Claire placed a hand over her pounding heart. "You scared me to death."

Gilly picked up the broom that had fallen from the cart. "I didn't have it in the holder well enough." He gave it a good shove. "It's not going anywhere now. Can I get you anything? More coffee? A valium?"

She let out a low laugh. Gilly had been working in the building for the last two months and she'd seen his sense of humor on more than one occasion. "It's all right. The valium might not be a bad idea, but I think I'll pass. On the coffee too. I'm jittery enough."

"Everything all right?"

"Not exactly, but it will be." She shot a glance in the direction of the conference room. "I hope. How are the classes going?"

He shrugged. "They're hard, but fascinating. I'm enjoying them." He glanced around with a smile. "Who knows? One day, I might have your job."

She laughed. "You sure might. Thanks, Gilly."

"No problem." He wheeled the big yellow cart toward the door.

"Oh, there you are, Gilly," Tara said, stepping just inside Claire's office. A dark brown stain covered her white lab coat. "I'm a klutz. Do you mind mopping up the area around my desk while I go in search of a new coat?"

"Of course not." Gilly nodded to Claire. "See you around."

"See you."

Gilly gave her a small salute, then followed Tara down the hallway toward the woman's office. Claire raised a brow. It seemed to her that whenever Gilly was around, Tara had quite a few accidents that required his attention. What was up with that?

Derek's face appeared around the doorjamb, distracting her, and she waved at him. "I'm fine."

"Just checking." He walked over to her. "Thought I'd update you."

"You found something?" she asked.

"Not sure. In one of the cases, you testified for the defense and got a guy off who'd been arrested for armed robbery."

"I remember that case. It was last year."

"He had a rap sheet a mile long."

"I know," she said, "but he didn't rob that gas station."

"I get that, but he did kill a pregnant woman two months later. We're looking for the husband."

Claire rubbed her eyes. "You think he could be holding a grudge? That he blames me for his wife's murder? That if I hadn't testified, the guy would have been in prison and his wife would still be alive?"

"It's a long shot, but . . ." He shrugged.

"But they eventually caught the guy who did the robbery. In fact, he's still in prison."

Derek raked a hand down his jaw. "Yeah. I know."

"And, like I said, the murder was nine months ago. Why come after me now?"

He grimaced. "All good points."

Claire offered him a sympathetic look. "I think you'd better keep looking."

"Will do."

She smiled and headed for the door.

"Where are you going?" he asked.

"I've had four cups of coffee. Figure it out, Detective."

His laughter followed her down the hallway. Her lips twitched again and she was amazed she could find something to smile about.

Franklin Greene came out of the men's restroom just as she was about to go into the ladies'. "Claire," he said. "Glad to see you're back."

Was he? She shoved the ominous thought aside. "Thanks, Franklin. I appreciate that."

"Do they know who broke into your house?"

"Not yet, but they're working on it."

He shoved his hands into the front pockets of his khaki pants. "You're doing a really good job in the supervisory role. I'm glad to see my instincts were correct."

His instincts? She raised a brow. "Well, thank you."

Franklin offered her a small smile, turned on his heel, and headed down the hallway.

Weird. And a bit creepy?

Or just a nice guy offering her a genuine compliment? She groaned. She didn't know what to think anymore.

She pushed into the restroom and let the door shut behind her. The place was empty and she drew in a deep breath for the first time in hours. Once she was in the stall, she braced herself against the wall and leaned her head against her hands. This was crazy. She had to stop thinking everyone she knew had ulterior motives.

A minute later, she exited the stall.

A spray of liquid hit her in the face. "What—" She lifted a hand to wipe it away as a wave of dizziness hit her. The room tilted. Spun.

Claire gasped and turned, stumbled. Caught a glimpse of a familiar face just as the darkness closed in. Her knees trembled, then gave out. A hard hand shoved her backward and she tumbled into the blackness.

Derek stared at the screen, then rubbed his eyes. With the others working on the list of currently released cons and their families, Derek had decided to move on to cases where Claire had testified for the prosecution. Not that someone couldn't be mad that she testified for the defense, but he had to start somewhere.

He'd narrowed down the possibilities to four. All four defendants had been found guilty and sentenced to prison. Two had died behind bars and two were still there. The two in prison still maintained their innocence. Of the two who were dead, one had confessed and apologized to his victim's family. The other, a woman, had hung herself, leaving behind a note to her two children, admonishing them to live good lives and to let her death free them to do so.

"What'd she do?" Linc asked.

"Killed her husband."

"Self-defense?"

"No, doesn't look like it. The defense tried to argue that, but the evidence Claire presented showed she planned it right down to the type of wine she would buy to drug him. Those pesky internet searches give it away every time. People think they've erased their history, but they haven't. Most of the time."

"So the evidence was clear."

"There was no question in anyone's mind. The jury debated for only an hour and a half before coming back with a unanimous verdict."

Allie let out a low whistle. "Wow."

"No kidding. That was fast."

"But why'd she want him dead? Was he abusive? Was she seeing someone else?"

"Got him," Daria said.

Linc looked up and exchanged a look with Allie. Derek slipped around behind her. "What do you mean you got him?"

"Well, sort of. So"—she looked at Nolan—"you said the car belonged to Brad Stevenson and he had a rock-solid alibi at the hospital."

"Yes."

"Well, you're right. It doesn't look like he's involved. If that's the case, then the person who took the car got really, really lucky and picked the right one that wouldn't be missed for many hours . . ."

". . . or he knows Brad," Allie said.

"Exactly. So I simply wrote a program to find every time Brad has been tagged by one of his friends on social media, then cross-referenced those with the people from cases where Claire has testified."

"I'm sorry," Nolan said. "You wrote a program?"

Derek waved a hand. "Don't ask." Back to Daria, he motioned for her to continue. "And?"

"And social media is awesome for finding people who think

they're anonymous. The woman who committed suicide in prison was best friends with Brad Stevenson's mother."

"What?" The word echoed around the room.

Nolan leaned in, eyes wide. "You put that together just like that?"

Daria shrugged. "It's really quite simple when you know what you're doing." She lifted her chin, a wickedly pleased gleam in her eyes.

"Watch out," Derek said, "your head isn't going to fit through the door before too long."

She smirked. Linc and Allie simply looked proud.

Derek, who'd gotten to know the imp very well in the last two years, barely refrained from rolling his eyes. "All right, squirt, give. You said you got him. What'd you mean by that?"

Her smirk faded and her brows pulled together as she focused back on the screen. "Well, with a little more digging, social media also revealed that Brad Stevenson is dating Marie Gilmore, who is the sister of one Hank Gilmore."

Derek raised a brow. "You say that like his name should mean something."

"Amanda Gilmore's children. Amanda is the woman who committed suicide in prison," Nolan said.

"Exactly. And I think Hank's the one who's after Claire."

Derek exchanged a confused look with the others in the room. "Why's that?"

She hesitated.

"It's all right, Daria," Allie said. "Just show us."

"Well, since I had the password to the system, I did a little more snooping and found this." A few more clicks on her laptop and she projected an image on the far wall. "Here, here, and here, on three different occasions, he's on camera watching as Claire leaves the building. Each time she drives away, he follows." She zoomed in on the driver of the white Ford truck that was in all of her shots.

Hank Gilmore was easy to see. "And," Daria said, "it looks like he just got a job here at the lab a couple of months ago."

"Here!" Derek narrowed his eyes and glared at the man on the screen. "What's he doing here?"

A grunt of surprise drew their attention to the doorway. "What are you doing?" Brandon said. "That's Gilly."

SEVEN

Claire woke with a groan and tried to press a hand to her pounding head, but her hand wouldn't budge. What in the—

Memory flashed. Terror spiked.

She stilled, trying to keep her breathing even as her thinking became more clear with each passing second.

Gilly. Hank Gilmore had done something to her.

In the bathroom. The liquid in her face. The smell. The darkness.

Panic escalated, tumbling through her, and she tugged at the bonds around her hands. Pain shot through her wrists and she stopped to catch her breath, attempting to slow her racing pulse. *Don't. Stay in control.* The order helped a fraction. Instead of bolting upright, she cracked her eyes open, letting her blurry gaze roam the area. She was in a room.

What kind? She let her eyes shut once more and took inventory.

Concrete beneath her cheek.

And she was cold. Shivers wracked her and goose bumps pebbled her skin. Yes, definitely cold. The only thing between her bare skin and the floor was the fisherman heavy cable-knit sweater she'd chosen to throw on over her long-sleeved T-shirt. And she was still cold.

Claire clamped her lips, trying to keep the mounting scream from escaping.

Stop. Be smart, stay calm, and think.

The pep talk kept the scream inside, but that was about it. She closed her eyes. *Okay, Claire, you need to get free. How are you going to do that?*

Her hands were taped behind her back. Her legs were also held immobile. Probably by the same tape that trapped her hands.

Get your bearings and figure this out.

She heard the hum of . . . something. The air conditioner? Maybe. She opened her eyes and noticed she could see, thanks to the exposed single bulb hanging from the ceiling

The walls were unfinished concrete. Behind her, a metal door with a padlock at the top said she wasn't going out that way. Opposite of that door were wooden steps leading up to . . . where?

It didn't matter at the moment. She pictured the nice young man from work who always seemed to have a smile or a witty one-liner.

Gilly.

Why? She wracked her brain, trying to figure out what she'd done to make him hate her like this.

Shudders rippled, nausea churned. Minutes passed as she struggled to ignore the crippling fear and figure out a plan.

Think!

Why was she still alive? Why drug her rather than just kill her? He sure hadn't hesitated to attempt to end her life the night he'd broken into her home. The grenade through the window would have surely killed both her and Derek, had Derek not reacted like he had. So, why snatch her from the bathroom at work and give her time to wake up?

Unless he'd had no choice.

More time passed in silence. No footsteps, no feeling of being watched. Just the feeling of time running out. A sense of urgency.

She'd always hated surprises. Every Christmas, she snuck around to find the presents. Every time her parents argued, she found a way to eavesdrop. Because with knowledge came power. And she really needed some power right now. She wished she had someone or something to eavesdrop on at the moment. She couldn't shake the sheer horror of the unknown.

The nausea faded and strength began to return.

Claire struggled into a sitting position, waited for the resurgence of nausea to pass, then got another look at her prison.

The high windows suggested she was on a lower floor. Maybe in a basement. But the windows had bars on them. Shoving the incapacitating fear aside, Claire looked for a weapon—or anything sharp.

Nothing.

Then she'd have to make something.

Out of . . . what?

An old washer and dryer sat in the corner. A wrought-iron bench with a missing seat that had probably been wooden slats. Wooden, unpainted steps led up.

Definitely a basement. She shivered. A very cold basement. And a mostly empty one. Had someone just moved? Or had they simply cleaned it out and used it only for laundry?

While she scanned the room and grappled with her fear, she managed to slide her arms under her rear, pausing when the pain of pulled muscles and unhealed bruises arced through her. Bracing herself for another wave of agony, she bit her lip and pulled her legs through.

Spots danced before her eyes and weakness returned. She paused for a moment, gathering her strength and waiting for it to pass. How much time did she have?

Don't think about it. Just act.

Using her teeth, she gripped the edge of the duct tape and pulled. It took longer than she expected, but finally, her hands were free. Quickly, she released her feet and tossed the tape aside. Her eyes returned to the lightbulb. Then the window. It was light outside, so did that mean she'd been down here only a short time? She was hungry but not starving. Maybe a couple of hours? Derek should have missed her by now.

Please, Derek, miss me.

She couldn't reach the bulb, but the window was only about a foot above her head. Claire pushed herself to her feet and swayed, blinking and waiting for the room to stop spinning.

Footsteps on the floor just above her head froze her, then sent her pulse pounding even faster. With no place to hide, she was a sitting duck, which meant she needed to stop thinking and start moving. Fast. She darted across the room and opened the dryer. A load of towels sat there. She stared for a second at the completely normal sight in a world gone crazy. Then she grabbed the thickest towel and wrapped it around her hand.

Stepping to the window, she drew her arm back, then paused. Would the noise alert her attacker? Set off an alarm? Not seeing any sign of a system, she punched the window. It cracked, but held. Another sharp jab sent glass raining down on the other side; however, a nice chunk still hung from the wood. Carefully, she worked it loose, then placed it under her shoe to break off a smaller piece that resembled a triangle. It might slice her hand up, but at least it was a weapon. While her ear continued to tune in to the sounds coming from the floor above her, her gaze swept the room.

Landed on the duct tape.

An idea began to form, and as long as she had the time, she might actually make it work. Claire returned to the dryer and pulled the lint catcher from its space in the front. Plastic outlined the screen. Working quickly, she fashioned a piece of the cream-colored plastic into the size she wanted, then returned to the duct tape.

With shaking hands, she wrapped the tape around the plastic and the lower part of the glass triangle. While she worked, she listened.

When she was done, she hefted the makeshift knife—or *shank* as they'd call it in prison—in her right hand and drew in a slow, shaky breath. Could she really kill someone with it? Stabbing was up close and personal—very different from standing behind a gun. But dead was dead no matter how one looked at it, and Gilly had made it extremely clear that she was to die.

Her fist tightened around the handle of the shank. Well, not if she had a chance to defend herself first.

She flipped the light off, then raced back to the bulb. Hefting the remaining plastic from the dryer lint screen, she connected it with the lightbulb. Once more glass fell. She gripped the handle of her newly fashioned weapon and hurried to the stairs to wait.

"Where'd she go?" Derek asked. Panic was starting to set in. As soon as they'd realized Hank Gilmore was Gilly—and had access to Claire—Derek and the others had rushed to her office only to find it empty. "The last time I saw her, she was heading to the bathroom," he said. "Allie, will you check it?"

Allie had. Only Claire hadn't been there either. Of course not. That had been a while ago.

"Shut the building down," Derek said, knowing they were probably too late, "and get security footage of her going into the restroom and coming out. Follow her and see where she goes and who she's with. She wouldn't have left without letting us know. Not willingly."

"I can do that," Daria said, still holding her laptop. She dropped into the chair opposite Claire's desk and eyed Brandon, who stood in the doorway open-mouthed. "What's your password for the security cameras?"

"I . . . I'm not supposed to . . ." At her intense stare, he stuttered to a stop. "Never mind. But just that part of the footage, okay?" He gave it to her and Daria's fingers flew over the keyboard.

"Okay," she said, "I'm in." More tapping and then she stopped.

Derek leaned in. "What'd you find?"

"She went in, the cleaning guy went after her—"

"Gilly," Brandon said.

"Yeah. Him. He comes out about five minutes later, but Claire never does. Watch."

They watched.

"She came out," Derek said. He slammed a hand on the desk and Daria jumped. "Sorry," he said. "But she came out right under everyone's nose."

Daria frowned, then gasped. "The cleaning cart."

"Exactly. He must have done something to knock her out, then shoved her in the cart."

"And walked her out of the building with no one the wiser," Allie muttered.

Brandon's head swiveled as he tried to keep up with them. Every so often, he'd open his mouth as though to say something, then snap it shut.

"Brandon? You want to say something?"

"Uh . . . no. Sorry. It's just I noticed Gilly paying attention to Claire and I didn't do anything about it." He looked away and gave a small shrug. "I thought it was just that he had a teenage crush on her or something." He swallowed and met Derek's gaze. "If I'd known—"

"I know. It's okay. This isn't your fault."

Brandon nodded and Daria thumped another key on the laptop. "Looks like he used the service elevator," she said. "Rode to the bottom floor and out the back near the dumpsters."

"And no one would have thought a blasted thing about him doing so," Derek muttered. "I can easily get his address, but we're going to need more info. Linc, I think it's time to bring Annie in on this." Their IT expert at Quantico.

"I've got his address," Daria said. "I just sent it to your phones. Working on the other stuff." Their phones buzzed and pinged as if on cue.

"I don't think we're going to need Annie," Linc said.

"Sent you the address his license plate's registered under as well."

"How—" Derek's jaw sagged.

"Easy. The first address is what's on his driver's license, but . . ." More clicks sounded. "He doesn't live there anymore. The second address belongs to Amanda Gilmore and is the one he put on his employee application here. Hold on . . ." They waited, watching her fingers fly over the keyboard. "Okay, don't bother going to the first address. It's rented to someone else now. I'd be willing to bet he's living at his mother's house."

"We'll head there."

"He's single, a friendly guy, well-liked by those who know him. Described as having a good sense of humor and they all feel terrible that his mother would do such a thing."

"Again, how did you . . . ?" Derek asked.

She glanced at him. "Transcripts from his mother's trial and interviews of neighbors the detectives did while they were investigating the death of his father. Looks like he's seeing a counselor, but I can't seem to access those records."

"Don't," Allie said. "If he's done this, and it looks like he has, we'll need to do everything by the book to make it stick in court. Focus on finding Claire right now."

"Okay." She started clicking furiously once more, almost pounding the keys in her desperate race against the clock.

Nolan hung up. "I've got local officers heading to both addresses just in case."

Derek squeezed Daria's shoulder. "You did good, kid."

"Thanks." More clicking as he hurried to the exit. "Wait!"

He froze.

"I found him on the traffic cams. He's heading away from his mother's address."

"Daria—" Linc started.

"I know, I know. Just give me five more seconds. And . . . there. Brad Stevenson's mother owns a small house about ten minutes from here. It's on five acres surrounded by trees, but close to the city." She looked up. "And it's in the right direction indicated by the traffic cams."

Nolan nodded at Derek. "Let's go."

"I sent you the address," she said.

Their phones went off once more and this time Derek didn't stop running until he threw himself into the driver's seat of his vehicle.

EIGHT

What is he doing?

He'd opened the door at the top of the stairs, then just . . . stopped.

Her heart thudded a painfully fast—and loud—rhythm. Could he hear it? He'd flipped the switch and, of course, nothing had happened. She held the homemade knife in her right hand. What she wouldn't give for her SIG Sauer.

Voices reached her. Two of them? She swallowed and tightened her grip on the metal. One she might have had a chance against, but two wasn't going to happen.

The voices faded and the door shut.

Her pounding pulse slowed a fraction.

Until the door opened once more, a beam of light split the darkness, and footsteps started down the stairs.

Claire moved to the highest part of the steps that would give her cover without allowing him to see her.

The footfalls grew closer. Claire waited, pulse racing, trying to ignore the images from the last time this man had gotten his hands on her. She wouldn't survive a second time.

And she desperately wanted to survive. Derek's handsome face flashed before her and a shudder rippled through her. *Please, God, give me a chance with him.*

Focus.

His calves came into view. For a brief second, she thought about trying to slice his Achilles tendon, but what if she missed?

Knees. Thighs.

The beam swept to the place where she should have been and a curse slipped from him.

He hit the bottom step.

Claire's nerves tightened. *Move!* her mind screamed at him.

If he turned the light toward her, she was dead—or at least in a fight for her life.

But the light stayed on the spot where she should have been as though keeping it there would make her appear. He took two or three steps forward. Claire edged behind him, trying to breathe without making a sound. With a roar, he rushed forward, swinging the light back and forth. "Claire!"

His bellow sent her hooking around the end of the wooden banister and pounding up the stairs.

She burst through the top door and into a kitchen from the 1970s.

"Come back here!"

The kitchen door to her left held a padlock. Not going out that way. He was right behind her. Still gripping her homemade weapon, she spun right and bolted into the foyer. Another padlocked door. Bars on the window. Panicked, she darted into the sunroom.

"You can't get away, Claire."

The female voice stopped her, and she turned to see a woman in her fifties. Salt-and-pepper hair was pulled into a ponytail. Blue eyes gleamed behind black-framed glasses.

"Who are you? Why are you doing this?"

Gilly huffed to an enraged stop next to the woman. He lifted his weapon and she placed a hand on his arm. "Let me answer her questions," she said without taking her gaze from Claire.

"I'm ready for her to be dead." His eyes spat his mammoth-sized anger.

"It's okay, Hank. A couple more minutes won't matter. And

I have to admit, I'm not opposed to watching her suffer a bit."
She narrowed her eyes. "You want to know why we're doing this?
Because Amanda Gilmore was my best friend and you killed her."

Amanda Gilmore. The name was familiar.

The woman scoffed. "You don't even know who I'm talking
about."

It clicked. "Amanda Gilmore," Claire said, "mother and wife,
age fifty-one, poisoned her husband bit by bit until he finally died.
She received life in prison."

Surprise flickered. "So you do remember."

"It was an open-and-shut case."

"For you maybe, but not for us, the people she loved and had
to leave. Not for her children who were free of that monster but
now had no mother."

"There was no evidence of abuse that the defense attorney could
find." The details were becoming sharper.

"That's because he wasn't looking in the right places." And
the places he had looked had shown Amanda to be the abuser,
not the abused.

"Look . . ." She held her left hand up as though in surrender
while her right hand stayed curled around the weapon. "All I do
is gather and follow the evidence—and sometimes I don't even
gather it. I have no control over what goes on in court or behind
a closed jury door. I just present my findings, that's all."

"Well, it shouldn't be all! Your findings sent an innocent woman
to prison. She said so!"

"She confessed!" Wait. "Who said so? What are you talking
about?"

"It's your fault!" With a roar, Gilly charged her. Claire brought
her hands up to block him, belatedly remembering the homemade
knife. She felt it sink deep into his belly even as he slammed into
her, his forward momentum carrying them through the glass window behind her.

She hit the ground hard. The breath left her. Blood soaked her. The woman's screams echoed around them.

Derek heard the screams coming from the backyard and changed his course, motioning for Linc and Allie to go to the right while he and Nolan bolted to the left.

Derek rounded the side of the house. "Police! Show your hands! Show your hands now!"

Nolan added his orders, and together, they rushed the two on the ground.

While local officers and Nolan cuffed the woman and the bleeding man, Derek raced to check on Claire. "Are you all right?"

"Yes." Gasping, she let him haul her to her feet.

A sharp crack from the tree line jammed his pulse for a split second. "Shooter!"

Derek grabbed Claire and pulled her back to the ground. Another shot sounded. Derek saw Hank Gilmore hit the ground, the right side of his face missing.

"Who's shooting?"

"Shooter's in the trees!"

"Stay down! Stay down!"

Voices and orders merged as one. Bodies moved, weapons turned in the direction of the gunshots.

Claire pushed to her feet and took off.

"Claire!"

She didn't stop but aimed herself toward the shooter.

Another crack sounded. When Claire didn't fall, Derek swiveled around in time to see the woman—Mrs. Stevenson?—jerk, then lie still on the ground where she'd been pulled by the officer. Shouted orders, bodies diving for cover, and screams to hold fire.

"Claire, get down!"

She dove for the ground. All Derek could see was that the shooter was hitting whatever he was aiming at. Any moment, he expected that to be Claire.

He put on a burst of speed in time to see the figure disappear around the nearest tree. He reached Claire and she waved him off. "I'm fine. We have to stop her."

Her?

She shot to her feet. "I don't know what's going on, but she's not getting away."

Derek stayed with Claire, dodging trees and keeping his eyes open, his weapon ready, until he was finally able to yank her to a stop. "Claire," he yelled. "I need you to stop and stay put. Let me do what I'm trained for." She glared up at him, but beneath the laser look, he could see the fear. And determination.

And finally, her resignation. She gave a short nod and hunkered down behind the tree. While he'd been talking, he'd been scanning the area. Looking for any sign the shooter was still moving. But everything had gone quiet. No sounds, no movement, not even a hint of a breeze whispering through the leaves.

The chill in the crisp winter air seeped into his bones. The cold came from more than just the weather, pressing in, freezing his very spirit.

It was time for this to end. He called Nolan and let him know the situation. "Stay back, but circle around. Create a barrier this person has to cross to get off the property."

"10-4. And Derek?"

"Yeah?"

"The woman's dead and so is Hank Gilmore."

"Thanks."

He was sorry for it, but they'd chosen their paths.

As had the person still out there. Armed and ready to put a bullet in anyone who got too close.

Crouching next to Claire, Derek waited.

Claire stayed still. So still that if he hadn't known she was behind him, he would be oblivious to her presence. He shot a quick glance over his shoulder to make sure she was really still there.

She was. Clasping her hands in front of her as though in prayer. Prayer was good.

A flash of movement just ahead snagged his attention. A deer? Or a killer?

"All right," he said, "I'm going to get this person. Please don't move. I need to know exactly where you are so I don't shoot you by accident. Got it?" A faint nod answered him. "Good." He locked his gaze on hers. "I'll be back. Trust me, okay?"

She leaned in and kissed his lips. A short, quick peck. "Be careful."

"Absolutely."

NINE

Claire watched him go, heart pounding, blood rushing. She wanted to follow, but she'd promised to stay put. Derek was right. He was trained for this kind of thing. All she would do was get in the way and get herself shot. Or get him shot.

So she'd keep her back against the tree and do her best to be his lookout.

Another thing he was right about. This needed to end today. Constantly looking over her shoulder had gotten old very fast.

She could see him just ahead, his dark head tucked low.

Please, please, be careful.

A flash of movement behind him. "Derek! Duck!"

The gunshot sounded and the figure spun to fire off another round in Claire's general direction. She scuttled to another tree, hoping she'd stayed low enough that the shooter hadn't seen her move.

A loud crash, a grunt, and a scream came from Derek's direction. Heart thudding, Claire pushed to her feet in time to see him wrestling with the woman on the ground.

"Stop! You're ruining everything!"

Derek didn't bother to answer as he worked to keep the weapon aimed away from him.

Do something! Frantic to help, Claire let her gaze roam the ground. There. She snatched the heaviest branch she could spot nearby and raced over to bring it down on the woman's head.

The masked woman went still. Stunned, but still conscious. Derek yanked the gun from her fingers, tossed it aside, then pulled the mask from her head.

Claire gasped. "Tara Scholtz?"

"It should have been me! Not you! It should have been me!" Fiery green eyes glared up at her. Tara jerked against Derek's hold, but his grip held fast.

"What should have been—" Claire stopped, gaped. "The supervisor's position? That's what this is all about? That's what you killed people for?" Claire heard the screech in her last question but couldn't seem to help it.

"I was next in line." Tara's shoulders heaved. Spittle flew from her lips. "I was there the longest after Franklin. When he turned it down, I should have been next to be offered the position." She gave another keening cry and flailed unsuccessfully in Derek's grasp. "Let me go!"

He flipped her over and placed a knee in the middle of her back. With effort, he managed to grab her arms and pull them behind her back. "Calm down," Derek said. "You're not going anywhere."

Linc and Allie hurried over to them, and Linc handed Derek a set of handcuffs. Derek expertly applied them to Tara's wrists while reciting her rights.

When he fell silent, Tara began to scream. "I'll have your badge! I'll have you all up on charges of police brutality! I'll have you—"

"Shut up!" Claire yelled at her. "Shut up, shut up!"

The screams broke off and Tara stared. They all stared, but Claire wanted answers and Tara's drama was on her last nerve.

"What do you mean he turned it down?" she asked calmly as though they were seated at the dinner table.

"Just what I said," Tara said, lowering her voice to a bearable decibel level. "He didn't want the job because it would require more hours and more time away from home. His daughter is a single mother whose son is constantly getting in trouble. He turned it down because he said it wasn't the right time for him. That's because it was *my time*! It should have been mine! Mine! You hear me? Mine!"

She sounded like a tantrum-throwing three-year-old instead of a fortysome-year-old professional. That and the cuffs she wore made her seem much less terrifying.

"But . . . I don't understand. What did Gilly and that woman have to do with anything? Why did you shoot the woman?"

"That was Jane Stevenson," Derek said. "She was Amanda Gilmore's best friend. My guess is she didn't want the woman talking. Tara shot her and then ran, hoping to get away in the confusion." He glared at Tara. "At least that's my theory."

Claire's mental lightbulb flickered. "Mrs. Stevenson blamed me for Mrs. Gilmore going to prison, that's clear, but I'm still confused. How did everyone get connected like this? With Tara especially?"

"It was me, of course," Tara boasted. She seemed to have accepted that it was all over for her and was willing to talk. She scoffed. "I'm a lot smarter than Franklin or anyone else wanted to give me credit for. I overheard Franklin recommend you for the job. I was stunned, hurt, *furious*."

"So you decided to have me *killed*?"

"I knew there had to be a way to get rid of you without it looking like I had anything to do with it. I simply searched your court cases until I found one that I could use."

"So you could manipulate the emotions of those involved," Derek said.

Tara sighed and a tear slipped down her cheek. "It was a truly brilliant plan."

"So, you what?" Claire said. "Called them up and said, 'Hey, your mom's imprisonment and death were Claire Montgomery's fault. Let's plan to kill her and get revenge'?" She stomped a foot. "Who says yes to that kind of insanity?"

For a moment Tara simply stared at her. No one moved, no

one breathed. She hadn't asked for a lawyer after Derek had read her rights.

Tara huffed a laugh. "Insanity? If it had worked, no one would have any reason to connect your death to me. Or to the deaths of the two sad people who just couldn't go on any longer without their beloved Amanda Gilmore."

"All right, that's enough," Derek said. He pulled her to her feet and passed her off to Nolan, who gripped her bicep. "I'll fill out any paperwork you need from me in a little bit. I want to get Claire home—or someplace comfortable anyway."

"Home sounds good," Claire said. "I need to take a look at what's left of my house and pack a few boxes."

"And we need to say thanks to Levi. His description of the car is really the thing that enabled us to find you so quickly."

"Levi. Yes. I need to make a stop on the way home then."

"For a dinosaur?"

She smiled. "Yes. And one other thing."

"All right. I'm driving?"

"Might be a good idea since Gilly didn't let me bring my car."

He scowled and led the way to his truck. "How did you know it was a woman shooting?"

She climbed in and buckled up before rubbing her head. "It was something they said. Something like my findings had sent an innocent woman to prison. And then Mrs. Stevenson said, 'She said so.' I knew it was a woman, I just didn't know who."

"I'm sorry."

She nodded and swallowed. "Did I kill Gilly? I know I stabbed him, but did I kill him?"

"No. Tara did."

"Oh." She sighed. "I didn't want to kill him. I didn't even mean to stab him, but he just . . ."

He took her cold hand in his warm one. Then pulled her into a hug. And she released the tears.

Derek held her. "Cry it out, Claire, it's okay. It's normal." He knew from experience that her emotions were all over the place right now.

She sniffed and swiped her tears. "Sorry."

"You don't need to apologize," he said softly. "I've shed a few tears myself after the intensity of a job."

"You?"

He shrugged. "It's a healthy release. I just make sure I don't do it in front of any of the guys."

She let out a short chuckle. "Yeah, I can see how you might not want to do that." She paused. "Although I'm sure they've shed a few of their own."

"They have." He squeezed her fingers. "Ready to go?"

She blew out a low sigh. "Ready."

He put the truck in drive and pulled away from the scene. "I have a question for you."

"Okay."

"You know what two weeks from now is, right?"

"Um . . . no?"

No? He gaped. "Really? Two weeks. From now. As in from today."

"What's today? Thursday?" She frowned. "What am I missing?"

"It's Thanksgiving! The all-time best holiday of the year in the South."

"You look absolutely scandalized that I didn't know that."

"Well . . . yeah." Who didn't know that?

She gave a small laugh. "And what makes Thanksgiving rank so high on the list?"

"Because in November in Columbia, there's always a chance you'll get a perfectly amazing weather day."

"Which means?"

"Football, baby, football!"

Claire lifted a brow. "You say that with such reverence. Why do you need good weather to watch football from the couch?"

"Watch—" Clearly, he had some work to do. "No, my dear. I come from a very large family. We don't watch football, we play it."

"Where?"

"In the backyard!"

"And if it rains or snows?"

"Bite your tongue."

"No, seriously," she said, turning in the seat, curiosity animating her lovely features.

He pulled in a breath to slow his suddenly racing pulse. "Ah, well, if it rains or something, then we play Phase Ten."

"What is that?"

Derek shook his head. "I'm flabbergasted, utterly flummoxed. We obviously need to talk."

"Why?"

"Because you're coming home with me for Thanksgiving, and the more you know about the St. John family, the better armed you'll be. And the better armed you are, the less likely you are to run away."

"Coming home with you? Run away?"

"Yes. You haven't really lived if you haven't experienced a St. John Thanksgiving. Or Christmas for that matter." A pause. "Of course, Easter isn't so bad and neither is Mother's Day or Father's—" He shook his head. "Never mind. Back to Thanksgiving."

For the next hour, in between stops to ensure she had the appropriate gifts for Levi, Derek told her everything he could think of that would prepare her for his family.

Finally, he pulled to a stop in front of her home—and the noisy chaos of reconstruction. Hammers pounded, a SKILSAW whirred, and a country music station blared from a portable radio. She turned wide eyes on him. "What in the world?"

Bart Wells slipped out from the back of the house and shoved a hammer into the tool belt around his waist. Claire stepped out of the car and faced the man.

He stared at her a moment, then a smile slipped across his face.

TEN

Claire blinked. Wait. A smile? "Bart?"

He shrugged. "I own a construction business. Thought I'd be neighborly and put your house back together." A flicker of unease flashed in his gray eyes. "I hope you don't mind. The insurance company was already out here so . . ." Another shrug. "I mean, I know it's a rental and there's the rental insurance, but I also knew you'd feel responsible and want it fixed for your landlord—who gave me permission to do it. I mean, I didn't know how much the deductible was so I figured if I could save that for you—okay, I'm going to shut up now."

Tears pooled in Claire's eyes. She didn't care if the man wanted a hug or not. She stepped forward and wrapped her arms around his waist and squeezed. When she stepped back, he had a deer-in-the-headlights expression. "Thank you, Bart."

His neck flushed. "Aw, Claire, you're welcome. I'm sorry I've been so hard on you about Levi. I was just afraid you'd be like a lot of other people and . . ."

"Make fun of him?"

He nodded. "Or hurt his feelings."

"I'd never do that. Not on purpose anyway."

"I think I've figured that out. Levi's a pretty good judge of character. I need to trust that about him."

She smiled. "So, is it okay if I give him a gift?"

Bart groaned. A longsuffering one that held no real heart. "Sure." He turned. "Hey, Jake, tell Levi to come here a minute, will you?"

When Levi rounded the corner of the house and spotted Claire, his face pulled into a huge grin. He ran forward only to stop inches from her. "Hi, Claire."

"Hi, Levi."

"Did you bring me a dinosaur?"

"Levi—" Bart sputtered.

Claire winked at the beleaguered cousin and turned to find Derek standing beside her with the gift bag. "Thanks." She took it. "What do you think it is, Levi?"

"A dinosaur?"

"Yes, there's one in there. What else do you think might be in there?"

He frowned and shook his head. "I do not know."

"It's a microscope. A real one. And I'm going to teach you how to use it if it's okay with Bart."

"It is more than okay," Levi said before his cousin had a chance to open his mouth. He grabbed the bag, then gave her an awkward hug. "I am done working today, Bart." He took off for his house.

"Oops," Claire said softly. "Sorry about that."

Bart shrugged. "We were just about to finish up here anyway."

"Levi!" Claire waited until the young man turned around. "Don't open it yet, okay? Promise?"

"I promise! I just want to look. It is okay to look, right?"

"Sure."

And then he was inside.

"So," Bart said, "we got your new wall up and replaced all the brick and siding that was destroyed."

For the next fifteen minutes, he walked her through what he and his crew had done. Claire was astounded at the progress they'd made in such a short time, but the place looked like it had been

348

invaded by ants. Workers were everywhere. "We just need a couple more days and you can move back in." He shrugged. "Actually, you can stay here now, but it's awful dusty."

"I'll be fine," Claire said. Another tear slipped down her cheek. "I don't know how to thank you," she said softly.

"You've already thanked me. You gave Levi something he'd been sorely lacking lately."

Claire raised a brow.

"Hope and happiness," the man said.

He walked away and Claire felt Derek's hands settle on her shoulders. She turned to look up at him and he claimed her lips in a long, lingering kiss.

When he lifted his head, she grinned. "Not that I mind, but what was that for?"

"You're amazing. Hands-down amazing."

She reached up to curl her arms around his neck. "And I think you're pretty incredible too, so maybe we make a good team?"

"The best."

He started to kiss her again and she stopped him with a finger on his lips.

"What?" he asked.

"I think we need to save the kissing for a bit later and you need to keep telling me about your family. I don't think my arsenal is near as full as it needs to be."

Derek snorted, then nodded. "Fine. Let's go to Nolan's house. We can crash there and eat his food while he and Kallie are over at Jason and Lilly's this afternoon."

"Nolan and Kallie are the best, aren't they?"

"Yeah. And they always have good stuff in the fridge."

"Ah, now we know the real reason you wanted to come visit."

He laughed and squeezed her fingers. "It's going to be fun getting to know you, Claire."

Her heart thundered. "Yeah, I think you're right."

"No desire to run away from us?" he asked, suddenly serious. "From what we might have? From the future?"

"None whatsoever." She paused. "In fact, I honestly can't imagine my future without you in it."

His features relaxed and he kissed her again. "I like the sound of that. All right then, let's go."

Two weeks later, Claire let Derek lead her up the porch steps to his childhood home and he closed the umbrella. "I can't believe it's raining. Of all days it could pick to rain, it had to choose today."

Claire laughed. "Hush. It's just a little drizzle."

"But it means no football."

She stared at this man she'd spent almost every waking hour with over the past two weeks. "Are you actually whining?"

"No, but—" A sigh. "Yes. Yes I am. I wanted football."

"I'm kind of looking forward to the Phase Ten game. I read the rules online." She glanced around. "This place is amazing. It's Thanksgiving, but your parents have Christmas lights up. And I saw a tree in the window!"

"It's my mom. She loves Christmas. And Thanksgiving. And any holiday, really. Or Sunday dinner. She and Dad put the tree up every Thanksgiving Day morning. Well, Dad kind of does. And any kid available who wants to help. Mom pretty much stays in the kitchen." He rubbed his hands together and cleared his throat.

"You okay?"

"Yeah, yeah. I just . . ." He put his hands on her shoulders. "It's been an amazing two weeks, Claire. I can't remember when I've had more fun—or felt so deeply. Thank you for that."

She opened her mouth. Then shut it. Then opened it. "I feel the same way. Thank you for not letting me run away."

He hugged her. "There's just one more thing. I sort of . . . um . . ."

"What?"

". . . left something out. About my family."

"Derek, you talked for hours about your family. Each person, their role in law enforcement, Ruthie's choice to go into medicine, the cutthroat Phase Ten games, everything. What could you have possibly left out?"

He sighed. "Two-year-olds."

She blinked. "What?"

"How do you feel about two-year-olds?"

"Specific ones or just two-year-olds in general?"

"Lively ones."

"Um . . . sorry?"

"Never mind. I think it's best just to rip the Band-Aid off." He opened the door and Claire froze. Music, laughter, and the occasional outraged scream quickly followed by peals of giggles greeted her. And that was all within the first several seconds of the door being opened.

A blur of movement whipped past her, followed by another and another and another—and yet another. Followed by Daria, who waved. "Hi, Claire! Hey, Derek!" Allie pulled up the rear and stumbled to a halt when her eyes locked on Claire's. She grinned and snagged Claire's wrist to pull her into the foyer. Derek followed and shut the door.

"Derek?" Claire asked over her shoulder.

"Just go with it."

"Those little people that just went past," she said. "The ones moving faster than a speeding bullet? Those are two-year-olds?"

He shrugged. "Yeah. Five of them."

"Who does that?"

"Siblings who get pregnant all within a few weeks of each other. Then throw in a set of twins . . ."

"Oh."

"Unca Derk!" One of the two-year-olds threw himself at Derek's shins, and Derek leaned down to pick up the grinning munchkin. "Hiya, Timbo. How's it going?"

"I'm hungry."

"You're always hungry."

By this time, Allie had moved Claire into the large living area. She placed her fingers in her mouth and gave an ear-piercing whistle. When everyone fell silent, Allie smiled. "Thanks. I want to introduce you all to Claire Montgomery. She's a new friend and probably family one day if Derek has anything to say about it, so try not to scare her off."

Claire's cheeks lit up with a heat she'd never experienced before.

"Like you just did?" Linc asked.

"I didn't," Allie said, turning a suddenly contrite gaze to Claire. "Did I?"

Before she could answer, Derek grabbed her from Allie and everyone's welcome yells. He pulled her into a semi-private area off the den and wrapped his arms around her. "I'm sorry."

She giggled.

He placed a hand under her chin and tilted her face up. When she met his eyes, a half laugh, half snort escaped from her.

"What?" he asked.

"This place is exactly like I imagined. But, Allie . . . I didn't expect that after meeting her in Tanner Hollow. She was so professional and . . . and . . ."

"And?"

"I'm not sure, but not *that*."

A smile curved his lips. "Actually, she's kind of scary with that Dr. Jekyll, Mr. Hyde thing she does with her personality. She's come a long way since Linc brought her home."

"You make her sound like a puppy."

He sighed and a laugh slipped from him before he pressed his forehead to hers. "They didn't scare you off? You don't want me to take you back to Tanner Hollow?"

"No way. And if you hadn't dragged me out of there, I'd probably be knee-deep in conversation and asking them all kinds of questions."

"Oh."

"Son"—a woman who could only be Tabitha St. John stood in the door—"do you think you might bring Claire back into the den so we can all get to know her?"

"I'm sorry if I embarrassed you, Claire," Allie said softly from behind her mother-in-law.

"You didn't," Claire said. "I can see you're a lovely group, and I'm coming just as soon as I can convince this guy I'm not going to slip out the back door."

"Oh good," Allie said, looking distinctly relieved. "Almost three years ago, I never would have done something like that, but the St. Johns have a way of loosening you up."

"Grammy, I'm hungry," one of the two-year-olds said, pushing his way through to Tabitha.

She picked him up. "This is Tim. He's Ruthie and Isaac's son. His twin sister, Faith, is around here somewhere—probably being chased by Penny, Rachel, or Daria. Penny is a cousin to the St. Johns and Rachel is Blake and Chloe's daughter. Well, Chloe's stepdaughter, but . . . oh, never mind. You'll figure it all out."

Claire blinked. "Tim and Faith?"

"Yes. And before you ask, yes, they're named after *that* Tim and Faith." She shook her head. "I never would have guessed I'd have grandchildren named after country music stars. Whatever happened to family names?" She shrugged. "But that's Ruthie for you. Always marching to the beat of her own drum."

"Ruthie. The surgeon, right?"

"My little black sheep in the family." In reality, Tabitha didn't seem all that bothered by it—Ruthie's profession or the kids' names. "Well, join us when you feel like it. Since it's raining, it will be a Phase Ten day instead of football. Brace yourself, things might get a bit wild around here."

She disappeared with the little boy still on her hip, looking nothing like a chief of police and everything like a very contented grandmother. Allie followed them and Derek raised a brow. "All right then, let's do this," he said.

He took her hand and led her back into the middle of the chaos.

"I'm Izzy," a pretty dark-headed woman said. She snagged a little one. "And this is Christopher. He just turned two a couple of days ago. Christopher, say hi to Claire."

The little boy grinned at her. "Hi." Then frowned. "Down, Mama. Pweeze?"

She kissed his dark curls and set him on his feet. He was gone so fast Claire blinked.

Izzy laughed. "Yep, faster than a speeding bullet."

"Wow."

"Hi, I'm Emily," a voice to her right said. "I'm married to Brady and this is Angela Noelle. She'll be two December fourth. And that's Chloe over there with her little girl, Brianna."

Head spinning, Claire took it all in, doing her best to match the names she'd memorized with the faces they belonged to.

The day passed in a blur of new faces, sibling bickering, and more laughter than Claire thought was possible to pack into such a short span of time.

Tears filled her eyes and choked her throat.

"Hey," Derek said, slipping an arm around her shoulders. "You okay?"

"I'm wonderful." She leaned into him and kissed his cheek. "I never knew families like this really existed—off of reality television anyway."

"We're not perfect."

"No, but you love each other."

"Yeah, we do." He paused. "So, you're going to stick around?"

"Absolutely. I've just been schooled in the rules of Phase Ten."

He stilled. "By who?"

"I think it was Ruthie and Isaac."

"Oh. And that's it? They just told you the rules?"

"Hmm."

He narrowed his eyes. "What else?"

"Just to keep an eye on you because you cheat."

"I knew it!" He let go of her and turned to face the room. "Hey, Isaac! Detective Isaac Martinez!"

The man looked up, startled in the middle of wiping a child's nose. Claire didn't think it was his kid. "What?"

"I'm calling you out, man."

Derek's meaning dawned on Isaac and a huge grin slid across his face. "You're on!"

"Get the cards! Get the cards!" The chant came from Penny, Rachel, and Daria, who looked up from where they'd huddled in the corner of the room.

Claire let out a contented sigh and closed her eyes, basking in the world she'd been invited into.

And realized something.

Finally, she was home.

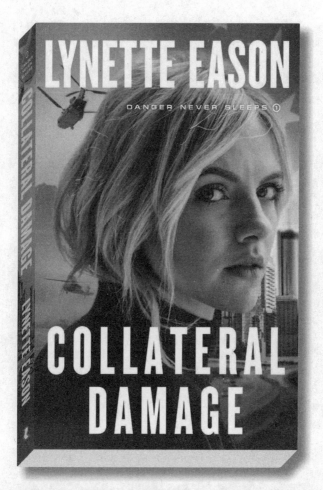

LYNETTE EASON

DANGER NEVER SLEEPS ①

COLLATERAL DAMAGE

READ ON FOR A SNEAK PEEK FROM

A NEW SERIES BY

LYNETTE EASON

ONE

FORWARD OPERATING BASE (FOB) CAMP CHARLIE
AFGHANISTAN
SEPTEMBER

Sergeant First Class Asher James stared at Captain Phillip Newell, sure that he'd heard wrong. "Sir? Isaiah Michaels? He's in sick hall." He let his gaze jump back and forth between his superiors. Asher was surprised to see the task force commander there, along with Mario Ricci and his unit led by Captain Gomez. Ricci nodded a greeting and went back to his laptop.

"Michaels never showed up to sick hall. One of our interpreters radioed in—he spotted Michaels at The Bistro restaurant in Kabul. You've got your orders, Sergeant James," Captain Newell said. "Bring him in."

Asher hesitated only a fraction of a second before nodding. "Sir, what's he being accused of exactly?"

"Being a traitor and selling information to the jihadists."

Stunned, Asher swallowed his shout of disbelief. "Sir, you know as well as I do that's not true." He was proud of the even tone he managed to keep.

"Not my call. And James?" Newell said. "You're leading this one."

"You're not coming?"

His captain hesitated. "No, I'm needed here. Waiting on a call from home I don't want to miss."

"Forget an anniversary again?" Asher wanted to recall the words as soon as they left his lips. "Sir?" Newell was one of the most private men he'd ever met. All he knew was the man's daughter had been very sick about six months ago, but it wasn't his place to ask.

"No." Newell's eyes met his. "I didn't."

"Good to hear, sir. I'll just mind my own business now."

The man's stance softened a fraction "You're a good man, James, I'm just a short-tempered son of a gun these days. Getting word about Michaels has made it worse." He glanced at the lieutenant colonel and Captain Gomez. "But we've been presented with proof. I've seen it with my own eyes, because if I hadn't, I'd be reacting just like you are. But this . . . I don't even know where to start explaining, so I'm going to have to let Michaels do that." He waved a hand toward the door. "Now go get him." He turned to Gomez. "I'll be ready for the debrief in five minutes."

Gomez nodded. He looked at Ricci. "Get everyone together in the CMOC. I'll be there shortly."

The Civil Military Operations Center. Why they didn't just call it a conference room was beyond Asher.

"Yes, sir." Ricci stood and grabbed his phone, dust flying from the sleeve of his uniform. With a growl, Ricci swatted at his sleeve, sending another dust plume to the floor.

Whenever Asher decided he was done serving, the one thing he wouldn't miss was the dust. And the death. And the occasional order—like this one—that made him want to revolt.

With a final nod to the men, Asher exited the building. Isaiah Michaels? No way. He didn't believe it for a second. The man was as squared away as they came.

But he'd obey the orders whether he liked them or not. He walked across the dusty yard to the twenty-two-ton MRAP and settled into the vehicle commander's seat with a grimace. The monster machine's air-conditioner hadn't yet had a chance to penetrate the suffocating interior heat. The other MRAP, with vehicle commander Sergeant B. J. King, the squad's fire team leader, would also participate in this mission.

Private Jasper Owens sat in the driver's seat next, frowning at Asher. "What's wrong, sir?"

"You got the target, Sarge?" The shouted question came from Staff Sergeant Mark Dobbs before Asher could answer Owens. Dobbs was their squad medic and was seated in the far back, finishing off an apple cinnamon ranger bar from his MRE.

"I got it," Asher said, turning to face the guys in the back. They sat along the walls of the vehicle, facing each other with their eyes on him while he struggled to push the words past his lips.

The guys exchanged glances. "You going to fill us in?" Owens asked.

Asher shook his head and lifted the radio to his mouth. "King, this is James. How copy? Over."

"James, this is King. That's a good copy. Just waiting for our orders. Over."

"Ash?" This prompt came from Sergeant Mitch Sampson, their gunner and resident artist—also known as Michelangelo—who was seated behind Owens.

"I . . . yeah. It's . . ."

"What, man?" Owens said. "Spit it out." A pause. "Sergeant."

Asher met each one of his unit member's eyes before locking gazes with the engineering sergeant of the team—and Asher's best friend—Gavin Black. Raking a hand over his buzzcut, Asher finally said into the radio so King could hear as well, "It's Michaels. They're saying he's a traitor—selling off information to jihadists—and we're to bring him in for questioning. Over."

Protests erupted, in the vehicle and over the radio. Asher let them vent before raising a hand. "I agree, but Captain said there's evidence and he's seen it."

Silence fell. The only noise came from the rumbling engine.

Finally, Dobbs blew out a breath. Asher met each man's gaze. "I don't believe it either, but these are the orders."

"Then let's go do what we've got to do," King said. "Over."

"I'm not doing it," Owens said.

The others stayed silent. Owens was the youngest of the group and gave the appearance of being unconcerned about the consequences of disobeying a direct order.

Asher knew differently and lasered him with a hard glare. "I get it, Owens. I feel the same way you do, but let's at least be the ones to find him and ask him what's going on." Owens finally nodded and Asher met each pair of outraged eyes. "Because if we don't do it, someone else will."

Heads bobbed in agreement. Owens set his jaw and cranked the engine, then lifted his radio. "King, this is Owens. You take the lead. We'll be right behind you. Over."

"That's a good copy, Owens. Stepping off in two mikes." King acknowledged the plan, and two minutes later the MRAP in front of them started to move.

Fifteen minutes later, the dust beat against the ballistic glass windows as they rolled along at five miles per hour in the Baraki Barak District in Logar Province, Afghanistan. Asher gripped his Colt M4 rifle. The MP4 at his feet would be for close quarter fighting and the Beretta pistol for even closer. He hoped he wouldn't have to use any of them. His nerves twitched as he strained to see through the plumed cloud ahead of him.

Owens drove with tense fingers wrapped around the wheel. They rode slowly through the wide-open expanse of land that had become known as a death trap, thanks to the improvised explosive devices that were often planted along the route. Asher would have recommended taking a different way; however, this was the fastest course into Kabul and they could speed up shortly.

"Hey, what's that?" Sampson shouted over the engine noise

and pointed. "You see that? A vehicle just went behind that hill. White SUV."

Asher squinted, trying to see what his buddy had managed to spot out the side window through the dust cloud. "Hill? What hill?"

The tension in the vehicle grew to mammoth proportions, and while the air-conditioner had finally cooled the interior, sweat started to flow again.

"King, this is James. Did you or your unit notice a civilian vehicle? White SUV. Over."

"Negative. Over."

"I don't see anything." Asher looked back at his friend. "You sure you saw something?"

Sampson rubbed his eyes, then shook his head. "Yeah, but I don't see anything now. I'm sorry, I've been at this too long. It's not good for my blood pressure. Time for me to get out of this business and go home."

"I know what you mean."

The MRAP in front of them began moving once again and Owens followed. Asher rotated his head, trying to loosen his locked muscles. The thought of home beckoned, and for the first time in a long while, he allowed himself to envision it, allowed the longing to see his family to sweep through. Even though they didn't understand him, they loved him—except maybe his brother. Definitely no love lost there, but Asher wished things were different.

The explosion came out of nowhere, hitting the MRAP in front of them, lifting it into the air and shoving it over on its side, then the top. Owens hit the brakes as the wave from the blast sent them rolling backward. They rocked from side to side, and for a moment, Asher thought they'd roll over as well, but they finally came to a shuddering halt right side up.

"King!" Asher shouted into the radio. "Give me a report! Over!"

Silence. Owens slid out of the driver's seat to the floor.

Asher radioed a 9-Line Medevac request for help, while Sampson pushed Owens aside. "What are you doing, man? Get your weapon." Sampson scrambled for the passage that would take him to the top of the vehicle where he could man the mounted assault rifle.

"They're coming from everywhere!" Sampson's warning came just as Asher caught sight of the Taliban fighters spilling in behind them. "They've got some kind of grenade launcher," Sampson yelled. "Sir, if that thing hits us, we're done for!"

"Air cover is on the way. Three mikes out!" Asher yelled. They didn't have three seconds, much less three minutes, before they'd be hit.

"Then start shooting!" Sampson said. "Aim for the third vehicle in that row coming toward us. See it?"

Asher saw it. Sampson opened fire. The line scattered, but the third vehicle continued to bear down on them. The weapon mounted on the bars of the jeep fired.

"Get out! Get out!"

Asher and his men rolled from the vehicle and found cover behind a hill as the first grenade hit. Then the second and a third. They all continued to return fire, but there was nothing from the occupants of the MRAP in front of them. Asher pushed down the sick knowledge that every man was dead.

And they were next.

Sampson let loose another volley of bullets while Asher and the others fired back. Bullets pelted all around him and overhead.

"Where are those birds?" Sampson cried. His voice carried over the radio, along with the spat of the 240 he fired.

"One mike out!"

"They're getting ready to hit us again with that RPG!" Sampson continued to man the assault weapon while Asher joined him in trying to take out the jeep holding the weapon that would sign their death warrants.

The man behind the launcher fell, hit the dirt road, and didn't move.

For the next sixty seconds, they defended their position as the enemy pushed closer.

Then the sound of the helicopters roaring overhead penetrated the chaos. Sampson fired off another spate of bullets and the choppers joined in. At the launch of the first rocket dropping from the sky, the attackers turned and ran. The birds followed and would make sure they didn't return.

Asher bolted to his feet and ran to the smoldering MRAP thirty yards away.

He could hear his captain's voice over his radio checking in. The others were right behind him, heading to find their buddies. Asher stopped to answer his captain as sweat dripped down his face, dust caked the inside of his nose and lungs, and his heart pounded with grief for the lives he knew were lost. "Captain Newell, this is James. It was an ambush, sir," he said, doing his best to keep the tears out of his words. "They knew we were coming. They hit King's MRAP. He's dead. They're all dead. Over." He gritted his teeth and let his gaze sweep the area. He could grieve later.

Curses blistered the air waves and Asher listened as the man ranted. "All right," the captain finally said, "I've got this covered. Abort the mission and get back here."

"They knew we were coming, sir. Someone told them. And if Michaels had anything to do with it, I want to find him." But Michaels couldn't have known anything about it. Their friend was in trouble. "We're going to get him, sir. Over."

The captain didn't protest. None of the others did either. They were with him.

Asher closed his eyes, blanked everything from his mind except the orders he and the others would follow before they could process what had just happened. "We're on our way."

Sampson stood next to him. "Michaels?"

"Michaels."

"I'm getting a couple of souvenirs from that IED, then I'll be there."

Asher frowned. His friend's affinity for collecting pieces of any bomb that didn't kill him was weird, but whatever. He had more pressing matters to worry about. Like bringing in a buddy accused of treason.

Military Psychiatrist Captain Brooke Adams was ready to go home in spite of the fact that she'd come to appreciate the Afghan people, their country, and their determination to survive—and thrive. She'd been in Kabul for the past six months, doing her best to help the men and women in the United States Army serving on the front lines, and she was tired.

No . . . *drained*.

No, that wasn't it either.

She was . . . empty.

Done.

And tired of having a male escort every time she went off base. Three more weeks and she could go home. She almost felt guilty about the way she just couldn't seem to adapt; then again, she was aware of her limitations and she'd reached them. It was better to leave before . . . well, just *before*.

But first, she'd promised to meet her friends. The ladies she now considered family in this war-torn land. Sarah Denning and Heather Fontaine would already be at the café waiting for her, along with Kat Patterson, the combat photographer they'd come to love and appreciate. Rarely did any of them venture away from the base—other than Kat—but things had been quiet, and they all needed something other than military rations and Kentucky Fried Chicken. Okay, the food wasn't that bad, but The Bistro fare was amazing. The café, set on one of the busiest streets in Kabul, offered a variety of French-Afghan deliciousness that had her mouth watering just thinking about it.

Brooke pulled her hijab a little tighter at the neck and stepped through the door. Her escort headed to the men's side of the restaurant where he'd wait until she was finished.

"Brooke." Sarah waved. "Over here."

The three ladies sat toward the back away from the windows in the section reserved for women only. On the positive side, things were already changing for the better for this country. She just hoped that would continue.

The red walls boasted lovely paintings of desert landscapes—probably done by a family member of the owner. The wood-burning stove in the middle of the room definitely wouldn't be necessary today. Brooke ducked between the stove and the nearest table to wind her way to the corner table.

She dropped into the one empty chair and let her breath out slowly. "Whoo."

"Everything okay?" Kat asked.

"Sure."

"Liar," Heather said.

Brooke hesitated. "Okay, so no," she finally said, helping herself to one of the cinnamon rolls from the bread basket someone had so thoughtfully placed at her seat. "Everything's not okay." She waved the roll. "But this helps."

Heather raised a brow. She'd changed from her surgical scrubs and wore a simple pair of khaki pants and a blue long-sleeved collared knit shirt. The hijab wrapped around her head held matching colors and brought out her eyes. Which probably wasn't a good thing in this area.

"Wanna share?" Heather asked. Her eyes held compassion—and a keen intelligence that a lot of people missed when they focused on the woman's outward beauty. Built like a runway model,

Heather had chosen medicine over the modeling career that had funded her first two years of medical school.

The Army had paid for the rest of it, and now Heather devoted herself to helping put the wounded back together. She took care of the physical brokenness and Brooke tried to help with the mental. Being a military psychiatrist wasn't for the weak or the easily wearied. "It was a hard morning. I had to recommend a soldier be sent home for suicidal reasons." And just like that, she'd managed to suck any levity right out of the atmosphere. "Sorry. Forget I said that. Let's not talk shop." She lifted her glass of water. "So, who's excited about going home? What's the first thing you plan to do when you get there?"

"I'm going to walk down the street and not worry about getting blown up," Sarah said.

Kat rolled her eyes. "I'm from the worst part of Chicago. I can't walk down the street without worrying about getting shot or something. So"—she drew in a deep breath—"I'm going to find different streets to walk down, I think."

"Come walk down my street," Brooke said with a grin. "I just bought a house."

"What?" Kat gaped. "When?"

"Yesterday. Well, the offer was accepted, and all that's left is to do the paperwork. My lawyer has been granted power of attorney and is taking care of all of that for me."

After a round of congratulations and cheers, Sarah grimaced. "But that's going to have to wait for me."

Kat frowned. "What do you mean?"

"I'm here for at least another year."

"What!" Brooke and Kat said together.

Sarah shrugged. "I don't have anything I need to rush home to and I love my job. Besides"—she glanced around the restaurant and lowered her voice—"I'm working on something and I'm not

going to have it wrapped up by the time I'd have to leave. So . . .
I requested to stay in for a while longer."

"What are you working on?" Brooke asked.

"Something big. Something that's going to make a lot of people
unhappy—and probably put some people in prison." She paused.
"In prison and unhappy. Kind of goes together, doesn't it?"

Brooke leaned in. "Sarah, what are you doing?"

"Well, originally, I was doing whatever was necessary to get
a spot with a major newspaper that would lead me to Morning
Star Orphanage, where I was going to do a story on some of the
kids there. Instead, I wound up in a part-time volunteer position
that has led to—" She stopped and met each friend's gaze. "Never
mind. Suffice it to say that this is serious and it's going to blow
up a few careers if my source is being truthful with me. And I
think she is. "

"What source?" Kat asked. Her eyes narrowed. "What's going
on at the orphanage?"

Sarah shook her head. "So far, my evidence is circumstantial.
But I know—" She held up a hand. "Never mind. My turn to
change the subject." A pause while everyone stared silently. "But
if something happens to me, it's probably because of this story."

"What?" Heather narrowed her eyes. "I thought you were coming to the hospital to see me. Are you saying you've been coming
for other reasons?"

Brooke snorted. "Of course she is." Sarah was always investigating. She was a good reporter and didn't generally overreact to
things. The intensity of her words and facial expressions made
Brooke wonder if this time she might be getting in over her head.
"Your life's not worth a story, Sarah," she said.

"Normally, I'd agree with you, but this . . ." Sarah looked away,
blinking back tears. "Just pray I'm wrong."

Kat and Heather continued to press Sarah for details, but Brooke
tuned them out, having a hard time focusing on her friends' words.

Not that she didn't care, but her heart was heavy, her mind on the fact that she'd ruined a man's career this morning. That he was from her hometown of Greenville, South Carolina, just made him all the more special—and her responsibility all the more heart-breaking.

Heather's hand clasped hers under the table and she looked up to find the three ladies staring at her. "Sorry, I did it again, didn't I?" She stood. "I'm afraid I'm not going to be very good company today. I think I'll take off." Amidst the protests of her friends, she turned to go.

The little bell over the door jangled as it opened to admit three soldiers dressed in Army Combat Uniforms. She recognized the first one. Isaiah Michaels. His eyes caught hers and he nodded as he took a seat at the bar. His friends settled into the two seats next to him. They didn't acknowledge her, but the fact that Isaiah did was more than if he'd shouted her name.

Brooke returned the slight nod and sat back down. "Or maybe I'll order my food and enjoy myself."

"That's the spirit," Kat said. She moved her ever-present camera to the side of her plate and held up her water. "A toast. To home."

"To home!"

"And to Brooke's new place. May we eventually spend many a hot summer's day gathered around her pool."

Brooke gaped. "I didn't say anything about a pool."

Heather laughed. "Are you kidding? I'm surprised you're not in the Navy the way you can't live without water. You have a pool, don't you?"

"Well . . . yes, but still . . ."

The others cracked up and Brooke couldn't help the smile that curved her lips, even as she shot another glance at Michaels sitting with his friends at the bar. He caught her gaze, held it for a brief second, then looked away. He wanted to talk. She almost snorted, her ire rising. Well, he could wait on her this time.

"What's he doing here?" Sarah asked.

"Who?"

"Isaiah Michaels."

"You know him?" Brooke asked.

"Mm. Yes. Met him on the base a couple times, then ran into him at the hospital when I was there covering something for a story, then again at the orphanage."

"What was he doing at the hospital and the orphanage?"

"That's not important." Sarah's eyes bounced between Michaels and Brooke. "How do you know him?"

"That's not important," she mimicked and ignored the eye roll from Sarah.

"He keeps looking this way," Sarah said. "At you. Like he's waiting on you or trying to get your attention."

"Well, he can keep waiting on me." He was a client and he'd called to schedule an appointment, which had shocked her socks off. She'd always been the one to schedule the appointments and then had to practically drag him to them—or threaten to report his absence. Then he'd failed to show up. Which hadn't shocked her nearly as much.

They ordered their food and, for the next forty-five minutes, talked and caught up before duty called Heather and Sarah away, leaving Brooke alone at the table with Kat. "You really think Heather will decide to leave the Army and go work in a hospital?" Kat asked.

Brooke lifted her hands, palms up. "Sounded like she wants to."

"She'll be bored."

"She's a trauma surgeon. I doubt *bored* is in her vocabulary," Brooke said with a wry smile.

"Seriously, I'm a combat photographer. You think I could just go home and start taking headshots?"

"It'd be a lot safer."

"Brooooke . . ."

"I know. What am I thinking? You never have been one to play it safe. I have a theory about that, you know."

"Hmm, so, who's the guy?" Kat asked.

"Which one?" Brooke had no trouble following her friend's deliberate change of topic.

Kat smirked. "The one you locked eyes and exchanged nods with. The one who's still sitting over there with his friends pretending he's not waiting on you. I mean, I know his name, thanks to Sarah, but anything else I need to know?"

"Nothing much gets by you, does it?"

"Not if I want to stay alive."

"I can't say who he is," Brooke said.

"Ah. That means he's a client."

Brooke smiled and took a sip of the hot tea the server had brought.

"And by that look he gave you when he came in, he has something he wants to talk to you about." She sighed. "Which means, I need to say goodbye."

"I don't know what he wants," Brooke said, her voice low. "I have a lot of clients who are ordered to see me and sit there in silence for an hour. Not saying he's one of those, but I do have a lot."

"I know."

"So you know what I do?"

Kat raised a brow.

"I talk," Brooke said. "And I talk some more. The whole time. About PTSD and coping strategies. I talk about faith and God, saying things like, 'I don't know if you even believe in God at this point, but if you do . . .' and so on." She swallowed. "I don't know if it makes a difference or not and I'm tired of trying. Tired of being treated like I'm an intruder who can't understand what they're going through, much less be able to help." She shook her head. "Nope. It's time for me to leave." She stood.

"Aren't you going to see what he wants?"

"If he wanted to talk, he should have shown up two hours ago for his appointment." Brooke heard the brittle hostility in her tone and took a deep breath. "And now I'm breaking the rules in even saying that."

Kat stood, too, and placed money on the table. "You're doing good, Brooke. I know you can't see it, but you are."

Brooke let her gaze linger on the soldier who refused to look her way but was clearly waiting on her, as noticed by Kat. She closed her eyes and let the words wash over her. "Thank you," she whispered.

"No problem. I'm going to scram. Let me get out the door before you leave so he won't think we're together anymore. Then your escort will follow you, the guy who wants to meet with you will follow him, and his friends will . . ." Brooke scowled and Kat gave her a sheepish smile. "Well, you get the idea." A single man and single woman didn't meet together in a public place. It would be fine to walk and talk with her within a group, and his friends would make sure that's what it looked like.

"I think I know how it works at this point."

Kat grabbed her camera and looped it around her neck. "See ya."

"Stay safe, friend."

"Always. You too."

"Always."

Kat left and Brooke waited a few seconds before following in her friend's footsteps. Just as Kat predicted, the moment she passed the man at the bar, he turned and followed her. And his friends did the same.

The window next to the section where she'd been seated exploded and she went to her knees. A hard body hit hers, covering her as debris rained down.

She managed to gasp in one breath and then another explosion rocked the building.

ACKNOWLEDGMENTS

Thank you to my awesome family.
I love you guys bunches!

Lynette Eason is the bestselling author of *Oath of Honor*, *Called to Protect*, *Code of Valor*, and *Vow of Justice,* as well as the Women of Justice, Deadly Reunions, Hidden Identity, and Elite Guardians series. She is the winner of three ACFW Carol Awards, the Selah Award, and the Inspirational Reader's Choice Award, among others. She is a graduate of the University of South Carolina and has a master's degree in education from Converse College. Eason lives in South Carolina with her husband and two children. Learn more at www.lynetteeason.com.

SECRETS AND LIES.
DANGER THAT WILL NEVER GO AWAY.

Join three beloved masters of romantic suspense for novellas of deadly betrayal where the past will not stay buried.

INTENSITY. SKILL. TENACITY.

The bodyguards of
Elite Guardians Agency have it all.